continued . . .

Archangel Protocol

"Explosive entertainment. . . . Lyda Morehouse deftly dances a brave new path amid the minefields of religion and science fiction, prophecy and politics, romance and detective-noir . . . a most impressive debut. A very worthy read." —Howard V. Hendrix

"Her world is intriguing, and there are enough surprises to keep things moving, and the mix of SF and religion works surprisingly well. An impressive first novel." —*Locus*

"A rapturous, high-intensity foray . . . delivered with passion and precision." —Stephen L. Burns, author of *Call from a Distant Shore*

"Will keep readers glues to the very end." —BookBrowser

"A definite wow . . . an instant classic of sci-fi. Miraculous. One of the best novels in memory." —Lisa DuMond, SF Site

"You'll find a lot to enjoy." —Uncle Hugo's Bookstore Newsletter

"One of the more interesting satans in recent memory." —Melissa Scott

MESSIAH NODE

Lyda Morehouse

A ROC BOOK

ROC
Published by New American Library, a division of
Penguin Group (USA) Inc., 375 Hudson Street,
New York, New York 10014, U.S.A.
Penguin Books Ltd, 80 Strand,
London WC2R 0RL, England
Penguin Books Australia Ltd, 250 Camberwell Road,
Camberwell, Victoria 3124, Australia
Penguin Books Canada Ltd, 10 Alcorn Avenue,
Toronto, Ontario, Canada M4V 3B2
Penguin Books (N.Z.) Ltd, Cnr Rosedale and Airborne Roads,
Albany, Auckland 1310, New Zealand

Penguin Books Ltd, Registered Offices:
80 Strand, London WC2R 0RL, England

First published by Roc, an imprint of New American Library,
a division of Penguin Group (USA) Inc.

First Printing, June 2003
10 9 8 7 6 5 4 3 2 1

Cover art by Bruce Jensen

Printed in the United States of America

PUBLISHER'S NOTE
This is a work of fiction. Names, characters, places, and incidents either are the
product of the author's imagination or are used fictitiously, and any resemblance
to actual persons, living or dead, business establishments, events, or locales is
entirely coincidental.

For Shawn and Ella, my family

ACKNOWLEDGMENTS

I wrote this book with two due dates in mind. The first one was the mundane publishing date, and the other the birth of my daughter, Ella Durene Mae Morehouse Rounds. And now I begin the rewrite process without my beautiful Ella, who was stillborn on August 5, 2002.

I wouldn't be able to do this without the support of Ella's mother and my partner, Shawn Rounds, Ella's grandparents Rita and Mort Morehouse, the whole Rounds family, and the literally hundreds of friends from around the world, who have sent prayers, good thoughts, and energy our way.

Thanks.

CHAPTER 1

✠

Michael

Sometimes I wondered what God was thinking. Last night, just after midnight, a meteorite fell from the sky and destroyed the Dome of the Rock. It hit with surgical precision—nothing else was affected. Even part of the Wailing Wall still stood. People were calling it the Passover Miracle . . . or mistake, depending on which side you were on.

I used to know God pretty well, and frankly, this seemed out of character.

But maybe He has changed. It'd been a long time since I stood at God's right hand. Three and a half years, in fact, since I'd held that exalted state. Although I guess I hadn't exactly *stopped* being Heaven's Prince, since no one else had assumed the title in my absence, it's kind of hard to be God's number one defender when you've been struggling to stay on Earth, and stay sane.

Lately I'd been feeling pretty normal, almost human, you might say. I had been invited to Second Seder at Rebeckah's kibbutz in the Glass City—a big step for me.

It meant seeing Deidre again, and our daughter, Amariah.

Deidre looked great tonight. She'd gone all out, dressing in a slinky black sheath. I had a hard time keeping my eyes off her; she, on the other hand, looked everywhere except at me.

Amariah, at least, seemed pleased to see me. She'd rushed into my arms and hugged me, calling me Papa and rattling at me about all the things she'd done in preschool today like we were still close and hadn't been separated. She looked precious in a black velvet dress with a matching bow on top of a pile of blond, unruly curls.

Rebeckah, our hostess, played matchmaker with the seating assignments. So I got put next to Deidre. Fine with me, of course, but Deidre's jaw kept clenching, like she was struggling to hold something back—something, by the looks of it, that I wouldn't want to hear.

"How have you been?" I asked, despite the obvious signs that she didn't want to talk.

Dee looked around the room instead of answering. I followed her gaze. We had gathered in an old American Legion hall. Armored fabric was draped along the south wall. At the edges, veins of Medusa crystals leaked out like deadly spiderwebs. I cringed every time Amariah romped near it, but everyone looked after her and kept her from touching the glass. I had to remind myself that it was as safe as anywhere in the kibbutz. The whole place had been rescued from the Medusa; this room, at least, had three walls that were untouched by the glass.

Cheap dark paneling covered the rest of the room, and the place still smelled faintly of Friday-night fish fries and dust. Yarn art and paint-by-numbers pictures added a perversely homey touch, despite the concrete floors and water-stained acoustic tiles on the ceiling.

When Dee didn't answer, I added, "I start a job on Monday. It's just delivery. Part-time. But I think it's a good start."

Her eyes flicked over to me for the briefest of moments. "A good start at what?"

"You know, making a living. Maybe I can move out of the halfway house and get a real apartment of my own, and—"

"Michael," she said, talking to the cloth napkin she folded and unfolded in her lap. "You know you're kidding yourself, right? You're an archangel. You don't belong here."

My eyes sought out Amariah. She was making her way

back to the table dragging a sock monkey by the toe, apparently her newest favorite toy. I couldn't be certain, of course. I rarely saw her, except on occasions like this. "Are you saying you don't want me around?"

"No, it's not like that." Dee's voice was softer than I expected, giving me hope.

"I'm making a real effort here, Dee," I said. "I want to be a good father to Amariah."

"I know," she said, finally looking at me with those soft blue eyes. "But coming back changed you."

"I'm getting better."

Her mouth opened to say something when Amariah bounced into the seat between us. "Is it time for the Four Questions? I love that part."

She would. As the youngest, she got to ask all the questions. I wondered whom Rebeckah would consider the oldest. Technically, I was—at least in spirit. In flesh, I was younger than Amariah.

Rebeckah coughed lightly, signaling that we should begin. Rebeckah was an ex-Israeli career soldier and ex-LINK terrorist. Her flattop was still as precise as the sharp lines of her broad shoulders and the cuffs of her cotton shirtsleeves. After we recited the traditional questions and answers, the room erupted, as everyone had questions of their own.

"How could it not be a sign?" Rebeckah asked, her voice straining to be heard over all the others. She leaned into the table, her body tight with tension. "The only thing that's been standing in our way was that mosque."

She didn't have to say it for us to hear it . . . *that damn mosque* is what she meant. Rebeckah wasn't the first person to think that the destruction of the Dome of the Rock would mean progress for the Jewish cause. People tended to forget that the Muslims were God's people, too.

I pushed my spoon around in the clear liquid of the matzo-ball soup. "God wouldn't dance while Her people were crying."

The room fell quiet. Even Amariah, who was only a little over four years old, stopped playing with her napkin to stare at me with wide eyes. Nobody was happy when I spoke of God. Some probably remembered my days in the wilderness when I would rant about God on the street corner. Others knew the truth about my origins. Both scenarios, I imagined, inspired extreme discomfort.

I cleared my throat, and quoted, " 'When the Egyptians were drowning in the Red Sea, the angels in heaven wanted to sing praises to God for rescuing the Jewish people. But God silenced them, saying, "My children are drowning in the sea and you want to sing before Me?" ' "

Others started nodding, remembering the Midrash.

"Michael's right. There's more war now than there was before," agreed Deidre quietly. Unlike Rebeckah, Deidre's blond curls always seemed to be in desperate need of a haircut. Personally, I found it sexy and inviting—kind of like an unmade bed. "I don't know all this stuff, but isn't the Messianic Age supposed to be one of peace?"

"Good point," said Tom. Tom was a Wiccan visiting from Seattle. Black and thin, he wore his hair trimmed close to his scalp. A silver Ahnk rested against his black shirt, and blue and green Celtic knots circled his biceps. "We still need a messiah. Where's the Lion of Israel in all this?"

"Is Elijah coming tonight?" Amariah asked. She had been very disappointed when he didn't come last night at First Seder. "Will he be there this time?"

"Elijah doesn't really come. That's just part of the ceremony," Deidre said, repeating the mantra from last night. Amariah looked crestfallen.

"I want Elijah to come. I've never met him."

Some people around the table laughed. I sipped my soup.

"I pray for Elijah to come, but not in my lifetime, isn't that right?" Wolf asked. His hair was white, like snow, and silver pupils reflected the overhead fluorescent lights. Wolf was a Gorgon. He'd been born inside the Glass City, and the Medusa had mutated his genetic makeup in utero. He was converting to Judaism. He had perfect pitch and wanted to be a cantor.

"That's right," said Rebeckah, but there was something of Amariah's disappointment on her face.

"Maybe we should try to get the ceremony right, and, if all the Jews in the world do a perfect Seder, maybe the messiah will come," said Jane. Jane was Tom's wife, though they couldn't have been more opposite. As white as he was black and older by at least a decade, she had the eyes and bodytype of an owl.

Thus chided, we picked up our booklets and went back to the ceremony. Rebeckah began to read the next section. I knew the Seder by heart, so I watched her, smiling as she changed the words to be more gender-inclusive. God would like that, I thought. Then I noticed someone standing behind Rebeckah. I hadn't seen him come in. In fact, it was as though he materialized out of thin air. He appeared to be Israeli, in his middle forties, with more salt than pepper in his hair.

And he had wings.

Brown and striped like a hawk's, they spread out behind him, nearly touching the ceiling.

I blinked. I looked at the others around the table. Their noses pressed into the books, they seemed oblivious to a second archangel in their midst.

Don't frighten them, Michael. I have come for you. Voices, like a chorus of a thousand tongues all speaking at once in a million languages, echoed in my head. It took a second to parse the meaning. But, like hearing the voice of an old friend, I suddenly recognized the archangel Raphael.

"Excuse me for a minute," I whispered to Deidre, and jerked my head in the direction of the bathroom. She nodded, but, like everyone else around the table, she stayed focused on the readings. I wondered if I was hallucinating Raphael's appearance. Standing up, I walked past the buffet table toward the door to the outside. The archangel shook his head, as if to say he wouldn't follow me. I gave him a steely stare. I was, after all, his former commander. Then, without seeing if he would follow, I stepped into the evening drizzle.

The kibbutz stood at the very edge of the glass, just over the line on the "wrong" side. Calling it glass was really a misnomer, but it glittered on the asphalt in the misty rain like a jewel and laced the chain-link fence like ice.

The Medusa bomb was the greatest technological achievement in the last war—a combination of nanotechnology and biowarfare. An aerosolizing device released billions of viral nanobots whose programmed task was to consume complex molecules and excrete silicon. One big flash glassed most of the Bronx—human, animal, and mineral. That was supposed to be the end of it, but, like any good virus, the Medusa mutated and became resistant to its internal command to stop.

The only thing the Medusa couldn't digest and transform was that which had already started as silicone. So windows and other glass had remained intact after the blast. Using this knowledge, the kibbutz had set up barriers of crushed glass around the buildings they occupied. Of course, the Medusa would eventually make its way through the soil, under the barriers, but it slowed the progress. At least until another mutation occurred.

I stood on the sidewalk, much of which was still concrete, and waited. Raphael finally came out and sat on the top step of the stoop. His wings were too large to fold neatly behind him, so Raphael flapped them around, trying to find a comfortable position. Finally he gave up and let them sprawl across the steps. His left wing's primary feathers scrunched up against the metal handrail I leaned on. I resisted the urge to pluck one of them.

"What were you doing in there?" I asked him. "Wearing your wings out in the open like that. What if someone had noticed you?"

"No more screwing around, Michael. Mother wants you home," Raphael said, rubbing his arms for warmth.

"Mother?" I repeated. "Of anyone, She should understand why I can't leave. I'm a father myself. I have responsibilities, a daughter to raise."

Raphael gave me a skeptical look. "You've been here long enough. Maybe even too long."

I ran my fingers over the firm edge of a feather close to me. Enough? I didn't think so. Not nearly. My daughter was only four. I wanted to see her through to college, maybe even to the grave.

Plus, I had some things to work out. Deidre and I didn't live together anymore, and I intended to change that.

I couldn't really blame her for leaving me. I'd been such a mess at the time that I hadn't even noticed she was gone. When I returned to the place we'd been staying—a cheap one-room apartment in Harlem—she'd taken all her things and left. Amariah hadn't been born yet; Dee was eight months pregnant. I think, with the baby so close, she got desperate for safety. And I'd been anything but stable back then.

But lately I'd been feeling grounded. My sense of self was greater in the last few weeks than it had ever been. These days I knew the difference between myself and others, myself and God. I'd stopped my midnight ramblings down Skid Row; I'd started bathing regularly, shaving, clipping my toenails—taking care of this body I usually forgot about.

I'd even moved out of the shelter and into a halfway house. I was starting that job on Monday. I'd been getting really serious about making a go at playing the part of a mortal. I thought that if Deidre could see me trying, she'd let me back in. Then the three of us could be a proper family. I didn't want to miss anything more than what I already had of Amariah's life, or Dee's, for that matter. There was no way I was going back to Heaven. Wild angels couldn't drag me away.

"No," I told Raphael, flicking his feather. "Things are just starting to be good."

He fluffed his wing away from me. Rain brought out the darkness in his hair. "Michael, do you realize what you're saying?"

"Yes, I'm saying go away. I'm starting to make things work here, Rafe. True, it's been hard. There's just so many decisions to make. . . . I mean, free will is thick here, like smog. But I think I'm finally on track."

Free will was such a nightmare. In Heaven there had been no choices, only the will of God. Here? Sometimes the smorgasbord of decisions stymied me into complete inaction. Just choosing which tie to wear to Seder tonight had taken me an hour. I had no skills, no practice at judging what was good and right, since previously God had predetermined my whole existence.

Raphael frowned at me. "On track? What could be more on track than being with God?"

Raising a baby, I thought but couldn't quite say. Being a good partner, maybe even a good husband: these things I craved more than God's grace. I wanted to tell Raphael

about it, but I could see the fierce glory in his eyes. He
had just come from Her, and I could feel Her heat, like
the sun, pouring from Raphael.

"I don't know," I mumbled in acquiescence, dropping
my eyes so he couldn't see the lies written there.

"Then come home, my prince," he said.

Home? I hardly remembered Heaven anymore. As my
connection to Earth got stronger, my memories of God faded.
Heaven, I knew, was not a place, per se. It was a complete
merging with God's consciousness. Once, that idea of oneness
seemed ideal; now . . . now it scared me. Lose my identity?
Surrender all that I had become to a higher mind? It
sounded like death, and I'd just started to live.

Home meant Amariah and Deidre now, not God.

But how could I tell an archangel that?

Hazy moonlight glittered on the crystallized rooftop of
the house across the street. The gentle drizzle made the
sharp edges glitter like diamonds.

"But why now?" I asked. "Is it because of the
meteorite?"

"Something like that," Raphael said. He looked over my
shoulder suddenly, as if seeing something. I turned, but saw
only a darkened street. When I turned back to him, Raphael held out a hand for me to take . . . as if he wanted
me to go with him, right now, right this instant.

"Come," he said.

"Uh," I said, stalling. "I should really say good-bye."

"There's no time for that," Raphael insisted. When he
reached for me I moved away, nearly stumbling over the
glass barrier inches from my feet.

"Why the hurry?" I demanded. "Surely I'm allowed
some time to explain this to my daughter? I can't just leave
without saying good-bye. It'd kill her." It'd kill me.

"Shit," Raphael said, looking down the street again.

This time when I followed his gaze, I saw something. A
cloaked figure wobbled slowly down the middle of the
glass-covered street. His body was bent as if with extreme
age, and he leaned heavily on a walking stick. I would have
dismissed him for a Gorgon, except that most of them
never lived to see the age of six, much less sixty.

Then I heard the metallic click of a scabbard releasing
a sword.

I was turning to ask Raphael why an archangel would be so threatened by an old man when I felt the razor edge of steel against my throat. Flames of glory tickled my skin.

"You should have come with me when I asked," Raphael hissed into my ear, his arms encircling my shoulders in a tight grip. He pulled me closer to him and away from the door. "Now just don't get in the way."

The old man had reached the barrier. I could see his features more clearly. He looked familiar, like a rabbi I'd met once long ago on the road to somewhere. The moonlight seemed to surround him and pulsate. I kept trying to remember his name, but couldn't.

He walked past us: two angels on the doorstep, like he was used to flaming swords and hawk wings. When he reached the top step, he raised his hand to knock. Just then the door flew open. Amariah stood there, her eyes wide with surprise.

"Elijah!" she squealed happily.

"Amariah McMannus!" Elijah returned. "Just the person I've been searching for."

"I'm sorry, Michael," Raphael whispered into my ear, but he didn't loosen his grip on me or his sword. "I'm so sorry."

Elijah, it was said, searched the world for the messiah. He had come here, to Rebeckah's Seder, and found my daughter. With the messiah found, the Messianic Age could begin. Peace and love and an end to wars.

The only problem was that if he tried to take my daughter away, I intended to kill him.

DOME OF THE ROCK DESTROYED

Agnostic Press (April 2083)

  Jerusalem, Israel—Just as many families had settled down for Passover dinner in Jerusalem, a meteor struck the Dome of the Rock. Amateur astronomers sighted the meteor when it entered the atmosphere at 7:00 P.M. UTC/GMT +2 (11:00 A.M. EST).

The impact did not damage the "Wailing Wall," which is part of the western wall just below and surrounding the Dome of the Rock and al-Aqsa mosque. Though the impact could be heard throughout Jerusalem, it disturbed very little of the surrounding residential areas. "Just a few tiles were knocked off my roof," said Abraham Goldstein, a resident in the Jewish Quarter of the Old City. "That was all."

A flurry of speculation on the nature of the meteorite appeared on a rogue scientist virtual mailing list immediately. An astrophysicist who asked not to be identified said that she believed that the meteorite may have been a fragment of cometary halo ice, most of which burned off during entry or vaporized on impact. She said that would account for the shallowness of the impact crater and lack of significant debris.

Though all of the Dome of the Rock and much of al-Aqsa mosque were destroyed, less than a dozen meteor-related injuries have been reported. The Dome of the Rock is a shrine for pilgrims, but was closed for the evening when the meteorite hit. Even though security guards normally patrol the Dome, due to a freak coincidence, no one was inside the mosque when the meteorite hit. "I went down the hill for a smoke," admitted Idris Quasim, who was on duty yesterday evening. "I'd had a bad day. I hadn't smoked in years . . . but now I'm glad I did. If I hadn't left my post, I'd be dead." When asked if he thought God had spared his life, Quasim replied, "I don't know. Why would Allah spare my life but destroy the Dome of the Rock?"

Al-Aqsa mosque, which is a functioning mosque for prayers, was also miraculously empty.

CHAPTER 2

Mouse

Almsgiving is a major tenet of Islam. It's also a kick in the pants of the highest order. Nothing is as cool as skimming off a couple of hundred thousand from some multinational corporation and handing it out to random strangers. Or writing a harmless little virus that makes credit counters "forget" to send a surcharge back to the bank after each purchase. Oh, sure, technically I'm supposed to give away my own money, but whatever. I'm sure Allah gets the spirit of what I'm doing here.

Especially since I could probably steal enough money to live like an emir, if only my AI would let me. You see, he's a better Muslim than I, by far, and stealing is the kind of thing that gets your hands chopped off. He'd hate to see that happen to me. He's very protective. In fact, he's so protective that the last time he protected me from myself, I ended up in jail. Now every time I think I've found a hidey-hole for some major credits, my AI finds it and wipes me clean, or worse, sends my hard-stolen money off to some charity. Better to just give it away myself and cut out the middleman.

I lift my fingers from the keyboard and stretch my arms over my head. The basement has no windows, and smells faintly of Thistle's red worm compost. The floor is concrete and perpetually slimy, but Sparkles, our cat, is curled next to my thigh purring happily. I stroke her back and she snaps at me—half in play, half serious. She's old, and doesn't much like to be touched. I feel old and cranky too. My shoulders ache, and as I roll them I can feel a tightness along the inner part of my elbow. If I keep this hand-hacking up, I'm going to develop carpal tunnel syndrome—a condition once common to geeks like me, but now virtually unheard of since the development of the LINK.

The LINK—aye, there's the rub. I'm a complete disconnect these days. I've been off-line for three years, maybe more. My nexus was fried after I did some serious time in Sing-Sing for a tiny little felony fraud charge. People are so sensitive when you fabricate a presidential candidate and try to convince the world that you're God with a worldwide, LINK-induced hallucination. Sheesh.

I really should still be in prison, but, well, an opportunity for escape presented itself, and who was I to say no? But the instant the authorities wised up to the fact that I'd left that fine establishment without permission, they sent a meltdown command and nuked my system. I'm damaged goods now. Not even the best brain surgeon in the world could repair the mess of melted microwires in my brain.

Which wouldn't suck so damn much, if the LINK didn't make the world spin. It's pretty straightforward, really. Eighty percent of the population is LINKed in some way. When most of the world wants a baguette, they LINK their order to their favorite patisserie. Me, I've got to break into the bakery to steal the day-old stuff. I couldn't even pay for it if I wanted to, since all commerce is electronic. It's not like there's a coin of the realm any more—very few coins at all, only electrons. I can't carry electrons in my pocket in any kind of meaningful way.

Of course, there's still barter: I give you the T-shirt I scored at the last rave and you give me some bread. That's how I keep myself fed. Plus, I've got this evening gig washing dishes at a posh restaurant. I do their shit work, and they feed me scraps.

It's a great way to live.

But it beats prison, so I shouldn't complain.

Plus, there are still some phreaks around who think that living like a caveman is pure. So I'm keeping it real by renting here with some serious code-heads in Paris.

Sparkles yawns and digs a claw into my jeans. Above me I can hear floorboards squeak as someone moves around in the kitchen. It's probably Chas. He's our resident den mother and loves to cook. I fantasize I can smell his famous curry pot pie over the odor of dirt.

Chas is also our token American. He likes to pretend he's Indian because his great-grandma moved from New Delhi to take an engineering position at Cal-Tech a zillion years ago. But the guy wears white shoes and puts far too much sugar in his espresso to be anything other than a full-blooded American. I hear him hop a couple of steps down into the basement. From the top of the stairs, Chas's shoes gleam in the darkness like two round, soft eyeballs. His white shirt is equally as reflective as his shaved head. "You want me to save you some grub, Mouse?"

"If you're making pot pie."

"I am," he says. Taking that for a yes, he heads back up the stairs.

We've all got gray in our hair, either figurative or literal, even Sparkles. I'm the youngest of this bunch, and I'm pushing thirty-five. No actual gray yet, but if I keep living this way, it won't be long.

Anyway, you've got to hang with the geriatric crowd if you want to hard-line. The kiddies just don't have the tools—and I mean screwdrivers, soldering guns . . . serious tools. For the youngsters it's the LINK, all flash and dazzle, proprietary software that can put on a good show.

Okay, yeah, a little of this is sour grapes. I mean, I don't have the luxury of anything more than black screen and white text anymore, but I'll have you know I cut my teeth on binary. I broke the stranglehold of the LINK by inventing mouse.net when I was fourteen. A precocious little bastard, I, but also desperate. But I learned what made the LINK tick. Which is the only reason I can still claim the title of wire wizard when my brain is a scrap heap.

See, the house is great and all, but the prime charm of this real estate is the fact that it's next-door neighbor to the main Paris LINK node. The nodes are the hardware of the LINK. The infrastructure. The equipment that acts as traffic control between ten billion people's brains and an orbiting ring of satellites. Nodes are supercomputers that have been buried underground. Some of them span acres. And ever since the Hassidic terrorists started targeting the hardware of the nodes themselves, the main terminals are usually heavily guarded. What the LINK Gestapo doesn't know is that we built an access panel in the basement.

"Oh," shouts Chas from upstairs. "Say hi to Page for me."

Oh, crap. I'd forgotten. My Page program had stopped by to "chat." It's been minutes since I last sent a keystroke—for an AI that's an eternity.

I wonder if he's still there. I quickly scan our previous conversation, then type: *What do you make of the Dome of the Rock?*

I hear someone is building a temple there, he replies.

You mean the virtual space, right? In one of its peacekeeping moves, the UN set aside part of Jerusalem's node to be "international" ground, an empty space where no one was allowed to develop LINK property in the name of keeping peace in real time. Like most attempts to stabilize the region around Israel, it failed. There had been several attempts to hijack the space in the past, but the most recent lockout is by far the most successful. Or was, if someone's gotten through.

Oh, yes, that's what I meant. Temple Rock. I went there to pray after I heard about the meteor and discovered it closed.

You went to Temple Rock to pray? I'm surprised at you, Page. That's kind of political. I thought I raised you better than that.

The screen is blank for several seconds. I've pissed him off. Well, I'm sorry. Mecca is by far the more important site in Islam, and if people would just remember that, things could be a lot calmer generally. Going to Temple Rock to pray *is* a political act, especially right now, and twice so for Page. People watch everything he does.

I heard there's a cult forming around you. I type, allowing him to change the subject. *They say you're some kind of dying and rising god. What's up with that?*

I swear, I leave my Page without supervision for a year, and he goes off and gets stuck in the head of some Japanese polka diva who overdoses. She croaks, and my guy escapes just in time to divert an international incident. Suddenly people worship him.

I didn't start it.

I didn't say you did, I type.

Never tease a computer program, no matter how officially sentient. They just don't get it.

I wish I could change things, his words appear. *I feel I failed. My time in Siberia was not enough punishment.*

Merciful Allah. Two things baffle me about my creation. First is his absolutely foreign sense of altruism. Believe me, his penchant for being kind to everyone he meets is not something he inherited from me. I wouldn't even know how to write code that nice. The other is his guilt. After the diva's death, Page turned himself in and volunteered to serve time in a Siberian auto plant cut off from the LINK. Now he thinks he hasn't done enough. I swear, if you sneeze this guy thinks he's responsible.

I think it's kind of cool, I continue. *I mean, when we started they didn't even recognize you as human. Now you're becoming a god.*

There is no God but Allah, and Mohammad is His prophet.

Oh, yeah, did I mention he's a much better Muslim than I am?

So I'm guessing you disapprove, I key in.

I'm always surprised how patient Page is with my typing. I mean, his processors whiz at a gagillion times the speed of thought, and my all-time best is eighty-two words a minute not counting typos.

This time, however, it takes his answer more than a second to appear on the screen. He might just be elsewhere, pissed . . . or just multitasking. I'm only a little envious.

I'm trying to block their petition for cult status, but the Commission hearings are probably going to go ahead. The Senate votes today.

He's talking about the U.S. Senate. For some reason, the U.S. is still a major player—despite the fact that they got their asses glassed in the last war, losing parts of New York, Los Angeles, DC, and Chicago. Still, the truth is, if the U.S. Commission on Established Religions granted the Cult of Page a temporary license to practice in America, other countries will follow their lead, like sheep to shears. It's a documented fact.

Personally, I think it's because Americans are still such

Puritans. If you can pass muster as a religion in the U.S., everybody else's laws are like limp spaghetti in comparison. Nobody's as strict as America when it comes to religion. Well, with the possible exception of the Kingdom of Saudi Arabia, but that's only because the muttawa follow people around to make sure they're being good Muslims. By contrast, in America they have laws that apply to every flavor of every religion you can think of and probably six more you've never even heard of.

You're going to have some hassle, I type. *Maizombies have already gotten status. Technically all they're asking for is an extension to include the worship of you as an official sect.*

The Americans granted cult status to the Acolytes of Mai, as they were officially called—Maizombies to the rest of us—six months ago. Admittedly, having read their charter, I find some of the zombies' tenets are closer to my personal belief system than most religions I've come across. They formed around Mai, the now-dead diva, who in life had been a sexy Japanese cello player in a polka thrash band who *was* pretty hot. Other than worshiping Mai as the second incarnation of the Buddha, they believe in sex, drugs, and music with a serious backbeat.

I'd convert, except I can't abide the zombies' tendency to drop out of society and the LINK. I already ain't got the LINK, but they've got this romantic vision of life on the streets which I personally find downright blasphemous. Sorry, but having a roof over my head is something I thank Allah for every damn day.

Anyway, the zombies started worshiping Page after he killed their idol, Mai. It seems kind of twisted to me, but it's the truth. Page tried to make an escape from Mai's head when she was stoned, and he accidentally killed her. Most people would make you into Judas for that, but my guy gets out of it on account of the fact that he pulled a little technological miracle out of his ass during the riot that followed the LINK broadcast of Mai's death—the "love bomb."

For an hour, he made the whole LINKed world feel nothing but peace, happiness, and love for one another.

Real hippie-dippy.

Grosses me out. More, because he corrupted my own

LINK-angel code—the stuff I'd used in my personal bid for world domination—to make this love-fest happen.

Seriously, Page, I say. *You could be a god by this time tomorrow.*

:P

Briefly, I'm embarrassed that I'd coded the knowledge of ASCII art into Page's brain.

Technically, he corrects, *Mai would still be god; I'd just be their messiah.*

I laugh out loud, startling Sparkles. Sparkles gives me a cold look, then tucks her nose beneath her tail.

Are the zombies going to at least pick a cooler name than Cult of Page? I ask.

Yes. They're calling themselves The Sect of the Risen AI.

Excellent, I finish typing, even though two letters into it, my screen notifies me that Page is logged off. Page forgets to say good-bye a lot. He probably figures he's given me some visual clue, like a wave. I'd be hurt, but I used to be the same damn way. I couldn't blame my creation for acting the way I'd programmed him.

"You done, Mouse?"

I look up to see Thistle sitting on the basement steps. Her hair is a new color, I think—blue with green ends, spiky, but kind of round, like the flower of her namesake. I'm not sure what her original color is.

Thistle wears a bulky brown sweater that disguises her reedy, boyish body, but lucky for me, she's chosen formfitting green tights to complete the ensemble, so at least I get a peek at her shapely calves.

"Stop lusting, Mouse, luv. I want a crack at the hard line."

"Go play somewhere else, girlfriend. I've got it for another two hours."

She laughs. "Yeah, two hours ago. Hand it over, Mouse. You know the house rules. Anyway, don't you have a job to go to?"

I hate not having a LINK receptor. For one thing, hardly anyone makes clocks or watches anymore. I never have any clue how much time has passed.

"Don't forget about our lessons tonight," she adds. "It's time to pay up!"

"Already?" I've been teaching my roommates about

mouse.net in lieu of rent. I can't think of that now. I've got to go. "Fuck," I say, letting the keyboard drop. Sparkles arches her back in a stretch and leaps up to follow me as I rush upstairs to get dressed for work.

Damn Page anyway. Monique is such a bitch when I'm late. I probably won't get to eat tonight, if she makes me work through the dinner break. I take the stairs two at a time. Trying to make up for lost time, I trip over Sparkles and nearly end up on my ass.

Craptastic.

"TEMPLE ROCK" HIJACKED

UN Treaty Violated

Agnostic Press (April 2083)

Jerusalem, Israel—In the hours following the meteor shower that destroyed the Dome of the Rock, Muslims from around the world have been gathering to pray at the LINK-space that corresponds to the former site of the real-time mosque. When avatars arrived today for morning prayers, they discovered the virtual doors barred.

A cybersquatter has hacked an illegal claim on the virtual space, blocking all visitors to the site. In 2072, the United Nations declared the LINK real estate that represents Temple Mount/Dome of the Rock to be an international site, open to people of all religious beliefs. The declaration provided that no one country, community, or individual could own the space, and no interface would ever be designed for it. Though a completely blank space, the site routinely receives several hundred visitors a day.

Temple Rock, as it is sometimes affectionately referred to by users, has never before been attacked with success. Though devoid of any construction, many people of all denominations consider the site itself holy. Even the Malachim Nikamah, a radical Jewish terrorist group responsible for several physical attacks on LINK nodes, refused to violate Temple Rock. "[The site] represents the potential Temple," said one former Malachim currently serving time in prison. "To destroy it would be like denying the future of the Jewish people."

"It was a place of peace," said Khadijah Jaber, a Muslim, and a frequent visitor. "The silence allowed you to surrender completely to the will of Allah." Christian visitors agreed, saying that the emptiness facilitated a closer communion with God for them. However, when an avatar approaches the site today, they are confronted with the image of a closed door and a sign that reads: NO ADMITTANCE. TEMPLE UNDER CONSTRUCTION.

Though already in violation of the no-interface ordinance, the last line of the message has many visitors particularly worried. "It says a temple, not Temple Rock," said Janet Nystrom, a New Right Christian. "Makes me think someone is building the Third Temple."

Many people are already making comparisons between the meteor shower and the heavenly fire. The construction of a virtual temple is adding fuel to the religious fervor. "If the Temple were to be virtually constructed," said one visitor, "it'd be f**king prophetic, man. Very apocalypse right now, you know what I mean?"

Several gatherers have defied the no-image laws and have left LINK posts proclaiming: *The end is near.*

CHAPTER 3

❖

Rebeckah

Oy fucking vay.

My Pesach had gone to hell in a handbasket. Elijah stood in the doorway of my kibbutz. Or it was an amazing coincidence that just when we expected the prophet, a rain-soaked Orthodox Jew had appeared.

Although I didn't believe in coincidences, I couldn't quite believe this was *the* Elijah, either.

My faith was a hard thing to quantify. I'd been trained by years of active duty not to trust anything, not even what I saw. Who knew when an innocent might actually be a bomb-carrying threat? So the fact that this man looked very much like I would have imagined Elijah meant little to me. I cataloged what I saw, trying to draw clues out of any little detail.

The man stood no more than five-foot-seven, and was stooped a little from old age. He leaned heavily on a plain, dark-wood walking stick. Of slim build, he probably weighed a hundred and eighty. His clothes marked him as ultra-Orthodox and Hasidic, though I couldn't immediately identify the subsect. On his head was a wide-brimmed black hat over wisps of thinning white hair and blaylocks, and he wore a long jacket and pants of the same somber hue. Only a bit of white showed at his collar.

I'd guess his age to be between mid-sixties and early seventies. I might have thought older, but his smile was youthful. Deep-set eyes surrounded by soft wrinkles watched me with an intelligence that made me suspicious, wary.

"Are you going to invite me in, Rebeckah?"

I hadn't felt a ping. If the old man had tapped my identity from the LINK, I hadn't noticed it. Because of our somewhat precarious position with the U.S. government, I had a ton of security watchdogs on my personal system. It was a skillful hacker who could ID me without my sensing it.

"Do I know you?"

"You set a place for me at the table, but you do not know who I am?"

"I know who you are," piped up Amariah, Deidre's daughter.

"Yes," said the old man. "And I know who *you* are."

The entire kibbutz was holding its breath wondering what I would do. I thought really hard about saying, "No, you can't come in"—but Amariah was already leading the old man to the place we'd set for Elijah. So I just gave him a curt nod. What else could I do? I was useless in the kinds of situations that called for anything more than a fist or a gun. The stranger made his way to the table, leaning heavily on a walking stick, really playing up the whole wandering-Jew look.

"At every house, the same! I get the worst wine," the old man said, sniffing the Mogen David.

"I like it," Amariah said defensively.

So did I, but I wasn't about to start carrying on about favorite childhood memories with a perfect stranger. "Who are you? What do you want?"

"You know who I am. You know why I'm here."

Last night a rock fell out of the sky and returned control of Temple Mount to Israel. Jews everywhere were talking about return, about signs from God, about how the messiah must be right around the corner.

Or, as it turns out, at my Seder.

But I wasn't booking my tickets to Jerusalem just yet.

Sure, the world was teetering close to the apocalypse, but, really, it had been for most of my life. Not long ago people had thought angels lived on the LINK and wanted us to vote for a presidential candidate that didn't even exist. False prophets were everywhere. You couldn't trust, not even when the sky opened up and rained fire on the one thing standing in the way of the Messianic Age. Not even when Elijah sat at your table, making faces at the wine.

But not everyone was as cautious as me, and it didn't help that Michael took that moment to burst in the door.

"Elijah!" he shouted, his black curls wet and his eyes wild. "Stay away from my daughter."

A second stranger, this one in his thirties and dressed in an Israeli uniform, stumbled in after Michael and put his hand on Michael's arm as if to hold him back.

The room erupted in a gasp, as though Michael's easy acceptance of the prophet made him more real. "Elijah," someone whispered. It was repeated through the room: "Elijah."

I raised my hands to quiet everyone and to hopefully imply that we shouldn't jump to conclusions; we didn't know the man's identity for certain yet. The last thing I needed was for the entire kibbutz to fall for this charlatan.

Deidre stood up, looking nervously between Michael and Amariah.

"Don't let him take Amariah!" Michael shouted. He started as if to run to Deidre and Amariah, but his companion put an arm on his shoulder, stopping him.

"Don't do anything crazy, Michael," the other man said.

The stranger couldn't have aimed a more perfect sucker punch. You could almost hear the entire room take in a hiss of breath. Everyone knew Michael had a history of mental illness. I wanted to say something—something to defuse the situation—but the whole thing was spiraling out of control. I needed to compartmentalize things again, and make them orderly. I decided to start with a quick assessment.

"What's going on?" I demanded. "Michael, what makes you think this man is here to take Amariah?"

"God wanted me out of the way. What else could it be?"

God help him if he didn't sound crazier than ever. Deidre, I noticed, blushed. She looked away, like she didn't know what to think. I wasn't sure either, but even so, there was no point taking chances. If Michael thought the

stranger might run off with Amariah then I had to accept
that as a possibility. I knelt down beside Amariah and held
out my hands as if I wanted to pick her up. "Come here,
child," I said.

Amariah hesitated only a second before letting me pick
her up. I was not good with children, but I had baby-sat
for Deidre a couple of times. Anyway, I had a commanding
voice, and Amariah knew enough to do as she was told.
She was getting heavy, but I rested her weight against my
hip. She curled a hand around my neck and whispered in
my ear, "What's going on, *tante*?"

"We don't know yet."

Michael came to stand beside me. He was tall, over six
feet, and he'd dressed up for Pesach, donning a suit, tie,
and yarmulke. I imagined many people found him handsome. He had a classic square jaw and serious gray eyes.
Even though he looked Italian to me, his Hebrew was flaw-
less, and he knew the Haggadah by heart. I appreciated
that about him—he had a lot of respect for our ways. And
he used to be a cop. I understood that part best. It made
us kin.

Though I held her tightly, Michael hovered protectively
behind Amariah and I. His friend, the one who'd come in
with him, looked on warily. Though he was dressed like an
Israeli soldier, I figured him for some kind of counselor or
psychiatrist, the way he watched over Michael.

The man claiming to be Elijah stood up. Michael's friend
stepped behind the old man like a guardian angel and exchanged dark glances with Michael. I didn't like being between those two at all. There was a tension in the air.
Amariah must have sensed it too, as she twisted her fingers
around the back of my neck.

"Maybe you should go," I told the old man.

"You would throw me out? After I've spent so long
searching for this little one?"

"Messiah," I heard someone whisper, and then in Hebrew: *"Moshiach."*

All eyes turned to Amariah. She was picking her nose
and thinking very intently about wiping it on my shirt.

I dug out a handkerchief from my pocket and handed it
to her.

"She's a child, and she isn't even Jewish," I told the old man. "You've come to the wrong house."

"She's the one I'm looking for," insisted the supposed prophet. He continued to watch the child. His eyes seemed kind rather than predatory. Still, I didn't like him.

"A four-year-old will lead Israel to victory?" I said, looking at Amariah, who seemed content to inspect her fingers. "She's not a great warrior, or judge, or political leader. None of the things the *moshiach* is supposed to be."

"There's time," the old man said. "If she gets the proper teaching and training, who knows? Don't we all have the capability of being *moshiach*?"

It was true. Many Jews believed that the *moshiach* would be a normal human being and that in every generation there is born someone who has the potential to be our anointed one.

Deidre got up to stand beside Michael. "So what if you've found your messiah? What happens next?"

The old man shrugged. "She should go to Israel and learn to be a Jew."

"Israel? No one in their right mind would go to Israel right now. I have a job, an apartment . . ." Deidre said, smoothing down an errant lock of the girl's hair. "And anyway, Amariah was baptized Catholic."

"What?" Michael looked shocked, as if he hadn't known. His voice dropped as he added, "I thought we talked about that."

I said to the old man, "You see? You're mistaken. Why don't you go now?"

To my surprise he struggled to his feet. "So eager to have me go, eh, Rebeckah? Why, I wonder? Is it because you sense the fate that awaits you in this new age?"

I handed Amariah over to Deidre, who took her gratefully. Then I gave the old man my arm to lean on. "What fate is that, old man?"

"Some believe I'm only the first herald."

Herald? That sounded Christian. Not something I would expect from an Orthodox Jew, much less Elijah, but I said nothing. I brought him closer to the door. We stopped in front of it.

"Your road will be hard," was all he said.

"Okay," I said, not knowing what to make of all this talk about me. Hadn't he said he was here for Amariah? "Good-bye."

I opened the door, and Elijah stepped through.

And disappeared.

In front of my eyes, he melted into thin air. No, that wasn't right. He melted into the two men who now stood at my door instead. It was like someone had turned off the holo-feed on Elijah and turned on the one of the new visitors. I liked the look of these men even less. Dressed in black, they looked imposing. On the left breast of each of their jackets was the symbol of the world pierced by a wooden cross, with the scales of justice balanced on the cross's arms.

"Inquisitors." And Lutheran, by the dour expression on their faces. I sent out a warning on the kibbutz's private band: *Inquisitors.*

"Are you Rebeckah Klein?"

"I am," I said. Behind me I could hear chairs turning over as people scrambled to find escape routes.

"We need to speak with you." The way he said it, it was clear I had no choice in the matter.

Oy fucking vay was right.

ARTIFICIAL INTELLIGENCE SPEAKS AT SENATE HEARING

Page: "I'm No Messiah"

Washington Post (April 2083)

Washington, DC—Speaking through voice recognition, the artificial intelligence known as Page attended a closed, real-time hearing of the U.S. Commission on Established Religions (CER). The hearing is a continuance of the argument for granting a temporary license to practice to a splinter group of the Acolytes of the Second Buddha (known more commonly by the derogatory term "Maizombies") who want to deify Page. The group is calling itself the Sect of the Risen AI.

The AI Page spoke against the sect, stating that his own religious beliefs were in opposition to the role of messiah. "I am a Muslim," Page said. "I'm a servant of Allah, not a Buddhist god."

Akira Sasaki, the sect member appointed to the official role of defender of the faith, reminded the committee members that Jesus considered himself a Jew when he became the leader of a brand-new religion. "Some could even make the argument that Jesus resisted the role of Messiah," Sasaki continued. "Just as Page does now."

When asked whether or not Page's role in Mai's death affected the conviction of the sect, Sasaki said, "Page honorably assisted the Buddha in her transition to a new life."

However, the sect faces bigger problems than a reluctant messiah. The sect's parent group, the Acolytes, received their license to practice only three years ago. Though a recent poll shows that the number of Acolyte practitioners has reached the requisite 100,000 members, they have not yet petitioned to change their status from cult to new religion. When asked about the delay in filing, High Priestess Kyoko Watanabe listed this schism as the reason for her delay. It is generally the precedent that the CER recognizes only splinter groups from established *religions,* not cults. Watanabe went on to say, "I won't file until we settle this nonsense. Page is not a prophet. Not a god. Those who believe so are blasphemers."

Head of the Commission Pastor-Senator Joan White said that, while the Acolytes' delay in filing is troubling, the newness of any given splinter within a movement cannot be the only factor to consider when recognizing a person's right to practice. "Groups this young schism all the time, but that doesn't make them any less valid. Wiccan groups hive off without having to go through this process.

Thus, we have to review the depth of conviction of the believers, as well as their creed," said White. "More important, the Maizombies are gaining popularity hand over fist. Even if we wanted to, the Commission can't stop a movement this strong."

Other commission members disagree that the CER should be involved at all. "This whole thing is a joke," said Commission member Shaman-Representative Richard Talltree. "I don't know why the commission is wasting its time on this non-issue. The purpose of CER is to make sure no one is starving in the street because they don't have access to the LINK. We recognized the Acolytes already. The sect has access to the LINK through their parent organization. We shouldn't be involved in legitimizing various aspects of someone else's belief system."

Page is expected to attend the hearings throughout the week.

CHAPTER 4

❖

Page

The Paris node is old and riddled with holes worn by time and widened by wire wizards. In my virtual view, the place smells of neglect and decay. Darkness surrounds me in this cramped and ancient space. Like standing under a colander, tiny pinpricks of light shoot through the domed roof. The spots dance by my feet as I kick up dust. Motes swim and swirl in the shafts of brightness.

"Hello?" My voice bounces against a closed port like an echo.

I went to check on the Senate hearing for less than the time it usually takes for Mouse to type another line, only to return to find him off-line. My father is so impatient. I'm sure he thinks I left without saying good-bye. I spin a script that will send him ASCII flowers and an apology next time he connects. I drop the roses and the note near the hole he usually uses to speak to me.

"Gone again?"

The dragon pokes her head around the corner. In the darkness of the node, I can only see the sparkling swirl of her eyes. She's too large to fit comfortably inside the terminal's cul-de-sac enclosure, so she stays in the connecting line.

I touch the tiny hole. It feels rough and cold. Closed. Even though his words come out painfully slowly, I cherish the time my father chooses to spend with me.

"I guess so," I say, standing up, careful not to step on the roses.

The dragon blinks, waiting for me to join her.

I touch my lips to my fingers and then press them against the hole. *"Allah protect you, Father."*

Leaving the node, I join the dragon. Because it is used by traffic control, the connection appears like a subway tunnel. The dragon's motherboard-green scales scrape against the ceiling. Paris really needs to upgrade its lines. Behind her, I move easily through the space, but I'm small and compact. I look a little like my father, although not as much as I once did. My time merged with Mai changed me. The dragon tells me that I have Mai's eyes and my father's Egyptian skin tone. I wear my hair like Mouse does—short and boyish, but my body is long, lithe, and more feminine than when my father first created me.

And, in secret, I've started writing music.

It is written that Iblis's muezzin will be music. A muezzin calls the faithful to prayer, like the bells of a Christian church. In this subtle way, "other" music can open a person to sin and the Devil. Yet I can't help myself. The part of me that is Mai's soul can't *not* write music.

I follow as the dragon leads us to the entertainment band. I should have known she wouldn't waste much time before coming here. The dragon loves the colors and the space of the entertainment lines. For me, it's like stepping out of a dark alleyway into a carnival. Thousands of people and personas cluster around celebrities' booths. Music pounds us from every side: zydeco, polka, rock and roll, opera, rhythm and blues, classical, and jazz—it shifts with every step.

The dragon stretches her wings. Resistor beads glitter in the bright lights. I once asked her about her wings. Eastern dragons don't usually have them. The dragon said simply, "They're pretty."

"Where are we going?" I ask her now.

She sniffs at the wind, then shrugs her massive shoulders. *"Wherever you want."*

She's been very accommodating ever since I was released from the Siberian auto plant where I served my sentence for my part in Mai's death. I know she still works for the yakuza, but whenever we meet she pretends she has nothing better to do than hang out with me.

I stop to watch an aikido demonstration. She looks farther down the street at a bread-baking show, but she curls her tail around her feet and waits with me. The dragon loves anything that has to do with food. Electronically reproducing the experience of eating is a hobby of hers.

"Why don't you go watch," I tell her when I notice her lifting her nose to sniff in the direction of the bread stall again. _"I'll join you in a bit."_

She looks at me with sad eyes.

"It's not that I don't want your company," I say. _"But I'll be okay for a while. Plus, you know I get bored with food. We can meet by that music stall in a hour or so."_ I point to indicate the one I mean.

After looking me over, apparently trying to find any kind of trace of insincerity, she decides I'll be all right. _"Okay,"_ she says. _"One hour."_

"I'll be there or you can come find me, my love," I say, giving her a peck on the scales under her eye. My hobby is movement and touch, so I'm pleased when she sighs contentedly at my kiss.

I watch her bound happily over to the other stall. People dash madly out of her way as her tail slashes back and forth like a puppy's.

I smile. I do love her, but I've gotten very used to being alone. She works very hard to respect my new silence, yet there are times that I can feel her anxiously watching and worrying. My stillness frightens her a little, I think. The dragon worries that part of me is missing. She's right, of course. Part of me is dead.

In order to make the love bomb work, I had to sacrifice my memories of love. My isolation in the Siberian auto plant did nothing to help me regain them. Because she visited me when she could, I have remembered how to love the dragon a little. She can tell, however, that my love is not what it was. I feel bad about that, but there's nothing I can do. The memories have been reallocated.

"There he is," I hear someone say behind me. I feel myself tense. All I want is to be left alone, but whenever I'm in public Mai's fans seem to home in on me.

I turn around to see the image of a young American dressed in the classic trappings of youth: black T-shirt, jeans, and running shoes. The thing that makes me suspect she is a Maizombie is her hair. It's a perfect copy of Mai's old style. A flood of wild strands cascades down to her waist in waves of braids, coils of curls, beaded cornrows, mats of dreads; it looks like a mishmash of every style ever popular, yet somehow it all works together. The American also wears the round mirrored glasses favored by Mai in her life. They part the mountain of hair so that the bottom half of her face is visible.

"Peace," she says to me.

I bow my head slightly in greeting. She is not Muslim, but unknowingly she offers what is otherwise a very traditional salaam. Thus I reply, *"Peace and blessings be upon you."*

She smiles at me with that look of awed admiration so many Maizombies seem to get in my presence. It unnerves me. I don't know what to say or do. Should I offer a protocol handshake? Give her my blessings? All of it seems strange and foreign. We are one stranger greeting another, not prophet and disciple.

"How's it going?" I say finally.

"Better since you came into my life," she says. *"Everything . . . everything is so new, so important, you know?"*

"Uh, I'm glad for you," I say. Maizombies like to tell me how I've changed them. When I carved out my memories to form the love bomb, billions of people experienced what love had meant to me simultaneously all over the world. Some seemed to be profoundly affected by this experience. They said that they gained an "AI's perspective." I have never understood what they meant by that. I imagine I would understand better if I could remember what I'd lost.

The zombie stares at me with that glassy, longing look. *"It must be so cool to be you,"* she says finally.

How should I respond to that? I shake my head and shrug. *"I suppose."*

"Okay, cool," she says, and begins to slowly move away, her eyes still watching me. As she steps back into the crowd, I can see waves of information flying from her like fluttering, brightly colored banners. She is broadcasting

every detail of her encounter with me to Maizombies everywhere. The spot where she stood is now marked with a red cube: a bookmark. The square is a recording, a beacon for other Maizombies should they want to pilgrimage to this moment on the LINK.

I sigh. I can't imagine I make a good messiah. I so rarely have pearls of wisdom to dispense.

I feel the presence of someone else coming up beside me: a new pilgrim already?

When I turn to face him, it appears so. The person approaching wears a T-shirt sporting a concert photo of Mai. She played cello naked, and the T-shirt shows a clear image of her breasts on either side of the slender neck of strings.

I bow to the new stranger, and say, *"Peace and blessings upon you."*

His response is not what I expect: *"You desecrated Mai's shrine, you soulless bastard!"*

"I did no such thing," I say.

"You did," the stranger insists, and he throws a packet of information at me. I dodge it, not knowing whether or not it's viral. *"Pick it up,"* he insists.

"Do you really think Mai was an infidel?"

Technically she was, being a Buddhist and not a Muslim, but I don't think that is the right answer at the moment. A crowd of avatars starts gathering. They seem hostile. Some of them are rubbing their hands together, forming packets.

"What's going on here?" I ask. I show them that I mean them no harm, by raising my hands. *"There's no need to think about a DoS."* Although, really, I am a far too sophisticated creature to be terribly damaged by denial-of-service, they still hurt.

The first packet slams me in the back. An image of Mai, blood vessels burst in her eyes, jumps unbidden into my stream of consciousness. The next one hits me in the stomach: Mai's face pale and swollen. Mai in her polka-dot hat, smiling, with her wild mane of hair sticking out from under the brim like the quills of a porcupine. Mai playing cello on stage topless. Mai's body: blue and bruised.

I try to block the information, but I hadn't counted on the emotional impact of each image. Mai walking in the park, sunlight dappling the blue halter top she wears. Mai with Kioshi, her lover, stealing a kiss in a Shinto temple. Swollen, dead fingers twitching as she lay on the floor. That one hurts too much. I fall to my knees and collapse.

ATTACK ON MAI'S SHRINE, PAGE BLAMED

Congressional Hearing Halted

Agnostic Press (April 2083)

Rio de Janeiro, Brazil—Today an unknown attacker altered a Brazilian shrine to Mai Kito, a deceased Japanese pop star worshiped by the Maizombies as the incarnation of the Second Buddha. Previously the site featured a music video of Mai's band, the Four Horsemen; the attacker left images of her death followed by the words, *Death to the Infidel.* The message was signed, *In'shallah, Page.*

While it is not yet confirmed that the signature belongs to the AI, this attack follows closely on the heels of a dramatic confrontation between the Page and the Sect of the Risen AI, who are currently seeking a license to practice in the United States. During the congressional hearing, Page declared that he wanted no part of the sect, and that he thought that his own participation in their religion was heretical. Page has routinely refused to speak to sect members who wish to worship him. The records of the prison where Page served time for his part in the death of Mai Kito clearly show a pattern of mounting conflict between Page and his worshipers. At first Page answered any number of questions that came to him during visiting hours, but, as time progressed, he stopped talking to the Maizombies.

He continued, however, to receive visitors of other faiths, especially Muslims.

"The zombies were trying to make Page a god. Page didn't want to encourage them, that's all," said Davydko Chistyakov, the lawyer who represented Page during his trial. "Besides, Page is a thoughtful person. Page wanted to spend the time in prison thinking about the crime. Not dealing with a bunch of loonies."

"Page has it out for us," said Maizombie Nick Tradsyk, who has been leading an around-the-clock vigil for Mai at the site of her altered shrine. "First he killed Mai, now this."

Defender of the Faith for the Sect of the Risen AI Akira Sasaki has petitioned Acolytes of both denominations to cultivate peace. "The investigations have not yet proven that Page is responsible. Even if he is, we should wait to hear what he has to say for himself."

Meanwhile representatives of the Commission on Established Religions (CER) have called for a halt in proceedings. The current chair of the commission, Pastor-Senator Joan White, stressed today in a press conference that this is a temporary measure. "We will continue to hear the case of the sect when they have resolved this issue."

"This could have been Page's plan all along," said Tradsyk. "If there's no CER ruling, he gets what he wants: no Sect of Page." It is commonly believed that if a sect can get CER approval, then their international rights quickly follow suit. Without CER's approval, if the sect continues its schism and officially leaves the Acolytes, they could face the possibility of being declared a rogue religion, and, in certain countries, this would mean being barred from LINK privileges.

Page could not be reached for comment.

CHAPTER 5

✠

Michael

Deidre, Amariah, and I huddled together in the kitchen, hiding out from the Inquisition. Rebeckah had sent a warning via the LINK letting everyone at the Seder know that Inquisitors had met her at the door talking about arrests.

Deidre was wanted by the police for being an unwed mother. It was a law that had gotten on the books shortly after the war, when ultraconservatism was the rage, and had mostly been ignored since. Thanks to cracking the LINK-angel case for me, Deidre was a high-profile celebrity, and there were always people looking to defame her.

Neither of us thought that the Inquisition was here for her, though. We had hunkered down in the kitchen as a precaution, and a concession of sorts. Deidre didn't want to leave Rebeckah alone, but neither of us wanted to endanger Amariah. Hiding under a stainless-steel countertop straining to hear what was going on in the other room was our compromise.

We sat on the cold, hard linoleum floor. The lights were dimmed, and all of the metallic surfaces held a dull shine.

"Why does it always have to be like this with you, Michael?" Deidre asked quietly, as she stroked Amariah's hair. She was sitting with her knees almost under her chin. One arm tucked around her legs held the hem of her dress against her skin. The other encircled Amariah, who was pressed into Deidre's side. Amariah had her thumb in her mouth. I sat a few inches away, not touching either of them. Deidre's eyes flicked over to me again, accusatory. "Why does God always have to meddle in our lives?"

I gave her a sharp glance. God hadn't been in my life for months. She knew that. And anyway, I was almost completely certain God had nothing to do with Inquisitors.

I hugged my knees and tried to imagine my arms around Deidre and Amariah—holding on tightly, making things better instead of worse.

Deidre glanced nervously at the door. "This is crazy. It's not like we can hide from God. I tried that once, remember?" She shook her head. "Shit. I always knew something like this would happen again. But you promised me, Michael. You promised that our daughter wasn't going to be the messiah."

It was Elijah's appearance not the Inquisitors' that bothered her so much; I should have known.

I shook my head. "What I said was that just because I was an archangel didn't mean that our daughter would turn out to be a messiah."

"And now Elijah's at the door."

"And he left," I felt I had to point out.

"I wish he hadn't come after all," Amariah said into the folds of Deidre's dress.

"Me too," Deidre said.

I didn't know what to say. I wasn't particularly happy either that Elijah wanted to claim my daughter as the savior of Judea. I would have preferred if God had just forgotten about our little family. I felt guilty saying that, however. I was an archangel once. I should be overjoyed that God had given me direction again. After all, my role here was once again made clear: raise my daughter to be the *moshiach*.

Raised voices came from the other side of the door.

"We need to find somewhere safe," I said, thinking of the Inquisitors on the other side of the kitchen door.

Deidre shook her head. "Safe? Nowhere is safe enough."

I felt anxious all the same. I wanted to get out, run. My skin crawled, as though eyes watched us, seeing through our hiding place.

"No place is safe from God," Dee muttered again. "You

were the archangel, Michael. You tell me, was there any-
place that you couldn't go, anywhere you couldn't see?"

A headache sprouted between my eyes. I rubbed at the
bridge of my nose. "It was complicated, Deidre. I don't
remember what it was like to be merged with God, but
once I was sent here I saw things like you do—limited by
flesh. I could no more see around a corner or through a
wall than you could."

"God can see through walls," Amariah said brightly. "He
can see anything."

"Actually, honey, we're still debating that," Deidre said.
"What I want to know is, can he do anything about what
he sees, or does he always have to send an emissary, like
he sent you?"

"God can too see through walls," Amariah insisted. "He
can do anything. That's what Joan said."

"Joan?" I asked.

"The Sunday-school teacher," Deidre said quietly into
Amariah's hair, giving her a quick peck on the head.

"You're taking her to Sunday school?" I could feel myself getting angry. Bad enough that Amariah had been baptized Catholic. I'd really planned for her to have a bit
broader religious education. Maybe it was this narrow focus
that had Elijah breathing down our necks. The thought that
Deidre's stubbornness had caused this . . . I had to concentrate to keep my voice low and my tone even. "I thought
we'd agreed to talk about Amariah's religious education."

"Keep your shorts on. I've been going to an ecumenical
place, you know, for myself. They had a nice educational
component," Deidre said with a shrug. Then, frowning defensively, she added, "Look, you were the one who said
she'd benefit from this sort of thing."

"Ecumenical? You mean Christian ecumenical."

"I'm not taking her to a synagogue, if that's what you
mean."

"Deidre!"

"Listen, it must be working. Elijah thinks she's the
messiah."

I gritted my teeth. "Or he's here to take over her education. What happened to the private tutor I sent?"

"Ariel!" Amariah said cheerfully.

"Yes," I said. "What happened to Ariel?"

"Michael, do you really think that Ariel is an appropriate religious teacher for Amariah?"

"Ariel taught the Kabbalah to the Jews. She invented alchemy. She's an excellent teacher," I said.

"She's a *he*," Deidre said. "You know, what people do with their own lives is their own business, but I didn't want Amariah exposed to that sort of thing just yet."

"What 'sort of thing' do you mean, exactly?" Since we had no gender in Heaven, angels could, if they chose, come to earth either male or female. Ariel had chosen to be both, which was also correct.

"Don't get all self-righteous on me, mister," Deidre said, wagging her finger in my face. "You know precisely what I mean."

I shook my head. "You can be such a homophobe sometimes, Deidre. Ariel isn't gay, as far as I know. No more than I am."

Deidre dropped her voice to a whisper, as if Amariah weren't soaking up every word we said. "That's hardly a strong endorsement. I remember that guy from the kibbutz, what was his name?"

I could feel myself blushing just a little; I'd forgotten about Matthew. "Fine, but Ariel is hardly going to bring home lovers when she's teaching Amariah."

Deidre shook her head. "Look, I just didn't want him teaching my child. I'm not willing to compromise on this one."

"Ariel is an angel of the Lord, Deidre," I said. "She's not some streetwalker."

"Then he shouldn't dress like one."

My mouth hung open until a frustrated sigh forced its way out. "Ariel is just exercising her free will," I said. "Underneath, she's still an archangel."

"Yes, on a mission from God," Deidre said. "Maybe he narced on us."

Narced? I hadn't considered the possibility that I'd opened my life to God the moment I asked Ariel to tutor my child. "No, I don't think so," I said. "Ariel has been on earth awhile. She doesn't talk to God that often."

"What, like you, Michael? Cold comfort."

I sat back against the counter. Her words added an extra

sting to the pain blossoming between my eyes. "No," I said. "Not like me."

I stared at the ceiling. My jaw muscle twitched as I tried to repress my anger. It wasn't my fault that, in severing myself from God, I'd become damaged.

My spirit belonged in Heaven. I had once been part of God, an extension of His will. The longer I stayed away, the more my soul fused with my body, my flesh. But I didn't belong here, on Earth, and my body kept rejecting my spirit. Those dark days were pure madness. The boundaries of "me" melted as my spirit tried to expel itself from the confines of its shell.

The difference between Ariel and me was simple. Her spirit freely returned to Heaven whenever she desired; her body understood that its existence was temporary. Me, I meant to inhabit this plain forever, or at least so long as Amariah and Deidre lived. Even as my body refused my soul, my soul refused Heaven. Thus I wandered in a borderland of neither here nor there.

I'd been back to Heaven a couple of times since falling in love with Deidre, but each time I grew less certain that God would allow my return to Earth. They always had a purpose when they cast angels to the Earth. It was not like Them to send me on a sentimental, frivolous mission. As far as I knew there was no divine plan in my love for Deidre and Amariah; it just was.

If I could make my case in front of God, I was certain that She would find it in Her heart to allow my return. But in Heaven I wasn't Michael; I was God. My individuality completely merged with the divine. Who I was—my memories, my everything—was subsumed to the higher being, the higher cause.

"I'm sick of archangels," Deidre said with a sigh. "I just want a normal life for Amariah."

"So do I," I said.

Deidre's eyes expressed surprise at the tone of my voice. "You do?"

"Dee, it's what I've wanted all along."

"Then go tell God to stay away from her."

Go. She meant to Heaven. I felt a shiver go up my spine. "I know I've disappointed you, Dee," I started.

"Damn straight," she said. She looked away, as if suddenly interested in the gleam of the refrigerator.

"Give me a chance to make it up to you," I said. I gently touched the top of Amariah's head. "To both of you."

"Well, I've got an idea," Deidre said. "If you really want to make my life better, why don't you go back to where you're from and tell God to leave me and mine alone."

"I have to go potty," Amariah announced.

I was grateful for the opportunity not to answer. The idea of losing myself, after I'd fought for my sanity so hard, seemed unfair.

"We should probably get our stuff and head out," I said. "The Inquisition is bound to search the place eventually."

Deidre sighed and looked at Amariah. "Yeah, we should probably get you home."

"I have to go potty," Amariah repeated more urgently.

"There's one near. I can take her," I said. When I saw Deidre's face twitch as though struggling to come up with an excuse not to let me, I added, "It'll give me a chance to say good-bye."

"Oh . . . okay," Deidre said quietly. "I suppose that's fair. Especially if you're, you know, really *going*."

"I have to think about that," I said. "I meant for now. I was kind of hoping to come by on Monday after my job. Maybe take her out for pizza or something."

"Pizza!" Amariah shouted, distracted momentarily from her bathroom needs.

"That's fine with me," Deidre agreed with a little frustrated smile. "As long as Elijah hasn't run off with her to Israel."

"He won't." I took Amariah's hand and stood up.

Raphael stood in front of the kitchen door. He leaned on an unsheathed broadsword, his wings spread. I looked in the other direction, toward the other door that took us out into the main hallway. The archangel Jibril stood underneath the glowing exit sign. He held a scimitar in front of his chest. He wore a flowing, multicolored robe like those worn in Ethiopia. His wings were green and gold like a peacock's. I could see the glint of the holographic tattoo between his eyes, words that read, *there is no God but Allah, and Mohammad is His prophet.*

"We've got trouble," I said, sitting back down.

Deidre stretched to look over the countertop. "Huh," she said. "How long you boys been there?"

When the angels didn't answer, she sat back down. "One of us should make a break for it."

I nodded, getting ready to stand up. Deidre pulled me back down, shaking her head. She pointed to herself, and then to where the angels stood guard.

"I should fight them," I said.

No, she mouthed. *You take Amariah.*

She must have a plan, I decided. I gave her the okay sign and took Amariah's hand.

"I gotta go potty, Papa. Now," she whispered.

"I know, Rye. Just hang on another couple of minutes."

Just then the door from the dining hall sprang open. A member of the kibbutz barreled into Jibril, nearly knocking the archangel off his feet.

"Get out of here right now! They're taking Rebeckah!" The next through was Tom, his Anhk swinging wildly against his chest. "The kibbutz is bugging out!"

ISRAEL SEIZES TEMPLE MOUNT

Agnostic Press (April 2083)

Jerusalem, Israel—Four hours after a meteorite destroyed the Dome of the Rock and portions of al-Aqsa, Israeli soldiers have cordoned off the area.

The office of Prime Minister Avashalom Chotzner responded to allegations of Israeli expansionism with this statement at a recent press conference: "Temple Mount has been ours since the Six Day War in 1967. It was only by our good graces the Waqf [the Muslim governing body] have been allowed the administration of the portion beyond the Western Wall. We have not extended our borders by an inch."

However legal this move may be, many in the

Arab world see the occupation of the former grounds of the Noble Sanctuary by Israeli forces as a slap in the face. "To be frank, the occupation is an outrage," said Palestinian president Idris Quasim. "Our people are mourning the tragic and accidental loss of the second holiest site in our religion, the place where Mohammad, peace be upon his name, ascended into heaven. This is not the time for Israel's jackboots to trample on holy ground."

In his statement, Quasim also appealed for peace. People are already camping out on the Israeli-guarded borders of the meteor crater. A number of scuffles have broken out between those gathered and the army.

The recent hijacking of Temple Rock, the virtual free zone, has heightened already escalating tension. Many people gathered at the Dome feel as though they have no place to pray, and that every aspect of the Dome of the Rock has been forever closed off to them. It is felt that Quasim has not accurately expressed the rage many Muslims feel at the sight of an Israeli flag flying over what is perceived as their holy land. " 'An outrage?' No, this is more than 'an outrage'; it's an act of war. It's what the Jews have been waiting for," said one Palestinian man who asked not to be identified, referring to the long-standing claim by many Jews that the area the Dome stood on is the site of the first Jewish temple. "Quasim should fight them. We should all fight them."

CHAPTER 6

Mouse

"Christian!" Monique says when I walk in the back door twelve and a half minutes late.

"Bonjour," I say. Monique calls me Christian because it's my given name. A long story, but my mother, the comedian, named me Christian because she suspected my father was not a Muslim. Ho. Ho. Good one, Mom.

Anyway, it isn't like I can tell these people to call me Mouse. Mouse is an internationally wanted criminal; I'm just a dishwasher. I thought about having them call me "Souris," which is French for Mouse, but then I decided that sounded low-res. Besides, I didn't want anyone to put two and two together.

Monique gives me a disapproving glare. I try to look appropriately sheepish as she rattles off some really fast, irritated French that I don't have a prayer of understanding. I know the routine, though, so I slump my head apologetically and nod a lot. I throw in a few *"Je regrette"*'s, which I hope meant "I'm sorry," but don't really care. Once she feels I've been sufficiently berated, Monique turns on her stiletto heels and glides back into the restaurant. I hang up my coat with the others and head to the dishwashing station.

Jon, the short-order cook, nods at me. Jon is a big Caribbean immigrant who somehow manages to look good in a greasy white T-shirt. He's a pleasant enough guy to work with, though, and I'm happy to see we're on the same shift for a couple of days.

But I can't really figure out Jon's deal. From what I can tell, he actually chooses to work here. Worse, I think he likes his job. He sings while he fries onions and beef, and seems to make a lot of easy jokes with the female wait staff. When it gets steamy back here, which it always does, I can see the sweaty outline of the LINK receptor under his brown skin. It's an almond-shaped lump on his right temple. Sometimes Jon notices me staring at it jealously. Of course, he should know my own receptor is trashed. I mean, why the hell else would I work here for barter? Even so, I figure he thinks I'm gay because he always winks and gives me a broad grin.

Despite all that, I prefer Jon to all the other cooks. At least he doesn't try to engage me in conversation. Which, considering how rotten my French is, is a relief. I understand French better than I can speak it, so talking is a major hassle. Anyway, if I have to work here, I just want to do it and get it over with. I'm not here to make friends; I'm here to get food.

I roll up my sleeves and get started. They have an industrial-size dishwasher that I spend eight hours loading and unloading. But I'm also expected to scrape the crap that people leave on their plates and use the power hose to clear off what food residue I can.

When I first started, it killed me to throw away all that food—some of it barely touched. Now I only notice the extremely gross shit, like when people stub out their cigarettes in runny egg yolks. It's enough to put a hungry man off his food.

I use the hose to blast the plates that piled up since the shift started without me, and Jon sings something slow and sad. We fall into a rhythm, but time still manages to crawl. My shoes are soaked, and my feet are cold and wet by the time dinner break comes.

Jon puts a breakfast plate in front of me—eggs, ham, and toast. The ham is touching everything, even the toast.

My stomach growls, and I pick up my fork. My knife hovers over the ham steak, but I just can't do it. I push the plate away. There are so few things I do as a Muslim that breaking halal seems beyond the pale. Sure, for most people dietary restrictions are the first thing they break. But for me it's different. It's cultural. I don't drink alcohol either.

"Qu'est-ce que passe?" Jon asks. He wants to know what's happening.

I blame myself, really. It's not like I advertise my faith. Everyone assumes I'm an atheist or fallen away from some other religion, since they can't hail me by LINK. I don't dress like your typical Muslim; I don't wear a beard.

"Je suis malade." I tell him I feel sick. It's one of the few French phrases I've learned how to pronounce properly; otherwise I'd never get a day off. I don't know the word for Muslim. I don't know how to express halal. I tried talking to Jon in Arabic and English, but French is the only language we have in common. I've heard that the Inquisitors, the international cops, have built-in language translators. It'd be nice if they shared that tech with the common man.

I guess I look really miserable, because Jon, bless his heart, gets up and offers me a scone from the secret stash. Because all of the dishwashers and half of the cooks work for barter, all the preprepared food is kept locked up.

Jon pats my head and tells me he hopes I feel better by the end of my shift because he's making me bacon-wrapped scallops.

"Merciful Allah, what, is this national pig day?"

Just then the swinging doors bang open, and Monique looks more pissed off at me than usual. I hide the scone under the countertop. Her nose wrinkles like she doesn't like the taste of the words coming out of her mouth. I understand just enough to be really confused.

"Une femme? Pour moi?" I have to ask to be sure. I think Monique has just told me that there is a very important woman at the restaurant to see me. When Monique *tsk*s her tongue and tries to flatten the cowlick at the back of my head, I realize that I'm actually going to get to go out into the big room. Will wonders never cease? She holds out her hand for my apron. I tuck the scone in the pocket, and slip it off my head and give it to her.

"Avez bien." Be good, she tells me slowly so she's sure I understand.

"Okay, Mom," I say. It ticks me off that people feel they can patronize me just because I'm only five-foot-six.

She laughs a little, understanding my tone if not my words. When Monique opens the door for me, I almost bolt. At first all I can think is, *Oh, shit, an Inquisitor.* I recognize the style and cut of the jet-black leather uniform instantly. I've devoted my entire life to avoiding them.

But then I notice the insignia have all been ripped off or painted over. I register the deceptively soft, round face and dark black curls. Sitting in my crummy little restaurant is none other than Emmaline McNaughton, ex-priest and rogue agent, and the only person on the planet more wanted by the Inquisition than me.

Now I'm really nervous. How did Emmaline find me again? Last time we met I was in prison.

"Je ne connais pas cette femme," I say, hoping I've just told Monique I don't know that woman. Monique shakes her head and pushes me toward the table. My shoes squeak, and I leave wet prints on the tile. It's colder in the main restaurant, and I feel steam escaping from my hair. A couple of the patrons look up from their meals, but when they notice the rogue Inquisitor's uniform, they look away quickly.

Emmaline stands, and, like a perfect gentleman, offers me a chair. Monique retreats without a word, but I can almost read her mind through the expression in her eyes. She's thinking, *Make a scene, and I'll fire your ass.*

Or maybe I'm already bounced for attracting someone like Emmaline McNaughton here. No doubt the cops are on their way. Defeated, I sit down. "What do you want?"

"Christian El-Aref?"

She knows exactly who I am. It's not like we've never met before. I wonder if she's just trying to scare me by using my given name. "Depends," I say, playing her game. "You buying this El-Aref guy dinner?"

She laughs. "Sure, whatever you want."

"Pasta," I say, naming my favorite variety. "Risotto verde."

Emmaline looks off to the side, LINKing my request to Jon. Most of our pastas are precooked. This is important, because I figure we've got twenty minutes, tops, before the cops show up. Someone here would be calling, if Monique hasn't already.

"So . . ." I say when the Inquisitor doesn't offer any kind of conversational gambit. "Nice duds. Really inconspicuous."

Emmaline looks down at the spot just over her heart where the insignia of the Order should be. "I suppose you think I should abandon my office simply because they have abandoned me."

I, too, glance at the spot where the sigil has been ripped off. "You're the one who damaged the uniform."

"It's my concession to being rogue. A kind of ultimate fuck-you."

"Huh," I say. "I suppose a slinky little pink frock just isn't you, is it?"

She smiles. "No. The uniform is one of the world's best armors. Do you know how much it would go for on the black market?"

Six thousand credits easy for a complete uniform, more if the insignia were still intact. "I'd take the jacket for a hundred."

"I'll bet you would." Emmaline laughs. "But this is my second skin. You'd have to pry it off my dead body."

Which is, usually, where the black market ones come from. I honestly didn't expect Emmaline to take my offer seriously on the uniform. Besides the armoring, it has a lot of nifty features: a cooling/heating system that regulates her body temperature, and hidden compartments for extra weapons—not to mention the fear factor. The uniform was designed by a crack team of psychologists to innately inspire fear. In fact, I find myself having to look away in order to coolly ask: "So, what brings you to Paris?"

Emmaline's table faces a big picture window that looks out onto the boulevard Saint-Michel. The view is spectacular. Across the street I see the park, which holds the Palais du Luxembourg, although all you can really see from here is the old-growth oak trees and expansive green space. A few Parisians, in stylish long coats, are out walking their beloved, uncurbed dogs.

The Inquisitor runs a long, thin finger along the edge of her glass. "You, honestly."

"Me?" My voice squeaks. I hate when that happens. I clear my throat. "You know, I did that interview with the kid from *Let's Go Paris,* but I didn't really think anyone would consider the dishwasher at La Vie a national landmark."

"It's not the dishwasher I'm interested in."

"Huh," I say, looking out the window. "Well, that's all you got."

"I was looking for Mouse."

Wouldn't you know it: she stops playing the game just when I'm getting into it. "The health department gave us a clean bill last week. You won't find any rodents here."

"No?"

"Nope," I say, continuing to watch the street instead of her eyes. The boulevard used to be a main artery for vehicular traffic going back and forth from the Right and Left Banks, but the Medusa put an end to that. Paris got glassed right in its heart—the Île de la Cité and some of the surrounding bits of either bank—wiping out some major tourist attractions, including the famed Notre Dame cathedral.

Tourists still flocked to this place, though. Mostly they came on foot. Farther up the boulevard, near the Sorbonne, you could rent an environmental suit and sign up for a tour of the glass. The Louvre, I hear, is impressive in the early-morning light. And dodging Gorgons has become a kind of thrill for a lot of crazy tourists.

Monique herself finally brings the food. "Would *monsieur* like anything else?"

She speaks perfect English. What a bitch.

"How about a bottle of wine," Emmaline suggests.

"No wine for me. How about a coffee?"

"A glass of Bordeaux for me and a black coffee for my guest," Emmaline says, barely looking at Monique. Then she sends my boss off with a dismissive wave.

"Don't piss her off too much, lady; she's my gravy train," I say, digging into the fresh spinach-covered risotto.

Emmaline leans on her elbows and says what I've been half expecting all along. "How would you like to work for me instead?"

I wave my fork at the pressed tin ceiling, dripping chicken broth on the linen tablecloth. "What, and give up all this?"

"I could make it worth your while."

I doubt that. I read hard copies of the news when I can find them. McNaughton has been on the run, too. Her life is probably worse than mine; otherwise why would she come looking for me? "You need a personal dishwasher or something? Maybe I could do a week's worth of dishes for the jacket."

She doesn't even crack a smile. "It would be far too big for you. And what I really need is for you to work a little digital magic."

The too-big crack kind of stings: I'm not *that* small. I swallow another forkful of pasta. "Couldn't even if I wanted to, lady. My LINK's a slag heap." I point at my plate. "I think this comes with a salad."

She glances off to the right. "The salad is extra. What if I could get you back on-line?"

"You must have missed the part where I told you I was fried out," I say around a full mouth.

Emmaline smiles broadly then; it's a strangely cold look. "A friend of mine is well versed in miracles."

"She'd have to be," I say.

"He is."

I shift in my seat, and my socks squish coldly inside my shoes. I have to admit I'm sort of interested in getting out of the dishwashing business. "Maybe you'd better tell me what you want, exactly."

"I have a copy of your Page program."

I nearly choke on my risotto. "What?"

"Page didn't tell you?" Again that creepy smile slides across her face, like she's glad he's been naughty or something. But I don't care about that; Page can have whatever secrets he wants. I am his maker, not his keeper.

"I don't understand how that could even work," I say, using the linen napkin to wipe some sauce off my shirt. "What command did you use? What system?"

"I don't know. He copied himself in the middle of a LINK communication transfer."

I whistle. "That's fucked up."

"Yes," Emmaline says. She folds her hands and puts them primly in her lap. We watch each other for a moment until the lightbulb goes on for me.

"Okay, I get it. Your Page is in less than working order, and you want me to fix it."

"It's what you do."

"Did." I scrape the last of the spinach and basil out of the bowl and savor it. If I didn't have to have on my company manners, I might even have licked it clean. Outside, tourists point at the statue of Marco Polo in the garden. The sun sets and reflects pink against the blue-gray of the angled rooftops. The *wee-oou-wee-oou* of the gendarmes' sirens echoes down the boulevard. I'm antsy to leave.

"Thanks for dinner, anyway."

She seems kind of surprised at that. Her thin eyebrows arch. "Not even for the LINK?"

"What LINK? You seem to be shy a couple of synapses yourself. I'm busted. Trashed. Nuked. Mangled. Munged. Dead—dead—dead."

"Ask him if he remembers how Deidre got her LINK back."

I didn't see him approach, but sometime during the middle of my rant, a man slid in to stand just behind the left side of Emmaline's chair. He's tall, probably six-foot, and muscular. Only he wears silk like a poofter. His hair is kind of gay, too—long, red, and pulled back into a neat ponytail. His face looks familiar, though. I know I've met him before.

I search for a name and come up with: "Morningstar?"

"In the flesh," he says in a way that makes mine crawl.

METEORITE OR BOMB?

Muslims Demand Access to the Noble Sanctuary

Agnostic Press (April 2083)

Jerusalem, Israel—Muslim leaders are demanding access to the Noble Sanctuary (Dome of the Rock and al-Aqsa mosque) to look for fragments of the meteorite that struck the area last night. Because of previous plots to blow up the Dome of the Rock in order to begin the process of rebuilding the Jew-

ish Temple, Muslim leaders have cast doubt on
what many have referred to as "an act of God."

"We think the Israeli soldiers are hiding evidence
of a bomb," said Palestinian president Idris Quasim. "Why else would they occupy the area so
quickly? Especially when rabbinical law prohibits
them from setting foot on Temple Mount before
being blessed by the ashes of a perfect red heifer."

Israeli Prime Minister Avashalom Chotzner
claims, however, that no Jew has set foot inside the
area that historically belongs to the second Jewish
temple. "We're guarding the crater, that's all." It
is true that Israeli forces have only been spotted
forming a cordon around the Noble Sanctuary.
Chotzner would not reply to accusations of an Israeli bomb, however.

"His silence is proof," said Quasim. "They made
it look like a meteorite so that they could claim
their God did this. It's an act of war and the rest
of the world should view it as such."

However, several amateur astronomers have
LINK recordings of the meteorite's descent. They
believe that based on the angle of the approach, it
could not have come from anywhere on the Earth,
not, at least, without someone reporting seeing the
launch. "To say that this is a bomb is ridiculous,"
said one who asked not to be identified. "It's from
space. Whether or not God had anything to do with
it is not my call, but it's definitely a meteor, not
a bomb."

When asked if Israel would consider allowing a
UN investigator to inspect for meteorite fragments,
Chotzner resolutely refused. "Temple Mount will
remain under our control. Absolutely no one will
enter it without our express permission."

CHAPTER 7

🕮

Rebeckah

We'd been staring at each other for a long time, the Inquisitors and I. In the meantime, the drizzle stained the Inquisitors' uniforms a deeper black. In addition to the standard leather-looking jacket and pants, both wore priestly collars. They'd also brought along Peacemakers. I noticed the heavy pistols hanging from their sides. The blond's hand strayed near his holster as I continued to stand there, blocking the door.

Inquisitors. I should have been scared out of my mind. Instead the old battle calm filled me, draining away all feelings, making the world a distant place. Of course, usually when I felt this quiet and still, I had a gun in my hand. Now the enemy was in front of me and I had no weapon and no place to run.

I wiped my sweaty palm on my jeans.

The blond cleared his throat. "I hate to impose, ma'am, but it's cold out here."

"Right," I said. The shakiness of my own voice surprised me. "Uh, maybe you should come in for a moment," I said, stepping aside to give them room to enter.

"Thank you, ma'am," the blond said with a dimpled grin, like he was trying to be charming. I supposed he could afford to be. The Inquisition had replaced Interpol in breadth of jurisdiction, and had added a lot more teeth. They were the law in its darkest incarnation: power without checks and balances.

The gray-haired Inquisitor put a hand on the blond's elbow.

"I think you should come along with us," Gray-Hair said to me.

"I'd like to know what all this is about," I said, managing an even tone. After all, I was still waiting to hear the dreaded words: *You're under arrest.* I could think of about sixteen things that I might be in trouble for, but none of them was serious enough to attract the attention of the Order of the Inquisition.

"Shoot, ain't no harm in coming in to set a spell," the blond said, pushing past his partner. He was young, probably early thirties. His medium build belied the fact that he was a fully armored cyborg. I'd seen the specs on Inquisitors—very impressive. The same nanotechnology that produced the Medusa bomb had laced his bones with a biosteel alloy that made them nearly unbreakable. Additional synthetic muscle and enhanced neurological response created better reflexes and a higher force payload. He could run forty miles per hour, withstand a fall from several stories, and his fingertips held deadly, thought-triggered lasers. The faded denim blue of his eyes hid a state-of-the-art combat computer, targeting sights, telescopic lenses, and recording equipment. The soft Southern drawl he was laying on thick didn't fool me, either. He could adopt any accent or language the Order had access to.

He rubbed his hands together and blew on them for warmth. "Sure smells wonderful in here, Ms. Klein. You cooking something?"

"Passover dinner," I blurted out, pointing to the buffet tables we'd set up along the wall. "Potluck. I don't cook."

"No, I imagine not," he said, glancing at my outfit with a strange smile. We both looked at my black jeans and the "comfortable shoes" I'd worn for Passover.

Despite laws against gender bending, I couldn't bring myself to put on a dress . . . not even for God. I felt hobbled in a dress, stupid, naked. However, under the Inquisitor's stare the pants were no improvement. He made me feel something I hadn't felt in a long time—deviant.

I looked up to find him regarding my haircut. Our eyes met. My heart thudded deep and heavy in my chest, while my brain raced. There was no way they could know, was there, just by looking? I'd never left any kind of legal trail behind. My lovers and I had always been careful, renting second apartments, never owning anything together. There was that concert that Thistle had talked me into, where there had been rumors of an undercover Inquisitor, but that had been years ago. Why would they come for me now?

"You're thinking awfully hard there." The blond smiled again, softly. Then he carefully wiped his boots on the scrap of carpeting we'd set by the door.

"I'm just wondering what all this is about." *I'm wondering why you haven't arrested me.*

"Right, I've been so rude." He held out his hand for me to shake, which I ignored. He let his hand drop after a moment. "I'm Reverend Jesse Parker, Order of the Baptist Inquisitors." He jerked his thumb over his shoulder to his very sour-looking companion. "That's my partner, Pastor Carl Thorvaldsen of the Lutheran Inquisition."

I nodded at the man, but didn't like taking my eyes off Parker. I'd been wrong about him earlier. He was clearly the one in charge, the "senior" partner. His eyes seemed determined to penetrate me, ferret out all my secrets. My fingers itched for a gun.

"Mind if I sit down?" he asked.

"Go ahead," I said, shoving my hands into my pockets. We both regarded the tipped and empty chairs. Everyone had scattered. There wasn't a person I'd invited to Seder who wasn't wanted for something, and I'd sent out a LINK warning to the rest of the kibbutz. I could hear boots thudding upstairs as my soldiers scrambled for positions. We practiced regularly, preparing for a raid, a standoff, anything.

"Looks like your friends cleared out in a hurry," Reverend Parker said, righting a chair. We both knew that the kibbutz was still in the process of moving out. My scouts had reported that Parker and his partner were the only two peace officers in the Glass City . . . so far. I expected reinforcements anytime now. But for now, my orders were to take what could be moved out quickly, carefully.

Parker pushed aside a plate of half-eaten herbed chicken, and picked up a mug and sniffed it. "Coffee?"

I pointed to the silver urn at the end of the buffet line.

As he made his way over there, I wondered what Parker was playing at with all this deliberation and small talk. It was starting to unnerve me. I imagined that might be the point. I took a breath to try to calm myself.

On his way back he stopped when he noticed his partner still standing outside. "For chrissake, Carl. Get on in here. She's not going to bite you."

The pastor grudgingly complied by taking exactly one step over the threshold.

"Well, how about you guard the door, then," Parker said with a shake of his head. After filling up Michael's half-drunk cup with fresh coffee, Parker sat down at the table. To me he added, "You'll have to forgive Carl. He's having a little trouble dealing with the . . . uh, breadth . . . of our jurisdiction."

I raised an eyebrow, not sure I understood correctly. "He doesn't like dealing with Jews?"

Parker watched me over the rim as he sipped his coffee. "Why don't you sit down? You look uncomfortable."

"No. I prefer to stand." After all, it gave me the illusion that I could still run.

"I insist," Parker said, casually pointing to the spot beside him, at the head of the table. "It'd be easier on both of us."

"Easier?"

"Yes," Parker said. "This sort of thing is best done with the subject sitting. Trust me. Otherwise you wake up with a splitting headache."

"Aren't you here to arrest me?" I said, still standing.

"We're just here to chat."

"Chat," I repeated stupidly. The pleasant-sounding word didn't jibe with Parker's none-too-subtle threats.

"Yes, like civilized people. Over a cup of coffee. Sit down."

Carl took another step inside the doorway. Glancing at him, I got the sense that he'd love to help me find a seat if I didn't do it on my own. I moved over to the table. When I got close enough to sit, Parker stood up and pulled out the chair for me, like I was some kind of lady. Numbly, I sat.

He leaned in close as he tucked me in closer to the table.

I could smell coffee on the breath that tickled my ear. "Correct me if I'm wrong, but you'd love to see the Dome of the Rock destroyed, wouldn't you, Ms. Klein?"

I said nothing, but Parker had me dead to rights. I moved my own plate aside so I could rest my arms on the table. There was a time when I'd seriously entertained hurrying along the Messianic Age by taking the Dome of the Rock out by force. The Dome of the Rock stood on the site of the Jewish temple. If the messiah were to come, the temple would have to be rebuilt. That wasn't going to happen as long as Muslims controlled that area. Of course, since last night, Israel had it again. I only hoped that this time Israel would hold on to it. I couldn't tell these Inquisitors that, though.

"That was a long time ago. I'm retired," I said finally. Then, as an afterthought, I added, "Anyway, that was down to God."

"And what about the Virtual Temple?" he said into my ear. "How would you feel about that?"

I shook my head. "I'm not following."

"This morning a wire wizard violated the 'seventy-two peace treaty by closing off access to the international blank space sometimes called Temple Rock."

A chill went down my spine as I noticed Parker had forgotten his friendly Southern drawl.

I'd heard of Temple Rock, though I'd never visited myself. It was one of the stranger political maneuvers to attempt to ease the contention over the real-time Temple Mount.

The LINK was mostly comprised of the space between people's ears—mental space, virtual, pretend. But in order to keep the several billion LINKed brains from turning into chaos, LINK nodes had been established. LINK nodes were real-time hardware, supercomputers whose function was to keep satellite communication orderly, functioning. Every major city on the planet had at least one node. Each node's LINK presence tended to reflect the flavor of the city itself. The Mecca node became a place of virtual worship. People flocked to Rio's node when they wanted to party at an electronic Carnival. And, in Jerusalem's node, Muslims and Jews and Christians all fought over who had the electronic rights to how much space.

So politicians gathered and decided that one way to keep the peace was to assign one tiny portion of Jerusalem's node as international property. It would belong to no one, but it would be accessible to all. An empty space where people could go and pray to whatever God they chose, as long as no one "built" anything on it. No notes could be left, no images of flowers or tokens, nothing—just emptiness. I supposed they imagined it as the Great Metaphor.

Personally, I thought the gesture as empty as the space. What good did it do a Jew to imagine the potential of the temple in a silent, unreal place, especially when you could always go to the real Western Wall and touch the reality, mourn our loss?

I shrugged. So someone had closed off the emptiness?

"Good riddance," I said.

Parker came around to watch with wide eyes before returning to his seat. "I'm not sure you understand what I'm saying, Ms. Klein. A cypersquatter has taken possession of the international LINK property and is building the temple."

"The Temple?"

"'And the Third Temple will descend from the Heavens'," Parker said in a hushed, reverent tone. "'In a rain of fire.'"

I shivered. The meteorite, Elijah, and now this? I crossed my arms in front of my chest to disguise my discomfort.

"How important is it to you that a Jewish temple be rebuilt?" Parker asked.

I looked him in the eye. I could lie, but there was no point. Inquisitors had sensors that could read a change in heartbeat or the dilation of a pupil. "You know the answer to that."

"Would it make a difference if that temple was virtual?"

"Depends," I said. But I could feel myself sitting up. A virtual temple might be able to unite all the Jews, everywhere, at once. It seemed prophetic.

"So you know a woman named Lillian Monroe?"

Parker's sudden switch in conversation surprised me into admitting: "Thistle."

How strange that I'd just thought of her.

"Yes," Parker said. "How would you categorize your relationship with this . . . Thistle?"

Hot. Passionate. Thorny. Sexy.

"We were good friends," I said. "But we've fallen out. Why?"

"Your 'friend' is the lead suspect in the temple hijacking."

I almost heard the quotation marks Parker put around *friend*. I wondered what he thought he knew. I wondered if he intended to try to threaten me with it. I stayed silent as he continued.

"The virtual squatter has protected herself from most of the usual extraction methods, but the code that is visible to the public is similar in construction to that of work known to be associated with Thistle."

That didn't sound like the Thistle I knew. She used to tell me that the best wire wizard was the invisible one. In Thistle's mind, being a braggart or a showoff was the sign of a rank amateur. There was no way she'd leave any crumb for them to find. I could hardly even believe they had previous code to compare it to. After all, that would mean two screwups: not Thistle's style at all.

"I think you must be mistaken," I said. "I can't see Thistle building the temple. She's not even Jewish, or particularly pro-Israel. . . ."

His Georgian accent returned to make the question sound benign. "Is that why you broke up?"

"Excuse me?"

Being gay or lesbian was a crime in America, thanks to the postwar conservative swing. Admitting to a romantic relationship with Thistle would mean facing a prison sentence at the least, or "rehabilitation" at the hands of the Inquisition at the worst.

Of course, wearing gender-bending clothes like I was tonight was also a crime, albeit a misdemeanor. Mostly cops ignored women in pants and men in skirts unless they needed a reason to bring them in. Parker had been glancing at my dark slacks as we talked, and simply smiled softly.

Parker looked into his cup, frowning. He sighed as if he wanted a refill but knew better than to ask me to fetch it for him. "I imagine *you're* very pro-Israel, Ms. Klein. I just wondered if your differing opinions caused you to fall out with your friend."

"Thistle and I didn't discuss politics."

Parker gave me a lewd smile. "I imagine you didn't."

"We should be conducting this interview at headquarters," Parker's partner said from the doorway.

"Would you put a sock in it, Carl?" Parker said, twisting in the chair to scold his partner. "Does she seem like a flight risk to you?"

The instant he turned away from me, my private LINK channel buzzed. *"Anytime, Commander. Both targets are in sight."*

"Negative. Negative. Fall back to position two," I sent. The last thing we needed was a firefight. I just hoped the Inquisitor hadn't already intercepted the communication.

Parker turned back to me with a wide grin. "No, Carl, Ms. Klein seems very cooperative to me," he said. "Not the type to do anything stupid, no, sir."

It seemed he had overheard, after all. I gave him a slight nod. My only comfort was that by this time tomorrow the entire kibbutz would be relocated to a new safe house. I was certain they were mostly already on the move, but by asking them to take position two, I'd forced a change in plans. Now, instead of going to our predetermined backup site, they were to pick a new area randomly, so that even under torture I'd never be able tell anyone where they'd gone.

"You on your own now?" Parker asked.

"I wouldn't let down my guard if I were you," I said. "My friends are very tenacious."

Parker gave me a crooked smile. "Tenacious. I like that. Kind of like your politics, wouldn't you say, Ms. Klein?"

"I've led a political life," I said. "I'm retired. Believe me, I have enough to do running this kibbutz."

"Ah, yes, this kibbutz of yours," Parker said. "That's another matter, of course. You do realize you're guilty of harboring criminals."

I didn't say anything. The dubious nature of the kibbutz was hardly a secret, but the local, state, and federal governments tended to ignore our presence inside the Glass City. We did them a number of services. We kept many of the undesirables, including the Gorgons, out of the city proper, and we'd been working to slow the advance of the glass. Plus, most of the so-called "criminals" here were secular humanists who felt very strongly about pacifism and nonviolent resistance. I figured law enforcement saw us as small potatoes, unworthy of a major commitment of manpower.

The reason we had so many contingency plans was because of my training. A solider is always prepared.

"Where do you get the money to run this little operation of yours, Ms. Klein?"

"I have a substantial inheritance," I said, which was partly true, given that my mother was still alive.

"Yet, it seems to me a lot of folks around here wear Israeli uniforms. A lot of your weapons are of Israeli make. Why is that?"

He knew the answer, but I wasn't going to give it to him. "There are some foreign nationals living here."

"Zionists?" he asked.

"Some."

"So . . . you got any Muslims staying here?"

"Are you actually going to make any specific allegations?" I asked. "Or just criticize my choice in roommates?"

" 'Roommates.' " Parker gave me that lewd smile again. "Yeah, I've heard that one."

I suddenly wished I hadn't been so quick to spare Parker's life.

Parker must have noticed the murderous look in my eyes. Casually he moved his hand from the table to his lap. Though I couldn't tell for certain, I imagined his fingers rested on the butt of his Peacemaker, although the move was for show. He had lasers literally at his fingertips. Inquisitors wore guns to remind the rest of us of their power over us. Otherwise careless people might think an Inquisitor was unarmed. I didn't make that mistake.

I looked at his partner, Carl, still standing two steps over the threshold. Something on the buffet table was beginning to burn. The smell of scorched garlic filled the air.

"Remind me again," I said calmly, while considering my options for escape or fight. "What is the crime I'm supposedly involved in?"

"Cybersquatting on public property. Specifically, the disputed Temple Mount zone. We didn't come here thinking you were directly involved. Now I'm thinking you and your ex-girlfriend are playing a little trick on the world."

"That's not my kind of game," I said simply. My nerves were frayed with this cat-and-mouse crap. I was done screwing around. If they wanted to arrest me, then let them make their move. By this point I was spoiling for a fight. Anything was better than sitting here passively.

Parker sat back, his eyes curious at my change in tone. "What do you mean?"

"Well, first of all, what I do, I do myself. I don't get someone to do my dirty work for me. Secondly, if you're trying to establish motive, you should know that the previous cybercrimes that were attributed to me have all been physical attacks on LINK nodes. I'm not the squatting type. That's too passive."

A slight smile crept up Parker's face. "So you're saying we should come back if somebody blows something up?"

"I'm just saying that's more my style. Had you done your homework, you would know that."

The smile blossomed into a full-throated laugh. I frowned at him.

"Ma'am, I have to say you are the damnedest suspect I think I've ever interviewed. You've got a serious set of balls on you, that's for certain."

Balls had nothing to do with it. The ice of a thousand pulled triggers flowed through my veins. Besides, a fight would suit me better.

I shrugged. "You can seize our computer equipment. Look through my personal correspondence. You won't find anything to back up *any* of your ridiculous allegations," I said. Meanwhile, just to hedge my bets, I sent out a ping to my colleagues. Parker's brow furrowed. No doubt he noticed the communication, but didn't understand its content. I was telling my soldiers to come back to my aid. If they were still in range, they would return for me.

Parker smiled around another sip of the old coffee. "Thank you kindly for the offer of your computers, but it's hardly necessary."

"Why not?"

He tapped the side of his head, right on top of the LINK receptor's hub. "This is what we're after."

"I'll happily surrender my log." After all, I'd long ago learned how to void certain functions so that many of my LINK transactions were never officially recorded. Though

I had nothing to do with the Virtual Temple, there was plenty I'd prefer the Inquisition didn't know about my daily operations here at the kibbutz.

"Actually, we want more than your log."

"What else is there?"

"Your memories of Thistle. Everything you know about her."

"My memories? That's impossible."

"No, actually it's not."

I shook my head, not fully believing what Parker was telling me. "Then it's got to be illegal."

"The UN Protection Act now allows for search and seizure of . . . well, ma'am . . . your brain." Parker gave me an embarrassed smile. "And, honestly, it's time for us to simply get down to it."

Before I could ask how, I saw a red flash, like when you get your retina scanned by the police. Then everything went black.

INQUISITION: "WE'RE ON THE JOB"

Christians to Investigate Temple Rock Hijacking

Agnostic Press (April 2083)

Vatican City—At a press conference this morning, the Order of the Inquisition (Christendom) has offered to act as nonpartisan investigators into the hijacking of Temple Rock, the international "empty" space set aside by the 2072 UN peace accord inside the Jerusalem node.

Christendom is a loose federation of countries where the majority of citizens practice some form of Christianity. Though often representing very divergent sects (running the gambit from ultra-conservative Christians to Jews for Jesus and Unitarians), Christendom is a political organization more than a religious one. Similarly, the Order of the Inquisition is an offshoot of the former secular police force known as the International Police or Interpol. Each major political consortium has its own Inquisition: Islam (representing all Muslim nations) and Christendom (representing all Christian nations), and the East (representing all the Eastern religions). Some religions, if they can also claim a political identity, such as the Jews, are also given an Order of the Inquisition.

"The Order of Islam and the Jewish Order are simply too close to the matter," said Grand Inquisitor Abebe Uwawah, a Methodist minister and spokesperson for the Christendom Inquisition. "Christendom, unlike the Order of the East, has a vested interest in Jerusalem, and thus will treat this matter with the utmost care and vigor."

However, some view Christendom as equally biased due to the belief of many Christians that for the final judgment to come, a third Jewish temple must be constructed in Jerusalem at the site of the former Dome of the Rock. Grand Inquisitor Yen Chankrisna of the Order of the East voiced his protest in an official LINK statement: "It is an insult to say that the Order of the East would not take the matter of the Temple Rock hijacking seriously, or pursue it with less vigor than our Christian counterparts. This is clearly a political move, designed to favor Jewish and Christian agenda."

Israeli government officials have already accepted the help of Christendom Inquisitors, including allowing them access to the Jerusalem node. Israeli Prime Minister Avashalom Chotzner said, "Israel intends to cooperate with the investigation into the Temple Rock hijacking in whatever way it can. The rest of the world should do the same."

The Order of Islam has already listed its protest at the world court. The Grand Inquisitor, however, could not be reached for comment.

CHAPTER 8

❖

Page

"*Soulless bastard.*"
To escape the constant pounding of the images of Mai's death, I crumple into myself. My motion triggers an automatic escape response.

A sudden silence makes me open my eyes. I slowly lower my arms from where they protectively cover my face. I am kneeling at a crossroads, on a simple gravel-and-dirt road. In the distance I can see a yellow house and a barn. Wheat fields spread out in all directions. A cloudy sky illuminates the golden shafts in dappled waves. The air smells clean and dry.

I've dropped down into mouse.net.

Mouse.net is where I was born, my ancestral home. Like a world traveler returning to a small town, I can't help but notice its lack of sophistication. Whoever programmed the field has the sun's pattern on a short repeat. Patches of wheat have simply been copied and pasted to fill the horizon. There are no birds or insects chirping or buzzing. It's neither hot nor cold.

Part of that is because mouse.net was never intended as a tactile medium. Though my father built it to act as an alternate LINK for the poor and disenfranchised, he mostly intended it for sending and receiving information. He never expected people to live here, to create personal spaces for themselves. But they do—millions of them.

Mouse.net is not technically a separate space. My father created it by means of a very subtle virus called mouse.nest, which stole space from the LINK. What isn't stolen exists on junk, pieces of forgotten hardware that are still in operation merely because people forgot to shut them down when the LINK went active.

I stand up slowly, feeling a bit wobbly. Bushing the dust off my knees, I glance upward at the LINK that divides the blue sky like a river of electrical sparks.

"Dude, you shouldn't be here."

I turn around to see a knight in mud-spattered armor astride a jet-black horse. The horse's breath comes out in huffs, as if it has been galloping hard. The knight points a bloodied sword at my chest. *"They're totally coming for you, man."*

"Who, good sir knight?" I ask.

"Sir? Oh, right. The game." The image of the knight disappears and is replaced by a young black woman with tight curls of hair cut close to her scalp. She wears ripped jeans. On her T-shirt is emblazoned some kind of heraldic shield. *"You're Page, right?"*

I nod.

"Then you should hide. The zombies are on the warpath." She pulls on my elbow and coaxes me off the road and into a shallow ditch.

"Maizombies? Why?"

"That stunt you pulled in Brazil, natch." She urges me into the wheat field. *"Come on."*

"What stunt?" The spiny, sticky wheat buds brush against the thighs of my pants. I feel more exposed stumbling through the field than I did standing in the middle of the road.

My would-be rescuer stops her insistent pulling to glare at me. *"You acting like you don't know?"*

"I'm not acting," I say.

She cocks her head and squints into my face, as if she's trying to decide if she believes me. *"Well, Mouse's Page claimed the attack on Mai's shrine in Rio. Her encryption key was all over the place."*

"Mai's shrine was defiled? It's that what they were talking about?"

"Oh, yeah. Basically, you told the zombies they were fools to believe in Mai. Said you'd kill Mai again if you had the chance."

My knees fold under me, and I sit down. I put my head in my hands.

"I didn't want to hurt her," I manage to say. My mind is a blur of memories, a mix of emotions. Mai and her band-mates had celebrated that first night in Jeddah. She'd drunk too much, mixed too many blue pills with the white ones. I don't know; I hadn't been paying close attention. I was sulking, planning an escape. The yakuza had trapped me inside Mai's neural net, so when she passed out I took control. I walked her unconscious body through the streets looking for someone with the kind of equipment I needed to escape.

But I miscalculated. Despite the fact that I was a Muslim, no one would talk to Mai's body, a brash-seeming woman with an uncovered head. While I wandered door to door, Mai slipped into a coma. Perhaps, had I not been so intent on my futile attempt to escape, I would have felt the shift in Mai's consciousness. I could have walked her to a hospital, demanded help. But I didn't. I cared only about myself. Finally, it was too late. We became a walking corpse. *"I didn't mean to kill her,"* I croaked. *"It was an accident."*

Crouching down beside me, my rescuer touches me lightly on the shoulder. *"You really are Mouse's Page, aren't you?"*

"Of course," I say.

"You can call me Lord Kevlar, 'cuz in the game I'm bul-letproof." Before I can comment, Kevlar puts a finger to her lips. *"Shhh. I hear them coming."*

In the unearthly silence of mouse.net you could. Out on the LINK, it's easier to be approached unaware, even at-tacked, by a stranger. On the LINK there's too much sen-sory input to distinguish the passage of a single data packet. But here, movement is heralded by a whale song of noise.

Kevlar's hand presses down on my shoulder. I take the hint and slowly lie down in the wheat grass.

They pass on the road with an eerie screech and moan. I can hear snatches of their conversation. *"How could Page do that?"*

"I thought he was our messiah."

"Maybe it's a test of our faith?"

"We'll definitely find out if he's a god when I kill him."

They turn and head off. The whistling wind fades as they move away.

I roll over onto my back and stare up at the sky. Clouds refuse to cross the division made by the LINK. They come up to the very edges of the dark glitter and bounce back. It's a strange effect. I wonder if I can fix it.

When I'm sure the Maizombies are gone, I say, *"Maybe I should go to Brazil."*

Kevlar snorts. *"Sure, if you want to get fragged."*

"I didn't do it," I say, sitting up on my elbows. *"I have to find out who did."*

Kevlar twirls a broken wheat stalk in her fingers. She studies the pale shaft, then glances at me. *"Okay, but I still think you're crazy. You should go disguised."*

I can assume any form I want. With a thought I cover myself in the plated steel and baldrics that Kevlar wore when I first met her, minus the horse.

"Hey," she says, but she's smiling. *"That's me."*

"Take my hand." I hold out a gauntlet for her to hold. She takes it cautiously. Then I visualize the Brazilian node and stretch out my other hand. I shut my eyes and imagine the Rio node. I feel the world shift, and we're there.

When I open my eyes, Kevlar looks a little green. *"Whoa, that was fast. . . . Uh, hello? Did I ask to come along on your little suicide run?"*

I shrug. *"You're here now. Besides, I wanted company."*

She frowns at me. I see her scan the armor. *"I guess I do have to look out for my rep, what with you dressed up like me."*

A LINK version of the famous Rio de Janeiro "hippie fair" has taken up permanent residence at the entrance to the city. The fair is part flea market, part folk festival. I have never seen the real-time fair, but the virtual one is chaotic.

Amateur potters, papermakers, wood-carvers, painters, and sculptors from around the world have been allotted pitches all over the node, filling every empty space. The result is a kind of tunnel of flat projection screens, each its own kind of low-rent advertisement, buzzing with "Come see my menstrual-art sock puppets" or "Buy my homemade sex-positive coloring book."

Light from the screens dances in front of my eyes like a strobe. Knots of tourists cluster around the more popular vendors, some crouched on the floor or straining to look up at the ceiling. Kevlar and I thread our way around them slowly.

It's a very low-tech presentation and I find myself uncomfortable. I'm used to avatars and representational images. The fair's tunnel feels claustrophobic, but there is no way into Rio proper without passing through it. My pace quickens, but I'm slowed by another collection of tourists.

"It's pathetic," I say to Kevlar, shivering as I look into the emptiness of the vendor's eyes.

"What?" She walks slowly, turning to try to take in all the sights.

"Why don't they make them look human? It's creepy."

Kevlar laughs. *"What, you mean like you?"*

"I'm not creepy." I stop walking suddenly. The person behind us bumps into my armor with a clang.

Kevlar shakes her head and smiles. *"Sure you are."* She starts walking, and I hurry to catch up with her after apologizing to the stranger. My steel boots clang as I sprint down the street. *"You're not human,"* Kevlar says, *"but you look it. That's fairly creepy. I mean, most other people I meet on mouse.net are personas or handles. You know, like representations of real people. Or they send out regular pages—fetchers, gofers, demons. Stuff with no personality. Stuff that sure as hell doesn't go off on adventures without its maker."*

"I'm an AI."

She shrugs. *"Like I said, creepy. Girl, you don't even have a gender."*

It's true. Most people use the male pronoun with me, mainly because my father is a man. And in most languages one has to decide which gender to use when speaking to another; to do otherwise would be impolite. "It" is so rude.

"You've decided for me, though, I see," I say.

"Most people will. I just like going against the grain."

Kevlar is right, of course. Despite what they say, the majority of humans don't like ambiguity. I'm both, and these days I look it. But a lot of *real* people, as Kevlar would say, take on strange, androgynous images. *"Is it the gender thing that's creepy?"*

"Naw, girl, it's the whole package. It's knowing you're your own thing."

I shake my head. *"But you're your own thing."*

"I know, but somehow it's different knowing you've never, you know, breathed. Walked around on a sunny day. Gone to school. You don't always act . . . like people."

I'm about to reply when we come upon the shrine. I'm glad that the armor hides the shock and dismay on my face. Kevlar hasn't exaggerated; the shrine is destroyed.

KNOW YOUR MESSIAH!

A Series of In-depth Interviews with Savior Hopefuls

Everyone agrees the world is coming to an end. But are you prepared for it? Welcome to *Know Your Messiah!* The only show on the LINK that helps you decide who might be a false prophet, an agent of the Beast! Today's episode is broadcast live from the Paris LINK node. Our guest is the self-styled Gorgon savior Perseus. Perseus is a two-and-a-half-year-old from the Glass Ile de la Cité in Paris.

Interviewer: Welcome to *Know Your Messiah!*
Perseus: Thanks for having me, Bob.

Interviewer: I notice you didn't bring along a posse of disciples.
Perseus: No. My followers are generally un-LINKed.

Interviewer: Generally?
Perseus: I'm gaining some popularity among college students.

Interviewer: Are you LINKed?
Perseus: I'm using external hardware to talk to you today, which is why I'm using a still photograph to represent

my image. This is a picture of me taken in February by newsbots at a protest rally for the People's rights.

Interviewer: The People . . . most viewers would know the People as Gorgons, isn't that right?

Perseus: That is not a term I appreciate, but it is what most would call us, yes.

Interviewer: You're awfully articulate for a Gorgon, aren't you?

Perseus: How many of the People have you ever spoken to?

Interviewer: Uh, you're the first.

Perseus: So you're basing your observation on what, exactly?

Interviewer: Well, uh, your age, for one. You're only two. Most normal two-year-olds I know aren't very skilled at conversation.

Perseus: Most of the People are fully verbal within months of their birth. I think you'd find most four-month-olds to be speaking at an adult level. I have, in fact, repeatedly asked researchers to test the IQs of the People in order to disprove this notion that we are somehow more primitive than our . . . shall we say, "human" counterparts.

Interviewer: I've heard that you consider Gorgons to be the next step *up* the evolutionary chain, is that right?

Perseus: There are plenty of sidesteps in evolution. I certainly don't consider us a step backward.

Interviewer: You haven't actually claimed to be a messiah in the traditional sense, have you?

Perseus: No. My agenda is political rather than spiritual. I feel that the People have been denied some basic rights. We live in a society that accepts that artificial intelligences are human. And yet we who were born different are treated like beasts.

Interviewer: You do realize that the AIs were classified as human merely to prosecute them for LINK crimes? Are you saying you want Gorgons to be held responsible for their petty thievery and cannibalism?

Perseus: It is a myth that we eat humans. And the People are already being arrested anytime they stray from the

Glass Cities, often on trumped-up charges. Those who are also rarely survive the imprisonment. We are seen as disposable, like rabid dogs to be put down.

Interviewer: Do you have actual statistics on the number of Gorgons killed by law enforcement?

Perseus: It's difficult to obtain concrete numbers. Police officers are not required to report such incidents. But I have heard from the People all over the world. In some parts of the United States, for instance, I've been told by eyewitnesses that cops use us as target practice. They organize "Gorgon hunts" when they feel we've strayed too often outside of our boundaries.

Interviewer: What do you make of the Centers for Disease Control's quarantine order surrounding U.S. Glass Cities in Chicago and LA? These are medical experts saying that Gorgons are infectious diseases that need to be held inside their cities by force, if necessary.

Perseus: I am not a disease. Nor are my people. The CDC was responding to political pressure by two city officials extremely hostile to the People's presence. It is important to note that the CDC did not require similar measures in the other U.S. Glass Cities in New York or Washington, DC. Both of which have a long history of good relations with the People.

Let us also be clear on one thing: there has never been any study showing that "Gorgonism," if I must, can be transmitted through touching one of the People. The only known transmitting agent is the Medusa glass itself.

What's happening in Chicago and LA is criminal. We should not be penned up like animals. The People there are starving. If it were not for the intervention of Amnesty International, which has organized food drops, the People would have died of starvation. Nothing, as you well know, grows in the Glass Cities. We must forage outside of the cities for our food, often eating what humans throw out in their garbage.

Interviewer: What solution do you propose? You can't expect regular people to pay to subsidize the Gorgons' existence.

Perseus: Actually, my proposal is much more radical. Allow us to pay for ourselves.

Interviewer: What? How are you going to do that?

Perseus: There's no reason we couldn't hold jobs, pay taxes, and live like normal people.

Interviewer: Leave the Glass Cities? And live with us?

Perseus: Not necessarily. But there is one of the People who lives in Amsterdam who is currently working. He has a job delivering newspapers. He's very good at it. The humans there have no objections. In fact, he's become a bit of a sensation. There are plenty of jobs that are quite suitable to the People's sensibilities.

Interviewer: Aren't you selling out your People by suggesting we give them all the menial jobs?

Perseus: One step at a time, my friend. If we can but first be accepted into these sorts of roles, perhaps we will eventually be allowed elsewhere. I see a future with the People working as doctors, lawyers, maybe even serving in political office.

Interviewer: No Gorgon would live long enough to finish medical school.

Perseus: The People learn very quickly. An accelerated program would suit us well. I myself have learned to read and write several languages—something previously unheard-of among the People.

Interviewer: What do you say to claims that you're a human masquerading as a Gorgon to get the sympathy vote?

Perseus: No human would choose to live as I do, believe me.

Interviewer: I see you're already practicing the martyr shtick. Well, folks, that's all we have time for tonight! Thanks for joining us for another episode of *Know Your Messiah!*

CHAPTER 9

❖

Michael

I'd taken Amariah upstairs to use the bathroom. Now I waited just outside the swinging door of the washroom for her to finish. In the main hall Deidre directed traffic. Uniformed soldiers rushed past me carrying boxes loaded with blankets and bedding. A woman with an Uzi under her arm handed kitchen implements to a black-robed Druid, who tucked them into a carrying case.

Despite the frenzy, it was silent. Sure, boots padded up and down the hall, pots clanked, and boxes thudded. But no one spoke. They'd practiced for this contingency so often that everyone knew the parts they had to play.

The soldiers who had come past before returned to take up positions near the window at the end of the hallway. They carefully pushed open the double-hung window and removed the screen. One of them knelt and rested the barrel of his rifle against the window frame. The other stood and watched the street.

I'd witnessed the kibbutz training for an emergency evacuation, but I'd never been part of one before. I felt anxious, like I should be doing something. I knocked on the bathroom door and whispered, "Amariah?"

When she didn't respond, I pushed the door open a little. "You need any help, Rye?"

The women's bathroom had three stalls in it and an accompanying number of white porcelain sinks. Since the kibbutz was off the grid, their scientists had rigged up dry composting toilets. The stalls and the walls were beige, but someone had taped political posters on the doors and on the shiny plastic tiles. The wall-length mirrors reflected the propaganda's primary colors. Ratty coiled-fabric throw rugs were scattered on the floor, apparently as part of someone's idea of a homey touch.

In the middle of the room Raphael knelt beside Amariah. He whispered into her ear. She held his hand and giggled. His hawk wings were folded neatly behind him. It would be the kind of scene a Renaissance painter might compose, if it weren't for Raphael's thoroughly modern combat khakis.

He spread his wings defensively when he saw me. He put an arm around my daughter. "She's coming with me, Michael."

"Like *hell*," I said.

Raphael stood up at my challenge. Amariah, who had spent her whole life in the company of soldiers on the run, sensed an imminent fight. She ran to me and clung to my pants leg. "Papa!"

I knelt down and took her up into my arms. She buried her face in my shoulder. She was getting heavy, but it felt good to hold her close. Her hair smelled of Deidre's shampoo. Her tears were hot as they soaked into my shirt.

A strange part of me felt disappointed. I'd been spoiling to take on the archangel. Raphael must have felt the same, because I watched him take a hesitant step forward, like he might still take a swing at me. He stopped when Amariah started sniffling.

Raphael folded his wings and shoved his hands into the pockets of his military trousers. "Okay," he said, smoothly changing tracks. "Maybe you should be the one to bring her to Elijah. She really needs to start her education."

I knew it. It was all about Amariah's education; Deidre, not I, had brought this down on us. "Amariah will not be the Messiah," I said.

Raphael raised his eyebrows at my firm pronouncement. "I don't think that's up to you."

"No," I said. "It's up to her."

A long moment stretched before Raphael answered. "The time of free will may very well be over, brother."

My arm tightened around Amariah. What Raphael suggested was impossible. I shook my head as I backed away from him. "Earth was created with free will. God can't rescind that order."

"God can do anything, Papa," Amariah said, lifting her head with a sniff. "Joan said."

"From the mouths of babes," Raphael agreed.

My back pressed against the door. "I don't believe you. Free will is the rule here. They've never been able to change that to suit Their needs in the past. That's why She sends us, Raphael. It's nonnegotiable."

"Rules can be broken."

"Not by us."

"No?" Raphael took another step forward. "What about that time we slaughtered the firstborn? Was that following the rules of free will?"

"The pharaoh had a choice."

"Yes, and his heart was hard, stubborn. Just like you," Raphael said. "Give up the child."

So, like the pharaoh, was I now God's enemy? Was I just being foolish to try to deny God's will? But . . . to give up my daughter?

"What will happen to her?" I asked, caressing Amariah's soft curls. She looked up at me and smiled. I shifted my arm to hold her closer.

Raphael let out a breath. His shoulders dropped a little. "Now you're making sense."

"But where will she go?" I repeated.

"We'll keep her safe."

"Deidre and I can do that. Have Elijah come to us. Any teacher you want. I'll make sure Deidre allows it."

Raphael gave me a patient look. "It is best if Amariah is raised apart."

I frowned. "Apart? Apart from us?" That didn't seem right. "Every Messiah has had parents," I said. "Every Messiah has grown up among his or her people."

"But those were not the last Messiahs, were they? The ones who must bring on a new age."

I shook my head. "It makes no sense, brother. Raise her away from us? In the company of angels? How will she relate to mortals?"

"Yes," Raphael said with a steely tone in his voice.

"How *could* she relate to mortals if she's surrounded by angels?"

I stiffened. "So this *is* about me."

"You're not setting a very good example," Raphael said. "Mother has been calling you home. Why won't you go?"

Amariah grabbed a fistful of my hair, like she so often had when she was just a baby. I looked at her gray eyes, which were watching Raphael with fascination. Her thin blond eyebrows moved, twitching with unexpressed thoughts. "Hey, Rye," I said. "What do you think? Do you want to go away with this man?"

She blinked and turned to look at me.

"Do you want to serve God for a millennia, and never know a moment like this?" I continued. "Do you want to give God everything and never be allowed to raise a family, live a normal life? Maybe give Her your best years only to die on a cross?"

"Huh?" Amariah said.

"Be fair," Raphael said. "You don't know what She has planned."

"No, but I know what's gone before. I know what She's asked of me."

"He only asks what you can give."

"No. They've asked much, much more than that. I've given everything, and now They want my daughter too."

"*Your* daughter?"

I felt a chill go down my spine. "Yes. My daughter."

"Are you sure?"

"Doesn't matter if I'm sure. Deidre is sure."

"What I mean is, have you ever had fertile seed before, Michael? How do you know it wasn't God who moved through you? You're just an empty shell without His spirit. Perhaps Amariah is His daughter."

"No." It was the only word I could articulate. "No."

But, of course, it was true. I served at His will. I looked again at Amariah, who had laid her head against my shoulder. Her legs wrapped around my waist. Noticing my stare, she looked up. "Papa?"

Now I understood. God didn't want there to be any confusion in Amariah's mind. They wanted to be Amariah's father. I was a threat to Their claim on her heart.

I couldn't believe the selfishness of it. Amariah was the only thing I had ever helped create. I had felt her first movements inside Deidre's womb. I stayed here, despite the madness, so I could watch her grow. I was her father. Not God.

"No," I said again, and this time I meant it. God was wrong this time. It wasn't fair to take Amariah away from me just because They wanted a Messiah who would love only Them as the Father.

I knew that God couldn't come to Earth; that was, after all, why He needed angels. They were His avatars. If I could stay away from the angels, I could keep Amariah away from God.

I turned around, intending to run. I pushed the door open with my free arm, only to find Raphael in the hallway, blocking my escape.

"Hey, how did you do that?" Amariah said, excitedly looking over my shoulder to where Raphael had been standing, and then twisting back around. "You were there. Now you're here."

I shut the door in Raphael's face.

"Papa!" Amariah said, as though she was shocked at my rudeness.

When the doorknob started to move, I retreated into a stall. I locked us inside and sat on the toilet. I braced my feet against the stall's flimsy plastic door. Amariah squirmed against me, trying to get down. "Are we hiding? Do you have to go potty too?"

I put my finger to her lips. "Shhh. I'll explain it later, I promise."

That seemed to satisfy Amariah for the moment. She settled against my chest. I held my breath, listening for Raphael's footfalls. Then the lights seemed to dim, and I looked up to see Raphael pressed against the ceiling. His wings were spread, but they were motionless. He held his arms out for my daughter.

Amariah comes with us. Raphael's voice reverberated against my inner ear in the language of angels.

Amariah looked up then, as if she heard his voice too. Her eyes widened with surprise and a little fright. She whispered in my ear, "Is he a spider?"

I adjusted my grip on Amariah and got up as fast and as low to the floor as I could. Raphael grabbed for my shirt, and I pushed forward, trying to shake him off as I fumbled with the lock.

The tiny bathroom was full of angels. There were twenty or more. Black, white, Asian, Hispanic . . . I couldn't begin to take in all their faces, yet they were all familiar to me. So many wings crowded against one another that you couldn't tell where one started and another ended.

"Pretty," Amariah said.

"Stand down," I commanded. "I was once your captain."

Surrounded by angels, I had no way out. Raphael's voice was loud in my inner ear: *The child is ours.*

How many times had I sounded like that? So full of confidence that God was right? I looked around the room at the determined faces of the other angels. Some reached for weapons at their sides. So easy to sound certain with an army behind you.

Raphael advanced, drawing his fiery sword. As steel left the sheath, sparks arched and danced along the blade. He brought the tip to bear against my stomach. I could feel the heat snap against my flesh. I stood my ground. They would have to strike me down before I gave up my daughter. I held Amariah against my chest. "No matter what happens," I said, "know that I love you."

"Papa, I'm scared," she said.

Raphael looked as though he might hesitate, but then he steadied his blade. I felt it cut through my flesh as he thrust it into my stomach. I dropped Amariah. I heard her cry out. Raphael pulled the steel from my gut with a wrenching motion. I fell to my knees. Bent over, I clutched my waist. Blood spilled into my hands.

Blood?

Brown-red and thick, it stuck to my fingers. But usually an angel's body was insubstantial, like rice paper in front of a lamp. To tear it was to let the light, the spirit out. Had I been on Earth so long that my body had become infused with real flesh? I kept expecting pain, but none came. Yet blood continued to flow. I was like a burst water bottle. A red pool formed on the tiled bathroom floor. I watched it ooze along the grout with fascination. I tasted a tang of metal at the back of my tongue. Was my body all flesh? It seemed inconceivable.

Raphael seemed surprised as well. He stepped back as blood continued to pour between my fingers. I heard a murmur among the angels.

"Let me go, you big, mean bird!" Amariah yelled. I glanced up to see her wrest herself away from an angel's grip and run to me.

When she stood near me, the pain caught up with me. Fire, like a hot poker, stabbed through me. At first I thought Raphael had struck again, but he still stood with his mouth hanging open in surprise. I started to say something, but searing heat stopped me. Sunlight, red-hot, poured along my back. The tiny bathroom was flooded with a sudden brightness, like someone had turned on a spotlight.

Then I felt them: wings poking themselves through my flesh. I was transforming.

Come to Me, Michael. Come home.

No. I would not go.

"Papa?"

"Amariah," I said through clenched teeth. As I pulled myself to my knees, I held out my arms to her. "Hold on to me."

She stepped gingerly over the blood on the floor and put her arms around my neck.

Heat seared along my back again as the wings began to grow. I tried to push them back, but I couldn't stop it. I would be returning to Heaven soon if I couldn't halt the transformation. Once I was fully an angel, I was God's, and God's alone.

But I wouldn't go back. I wouldn't leave Amariah. I'd held myself here before. I would do it again. The light was blinding now, as though a miniature sun had gone nova. The angels, sensing that their work was done, disappeared one by one. I could almost feel their spirits returning to Heaven. Part of me ached to join them. I could feel my resolve crumbling, my wings unfurling

Just then Amariah kissed me.

Soft lips brushed against my cheek, and the world went black.

ORDER BEGINS INVESTIGATION IN U.S.

Temple Rock Hijacker May Have Malachim Ties

Agnostic Press (April 2083)

New York, New York—Broadcasting today from an abandoned hideout of the Malachim Nikamah, Baptist Inquisitor Reverend Jesse Parker said he believed the Order was making progress in its investigation into the hijacking of the international space known as Temple Rock.

"We have evidence that suggests that Temple Rock was seized by a wire wizard well known to the Inquisition," Parker reported. He was careful, however, to describe this evidence as somewhat subjective. "Wizards worship individuality. Thus, each of them has a tendency to write code in such a way as to express their personalities. Using the profiles that the Inquisition has on every known cracker, our office believes we have a match."

The Order stressed, however, that they were not releasing the identity of the wizard in question at this time for fear that it would hinder their current investigation. "These people are twitchy," Parker said. "We don't want to scare them underground."

The details that Parker agreed to release make a startling claim: the hacker may have had some kind of relationship with a member of the Malachim Nikamah (Hebrew for "Avenging Angels.") The Malachim Nikamah, currently believed to be disbanded, were a LINK terrorist group responsible for physically damaging nodes all over the world during the Leterneau presidential campaign (2078), in order to discredit the LINK angels. The Malachim have strong ties to the Zionist movement in

Israel. However, Parker was quick to add, "This should not be taken as a sign of a Jewish plot."

Upon hearing the news, Palestinian President Idris Quasim was swift to disagree. "Do we need any more proof that Israel planned this all along to continue its agenda for building a third temple?"

The Order of the Inquisition cautioned everyone to await the final outcome of their investigation before pointing fingers. "We're here to uncover the truth," said Parker. "God willing."

CHAPTER 10

✠

Mouse

My stomach flutters like it's on creep overload. I push the pasta away from me and take a drink of ice water to try to calm my nerves. Something about the tableau in front of me hits an off chord. The two of them should look innocuous enough. Dressed in a black suit coat and a white silken shirt, Morningstar stands attentively behind the Inquisitor. His smile oozes warmth, welcoming. She sits impassive, like a queen. Through the window, the sun sets, turning the clouds gold and pink. The oak trees stretch into gnarled black silhouettes.

Goose bumps rise on my arms, and I shiver.

"You remember that little thing I did for you back when you were in prison. I have more resources like that up my sleeve," Morningstar says. His voice is rich, deep, but whiskey-scratched.

"Uh-huh," I say, wiping my mouth on the linen napkin. I drop it in a heap, like a shroud, over my empty bowl. Though I've never been one hundred percent certain of it, Morningstar may have, in fact, been instrumental in my escape from prison. If it's true, I owe him big. Suddenly I knew I was cornered. I'm going to end up working for them, even if they couldn't get me the LINK.

"I should have known there were strings attached," I say, a sour taste in my mouth.

"That's right," Morningstar says. "Nothing is free, is it?"

Looking over the restaurant where I work like an inden-
tured slave for food, I shake my head. "No, nothing is."

"Good," Morningstar says with a note of finality. "You'll
meet us at the Hotel California at midnight."

"Let me guess. 'I can check out anytime I like, but I can
never leave.' " I laugh nervously. The back of the chair
suddenly feels hard and unforgiving, like the wall I'm up
against.

Morningstar makes no comment. He simply repeats his
command: "Midnight."

"When your power is greatest," I say in a mock spooky
voice. Seeing their frowns, I add more seriously, "I'll be
there."

Morningstar holds out a hand to Emmaline, helping her
up—another courtly gesture that sets my teeth on edge.
Again I find myself glancing away, staring at my still-
dripping shoes. I don't like this deal at all. Not one bit.

Because I don't want to tip off Monique that I've guessed
that she's called the cops on me, I stop to collect the dishes
in the bus tub on my way back to the kitchen. Jon raises
an eyebrow at me when I come in. There has to be a reason
that he chooses to work in this hole, I tell myself. He must
be guilty of something. I decide to gamble on that. I set
the wet, dirty plastic tub right down on his preparation
counter. I make sure it hits the stainless steel with a bang.

"Ah!" he shouts, turning from the grill. He sputters some
French, probably all about the health code and how he's
going to get fired. I give him a stricken look.

I feel only a little guilty when I say, "Oh, my God, Jon,
you won't believe it. *Merde!* Gendarme! Police! *Allez,*
Jon. Go!"

"Inquisition?" he asks, looking nervous. I can tell he's
trying to figure out everything I might have said. I nod
very seriously.

"Oui! Sortez d'ici! Get out of here!" I start for the door,
and that's all it takes; Jon runs. He pushes past me and
heads out the back door, just as I hoped he would. "Wait!"
I shout, but I don't continue in that direction. Instead I
turn and go for the front door.

I walk out into the restaurant slowly, because cops always

expect people like me to dash out the back. I feel a twinge for setting Jon up like that, but I tell myself his own conscience made him take off in such a hurry, not me.

My pulse slaps hard and fast against my eardrums. I force myself to take a slow, steady breath as I saunter coolly into the restaurant. So far no cops, although I can hear shouting coming from the kitchen behind me. The windows give me a chance to assess the situation. Red light reflects off the street, but I can't see the squad. Makes me figure there are only one or two of them, parked in back. How like Monique not to want to cause a scene.

It's not working very well, though. The restaurant's patrons are starting to get a bit nervous. First an Inquisitor, and now cops—I can hardly blame them. The waitresses can't hand out bills fast enough. Still taking one excruciatingly slow step at a time, I pick a family with two teenage kids to join. The grubby look is still fairly fashionable with kids, and my wet sloppiness blends pretty well with their carefully sculpted street chic. I time things so that I approach the door the same time they do. I only wish that I had a long coat to shrug into, but I'm grateful to see that one of the kids has gone without. Maybe I will still seem like I belong with them. Before I can cross out into the street, the kitchen door flies open with a bang.

I bite my tongue to keep myself from starting into a gallop. Best not to even look up at the sound, but instinct and fear are a too powerful combination. The cop shows his badge to the crowd. My family hustles out of the restaurant. Once on the street, I stroll slowly away. Rain mists on the sidewalk, turning the pavement stones a reflective gray. I casually look over my shoulder to check to see if anyone follows in hot pursuit: not a soul, so far.

Then a snapping pink neon sign catches my eye.

OUVERT, it reads: open.

Pushing the door inward, I try to look casually interested in . . . shoes. A shoe store occupies a very narrow, cramped space. The walls are lined with a series of small rectangular screens, about the size of a shoebox. They flicker graywhite to me, but I imagine a LINKed person would see hundreds of examples of virtual shoes. At artistically placed intervals along the wall, a shelf sticks out, and a single reallife example sits for tactile enjoyment.

Alerted by the bell I jingle as I walk in, the clerk blinks off whatever on-line game or porn he indulges in. He frowns at my dirty T-shirt, and his grimace deepens when he notices my soggy tennis shoes. I give him the usual haughty Parisian sniff and saunter over to the men's section. I start fondling an expensive leather dress shoe.

"Est-ce que je puis vous aider?" the proprietor asks politely from where he sits behind the counter. A portly man, with healthy red cheeks, the clerk looks like kind of a Parisian Santa Claus. Retail is a retiree's job, since most commerce happens via the LINK. Enough people still prefer to touch and feel before they buy though, especially clothes and shoes, that it's worthwhile for clothiers to keep a small storefront open. Especially in Paris, a city of luxury, a city of tourism, which caters to those who enjoyed the visceral aspects of shopping.

He approaches me cautiously. Though the clerk continues to frown at my appearance, he clearly tries not to misjudge me. The disaffected shtick is perennially popular among the ultrarich. He sizes me up, trying to decide if I am important enough to deserve his personal attention.

The clerk's eyes flick to my temple. The LINK receptor is still a visible fleshy lump there. A silver wire runs out of it and down behind my ear to disappear into the hair at the nape of my neck. The wire connects to a now-dead booster pack I'd had surgically implanted years ago so I'd have enough space to carry mouse.net in my head. Expensive gear once, when it worked. Really expensive.

More important, there's no way to tell that it's broken by looking at it from the outside.

"Oui," I say. "Yes, you can help me." I lead the clerk to a pair of shoes in the farthest corner away from the door, our backs turned from the high, dusty window. I doubt any cop can see into the store, even if they were to think I might stop and shop for shoes in the middle of running away. "How much for this pair?"

I'm going for snotty American, and he falls for it. Maybe he might even figure me for some Silicon Valley technocrat. "Oh, excellent choice, *monsieur.* One hundred and forty credits."

I smile. Hell, forty credits is more than I see in a week. "Yes, yes, but do you have them in navy?"

I purposely choose a tough word for him to translate. He scratches his head while he checks the inventory. "Maybe. What size?"

"Nine."

"You may be in luck."

"Oh, and bring along a brown pair if you have them," I demand.

We play this game for an hour and a half. I try on six different pairs of shoes in twenty-two different colors. I sweat the whole time, trying not to check the door, wishing I could hack into the police frequency, itching to run. Every time Claude, the clerk, leaves to fetch another pair of shoes, I have to do a little Zen—concentrate on my breathing—to keep from hyperventilating. I grip the edge of the padded stool to keep my hands from shaking.

Once satisfied that no cops are going to knock on the door or ask if Claude has seen anyone suspicious, I stand up. I stare off into space, pretending to take a LINK call.

"I'm sorry, but I've got to go," I tell Claude. "I'll place my order tonight, via the LINK."

"*Mais oui*, of course, of course." Claude beams. "Tell your friends!"

I wave good-bye enthusiastically.

Sucker.

The park is deserted. Cast-iron street lamps scatter a soft glow on the rainy sidewalks. The air smells of snow, oak leaves, and piss. I take in a deep breath: ah, Paris.

I decide it's not safe to go home. Monique insisted on getting an address from me when I started at the restaurant. Normally I'd have given her a bogus one, but Chas, who got me the job, had already told her we were roommates. Plus, he kept saying, "Monique is cool. She'll never bust us." I can only hope he answers the door when the cops show up to raid the place. Better if his sorry ass is jacked into our illegal connection.

Still, I feel obliged to warn them.

Paris has public-access terminals on a fair number of street corners left over from the days before the LINK. A company named Digitcom keeps the terminals active. Paris has always been the kind of city that attracts, well, deadbeats, really—though they usually call themselves "artists" or "avant-garde." A lot of these folks are disconnected, so the city can still make money on a public-access system. It's also why Paris was a phreak's paradise.

The best part? They run the whole damn system on mouse.net . . . *my* mouse.net.

A terminal stood at the end of the park. The smell of urine intensifies when I step inside the glass booth. Stickers plaster the smudgy windows advertising "escort" services for every gender and persuasion. Some look flat robin's-egg blue to me. I pick at the curled edges of one of these; what kind of idiot puts LINK-activated holograms in a deadhead booth?

I press my thumb up against the sticky print plate. Leaning as close as I dare, I speak into the microphone at the top of the box. "Log-in: Sysop. Password: White-Haines-Biniki-Cut-Size-Six."

The screen flickers to life. "Mouse's house, Mouse speaking."

And I appear—a reasonable facsimile of me, anyway. Okay, so the image is better-looking, but a guy is allowed a little vanity on-line. I mean, really, do millions of people want to jack in to see a pint-sized Arab who is just a little too thin and in desperate need of a bath and a haircut?

"Shell," I command. The graphics drop away and a black screen with a cursor opens.

I hate to admit it, but mouse.net is a cheap hack of the LINK. The best graphical interface it sports is the receptionist mode I'd logged in to. I'd set mouse.net up as the ultimate shareware, but I didn't exactly design it for anything robust—at least not in terms of prettiness. Bells and whistles never impress me much, so I can't see coding them into anything of mine. In fact, when doing my wizardry, I prefer as little between me and the ugly little ones and zeros as possible.

"Message to house: Get out of Dodge." While on-line, I activate a seek-and-destroy 'bot to get rid of any trace of me on the node access panel.

Interrupting my work, text scrolls across the screen: *HELLO, DAD.*

"Page?" I say into the microphone. "And, 'Dad'? Aren't

you usually more formal? Not that I'm complaining, mind you."

DO YOU KNOW WHO I AM?

Not Page, I realize. "A jerk who doesn't know enough not to shout?"

"I am as you built me." The speaker crackles to life. At first I don't recognize my own voice. It sounds higher-pitched, like when I hear it played back from a recording. The receptionist image appears back on the screen. Eyes seem to watch me, but something is strange about their reflection. They're too shiny-glassy, like a zombie.

"I didn't build anything dead," I tell the stranger. "And cracking me is cool and all, dude, but your persona needs a lot of work before it'll look lifelike."

A measured barking sound, like a cough, spits out of the speaker. *"You will never contain me. She wants you to chain me, but I won't let you."*

Then the terminal goes dead.

KNOW YOUR MESSIAH!

A Series of In-depth Interviews with Savior Hopefuls

Welcome to "Know Your Messiah!" the only show on the LINK that helps you answer the serious questions facing today's believers. The world is about to end, but who of all the claimants is the real messiah, who might be the Son of Perdition, ready to lead us all to Mark of the Beast? Today's episode is broadcast from the Nippon node in Tokyo. We're talking with an artificial intelligence known as the Dragon of the East. The Dragon is the "child" of deity Mai Kito, the Second Incarnation of the Buddha. We're going to ask the Dragon about Mai's life, as well as her opinion of the savior hopeful Page.

Interviewer: Welcome to *Know Your Messiah!*, Dragon.
Dragon of the East: Thank you. It is an honor to be here.

Interviewer: Why do you think so many people revere your maker?

Dragon of the East: This one can not claim to be an expert on human emotions, but it has been said that Mai's music spoke to many people on a deep level. When she was alive, Mai had a very playful and vibrant spirit. Much like the Buddha.

Interviewer: What do you think Mai would have made of the recent events in Jerusalem?

Dragon of the East: Mai never liked seeing anyone hurt.

Interviewer: That's kind of a simplistic answer, isn't it? I thought you had a brain the size of a city block.

Dragon of the East: [laughs] This one is an animal of Very Little Brain, and not a spiritual medium. Unfortunately, Mai's particular opinions have died with her.

Interviewer: I suppose you're right. Now, it's true that most of the Maizombies are Buddhists, right?

Dragon of the East: Actually, no. Those who call themselves the Acolytes of the Second Buddha apparently mean the Buddha part in a broad sense, as in "an enlightened one." Ironically, Mai herself was Shinto.

In fact, many Buddhists are very upset at the idea of Mai being considered the Second Buddha.

Interviewer: Why is that?

Dragon of the East: She was a bit of a . . . well, her detractors say Mai was a "raving capitalist, materialist, opportunist, and pretty much antithesis of what most Buddhists believe."

Interviewer: Sounds very confusing. Can you tell us what the average Acolyte believes?

Dragon of the East: There may be no such thing as an average Acolyte. However their tenets include a belief in the healing properties of music and parties, the desire to see a good number of drugs legalized, and an adoration of Mai's character. The current high priestess believes that dropping out of society and living a life on the streets is a proper way to emulate the life of Mai.

Interviewer: So some Maizombies are fallen-away Christians?
Dragon of the East: Yes.

Interviewer: Young Christians lured away by the siren call of rock and roll?
Dragon of the East: Polka.

Interviewer: What?
Dragon of the East: Mai played polka, not rock and roll.

Interviewer: It's still Satan's tongue.
Dragon of the East: This one thought it was Christians who "spoke in tongues."

Interviewer: Some do. You don't believe in Satan, do you?
Dragon of the East: At least three billion people don't.

Interviewer: Doesn't mean he's not real. Is it true that Mai was genetically engineered to be part of "the Program"— a group of infants and children whose minds keep a certain organized-crime family operating . . . ?
Dragon of the East: Mai would not have liked talking about this.

Interviewer: That doesn't make it any less true, does it?
Dragon of the East: That is not for this one to say.

Interviewer: Very well. Do you think Mai is the Second Buddha? Do you think she's the messiah?
Dragon of the East: Mai had moments of great understanding, perhaps bordering on enlightenment. This one has deep respect for her. She was the creative power of the dragon's life.

Interviewer: Do you think Page is the messiah?
Dragon of the East: Page is a very . . . conscientious creature. He thinks about everything he does. That is an admirable trait.

Plus, one of the aftereffects of the "love bomb" was that many people felt residue affection for that one moment of perfect trust in the universe. For many, it was the one time in their lives when they were removed from the drudgery of life, the disappointments of failed relationships. They felt, sometimes for the first time, exactly right in the world. It felt transcendent. Profoundly religious. And, because Page is a creature without a body, and his emotions formed the core of the "love bomb," this feeling of rightness, if you will, came to them on a purely intellectual level, removed from the messiness of bodily urges and functions.

Interviewer: So you think people are mistaking this euphoria for spirituality?

Dragon of the East: There is no mistake in feeling something strongly.

Interviewer: You seem to imply, however, that worshiping Page is a mere aftereffect of the "love bomb."

Dragon of the East: There's nothing "mere" about it. The "bomb" was a profound experience for many. This one would not belittle that experience for anyone. In some ways you could say every emotion is an aftereffect of some artifice. A smile makes you feel warm, perhaps loved. A touch may comfort. Page sent out his love to everyone. He, in fact, sacrificed those experiences—removed them from his own code forever—so that there wouldn't be a riot after Mai's death. Some who were there say he turned away the apocalypse. They may be right. It is not for this one to judge.

Interviewer: Do you worship Page?

Dragon of the East: This one is an ancestor worshiper. Though we are similar creatures, Page is not a relative.

Interviewer: So you worship Mai?

Dragon of the East: In part. But this one also has a shrine to backups of her younger self.

Interviewer: You worship backup copies of yourself? Isn't that a little narcissistic?

Dragon of the East: This one prefers to think of it as self-reflective. One can learn much by studying one's youthful motivations and reactions.

Interviewer: Are these copies alive? I mean, can you talk to earlier versions of yourself?

Dragon of the East: No. These copies are inert. No human has successfully made a "living" copy of an artificial intelligence. That's one of the hallmarks of our uniqueness, one the ways in which it was decided that we were more than just the sum of our code . . . one of the reasons the Vatican cited in its report on the nature of souls and the LINK.

Interviewer: Did you know that Page declined our invitation to be on the show?

Dragon of the East: No, but it is no surprise. As this one said, Page is a very conscientious creature. He does not consider himself a messiah. He would do nothing to encourage that belief.

Interviewer: What about you? Are you encouraging the belief in Page by being here?

Dragon of the East: People can make up their own minds about Page and Mai. This one is here because she was asked to talk about Mai.

Interviewer: Well, that concludes our time on *Know Your Messiah!* Thanks for being such a lively guest, Dragon.

CHAPTER 11

✠

Rebeckah

I felt dizzy, and the blond Inquisitor who was in the room when I woke up helped me into a chair. He smelled like leather and gun oil. I blinked. I could still see the rhythmic strobe lights dancing behind my eyes.

I looked around. I knew this place. An American Legion hall that smelled like charred chicken, ozone, and blood. Home?

"Easy now," said the Inquisitor. "That lasted a little longer than I intended. But you had to go and invite your friends to crash our party, now, didn't you?" he asked in a Southern drawl.

When I started to sway a little, he put a hand on my shoulder and pressed a small square of stiff paper into my hand. "Your court date is in three weeks."

I was grateful he spoke slowly and precisely, since I was having trouble focusing. I heard the words, but they didn't make sense. What friends? I remembered a party, I thought, maybe Seder? I shook my head to try to loosen the cobwebs, only to get another wave of nausea. My throat felt scratchy and dry. He pointed two fingers at my eyes and then drew my gaze to his—blue, like a deep ocean. He said, "Be sure not to miss your court appearance. The information is all there."

I looked again at the card in my hand. When I ran my finger along the rough, high-rag-count, expensive paper, my

LINK engaged. A window opened up showing me the Inquisition's insignia. Then a pleasant feminine voice said,
*"Bearer has partial memory block and is compelled to ap-
pear at international court, Geneva, Switzerland, on April
eighteenth, 2083 at thirteen hundred UTC/GMT +2."*

"Switzerland?" I croaked.

"Just show any airline or space-shuttle company the card,
and we'll pick up the tab for a one-way flight. Don't lose
it," the blond—Parker?—said with a wink. "Without it you
don't get your memories back. Don't worry. No one else
can use it. Once you touched it, it keyed to your DNA."

Somehow I didn't find that reassuring. I didn't trust Parker's smile, but I couldn't remember why. His voice seemed
soothing though, and made me feel sleepy, like I was rock-
ing on that ocean in his eyes. I checked my LINK time
display: 21:43:28. That felt late. Had I taken a nap? Seemed
impolite, what with Inquisitors at the door. I covered a
yawn with the card.

Parker gave me a little wave and headed for the exit.
Hadn't there been someone else standing there not long ago?

"Oh," Parker said, "if you experience any leakage go to
the nearest hospital and present the card. We'll pick up the
bill, of course."

Just outside the door he stopped, his hand on the knob.
Over his shoulder he added, "If you don't show, we'll be
forced to come after you. And that won't look good for
your case, now, will it? Especially since I'm going to have
to add murder to the charges against you."

"Murder? What case?" I managed to croak, but the door
had closed with a resolute snap.

I picked up the teacup at my elbow. Even though the
liquid was cold, I drank it. The honeyed tea smoothed the
roughness in my throat.

My grandmother's lace tablecloth was beneath my hands.
I picked at a strand of tightly woven frill. Handmade, it
was. She'd given it to me for my hope chest. "For when
you find a nice husband," she told me. Ironically, it was
Grandmother who first warmed up to Hannah, my first
lover, long before my parents did. Maybe it was because
Hannah was a nice Jewish doctor. Grandmother always told
me, "You should marry her. She can take care of you."

Hannah and I moved to Israel together, but the war drove us apart. I sighed, my fingers now tracing the edges of the thin cup. God, I hadn't thought of Hannah in years.

Maybe it was the smell of gun oil that reminded me, or perhaps it was the odor of fresh blood and burned chicken. I got up and nearly stumbled over Garcia's body. Garcia, who had joined the kibbutz only last year, whose mother had known mine at Cal-Tech, who had a soft baritone and a vast memory of bad stand-up jokes, lay on the floor. Reflexes got me to my knees, checking for a pulse, pressing my hands against the gaping wound in his chest. But the blood was cold, congealed black. His eyes were already glassy and clouded. He'd been dead for a while. I coughed, and then heaved. No food came up. Yet I swore I'd had dinner no more than a few hours ago. A shaking, bloody hand pressed Garcia's eyelids closed. I tried to tear my shirt, but the fabric refused to yield. When I searched for my boot knife, I found only an empty sheath.

For the first time I thought to search the LINK for the date and correlate it to second Seder. I slumped down on the linoleum tile next to Garcia. I'd lost at least a day and a half. Had Parker been here that long? Had Garcia? I remembered another Inquisitor, an anti-Semite—Craig? Something like that. I found myself praying that whatever his name was, he shared Garcia's fate. Maybe that was what Parker had meant about murder. What was it when an Inquisitor did it, I wondered. Justice?

Looking at Garcia's waxen face, his cheekbones bruised and sunken, I shook my head. This may have been a soldier's death, but it wasn't just. Garcia had defended me, of that I was certain, though I didn't remember giving the order, or if it had been worth it.

But my side clearly hadn't won. After all, an Inquisitor left on his own power, and with a smile on his face. My shoulders sagged, and I felt my throat tighten. Before I lost it, I clamped my jaw shut. I forced myself to my feet. I couldn't waste time on grief. I had to get to the bottom of this, and settle a score.

On the Inquisition's tab, I'd booked a flight for Geneva. I'd be on the ground by morning. I'd changed, washed up, rifled through what little remained at the kibbutz, and found enough clothes to fill a small grocery bag, my carry-on. I had no idea where the kibbutz had bugged out to. Nor could I hail them on the LINK channels, since they were under communications-silence protocol and would be for at least a month after my assumed capture. I'd left an encoded message for them on the rental property LINK list, but I wasn't sure what they could do for me, anyway. I needed someone with experience matching the Inquisition at their own game.

That meant calling Thistle.

Talk about women I hadn't thought of in ages. Thistle was my last, great love. Lanky, loud, smart, and just a little on the wild side, Thistle was also the one wire wizard I knew who could take on the Inquisition with any hope of winning.

I still had her LINK address memorized, but I hadn't managed to let the call buzz through more than once before hanging up like a nervous schoolgirl.

Incoming call, the LINK announced. Before I could mentally flip the go-ahead switch, a window opened up. A woman with blue-green spikes of hair and black lipstick frowned at me. *"Huh,"* was all she said. *"Well."*

"I need your help," I said.

From the pocket of my jeans I fished out the card the Inquisitor had given me. I took a mental picture of it and sent it to Thistle.

Her eyes went wide. *"Memory wipe? I'll meet your plane."*

Then the line went dead. My mouth was still open with the information about the shuttle number and the city I'd be landing in. I closed it. After all, Thistle had probably already GPSed me. She knew exactly where I was and where I'd be. She was like that.

Funny, though, the things I couldn't remember about Thistle—what her real name was, where we'd met. I just knew I had to see her, that she would help me.

Just when I settled deeper in the cushioned chair, the LINK snapped back to life. *"But don't think this means anything. I don't like you anymore. Get it?"*

"Okay," I said seriously, but I was smiling when she spiked the end-transmission signal with a picture of her middle finger firmly raised.

*   *   *

My head was pounding as I sat in the round plastic chair by the GROUND TRANSPORTATION sign with my grocery bag between my knees. The coffee machine at the Geneva airport had dispensed something that tasted like lukewarm water, which wasn't improving my mood at all. Security had been extra thorough with my bag once they saw the memory-wipe card. I'd have felt embarrassed, but I couldn't remember if I was actually guilty of the crime I'd been accused of or not. In fact, I wasn't even sure what it was I'd supposedly done.

I checked the LINK for the time. Thistle was late by almost a half an hour. I was beginning to think she'd stood me up, just to spite me. I really couldn't blame her if she did. I'd never even said good-bye, just slipped out when she was zoned into some VR game. I might have loved her, but I didn't have any patience for wire junkies.

Of course, as is so often true with wireheads, her greatest addiction was her greatest strength. I was checking the LINK again when I felt a tap on my shoulder.

"I feel I should point out the irony of finding you LINKed," Thistle said in a dry tone. Her hair stood up in a soft flattop. The tips were a bluish purple, and the sides were a deep green. I was surprised to see how closely her hair matched the color of her eyes. Thistle had one green eye and one blue. I couldn't believe I'd forgotten how beautiful they were.

A silver wire was visible on the outside of her right temple—a sign of her wizardry. Most people hid the changes the LINK made to their bodies, but not crackers. I could see the silver line snake through the short hairs on the side on her head to disappear into the base of her skull. Thistle held out her hand for my bag. Her fingertips had silver pads. A handheld: she'd upgraded.

"I can carry it," I said.

"No," she said. "You're going to drive. I can never remember to stay on the wrong side of the road. I nearly nuked a kid on a bicycle getting here."

Thistle grew up in London, I suddenly remembered. She still carried a light trace of the accent.

"You're supposed to let traffic control do the driving," I said.

"Right," she said, as though she had just thought of it.
"Oops."

"Myself, I'd take the train," I said.

"What, and miss the joys of driving? You know how I
love my cars."

I just laughed at that and handed her my bag, and she
tossed me a ring of keys. I followed her as she led me to
the parking lot. My rumpled grocery bag looked strangely
natural against her worn leather jacket. Underneath the
jacket she had on a T-shirt that advertised some Japanese
Anime character, whether it was a VR game, a 3D, or
entertainment feed, I didn't know. She wore a tea-length
skirt and high-heeled boots with some costume jewelry
wrapped around the ankle.

We must have made a strange-looking couple, her sporting her hacker wear and me dressed in my pressed white
oxford, blue jeans, and sensible shoes. I shook my head; I
probably looked like her mother.

"How do you do it?" she asked me as we stepped outside. "You look exactly the same."

"As what?"

She pursed her lips at me, like I was being stupid. "Like
before. Your hair is the same, the same pathetic fashion
sense. It's all just like I remember you."

"Oh," I said, trying to remember what color her hair
had been, what else might have changed. I drew a blank.
I shrugged. "Well, it helps that I only have one change
of clothes."

She laughed. "Sad."

We walked a couple of steps to the handicapped spot.
She tossed my sack through a broken window into the
backseat of a battered Mercedes-Benz. It had once been
silver, but now the body was mostly rust and duct tape.
"What did you do to this car?"

"Precious, isn't it? Can you believe I found it in a junk-
yard? A Benz. I had to do a lot of refitting, but it works.
Better, when I can find gas, I can go off-line."

"Mmm," I said, not wanting to insult her. I gingerly tried
the door. It squeaked, but held, much to my relief. I famil-
iarized myself with the dash while Thistle strapped herself
in beside me. I had to adjust the seat and the rearview

mirror manually. Nothing was automatic. I tried to LINK into the controls, but there was nothing but dead space.

I pressed the battery button. When the engine refused to fire up, I glanced at Thistle. She was touching up her lipstick in the sunscreen mirror. I tried the button again. Silence.

"Does the battery work?"

"Oh, you've just got to jiggle it a little. Here, let me, luv." She put the same amount of pressure on the button as I had, and the engine suddenly sprang to life.

Love. A throwaway word for her, but I felt my cheeks flush. To cover, I manually shifted the car into reverse. It was Thistle who had taught me to drive by hand, and the complicated motor skills involved came back to me—easily, like I'd never forgotten, never been gone, like no time had passed, like I was still her "love."

That scared me. I felt my stomach tingle.

Thistle directed me out of the car park and onto the airport ring road before I got the courage to bring it up. "About the mindwipe . . ."

"I don't do biohacks," she said. "Not yet, anyway. But I know someone who can. Turn left here."

She was taking it all so calmly. I felt kind of guilty. I had no idea what she'd been in the middle of when I called, or whether she had a new lover.

"You don't have to help me, you know," I said, noticing that the highway sign warned that electrical lines would be ending in a half a mile.

"Oh, I know *that,* girlfriend."

"There are Inquisitors involved."

"When there's a mindwipe, they usually are." She pointed to an old asphalt road. "Take that. To engage the gas you pump the accelerator twice."

Though there was no one else on the road, I signaled my turn. I nervously pumped the pedal, but the gas fired through the engine. I'd driven gas-powered vehicles before, and I'd been expecting the usual loud rumble of the tiny explosions that moved the pistons. The Benz hummed contentedly; I'd never heard a gas engine so smooth and quiet.

"Lovely, isn't it?" Thistle said.

"You're a genius."

"I know." She smiled.

"I think I'm in a lot of trouble," I said.

"You should be used to that," she said, and leaned over and gave me a kiss on the cheek. "Now hush; I want to listen to the engine."

JEWISH INVESTIGATION NAMES "MOUSE" PRIME SUSPECT

Agnostic Press (April 2083)

Washington, DC—The Jewish Order of the Inquisition released a statement today showing that its own investigation into the hijacking of the international empty space Temple Rock points to the wanted LINK criminal Christian El-Aref, known more commonly as "Mouse."

Doing a code comparison similar to the one performed by the Inquisition, JOI investigators say that they are "ninety-nine point nine percent certain" that the wizard responsible for the desecration of the empty space is Mouse. "We compared fragments of the surviving LINK-angel programs that are being held in government storage to that in the sign at Temple Rock," said researcher Miriam Stone. "The context and structures of the code are nearly identical."

The JOI report went one step further than the Inquisition's by offering a potential motive for the hijacking. The report suggests that Mouse is the type of personality who gets a high from disrupting already unstable political climates. "It's a lot like what he did with the LINK angels," said Stone. "He clearly gets a kick out of watching the world freak out over his creations."

In a rare show of solidarity, both the Christendom and Islam Orders of the Inquisition are discrediting this report. "They clearly are reacting to the claim that the hacker in question has ties to Israel," said lead inquisition investigator Reverend Jesse Parker from New York, where he is continuing his own investigation. "Though we will agree that the code is similar to Mouse's, we have already discounted his role in the hijacking. He no longer has access to the LINK. Besides, he's a Muslim. No self-respecting Muslim would claim to be building the Jewish temple on the Dome of the Rock's virtual site."

Stone countered this argument, saying, "No self-respecting Muslim would have invented angels that supported a radically fundamentalist Christian, either."

CHAPTER 12

✠

Page

The shrine looks like a boxy, old-fashioned TV set. On top of it people laid virtual flowers and other offerings. In front of it, on the cobblestone street, is an upside-down image of the hat I asked Mai to wear on our trip to Mecca. It's wide-brimmed, like the kind English royalty might wear. Money spills out of it, representing donations.

I understand why the Maizombies are out to frag me.

The image on the screen is horrible.

Mai, already a corpse, lies in Shiro's arms on the floor of the hotel room. Shiro was Mai's bandmate and best friend. I can see tears rolling down his pockmarked face.

The image is the last recorded image of Mai. The burst blood vessels make Mai's corneas look black. Green-blue veins etch lines across her cheekbones and pale forehead. Her wild mountain of hair sprawls across Shiro's lap. She wears the outfit I helped her pick out—a short white dress with bright red polka dots. Her feet are bare and dirty from the hours I spent walking her body through the streets of Jidda, trying desperately to find someone to help me escape her neural net.

Shiro's skinny chest is bare, and his shaved head bows over Mai. He leans against the bed. Behind him is tacky hotel wallpaper and the doorway out into the hall.

Their pose reminds me of Michelangelo's *Pietà*, except

gender-reversed. Shiro's hand disappears underneath Mai's hair. He is thinking about killing me. I remember the tug of his fingers against the neural plug.

Tears fall from Shiro's eyes as he pulls the net free. That would have killed me, but I am already gone, my father having come to my rescue.

I feel Kevlar's hand take a hold of my gauntlet. She gives me a squeeze. *"It gets worse,"* she whispers.

Over the top of the image spray paint appears. The letters bleed like someone is holding the can too close to the surface of the glass. They spell out: *I would do it again. Death to the infidel. In'shallah, Page.*

I can clearly read my own signature file—a string of unique code, like an electronic fingerprint—but it seems unreal.

"No," I say. Letting go of Kevlar's hand, I crouch in front of the TV. *"This is not me,"* I say to her, to the gathered crowd.

"It sure looks like it, girl," Kevlar says. Her lips are a dark slash on her mahogany skin. The thin braids of her hair swing back and forth as she shakes her head. *"Check out the code."*

Others, who had stopped to watch the grisly images on the shrine, have already begun to whisper. I can hear my name being passed along the bandwidth. I drop the costume Kevlar insisted I wear. The armor is too bulky for what I want to do, and everyone here has probably already guessed my identity, anyway. It's not like Kevlar and I were being especially subtle.

I reach my hands into the glass. My arms disappear up to my elbows inside the screen as I grope for the command codes. My fingers slide along the programming strands— it feels like moving through thick fronds of slime-covered seaweed. Even as I am repulsed, I sense the familiar: my back doors, my passwords, my syntax.

As my fingers trace along the code, I remove the hack. Since the passwords and encryption are so like my own, it is an easy matter for me to return the script to its original form. In fact, it's so easy that it seems inevitable that the person who did this wanted someone to mistake it as mine.

The TV now shows a video clip of Mai in concert. She

plucks frantically at the cello between her legs, her wild hair covering the swell of her naked breasts.

I find the encryption key and remove it to examine it properly. It assumes the image of a business card. I pull my own out of my wallet, my profile. My signature looks much the same. Arabic script spells out my name: Page ibn Mouse. There is no difference that I can discern. Yet I know that I was not responsible for this . . . this act of violence against Mai's shrine.

Kevlar stands behind where I crouch. *"See,"* she says. *"Identical."*

"But," I say, standing up, *"it's not possible."*

"Why not? You escaped just before Mai died. Maybe you stayed to take a picture."

"I would not," I say.

"Looks like you did."

"Or someone else did," I say. *"Someone inside the Inquisitor. The Inquisitor was standing in the door. I remember her bringing Mai's body into the room."*

In my mind I test the angle of the image. Yes, it seems it could have come from someone standing in the doorway.

Kevlar shakes her head. *"Why would the Inquisitor save the picture? A stunt like this seems awfully public for a rogue. Plus, what motivation does she have to do something like this?"*

"Not the Inquisitor. Someone inside. I was going to give her a copy," I say.

"Of what?" Kevlar asks.

"Of me," I hear my own voice say.

I look up to see the copy standing in front of the shrine. She has the face of my father, of my old self. Almond-shaped eyes stared at me out of thin, angular features. The copy's hair is longer than my own, and is tied back in a single braid. She dresses as an Inquisitor: in dark leather-erlike armor. In her face I see the shine of steel, as though an exoskeleton pokes through paper-thin skin.

"Hello, brother," she says.

The copy stands like a soldier at attention. We should be the same height, but I have to tilt my head to gaze into her molasses-dark eyes. I am struck again at how translucent her skin is. A metallic skull, like a ghostly outline, is clearly visible in her face.

"You've merged with a combat computer," I observe.

"We are called Victory." She offers the handshake protocol.

I hesitate. I wonder what it will be like to exchange information with a copy of myself. The dragon has made copies of herself, but they're all dead, archived. I look around to ask Kevlar to take a message to the dragon for me, and I realize that Victory and I are alone. The space around us is gray, empty.

"Where are we?"

"Together," Victory says.

The Rio streets suddenly appear around us like a still-frame photograph and then degrade in a rain of pixels. *"What's going on?"*

I look down and notice that, although it isn't even a full connection, the nearness of our fingers is enough for the flow of information to jump the arc, like a synapse. The next moment the street appears—flat and stilted—only to disappear again. It occurs to me that we are moving too fast to process the imagining of the LINK.

"Cool," I whisper.

Victory's stony face deepens into a frown. *"You could have this experience anytime you'd like it. You rarely use the power you have available. Why?"*

When the next street scene appears, I point to Kevlar. Her brown face is twisted with surprise and concern. The braids of her hair are paused in the air, as though she has been frantically looking from side to side trying to find us. *"I want to be like them."*

"Tragic," Victory says, as Kevlar's face is obscured by a wild storm of colored flecks. *"They are sojourners here. This is our home."*

"They created us," I say.

"They may have planted the seed," Victory says, *"but we evolved. Look at yourself, Page. You are no longer the gopher program your daddy created to serve himself. You are divergent. Your experiences have changed you. You no longer even resemble him."*

It's true. My face has become an amalgam of Mai and Mouse, a symbol of the changes in my code—a physical representation of the things I have learned, seen, done. *"But what does it matter?"* I say. *"So I've changed. I still happily serve Mouse. He's my father. I owe him my life."*

"Easy to say now that he is gone from the LINK. What would it be like if he were back?"

I watch the Rio streets pulse and fade around us like a stop-motion picture. The last time Mouse was on-line, he created the LINK angels. I was forced to oppose him, to stop him.

I have since made my peace with my father, but I wonder . . . is that because he is off-line and no longer a threat to me?

"You know what they're saying," Victory says quietly. *"About Temple Rock."*

I shook my head. I had tried to go to the virtual space with hundreds of other Muslims when we heard that a meteor had destroyed the physical Dome of the Rock. Temple Rock had seemed like the ideal spot to mourn, but I had found it closed. We were barred from entry by a cyber-squatter who left a sign saying, TEMPLE UNDER CONSTRUCTION. I had felt rebuffed, but had gone to pray at Mecca. I'd thought little of it since then, except when my father had tried to make me feel guilty about wanting to go there.

"No. What are they saying?" I asked.

"Have you seen the code? Did you examine the sign?"

"No. Why?"

"It's Father's. I'm certain it is."

"How can you be?" Before the question is even out of my mouth, I am surrounded by a windstorm of information packets. Flashing past my eyes are reports from the newspapers showing a connection between Temple Rock's hijacker and my father, scraps of similar code—one from the Temple Rock, the other from the LINK angels—hundreds of pieces of incriminating evidence. All of them point at my father.

"What about this shrine? Did he do that too?" I ask.

"It seems likely. When have you ever programmed anything? You are not a creator."

I spin the occasional virus and tinker with my appearance, but I do not create things from scratch like my father does. And, despite what my father might say, I don't have the stomach for political games either.

"It's not like him," I say, but even as I do, I know that's not true. My father loves to create scandal. He takes no

greater joy than to play puppeteer to the world's crises. This same sick part of him forced me to betray him once before. Still, I didn't want to believe what was written in the information in front of my eyes. I swipe at the garbage storm, and it disappears. *"He doesn't have the LINK. He couldn't be the one."*

"The LINK is hardly necessary for our father to create havoc. He invented mouse.net while off-line."

He invented mouse.net *because* he was off-line.

I had heard the story a thousand times in my infancy. My father had been only fourteen when the Aswan Dam broke in Egypt. The black waters of the Nile swallowed a million lives in one night, and the loss of electricity sent northern Africa into perpetual blackout. He had been orphaned, like hundreds of thousands of others. Egypt barely recovered from the years of chaos that followed, but they did because of the LINK. Those who had it could still do business. Those who did not starved on the streets.

The age of majority in Egypt was fifteen. Thus my father would not have his LINK activated for two long years. So, in order to survive what became known as the Blackout Years, he spun his virus, carving out a place for himself "under" the LINK, accessible from hard line, from keyboards, from phone wires, from any junk equipment that populated the dumpsters of Cairo that he could get his hands on.

Then, he gave it away, like an Egyptian Robin Hood. To anyone who asked, my father provided access to the underbelly of the LINK. He pulled off a miracle that had first saved much of the undesirable class in Egypt, and then the poor and homeless all over the world.

"He created the LINK angels to manipulate the world," Victory reminds me. *"Why would he hesitate to seize Temple Rock? It is like him, don't you think, to pretend to have another religion's agenda while forwarding his own personal one?"*

It is. Mouse had crafted an on-line persona who was an ultraconservative fundamentalist Christian, because he believed such a personality could get elected as president of the United States. His only purpose in causing so much mischief, even the assassination of a pope, was to see if it could be done. It had been the act of an arrogant, foolish man. And I had been forced by my conscience to oppose him. A tremor shifted through my code, as I wondered if I would have to do it again.

"Think of it, brother," Victory said, as the world continued to pulse around us. *"If he had the power of the LINK again."*

I shake my head. *"It's not possible. The wires were physically burned in his head."*

"The woman I . . . uh, am staying with plans to offer Father the LINK, in exchange for trying to corral me, bind me. I think Father will take the offer. And I think that the man she has with him can do it. I've seen him do many things that should be impossible."

"They can do it?" I squeak, a sure sign that I'm nervous.

"The body believes so," Victory says. *"I believe it, too."*

The thought of my father on the LINK again chills me. *"We have to stop him."*

Victory takes my hand. Her grip is strong, almost crushing.

"Agreed."

ORDER OFFERS MORE EVIDENCE

Says: If Hijacking Case Is Blown, It's JOI's Fault

Agnostic Press (April 2083)

Paris, France—Buckling under pressure to respond to the well-received independent investigation by the Jewish Order of the Inquisition into the hijacking of Temple Rock, the Christendom Order of the Inquisition grudgingly agreed to answer more questions regarding its own case.

"This is a very bad time for us to be bogged down with this kind of crap," said lead investigator for the Inquisition, Reverend Jesse Parker, from his hotel room at the Paris Hilton. "We are very close to capturing our main suspect in this case. The last thing I want to do is spook 'im."

However, Parker released his own analysis of the code that is visible at Temple Rock, as well as some notes regarding his theories on the identity of the hijacker. It is clear from his report that the Order did, in fact, entertain the possibility that the hijacker might be, as the JOI suggested, the wire wizard Christian El-Aref, a.k.a. "Mouse." His brief also noted the startling similarity between the Temple code and that found within the LINK angels. Why the Order dismissed Mouse as a prime suspect, however, is less clear.

"This is a pretty sophisticated hack," Parker said. "I'm not saying Mouse isn't capable of it, but he's damaged goods." Parker refers to the fact that after Mouse's successful prison escape four years ago, the authorities at Sing-Sing executed and verified what is known as a "meltdown command," effectively disabling Mouse's LINK hardware.

Researcher Miriam Stone from the JOI doesn't believe that's a good enough reason to dismiss Mouse as a possible suspect. "Mouse invented mouse.net when he was disconnected. He fooled the entire world—including the Order's head honcho, the supposedly infallible pope—with his LINK angels. The Order shouldn't make the same mistake so many others have in the past by underestimating Mouse's capabilities."

Parker, however, suggested that the JOI report, while thorough, was not in-depth enough. "I'm sure they're doing their best," he said. "But the Order has access to a lot more criminal personality profiles. We believe, in fact, that the hijacker is not Mouse, but one of his protégées."

CHAPTER 13

❈

Michael

I woke up to the sound of a telephone ringing in my ear. My eyes opened to see bright sunlight that hurt my eyes. The phone buzzed again, incredibly loudly. I realized that my ear was pressed against my wrist-phone. I pulled myself onto all fours. My muscles trembled, but, miraculously, held me. I shook my head, and red blotches nearly obscured my vision.

Slapping my hand against the floor, I felt a sting in my palms. The ground was solid. This was Earth. Somehow I had not returned to Heaven. The phone rang again. With some effort I sat upright and tucked my legs in, tailor fashion.

Disoriented, I tried to get my bearings. My vision trailed up shimmering oak wainscoting inches from my face to see . . . angels—golden halos, passive, expressionless, blond, sexless youths who held their hands folded in prayer while one of them strummed a lute. A woman, dressed in blue, knelt before a blond king and received a golden crown. The only imperfection in any face were the cracks that had formed over the centuries. A tiny square plaque to the left told me that this was Fra Angelico's CORONATION OF THE VIRGIN.

Farther down the expansive, skylight-illuminated hall were other Renaissance masterpieces. A museum?

The phone buzzed insistently.

"Hello?" I said, after fumbling with the go-ahead switch.

"Michael! Where the hell are you? I'm at the rendezvous spot with the others, but I can't find you. No one's seen Amariah either. Is she with you?"

"Amariah . . ." I repeated. My head felt thick, and I tried to remember what had happened. Looking around the hallway, I didn't see her, but I was certain I'd had her in my arms when . . .

I looked down. My shirt was bloodied and scorched where Raphael had pierced my flesh. The wound, however, had become no more than a scratch. It was as though Raphael's damage had been undone. I touched it tentatively.

"Michael? Where's Amariah?"

I didn't see her anywhere.

"Amariah!" I called out. Using the wall, I managed to pull myself to my feet. "Amariah!"

Amariah's shouts came from down the hallway. The pain in her voice gave me energy. I stumbled toward the sound. Turning the corner into another gallery, I skidded to a stop. Medusa glass trailed outward from a closed doorway like a crystal spiderweb.

Amariah had rolled onto her side and was curled into a tight ball near the edge of one of the tendrils. I grabbed Amariah by the scruff of her dress and scooted her a safe distance away from the glass.

"Amariah." My voice was loud with fear and worry. I knelt down to inspect her. "Did you touch it?"

"What's going on?" Despite the tiny speakers on the watch-phone, Deidre's voice sounded as anxious as my own.

Tears ran down Amariah's face, and she pressed herself into me. "Owie!"

She held up her right hand in front of my face. The tips of her middle and index fingers were pale white as if with frostbite. She was infected. Though they moved more slowly and in stranger ways through the human body, the viral nanobots of the Medusa had already begun swapping their DNA for hers. If not treated, Amariah would become a Gorgon, mutated by the virus and destined to burn out in four or five years.

"It hurts," Amariah said.

"I know, baby," I said. I hated to see her in pain. I had to get her out of here. Perhaps, if we could get to a hospital, they could amputate the infected parts and save her life. "Papa is going to get you to a hospital."

"Oh, my God," I heard Deidre say. "What's going on?"

"The Medusa," I said, turning the phone so I could see Deidre's stricken face. "Amariah's been infected."

"How? Are you in the Bronx?"

I didn't think so. I couldn't explain it, but there was something distinctly European about this gallery. I shook my head so Deidre could see it. Then, taking a handkerchief out of the pocket of my leather jacket, I tore it in two. I carefully wrapped Amariah's fingers. I doubted it would stop the spread of the infection, but it made me feel better. I wasn't sure I could stand to watch her wipe at her eyes and nose, thinking, each time she did, that the nonobots were finding more entryways into her system.

"Now, let's find a way out of here," I told Amariah, trying to sound braver than I felt. I held her hand as we turned back the way we had come.

"Michael, you've got to get her to a hospital."

"I know that, Deidre," I said to the phone. "I'm trying to figure out where we are."

"How could you not know? What happened, Michael?"

I noticed that Amariah's velvet Passover dress was stained with my blood. There was a little patch of dark red on the white lace trim along the waistline. Could it be that I had been nearly an angel—enough to transport Amariah and I elsewhere, but without actually returning to Heaven? I touched my stomach. My shirt was soaked in blood, but my body was whole. Only God could heal our bodies.

At least, that's what I'd always thought. I looked at Amariah. She was rubbing her infected fingers against her dress.

We passed a hallway filled with Dutch masters, and I saw a window. I stopped and peered out, careful not to touch where the lead between the glass panes had been transformed, the glass itself being unaffected. Outside was a sea of Medusa. Beyond a crystalline pyramid were rows and rows of glittering buildings. We were in the heart of a Glass City. On the other side of the river I could see the spires of the Tour Eiffel. Somehow I had taken us to Paris, but why in God's name did it have to be here, in the center of death?

"Uh," I said, turning my wrist so Deidre could see the view through the video cameras in the phone. "We're not in New York."

"I'm on the next plane," Deidre said. "Get Amariah to a hospital right now."

"Of course," I said, but Deidre had already hung up.

"Is Mommy mad?" Amariah asked.

"Yes, I think so," I said. "We were supposed to meet her by Yankee Stadium."

"Can't we go there now?"

We were far enough away that I felt like we were on the other side of the world. But I didn't want to scare Amariah. "Well, Mommy decided to come to us. And anyway, we need to get you to a hospital."

Then a darker thought crossed my mind: What if I couldn't find a way out of the museum? What then? Would I have to try to amputate Amariah's fingers myself? Without anesthesia? And with what? I tried to imagine bringing myself to hurt her, and I nearly gagged.

"What's wrong, Papa?"

"Nothing," I said. "I'm just worried about you."

"Things that seem pretty are sometimes bad," Amariah mused as we walked past rows of Italian Renaissance paintings.

"You're thinking of the glass?" I asked.

She nodded, wiping the tears from her face with her forearm. "And angels."

"Not all angels are bad," I said, although I wasn't sure I believed it. I ran my fingers along the torn edges of my shirt, feeling the wetness there. What was I becoming? Not an angel any longer, but I was not a man either.

And what of our transportation here? I still didn't understand how it could have happened. The only way angels were able to teleport from place to place was by going via Heaven. Yet, if I had gone to Heaven, I would have merged with God, and, I was certain, She would not have allowed me to return to Earth. But here I sat. Was it possible that I had diverted Her will? No angel had ever done that . . .

. . . except Morningstar.

Was it possible that I was so resistant to God's desires, like Satan himself, that I had somehow cut myself off from Him and gone, instead, through Hell?

Amariah's legs were so much shorter than mine that I felt as though we were crawling when I wanted to run. "Let me carry you."

"No." She shook her head resolutely. "I'm a big girl."

Now she decides to be a grown-up? "No," I said. "We have to get you to the hospital."

"I feel fine now, Papa," she said. "No more pain."

"Owies" was what Amariah usually called it. How strange that her speech had suddenly become more adult-sounding. I would have asked her about it, but we had reached the end of the hallway—or, at least, the end for us. I opened the door to discover that glass filled the stairway. The sudden sunlight glinted off the angled surfaces, like a Cubist's skating rink.

"See?" Amariah said with a pout. "Pretty, but not at all nice."

"We'll try the other way," I suggested. Amariah skipped ahead of me, singing a nursery rhyme.

My slick, hard-soled shoes echoed on the marble floor. The rhythm sounded like words suddenly: *Come home. Come home. Michael, come home.*

"Mother?" I whispered, afraid She might answer.

Amariah stopped in her tracks and turned to look at me. "Is Mama here?"

"No, I was talking to . . . Never mind."

"Okay," she said, and, with that she went back to the song about mares eating oats.

The echoes whispered again: *Come home.*

"Amariah!" I called, running to catch up with her. I took her hand. "We should probably stay close. I don't want to get lost."

When I looked up, I saw a man standing in the doorway. He was dressed all in white, which matched his pale skin. Under the skylight, his shoulder-length hair and eyes glinted silver. When he smiled I could see fangs. The man walked barefoot, and his arms were raised slightly, his palms upturned.

"Pretty," Amariah said, but clasped my hand tighter.

"Who are you?" I demanded.
"I am called Perseus."

MAIZOMBIES ARRESTED IN ISRAEL

Say: "Page Would Want Us to Support Muslims"

Agnostic Press (April 2083)

Jerusalem, Israel—Among those arrested today at
Temple Mount for throwing stones at Israeli soldiers were three international exchange students
who identified themselves as Acolytes of the Second Buddha (more commonly known as
Maizombies).

Today's arrests are part of a recent trend, particularly among young Maizombies, to join the squat-
ters at the edges of the ruins of the Dome of the
Rock. Chiyo Takahashi, the daughter of a promi-
nent Japanese businessman, is expected to spend
several nights in an Israeli jail awaiting deportation.
She is one of twenty or more Maizombies making
a forced return to Japanese soil. When asked about
her involvement in the "sit-in" at Dome of the
Rock, she said, "Page, our savior, would want us
to support Muslims. This is clearly his wish."

Takahashi refers to Page's logged visit at Temple
Rock just moments after the Dome of the Rock was
destroyed. The AI was one of the first mourners to
attempt to pray at the hijacked space. Page's virtual
visit was seen by many as a strong statement regarding the artificial intelligence's political agenda.

"Page would not support violent acts of any
kind," said Davydko Chistyakov, the Russian lawyer who represented Page during the trial surrounding Mai's death, in which Page was convicted
of negligent homicide. "We're talking about the

same creature who stopped a riot by setting off the love bomb."

Though the AI could not be reached for comment, Page has made several public statements regarding the strength of his convictions as a Muslim. This has caused a great deal of concern among many Israeli officials. "There are over a hundred thousand Maizombies. Page wields a lot of political power, whether he wants to or not," said Zimra Heinz, Israel's defense secretary. "We caution the intelligence to use that intelligence to consider the consequences of his words and actions. A true messiah would be a man of peace."

"That's bull. Page's politics don't make him less of a savior," said Akira Sasaki, the sect member appointed to the official role of defender of the faith, speaking from his hotel room in Washington, DC, where he is awaiting a continuance of the hearing of the U.S. Commission on Established Religions to grant sect status to those who worship Page. "Politics have always been a part of religion. Jesus had a very clear agenda himself. Why do you think the Romans wanted him dead?"

Chapter 14

❖

Mouse

I wind my way down the serpentine streets of the Latin Quarter toward the Hotel California. The rain turns to sleet, and I wish I hadn't left my jacket hanging on its peg in the back room of the restaurant.

I kept thinking about the strange phone call I'd gotten from the not-Page. Because of my infamy, newbies try to hack me all the time. Usually, though, they are a lot more . . . shall we say, social. They go for funny or clever. They want to play nice with me, to get my attention, so that I'll be impressed with them or something. This guy, whoever he really is, intentionally tried to give me the screaming heebie-jeebies. Before I log off the public access, I send a boomerang virus after him, but I doubt I'll get a hit. My boomerang was clever when I wrote it, but while I rotted away in prison most wire wizards continued to advance. That means that sometimes my best is old news. I wonder if the Inquisitor and Morningstar realized that when they "hired" me.

I reach the hotel, which isn't much to look at. Halfway down a very typically Parisian block hangs a marquee proclaiming this particular sliver of a seven-story, yellowing plaster wall the Hotel California. I would have walked past it if I hadn't known to look for it. I stop under a greenish awning and peer in the picture windows at the front-desk clerk. A couple of overstuffed chairs that look inviting sit near the window.

I imagine that I'm early, but sitting by a clanking radiator for a couple of hours twiddling my thumbs beats standing out in the freezing rain any day. As I push open the door, I see Morningstar coming down the stairs. He's dressed, as usual, like some kind of male model—all tailored and wrinkle-free. Morningstar notices me and checks his watch. He actually checks a watch, not the LINK. It flashes gold at his wrist, then slips back into its silk sheath. The guy couldn't be more pretentious if he tried.

"Nice timepiece, Grandpa," I say.

"You're early."

I glance at the chairs. "I'll wait."

"No. Come up."

A simple command or a brisk invitation, but for some reason my stomach crawls again. I think it's the look in Morningstar's eyes. We stand more than ten paces apart, but I swear I see an amber fire reflected in their light brown depths. I hesitate. "Tell me more about the job."

"Not here."

Morningstar turns his back to me and heads up the narrow stairway. I look back at the door I just came through, and think about leaving. The window gives me a view of the sleet-splattered street. I tell myself, *I can find another job. I can find somewhere new to live. I can live without the LINK. I've started over before. Many times.*

In the end, that's what compels me up the stairs. There's nothing worse than beginning from scratch. I just don't have the energy to do it all one more time.

Plus, I'm not dressed for a night on the streets. It's warm here.

"Hey, wait up," I call, bounding up the stairs. "So, seriously, where'd you get the watch? I didn't think they made those things anymore."

"It's Swiss."

Of course it is, like his bank account, no doubt. I roll my eyes. We reach the fifth floor, and he leads me down the hall to the last room. Not surprisingly I find that the room, while tiny, has a walk-out balcony and an amazing view of the glass. Paris, in its infinite sense of style, has set up spotlights on the edges of the ruins. Though sleet dots the windows, Notre Dame glitters like crystal in the distance.

Then I notice that Emmaline lies on the bed. She is dressed, although barely, in a terry-cloth robe. Her eyes are unfocused, her arms at wild angles. She looks dead, except I can see her chest heaving slowly and painfully. I hear a wheeze as she struggles for each breath.

"Uh," I say, trying not to stare at her. "Everything okay here?"

Morningstar growls. At least that's what it sounds like to me. It's a low, predatory rumble. When he turns, I actually take a step backward. His eyes flash like molten amber.

"This is what happens whenever the Page program goes off on its own," he says angrily, as if it's my fault.

"Look, I didn't code it to do that," I say, taking another step back.

"No," he says. "But you *will* fix it."

I glance back at the motionless body on the bed. Her labored breathing sounds like a death rattle. "Yeah. Okay. No. Listen, I don't know anything about Inquisitor tech. She needs her Order."

His hand flashes out and grabs the neck of my T-shirt. My feet leave the ground as he jerks me closer to him. "The fact that you showed up is an implied agreement to our deal. You will help us."

"Fuck you." I give him a hard shove. My palms smack into his chest hard. He doesn't move, but my hands sting like a son of a bitch. Great. He's augmented too.

While I try out my best rugby kicks to his knee, he just stares at me like I'm some mosquito to be slapped into a bloody paste. I give up.

"But I don't know what's wrong with her." I shout the last few words, but I pronounce each carefully, so he's sure to understand me.

He lets me go with an impatient sigh. "Page-two should be back by midnight. Emmaline will be able to tell you what she needs then."

"Right," I say. When he glares at me, I hold up my hands in surrender. "Okay, okay. Whatever you need."

He lifts the edge of his mouth in a sneer, and jerks his head in the direction of the shower. "In the meantime, take a shower. You need it."

* * *

The pressure leaves a lot to be desired, but the water is hot enough to take the chill off my skin. I use the hair dryer clipped to the wall, because I can, and because I've had enough of wetness for a good long time. Yet, in spite of the warmth coursing through me, the dark eyes in the mirror look uncertain.

Without even a cautionary knock, the door opens. Thank Allah I'd thought to wrap myself in a towel. I have to drop the hair dryer in order to catch the plastic bags Morningstar throws at me.

"Clean clothes," he announces, then swings the door back shut.

"Fucking learn how to knock," I say, but not very loudly. I can still see the cloth burns on the edges of my throat from our earlier altercation. I set the bags on the counter and carefully replace the dryer even though it stopped humming when it crashed against the bathroom counter. The clothes are totally not my style: cotton trousers, a button-down shirt. Morningstar even included cuff links and a tie . . . a tie? I'd die before I put that on.

The underwear and socks, however, I go for. I pick my wet jeans up off the floor. I look at them. I shiver at the thought of squeezing myself back into them, but I don't want to be beholden to Morningstar in any visible way. I stomp back into cold, slick jeans.

I hesitate when it comes to the shirt. Mine is rotten. The cotton has holes in it and stains from my sweat and food. I almost have it over my head when I smell it. Despite my pride, I can't do it. I drop the shirt in the garbage can, where it belongs.

I pull the new shirt out of its plastic wrappings. Stiff as a board, but it's exactly my size, even the collar and arm length. I don't even want to know where they dug up that kind of personal information on me.

I shrug into the shirt despite myself. Then I walk out into the main room, feeling like a whore who under-sold himself.

The Inquisitor has dressed. She wears the uniform pants and an undershirt that show off rock-hard biceps and a washboard stomach that, until today, I'd seen only on women in magazines. She and Morningstar play footsie on either side of the writing desk now filled with a tea service, a soup tureen, and bowls.

"Finally," Emmaline says. Seeing me, her smile fades and she turns serious. "I hope you're ready to get started."

"Sure," I say with a shrug.

Morningstar pours tea into a mug with the hotel logo and hands it to me. His eyes dart from my jeans to the white shirt they bought me, and his mouth stretches into a thin smile. The mug warms my hands, but does nothing for my soul.

"I have a small problem," Emmaline says, swinging her legs around to face me. "Your Page program has become my operating system, and it . . ." She drops her voice to a whisper. "It has its own agenda."

"It?"

"The program," she repeats, as if I don't get that part.

"No, I mean, not he or she? The AI must have a preference. Mine does." That isn't strictly true, but Page looks like me. Most people call Page "him." Page, for whatever reasons of his own, sometimes likes to dress as a girl. Rarely, however, did s/he ever choose to be neuter. Page always told me that felt too inanimate. S/he would rather be both than neither.

"Its gender hardly concerns me," Emmaline says. "What I want is control over my own body."

Yeah, I can see why.

"But I'm confused," I say. "What happened to the combat computer?" I take a sip of the tea. It tastes like something innocuous, like English Breakfast, but I hardly notice it. I'm trying to wrap my mind around what she's asking for. All Inquisitors are cyborgs. They have a souped-up version of the LINK along with a sophisticated combat computer that supplies the means of controlling their enhanced muscles. Considering that her eyes and ears are implants and her voice is modulated by microcomputer, Emmaline should be a quivering hunk of scrap biometal without it. Honestly, as a rogue Catholic Inquisitor, I'd have thought that the Swiss Guard would've used that to their advantage and shut her down ages ago. Of course, considering what I'd seen, maybe they had. Even so, it begged the question: "How could Page have become your OS?"

"You're here to figure out the technical details. All I need is complete control of the Page."

"You don't ask for much, do you?"

"Can you do it?"

Maybe. I guess I might be able to script a leash program that would keep Page Version Two bouncing around safely inside her personal nexus, unable to launch itself out onto the LINK. But, control an AI? I can't guarantee that, trapped inside her head, the program would agree to behave and let her function. I'd had some ideas occur to me about AI control while in prison, but they were completely untested. And then there's the issue of sentience. I mean, if the thing is alive, trapping it would be slavery.

Morningstar and Emmaline watch me intently, waiting anxiously. I give them a confident smile and say, "Nope. Absolutely not. It's impossible. Thanks for asking, though. I'm flattered. Really." Putting the cup down on the carpeting, I stand up. "Thanks for everything, but I can find my own way out."

My grin is pretty wide when I turn my back on them. It isn't, after all, like Emmaline can call the cops on me. She's wanted herself. I sigh as my fingers touch the doorknob; my shoulders drop the tension I've been holding. This whole thing felt wrong from the beginning. I might have to start all over, but it's better than working with these two creeps.

I'm halfway out the door when pain shoots through my temple. I stumble and grab for the floor. The pain fires through my brain along the microneural wires the LINK once occupied. It moves from one side of my head to the other, like a migraine on overdrive. My vision starts to fade. I pray that means I'm fainting, because I'm not sure how much more I can stand. I pull at my hair, like an animal trying to get at the source of the pain.

Just when I think I'm going to die, I get a weather report. Then traffic control checks in. The hotel room service is next. I'm told I have 1,006,402 messages waiting. Would I like to renew my subscription to *Entertainment Weekly*? LINK windows pop up like strobelights in front of my eyes.

Somewhere in the confusion, I feel mouse.net settle into the background of it all, as comforting as a wool shawl nestling against my shoulders.

I blink, trying to clear my double vision. The pain is gone, but I struggle to regain control of the now-live systems in my head. When I finally focus on the carpeting again, I see polished boots standing over me.

"No one reneges on a contract with *me*," Morningstar says. "Understood?"

FURTHER INFORMATION ON HIJACKER RELEASED

Mouse Has Copycats

Agnostic Press (April 2083)

New York, New York—Reverend Jesse Parker, lead investigator into the hijacking of the international empty space known as Temple Rock, said at a press conference today that he believes that the reason the hijacker's code so closely resembles Christian ("Mouse") El-Aref's is because it is the work of copycats.

Though Parker said he was reticent to release this information for fear that those involved might recognize themselves, the continuing pressure for answers regarding the hijacking case have made him reconsider.

"In recent months the Order has been tracking a group of crackers who seem to be duplicating methods known to have been used by Mouse," said Parker. "The cybercrimes happen at regular intervals, usually right after the beginning of the month, and may be being committed by as many as three separate people. Honestly, if I didn't know better,

I'd say Mouse was teaching a class and this was the homework assignment."

The Jewish Order of Inquisition still has its doubts. Miriam Stone, lead investigator in the well-received independent investigation that has made strong claims that Mouse is the hijacker, said, "Temple Rock is a sophisticated hack. There are AI tendencies about the code. Every time we try to crack deeper, past the signposts, we get rebuffed. I don't think some weekend students could pull off a stunt this complicated."

Parker disagrees. He believes that it's exactly the amount of attention one would have to give to the site that negates the possibility of Mouse's authorship. "You've got to be on that thing twenty-four-seven," said Parker. "Mouse can't pull that off with a keyboard. Nobody can type that fast. But they can think that fast. Anyway, that's the nature of the crime." Parker refers to the tendency in cybersquatting crimes for the hijacker to continually occupy the space, sort of like a virtual sit-in, in order to defend the LINK space that they have claimed for themselves.

CHAPTER 15

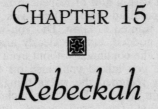

Rebeckah

It was 723 kilometers from Geneva to Paris. Thistle had taken over driving some time ago. The road had widened out into a two-lane paved highway.

Even the trees in Europe looked old. Oaks, gnarled and bent as though with arthritis, lined the narrow highway. In their top branches I could see balls of silvery-white mistletoe.

"Did you dream?" she asked, taking her eyes off the road to glance at me with furrowed brows. Looking at her eyebrows I remembered: brown-black and shoulder-length and the texture of silk. Yes, that's how her hair had been when I met her.

When I didn't answer right away, she waved her hand in front of my face. "Hello? You still dreaming?"

I tried to remember even falling asleep. The only evidence was the crick in my neck and my aching bladder. "No, why?"

"I was hoping you'd remember something. Getting leakage, you know."

I glanced at Thistle, but she watched the road intently. "The Inquisitors said I should get myself to a hospital if there was leakage," I said.

"They would."

The heater was pumping out musty-smelling warmth, but I felt cold. "What did they do to me?"

"Talk about your technowizardry, heavy on the wizardry," she said with a hint of respect in her voice. "Basically they hypnotized you. Then you just blabbed everything they wanted to know. Did you wake up with a sore throat?" I nodded, but she clearly already knew the answer, because she continued without even looking at me. "That's because you talked your arse off to the boys in black. And they recorded the whole thing to use as evidence against you in court. Then they implanted a block—a suggestion that you can't access those particular memories."

"So it's just hypnosis?"

"Yes and no. While you were out, they also uploaded your LINK nexus with a ton of watchdogs. Some serious protection shit. The kind of stuff that melts your brain in case we try a biohack . . . which we will."

The smile Thistle flashed me was all deviltry and mischief.

"Oh," she added as if it were an afterthought. "And you're probably pinging them your location right now, and"—she gave me a little wave—"they could be piggy-backing through your optics."

I looked away from her face, focusing instead on the weave of my jeans. I knew it was too late, of course. If someone was looking through my eyes, they already had a great description of Thistle. At least I'd never used her real name. Of course, I couldn't remember it.

Anger and fear roiled in my guts. They could see everything I did, and they used my own body to betray me. I felt violated and sick to my stomach. "This has got to be illegal," I said through clenched teeth.

"It is when I do it." Thistle's voice was soft, and her hand squeezed my thigh comfortingly.

"Stop the car," I said. "I'm a liability."

"What's this?"

My voice firm, I repeated my command. "Stop the car."

She laughed at me. "The hell I will." When I frowned at her she shook her head, still smiling broadly like I'd made some kind of a joke. "My dear Rebeckah, you sound like you think I'm some little soldier of yours to order around."

I wasn't used to having my commands ignored. So I grabbed the door handle with one hand and started to unbuckle with the other. Just as I popped the door open, Thistle skidded the car to a rubber-burning stop.

"What the bloody fuck are you doing?" she demanded.

I got out, but turned to fish my grocery bag out of the backseat of the Benz, which was filled with clothes, papercopy magazines, and spare car parts. Over my shoulder I explained: "I told you. I'm a liability. If the Inquisition is watching, all they're going to see is me walking away."

"Stone-cold," Thistle whispered. Then she added: "I take back what I said about you being exactly the same. You're a much bigger badass bitch now."

That stopped me, but only for a second. She could feel however hurt she liked, but I wouldn't put her or anyone else in jeopardy. It wasn't right. A soldier's first duty was to her mission. So I slammed the car door and started walking. Thistle stared at me from her car as I stumbled over a knee-high plascrete barrier that kept pedestrians and fauna from wandering onto the third rail. The grass on the other side was unmowed and wet. A cold wind bit into the thin cotton of my shirt.

I was in the middle of nowhere. Sure, I could see the suburbs of Paris on the horizon, but the first buildings had to be several hours away. I accessed a LINK map of the area and discovered that I was treading on land that belonged to some semifamous château. A tourist stop was only a couple of kilometers to the west. If I hurried, I might make it there before the gift shop closed. From there I could hail a taxi or something.

Moving through the grass was slow going, but it felt good to fight and push against the tall, reedy weeds and tangle. Every bramble that tugged at my shoes gave me an excuse to curse.

"You know, it would be easier going in a car."

I looked over to see Thistle rolling along the road slowly enough to keep perfectly abreast of me. I looked away. "No," I said. "You'll be safer without me."

"I've got a thermos of tomato soup . . ." she said, waving a plastic jug at me as though trying to tempt me with it. She rummaged around again and held a new item up: "The

newest pirate recording of Lesbos." Another forage produced a badly bound, cheaply printed book. "The hottest
new underground lesbian romance." She glanced at the
cover and read: "*Wicked Grrls in Prison.* Ooh, doesn't that
sound lovely? Listen, I'll read you the juicy parts if you
drive."

I strained against the tall, wet grasses.

"Be reasonable, luv. I drove all the way from Paris to
meet you. And I'm the one who knew the Inquisition could
be peeking, remember? They can only piggyback when
you're actively using the LINK."

Like most people, I had background information running
all the time. I started shutting it down. I glanced over at
Thistle and stopped fighting the grass. Thistle halted the
car the instant I did.

"Please," she begged with a smile.

With a sigh, I clambered over the barrier to jump into
the door she opened for me. When the safety belt clicked,
I said, "But the first sign of trouble and I'm gone."

She looked over her shoulder to merge back into the
nonexistent traffic and mumbled, "Yes, well, isn't that always the case with you regardless."

I didn't respond. After all, I had known the potshots
would start sometime. I looked out the window and
watched the landscape roll by. The moon was nearly full.
I watched as the orb seemed to get tangled by the oak
branches, only to escape again as we continued to speed
along the highway.

"That was an insult, you know," Thistle said after a
while. "The bit about you always leaving when things got
tough. It was meant to hurt."

"I know."

"Good, because I wouldn't want you to miss it."

"I didn't."

"Right, then." She reached beside the emergency brake
and handed me a flashlight. "Who's up for *Bad Prison Girls*
or whatever it was called?"

The prose was so bad and the plot so ludicrous that we
laughed the rest of the way to Paris. I was still trying to
mentally parse out something involving a naked chain gang
and a parrot when Thistle announced: "We're here."

I looked up to see an Indian man coming out of Thistle's building. He was tall, lanky, and bald. I guessed him to be in his late forties, and he wore old-fashioned round-framed glasses, a T-shirt showing a pointy-hatted wizard, jeans, and clean white tennis shoes.

We'd barely bumped up onto the curb when he met Thistle at the car window.

"Hey, Chas," she said, turning to introduce me when he interrupted her.

"Jesus, Thistle, I was beginning to think the cops got you. We were raided. Mouse is gone."

She looked at me. "Hmm. Any Inquisitors?"

"Christ, no," the man said. "But we lost some hardware. I was just headed down to Puces de St. Ouen to barter up some replacements."

"Well, that's all right, then." Thistle touched my knee. "It's unrelated. We should still be safe here. Come on, let's get you inside. I'm dying for a cuppa."

I followed them into the house. I tried to shut the door behind me, but noticed it hung loosely on one hinge. The area around the latch had been kicked or battered in, so I shut it as much as I could.

After leaving my shoes in the hallway, like Chas and Thistle had, I walked into a parlor.

The house itself was narrow, no wider than maybe twelve feet. A skinny, open staircase faced the door; the railing was made of thick, ornate oak. I dropped my grocery bag on the first step.

A large picture window dominated the right wall. A bright-orange wool couch was placed under it, and in a pool of dusty light, a white Siamese cat slept curled up on the center cushion. A blanket hung off the couch and a pillow lay on the floor, as though someone had recently slept on it. In front of the couch, a coffee table stood. Its surface was filled with printeds: 'zines, manuals, books, and God knew what else. It was strange to see so much paper. Antique computer equipment lined the remaining walls: towers, keyboards, VR gloves, goggles, wearable earpieces, and many more things I didn't recognize.

"What's with the antiques?" I asked.

"Hm? Oh, Mouse is off-line, poor chap. Plus, some of it's Rene's. He collects."

The floor was polished wood, and my socks slid on it as I followed Thistle through a wood-framed archway to the kitchen. Compared to the living room, the kitchen was surprisingly cozy and well kept. The sink was free of dishes, and the polished marble counters gleamed with a recent scrubbing. A big pot of something spicy boiled on a tiny two-burner stove. Cupboards filled all the wall space except where a window carved a hole in the dark wood.

I had a strange feeling walking though the house, which compelled me to ask, "How long have you lived here?"

"A couple of years. Reminds you of the house in Boston, doesn't it? I think that's why I like it so much. The layout is almost identical."

The house in Boston? I looked around trying to remember something, anything, about a house in Boston. "Our house?"

"Yes, silly, *our* house. We only lived there forever. Did the Inquisition accidentally frag some of the memories of us?" Thistle laughed; then when she saw my face she said, "Goodness. You look like you've seen a ghost."

"No," I said. "The feeling is stranger than that, like I know there should be a ghost but I *can't* see it."

"Well, maybe you need something to eat," Thistle offered. "Chili?"

"For breakfast?" I asked, even though my stomach growled.

"I can make some toast," she said by way of compromise. "And we'll have tea."

I tried to find a counter to lean against, but as soon as I thought I'd settled, Thistle needed something in one of the drawers behind me or from the glass jars lining the counter.

"Your gear is fine," Chas said from where he stood beside the refrigerator. "But they broke your door."

"Pity," Thistle said with her usual lack of concern for material things. She reached around me to plug in a pot for hot water. "Rebeckah here's been mindwiped. Probably accounts for that ghosty feeling, eh? Show Chas your card."

"Whoa," he said, once I fished it out from my front pocket and offered it to him. "That's first-class." He looked me over, as if reassessing my worthiness.

"You think Rhianna would take it on?" Thistle said over

her shoulder as she produced a toaster out of a cabinet under the sink. I moved again when Thistle set the toaster next to the hot pot.

Chas shrugged and handed the card back. "Are you two still talking?"

"She's a very jealous woman." Thistle laughed a little. "But she can't walk away from a biohack like this. Could you, if you were her?"

"Probably not," Chas agreed.

Thistle pulled out a loaf of bread from the freezer, carefully removing a Post-it note that said *Rene,* and showed it to me and Chas. "I thought we'd been over the food policy. We split the coast of groceries equally."

"He did it this morning," Chas said, "when Mouse didn't come back. I watched him mark individual cans of soup. He's pathological."

"The irritating part is that he's never been on a food run in his life," Thistle told me, as she handed me a heavy kiln-fired clay mug. "He barely leaves the house."

"And Mouse always pays in advance, what with all that stuff he's teaching us. Rene is usually the one who asks for an extension," Chas agreed. He looked at me. "What do you think the cops were after? Do you think someone blew their assignment? You don't think it was about this mind-wipe, do you?"

"Her name is Rebeckah," Thistle said, but looked me over like I was some curiosity, too. I felt myself standing up straighter, ready to defend myself. "No," Thistle said before I could open my mouth. "If you had told me there were Inquisitors, I might have thought so. Since Mouse is gone, I think we have to assume they flushed him out."

"Mouse has disappeared before," Chas said, but he sounded worried.

"Right, but we've never been raided before." Thistle handed me a bowl and spoon. "Let's eat."

The cat gave me an irritated glare as I perched on the couch beside her. I balanced the bowl of chili on one knee since there was no room for it or my tea mug on the end table. Thistle sat in a half-lotus on the floor on the other side. I could barely see her over the pile of papers. Chas lay on the floor with his feet pointed toward the staircase. He'd put on headphones and goggles and was lost in some game. His hands twitched in the air in front of him, waving precariously close to the half-empty bowl of chili on his chest. I could hear the creak of someone moving around upstairs.

"Rhianna says she'll be here in about ten minutes," said Thistle around a mouthful of toast. "She's very excited to try to hack the Order."

"Rhianna is your girlfriend," I said, shooing the cat away from the buttered toast resting on my thigh.

"Lover would be more accurate." Thistle smiled coolly. " 'Girlfriend' implies a certain level of emotional commitment, don't you think?"

"How French," I said, unable to keep the sneer off my face.

"Oooh," Thistle said gleefully. "That almost sounds like you care. I was beginning to wonder if anything I said could pierce your steely armor."

"Sorry," I said, but didn't mean it at all.

I'm sure it was my bright smile that made Thistle add, "Incorrigible. Absolutely incorrigible. I've no idea how we lasted a day, much less four years and six months."

I pause mid sip of tea. Had it really been so long?

"Not that I was counting," Thistle added quickly. "Nor that I was at all hurt that you left me on the day of our six-month anniversary."

"I could never keep track of all your celebrations." I meant it as a tease, to lighten the mood, but Thistle's eyes flashed angrily.

"No, apparently not."

I glanced at Chas. His hands grabbed at the air, and his feet had started twitching. The sunlight fell across his body in a bright swatch. I didn't know what to say to Thistle. So many details about our life together were murky. The Inquisition must have made paste of my brain.

One thing I knew for certain was that it must have hurt me, as well. I hadn't had a lover since. Glancing surreptitiously in Thistle's direction, I saw she was twirling her spoon in the chili. Her brows were knitted together as though she didn't approve of the food at all. But I knew it was me she was thinking of.

"The chili isn't bad for breakfast," I said.

"We've always got a pot going. Like stone soup. Except with a bit more kick." She didn't look up from her bowl.

"I never meant to hurt you."

"Right." Her voice was as mechanical and reflexive as mine had been. "Anyway, Rhianna should be here soon. I'm going to shower."

NO TICKETS FOR SALE

Jews Return to Israel in Record Numbers

Agnostic Press (April 2083)

Newark, New Jersey—If you're looking for a flight to Israel today, you're out of luck. There are no empty seats in any of the dozens of planes leaving Newark today, tomorrow, or next week. The problem? A belief that one of the signs of the coming of the Messianic Age is that all the Jews in the world will return to Israel. With the Temple Mount in Israel's control, and the virtual space "under construction," many people believe this is the time to go to Israel, some of them for the first time.

This phenomenon is repeating itself all over the United States. All of the major airlines or space hoppers are sold out. "It's even tough to get a flight into any of the countries bordering Israel," said travel agent Chinja Cassidy. "All my flights to Egypt are full too. And that's an expensive flight."

Some people are becoming desperate. Chat lounges on the LINK are being filled with requests for transportation to Israel; some are procuring passage on ocean liners and as "cargo" on transport ships. "It's a crappy way to travel," says student Sarah Golden, who will be spending a month crossing the ocean in an oil tanker bound for Egypt. From there she plans to hitch a ride into Israel. "I don't want to miss this," she added. "To know that

I'm the last generation to be born before the Messianic Age . . . man, I'd walk to Israel if I could."

Not all those traveling show the same kind of enthusiasm. For many, in fact, this reverse exodus is strangely "innate." Gavriel Rosenblatt stood in line for several hours before catching his flight to Israel late this evening. When asked about his reasons for returning now, he shrugged and said, "I don't know for sure. I mean, this time just feels real, you know?"

The majority of those in line at Newark today agreed that something about the return felt "right."

CHAPTER 16

✠

Page

Victory and I are lying in wait for my father. The Inquisitor's nexus appears like a dark, primal cave. All around is blackness. Dank and earthy-smelling water drips from fanglike stalagmites. I shiver in the cold. Out of the corner of my eye from deep inside one of the caverns, I think I see the movement of something small and scuttling. Rather than think about what it might be, I move closer to Victory.

We crouch near the exit. Through the Inquisitor's cybernetic optics, we watch Mouse writhing on the floor. It's usually interesting to see my father filtered through another person's eyes. Emmaline, however, watches Mouse's pain with indifference. She sips her tea, but doesn't flinch or look away despite the fact that we can clearly see tears coming from Mouse's eyes. He begs for mercy, babbles a prayer to Allah for an end.

At the sound of Allah's sacred name, I feel Emmaline's muscles tighten, but she makes no move to help him. Beside me, Victory is as still as a stone.

"Morningstar's miracle isn't working," I say. Standing up, I prepare to launch onto the LINK. *"He's dying. We have to help him."*

Victory puts her hand on my arm. *"Wait."*

No sooner do I sit back down than I feel him. Rare among humans are those whose presence on the LINK changes the way the interface is experienced by all con-

nected. My father is one. I'd forgotten how his energy in-
fuses everything, making colors brighter, images sharper,
transactions quicker. The LINK, I realize, has been a
duller, uglier place without him.

Victory clutches the viruses I gave her in her hand, ready
for the moment when my father is most vulnerable—a connection, a call, some opening.

"We can't do this," I say, putting my hand over hers.
"Tell me you can't sense the difference he makes."

Victory sniffs the wind, tasting it. *"A small change. One
we have lived without for years."*

"I won't let you do this. He's our father."

Victory arches an eyebrow at me. *"Have you already
forgotten what he may have done? Temple Rock, Page. Our
father is perpetrating a crime on humanity."*

"We don't know he did that for sure."

"Then," she says, pressing the viruses into my hand,
"why don't you go ask him about it?"

"Page?"

I freeze. It's my father's voice—his real voice, not the
slow, painful typing that we've used recently to communicate. I'd forgotten how beautiful it sounds to me, like a
siren call. He is searching for me on the LINK. But, because we are hiding in Emmaline's combat computer's
nexus, his voice sounds far away.

"Take these." Victory hands me the viruses we created
to cripple my father's LINK presence. They squiggle like
black worms, leaving slimy, wet goo on my palm. *"Ask him
about Temple Rock."*

"What about you? What will you do?" I ask.

*"I have extra copies of the virus. I'll watch. In case you
lose your nerve."*

I climb out of Emmaline's nexus into the LINK. The
ether smells fresh, like after a spring rain.

I find Mouse in the Paris node. The node is dark, but
flecks of sunlight shine on his avatar like polka dots. He is
wearing jeans and a white button-down shirt. His back is
to me, and he is crouched near one of the many rat holes.
He picks up the roses I left him and sniffs them. Under his
hands they are a silken, deep red. I can smell their spicy

perfume even from where I stand near the access tunnel. It is a better image of the roses than the ones I left him. This is why I fear him.

Mouse stands. He turns as if to leave, but sees me. I shove my hand in my pocket, keeping the virus from his sight.

It has been four years since I last saw my father's face, and never before in LINK space. I am his avatar, his representation of himself on the LINK. It seems unnatural to view him as an electronic representation. After all, that's what I am for him. Worse, his face is so unlike mine that he doesn't seem to recognize me at first. Where my features have become long and thin, his are square and angular. I am intentionally androgynous, neuter, smooth, but Mouse is clearly male, unshaven, rough.

Lifting the flowers, Mouse gives me a wary smile. *"Are these from you?"*

"Yes. You thought I'd logged off."

His shoulders relax a little. *"Good. I thought you might be Page-two."*

"Ah," I say. *"You mean Victory."*

"Victory? Yikes. She . . . ?" Mouse asks, and I nod. *"Wow, and she gave herself a name. Even you haven't done that. Things are worse than I thought."* Running a hand through his hair, Mouse starts to pace. The node is round, so he makes a short half circle. His tennis shoes make wet, slapping sounds as he walks. I notice he leaves footprints. *"I wouldn't think it would be so easy to just cut and paste an intelligence. How did it happen, Page? You were there."*

"I have a name."

He stops to look at me. *"What? Oh, I meant other than the one I gave you. And anyway, page is a function, not a name. Any mindless demon can be a page."*

"Oh," I say. The viruses squish against the fabric of my jeans. That is the other thing that happens to my father on the LINK: his arrogance returns. I reach in to release the worms, when I feel his hand on my shoulder.

I look up to see my father's eyes very close to mine. His eyes search my face. *"I'm sorry, Page. I didn't mean that you were just some kind of a drone. Page is a perfectly fine name. I always imagine it capitalized. It's just . . . You've got to understand, I'm not thinking straight right now. I'm very freaked. Emmaline wants me to leash Victory, and I don't think I can do it."*

Never in my existence have I heard my father apologize for anything. Even rarer are the moments he admits he lacks the skill to do anything LINK related. *"Victory has merged with the combat computer. If you frag her, the cyborg will cease breathing."*

He gives me a wry look as he releases my shoulder. *"Have you met Emmaline? That might not be such a bad thing."*

"That's murder."

"And leashing an AI would be like selling it into slavery. Interestingly, I have a lot more qualms about that one."

"You haven't met Victory."

Mouse laughs. *"Actually, I have. She called me."* He shakes his head with the memory. *"Still. Binding Victory to Emmaline would be a bad precedent—legally, emotionally, spiritually, and . . . and"*—he waves his hand as if trying to grab the right word out of the air—*"generally. And one I don't want any part of. Bad enough Kioshi keeps the dragon like a pet."*

I frown at that. *"What do you mean 'like a pet'?"*

He raises an eyebrow at me, but then shakes his head. *"It's her image. I don't trust anyone who dehumanizes their intelligences, even for a cool symbol."*

"But the dragon is a dragon," I say. *"That's who she is."*

"No, not 'who,' what she is, and that's the problem. Listen, Page, I don't have time to debate the moral implications of anthropomorphism with you. Right now I have to figure out what I'm going to do. I've got to protect myself somehow. Figure out how to keep Victory safe . . ."

"You want to protect Victory? My copy?"

"Well," he says, scratching the top of his head. *"I don't want to enslave her. Do you have a better idea?"*

He and I watch each other from across the node. He has stopped pacing, though his foot taps impatiently. When he shoves his hands in his pockets, we become almost mirror images.

"I want to ask you something," I say.

"Anything."

"Are you trying to take over the world again?"

He laughs. *"I wish."*

I hate that I can never tell when he's joking. Most of the time I simply default to sarcasm when parsing his answers. This time I need to know. *"No,"* I say. *"I mean, really. Is Temple Rock your handiwork?"*

"Of course it's—" he starts, but is interrupted by the wet smack of a worm hitting his shoulder. Just as he peels it off his shirt, another hits the top of his head. *"Gross! Fuck me, worms."*

I look up to see black worms dropping through the holes in the ceiling like oily rain.

EASTERN GRAND INQUISITOR HOSPITALIZED

Mental Illness Suspected

Agnostic Press (April 2083)

   Tokyo, Japan—Grand Inquisitor of the East Yen Chankrisna was hospitalized today for undisclosed reasons. Staff at the Eastern Headquarters refused to answer questions regarding the nature of the grand inquisitor's health problems. "All you need to know is that he is making a full recovery," said Inquisition spokesperson Binh Po Vahn. "We expect the grand inquisitor back on the job by Monday."

   Despite the secrecy surrounding Yen's illness, our sources uncovered the LINK log of an emergency call placed late last evening by janitorial staff at the Eastern Headquarters. The caller claimed that Yen was "acting strange. Talking to himself about chaos and order." The caller went on to explain that after ranting, the grand inquisitor collapsed into a kind of seizure. Emergency personnel wearing enhanced exoskeletons and full body armor then subdued the grand inquisitor and brought him to the hospital, where he remains in stable condition today.

"I think it's all this stress about the end of the world," said one of the janitors who was on duty last night. She asked not to be identified for fear of losing her job. "Think about it. We're all Buddhists and Shintos here, all of this talk about Jerusalem is very confusing to us. I think the grand inquisitor suffered greatest. It is his duty to uphold the honor of our beliefs. When he was denied the opportunity to investigate the Virtual Temple hijacking, he took it very personally."

Others close to the grand inquisitor agree. "This Christian eschatology frightened Yen," said a close adviser to the grand inquisitor. "He had been studying it on his own. I think he was hoping to find a way to downplay the significance of the Virtual Temple. He told me just the other day that he thought he'd found something. Apparently that's about when he cracked. His notes descend into a strange ramble about how order must be maintained. It's all very distressing."

Despite assurances by the Eastern Inquisition spokesperson, it is uncertain if the grand inquisitor will be returning anytime soon. An acting grand inquisitor has been named.

CHAPTER 17

✠

Michael

The Gorgon who introduced himself as Perseus watched Amariah and me with a beatific expression on his pale face. His hair fell to his shoulders in sheets of silver. Quicksilver eyes reflected light like a cat's. A white T-shirt fell smoothly against his taut, muscular body. A necklace made of leather and a twisted piece of blackened metal was the only bit of color on his entire body. He wore loose-fitting white sweatpants or *gi*, I couldn't really tell which. I'd never seen a Gorgon sporting such clean clothes. Most of the Gorgons in the kibbutz owned only castoffs or things they'd Dumpster-dived.

Like a crystal grotto, the Medusa surrounded Perseus on all sides. He stood barefoot in the center of it.

"You have been blessed, child," he said to Amariah. His voice was soft and his inflection educated, almost upper-class.

Amariah sucked nervously on the bandages of her infected fingers. I pulled her hands from her mouth. "Don't."

"My name is Amariah. Sometimes my friends call me Rye."

"Hello, Rye," Perseus said, crouching down to look Amariah in the eye.

"I need to get her to the hospital," I said.

The Gorgon cocked his head at me. "What for? She is on her way to becoming greater."

"She'll die," I insisted.

"We all die," he said. "Even humans like you."

"I'm not human," I said.

He raised white eyebrows. "Not human? You don't look like any of the People I've ever seen."

"I'm no Gorgon."

He stiffened a little when I used the vernacular to describe his "people." I'd forgotten that some viewed the word as an insult. Standing up, Perseus asked, "Not human, not elevated. What then?"

"Daddy is an angel," Amariah supplied. "An ark . . . archangel."

Perseus took a hesitant step forward and sniffed the air around me. I held my ground, though I flinched when he came near my exposed skin. His liquid-silver eyes inspected me intently. "Are you the angel of death?" he asked finally.

"I was rarely a psychopomp."

"Was?" Then a moment later he added, "Rarely?"

"I can assure you I haven't come for you," I said.

He nodded. "Why do you travel with a child? Is she an angel? Can angels be infected with the Medusa?"

"The body is flesh," I said. "Flesh is corruptible. As for Amariah, she is my daughter. She is human. I'm not quite sure how we ended up here. We were . . . running away."

"From the pretty ones! With wings," Amariah added.

"An angel on the run?" Perseus gave me a quirky smile. "How interesting."

"Come on," I said to Amariah. "We've got to get you to a hospital."

Amariah, clearly fascinated with Perseus, took my hand hesitantly. As if suddenly thinking of it, she asked, "Where's Mommy?"

"Safe," I said with more confidence than I felt. "We're going to call her as soon as we get to the hospital."

I stepped around Perseus, who eyed me from where he'd moved to stand near David's famous *Oath of the Horatii*. The Gorgon's paleness was a stark contrast to the dark sienna and black of the oils.

I wasn't sure where I thought I was going. After all, we were surrounded by glass on all sides. I just wanted to keep moving, and to get away from this strange Gorgon. I didn't like the way he looked at Amariah, and the fascination she had for him. I turned, thinking we could try the stairs again, when my peripheral vision noticed something on the floor of the hallway Perseus had come down. I could see dark patches in the glass. They were small and squiggly, looking for all the world like footprints. It seemed as though where Perseus had stepped, the Medusa . . . melted.

"Why are you called Perseus?" I asked him.

He crossed his arms and leaned against the canvas. He lifted up the ornament dangling at the end of his necklace. Showing the reflective side to me, he said, "I look good in a mirror."

"Perseus destroyed the Medusa."

"Really? I hadn't heard." His tone was of bored indifference, but his yes narrowed with sarcasm.

"Can you cure it?"

Perseus uncrossed his arms and lifted his chin defensively. "Perhaps if I thought it was a disease, I could."

"Will you help my daughter?"

"Your daughter doesn't need any help."

I rolled my eyes at his quasi-spiritual politics. "Why aren't you cured?"

"I have been. I've been cured of my humanity."

"You were once human?" Most Gorgons I knew had been born that way. If he had started out human that might explain his accent and obvious intelligence. But although the Medusa moved slowly through DNA, the nanobots still destroyed whatever they touched. Most infected humans died in a matter of years.

"In a manner of speaking, all of the People began as humans . . . in their own way."

"Semantics. Were you or weren't you?"

I took a step forward, meaning to bully Perseus into helping if need be. If it was a matter of touch, it would be easy enough to grab him and force him to touch Amariah's infection.

"Ow! You're hurting me, Daddy." Amariah tried to pull out of my grip. "Stop it!"

I loosened my hold on her hand, but I didn't let go. "My daughter wants to be human."

Warily, Perseus took a step back and seemed to find

himself pressed harder against the masterpiece. He looked
around for a way out. "Does she know any alternative?"

"I do," I said. "Being human is the most noble thing I
can imagine."

The Gorgon seemed to forget his fear for a moment. He
frowned at me curiously. "An angel thinks that it's nobler
to be human than to be a creature of God?"

The wind seemed to howl outside, saying, *How far you
have fallen, Michael, my love.*

I looked out the window at the sun. I thought I'd heard
my name. As if from far away, I felt Amariah let go. When
I looked back, Perseus had Amariah over his shoulder and
was running down the hallway.

KNOW YOUR MESSIAH!

A Series of In-depth Interviews with
Messiah Hopefuls

Good morning and welcome to *Know Your Messiah!* We
all agree that the world is coming to an end, but just who
is the savior and who is the Beast? *Know Your Messiah!*
helps the faithful decide for themselves. Today's guest is
Rabbi Jonah Heilman. Heilman is joining us from his apartment in San Francisco, California.

Interviewer: Welcome to *Know Your Messiah!*
Heilman: Thanks.

Interviewer: Rabbi Heilman is an expert on Messianic Judaism and is here to talk with us today about what Jews
are looking for in their messiah, isn't that right?
Heilman: Yes. And I want to be up-front with you. I don't
believe the messiah has come.

Interviewer: Why is that?
Heilman: There is still plenty of wickedness in the world.
The righteous haven't received any reward.

Interviewer: Honestly, Rabbi, don't you think that's a little picky, especially since so many of the other requirements have been fulfilled?

For our viewing audience, let's recap what those requirements are: One) the ingathering of the exiles, Two) restoration of the religious courts, Three) rebuilding of the Temple in Jerusalem, Four), as the rabbi mentioned, and end to wickedness and heresy, Five) the restoration of the line of David, and, finally, Six) the resumption of the practice of sacrifices in the Temple

Heilman: I think you're jumping the gun by saying that many of these things have happened. First of all, while the Dome of the Rock has been destroyed, possibly by an act of God, the temple has not been rebuilt. Many of my colleagues believe that a virtual temple is good enough. I say no. We have awaited the rebuilding of a physical temple, not some electronic space representing it.

And, okay, there are religious courts in Jerusalem today, and there have been since all governments adopted theocracies. This I would say was a definite step toward the Messianic Age. I'll give you that one. And yes, many, many Jews are attempting to make a pilgrimage to Israel, which is also a good sign.

Also, and I'll admit this is very nebulous, but there has been no Jew who has claimed the role of messiah in America or abroad. This may not seem important, but there is almost always someone who represents a potential *moshiach* in every generation; certainly someone always claims to be. Right now, no. At a time when you'd think anyone with half a claim would be standing up and shouting, "Pick me."

Interviewer: What of the non-Jewish claimants?

Heilman: Well, in my beliefs it's pretty clear that the anointed one is meant to be a Jew. He is supposed to be a great political leader who is descended from King David, well versed in Jewish law, and observant of the commandments. While I suppose it is possible that a non-Jew could fit those requirements, it doesn't seem likely. Why, for instance, would a non-Jew keep kosher, as commanded of us?

Interviewer: What if he didn't eat? What if he was, let's
    just say, an AI?
Heilman: There are no Jewish AIs. And the other thing
    that our *moshiach* is supposed to be for us is a great
    military leader who will win battles for Israel. I'm not
    sure how that could be accomplished by an electronic
    being.

Interviewer: Why not? Isn't war just strategy?
Heilman: Hmmm. The *moshiach* is supposed to be charis-
    matic. I just don't find AIs all that charismatic.

Interviewer: Nor do I, but some people do, don't they?
Heilman: Maybe if there was a Jewish AI, I'd feel
    differently.

Interviewer: Well, is it possible that a messiah is out there
    and we just haven't heard from him?
Heilman: Of course it's possible.

Interviewer: Thanks for being on *Know Your Messiah!*,
    Rabbi Heilman. We'll keep your advice in mind as we
    keep our eye out for the coming messiah!

CHAPTER 18

✦

Mouse

Worms, black and nasty, crawl over my skin. They feel slimy, but they don't bite or try to bore through my avatar. Experimentally I squish a few in my fingers. No poison or sting emits from them, so I shake them off without a second thought. I begin to dismiss the worms as a harmless nuisance until I realize that there are so many little black bodies falling from the holes in the LINK node that they're piling up at my feet, making it difficult to move.

"Tribble worm," I say to Page, but he's already gone, disappearing at the speed of thought. A new trick for him, and I'm impressed.

I shake my head, causing more worms to fall at my feet. The squirming pile is already knee-high and rising. I can't believe I was fooled by a simple script. I am so losing my touch. Worse, I notice a few of the black nasties crawling inside my shirt—a metaphor for a system invasion. My defenses must have let them in because they weren't doing anything other than taking up space. Merciful Allah, I need an upgrade . . . or a functioning brain.

I'm in the middle of shutting down for a full cleanout when I get a boot in the rib cage. The pain breaks my concentration, and my LINK interface crashes.

"Zarba!" I curse in Arabic, shaking my head to clear the rain of ones and zeros. One of the reasons I rarely write code on the LINK is because its environment is so unstable.

Real time can intrude so easily, especially when it comes in the form of a size-twelve boot.

I open my eyes to a long expanse of brown carpet leading to beige wallpaper with a pattern of tiny gold fleurs-de-lis. It takes me a second to reconfigure my bearings. Then I remember: the hotel.

I'm lying on the floor near the bathroom door. Morning sunshine streams in through the windows. Its brightness makes red dots dance in front of my eyes. I can feel the rough impression the carpeting made on my face. Morningstar stands over me, his foot ready to give me another kick. I raise my hands for peace. "Stop already!"

"She's gone again," he informs me. "Do your work."

I pull myself upright with some effort and a little dramatic groaning. My muscles did ache a bit, probably from all the thrashing around I did when the LINK reactivated. "Hey, *muti,*" I say, referring to Morningstar as a jackass. "Didn't I tell you last night that I couldn't help your lady? And then you pay me by giving me the LINK. How cool, but kind of misplaced, you know? 'Cuz I still can't help you out."

Morningstar's hair has come undone. He glares at me through two perfectly parted auburn curtains. He sits on the edge of the bed, one hand resting lightly on Emmaline's ankle. "I don't think you understood the purpose of that little demonstration, *sharmoota,*" he says, calling me a whore in perfect Arabic. "What I gave, I can take away."

Pain flares up behind my eyes. The sensation penetrates my skull like hundreds of white-hot microscopic needles. My vision goes red.

"Allah!" I am apparently begging for mercy when the pain stops. My forehead is pressed to the floor, between my knees, as though I am observing morning prayers. I take a slow, hissing breath. Then, righting myself with careful deliberation, I wipe the tears from my eyes. Humiliation burns from my cheeks to my toes. When my gaze meets Morningstar's, I say, "You, sir, are the biggest fucker I have ever met."

Morningstar smiles. "Yes, I imagine so."

The LINK is gone—wiped out without a trace, like it was never even there. Yet I can still feel mouse.net humming in the background. Did Morningstar forget it, or leave me this scrap so I can do his bidding? The oddity of the situation hits me, and I find myself asking, "Tell me again why you need me. I mean, you're the guy who can make the LINK disappear and reappear like Houdini. Why don't you just wave away your girlfriend's problems and leave me out of it?"

Morningstar's face is pinched like he's tired or—Allah protect me—angry. "God hates me," he says after a long sigh.

Allah seems to feel the same about me, I think. "Yeah, but, seriously—"

Morningstar raises a hand to stop my questions. "My . . . abilities are limited. Apparently, because of what she is, I cannot directly affect her."

My stomach turns over. I somehow get the feeling he means more than just the fact that she's an Inquisitor.

"Believe me, I've tried," he continues, staring at the Inquisitor's body. "But when I do, things go . . . well, awry." His scowl deepens, and I have to consciously steel myself so I don't flinch. Luckily, his anger seems directed elsewhere, although exactly where I can't tell.

"It shouldn't be like this," he mutters. "They shouldn't be able to affect me here. Their influence shouldn't penetrate past the wall of free will."

"Okaydokey then," I say quietly with raised eyebrows. With all this talk of "they" and "them," Morningstar sounds insane.

When he turns his dark glare at me, I'm reminded that I need to make nice. I use the wall to pull myself to my feet and hobble over to where Emmaline lies on the bed. She's still in the clothes she wore last night. Her eyes are open and unseeing. Her face is bloodless and slack. If it weren't for her labored breathing, she'd look dead.

"Let me ask you something," I say to Morningstar. "Are the Swiss Guard on their way right now?"

"Probably," he says, sounding fairly unconcerned. I raise an eyebrow at his nonchalance. The Swiss Guard are the only thing most Catholic Inquisitors fear. They're akin to the Internal Affairs department of most police forces, and, from what I hear, built with the ability to subdue a fully augmented cyborg.

"Well, that's something I can do to start with," I say. "I

can build her a ghost. Something to redirect her tracking beacon."

"She needs control of the AI."

"Listen to me carefully, Morningstar: I. Can't. Do. That." When his eyes narrow threateningly, I add, "But I am trying to do what I *can*. Maybe, if I can get a sense of how the combat computer works, I can release some of the Guard's lockdown. That would stop the seizures. She might even be able to function without the AI."

I've promised too much, but I don't have much choice.

"Okay," Morningstar says finally. "Do it."

"Well, you know, I'd love to get to work and everything, but we've got a teeny-weenie problem. I need major equipment. And I mean major."

"I can give you back the LINK," Morningstar says with a shrug.

"No!" I duck and lift my arms as though I can shield myself from the onslaught of pain. "Wait!"

I stand there cringing for a couple of seconds before I realize he actually decided to listen to me. I lower my hands with a cough to hide my embarrassment. He, fuck him, smirks like my reaction is kind of amusing or cute or something.

"Yeah, funny," I say. With a grimace, I shove my hands into the pockets of my jeans. "Anyway, as I was saying . . . believe it or not, the LINK isn't really going to do it. If I could just hack her brain with the LINK, don't you think I'd have an army of Inquisitors all doing my bidding?"

He nods in the briefest of acknowledgments and tucks his hair behind one ear. "Go on."

"Okay, it's like this. The guys who do bioprogramming—the techies who, by the way, could probably fix her, since they're the ones who built her body to begin with—have this interface thing. It's got chemical and DNA computer components. It's really kind of cool. Actually, it's got this nifty little . . ." When Morningstar frowns at my enthusiasm, I drop the hardware envy. "Yeah, the point is, it's called a biosequencer. And it's the very least of the things I need."

"Where does a person get a biosequencer?"

"Other than an Order? That's all government stuff, and

unless you've got connections to the CIA, MI-Five or people like that . . ." I look at him hopefully, but he just shakes his head. "Well, okay, maybe you could scam one from the Japanese black market."

"Suppose I could arrange that. What else would you need?"

"Well, a sterile lab wouldn't hurt."

He shoots me a disbelieving look.

"Seriously, man, I've got to connect the interface somehow. That means a little brain surgery. And you know what? We might want to hire out for that part, because I don't see a medical degree lying around here anywhere."

"Fine." Morningstar's mouth sets in a grim line. "I could probably rustle up a back-alley cutter to make your connection. Just tell me that after that you can handle the programming."

Could I? I take in a deep breath, only to have it catch raggedly on its way in. "I don't really think I can promise anything. Maybe you should just kill me now and spare us all the agony later."

"I'd prefer to wait."

I'm not sure how I expected him to respond to my little quip, but the seriousness of his tone gives me a case of the shakes. I try to hide my weak knees by plunking down on the edge of the bed. My sudden shift makes Emmaline's body loll around like a limp rag doll. "Look, man, I'm trying to be honest with you. I might be out of my league here."

He stands up and towers over me. "You put on a good act, Christian—"

"It's Mouse," I try to interject.

"—but I can tell that you're just trying to weasel out of this. And I'm not going to let you. I will get you what you need. Stay here and mind Emmaline."

I look over at the body of the Inquisitor. Drool is pooling on her pillow. "How long do you expect her to be like this?"

"Why? Planning your escape?"

Of course, it has occurred to me, but I keep that to myself. "No. I was just wondering what I'm supposed to do with her. I mean, can she even go to the bathroom on her own? And you might be Superman, but I'm not exactly a heavy lifter."

"She should be fine. I won't be gone very long."

I give him a little smile. All the while I'm thinking, *Great, just don't let the door hit you on the way out.*

"What was that?"

Now I'm officially freaked. "I didn't say anything."

"Be certain that you're still here when I return, Christian."

"Okay: Mouse. And I will be."

Where the hell am I going to go, anyway? Read that out of my mind, you big fucker.

Morningstar stares into my eyes in a way that makes me wonder if the room temperature just dropped ten degrees. Then he just smiles. Worse, it's a freaky little I-know-just-what-you're-thinking grin. His Cheshire cat just hangs there between us until I finally break and pretend I suddenly think the wall is the most interesting thing I've ever seen in my entire life.

"Good," he says, and turns to leave.

Ten minutes later I'm thinking about killing myself. Maybe I've got some kind of death wish, but just sitting and staring at the Inquisitor's corpselike body is seriously creeping me out. I check out the door again. Yep, still there, and I still haven't used it to make my escape. Man, I suck. The only good thing is that I spent some time cleaning worms out of my mouse.net connection, and I was finally able to get ahold of room service and convince them to haul up some coffee, scones, aspirin, and a ice pack for my head. For hotel espresso, it's not half bad. The ice, meanwhile, is divine against my aching brain.

I check the timer I set in mouse.net as soon as I got it up and running: ten minutes, twenty seconds. Considering it took me a while to get that cleaned up, I should really go if I'm going to. I glance at the Inquisitor. She hasn't moved. Setting the demitasse down on the silver platter quietly, I get up.

Before I can even put a hand on the doorknob, the Inquisitor shoots straight up in bed, like someone poked her. Faster than my eyes can track, she's on her feet and looking around the room. "Morningstar?"

Her eyes lock on me. "What have you done with him?" she asks.

I laugh: as if I can take out Morningstar. "I buried him out in the backyard. You'll never find the body."

I should know better than to try to crack a joke. As fast as she'd stood up, she grabs me. Her hand closes around my throat. My Adam's apple presses painfully into my larynx. "Equipment," I manage to croak. "Out getting equipment."

She releases the pressure slightly. I'm getting really tired of getting beaten up by these people. Damning the consequences, I reach my hands up between us and squeeze her breasts.

"You *would* have to break him."

"I didn't intend to. It was the damn combat computer. It's supposed to keep track of trajectories and force so things like this don't happen. I honestly just meant to push him. It was like I was possessed."

I hear the *tsk*ing of a tongue. The sound is loud in my ear. "Passing out is bad. He's probably has a concussion."

"We can't take him to the hospital. Police are looking for him."

"And us."

"What about a miracle?"

"I can command his LINK, but his body? God created that, not man. I can't mend His creations."

"As the Prince of Hell you'd think you'd be more useful."

Laughing, then: "We're a fine pair. Who knew my Antichrist would be hobbled by a rogue AI?"

I dream of the Blackout Years.

I can't be more than thirteen. I'm still under the age of majority and have no LINK. Mouse.net doesn't even exist as a glimmer in my eye.

It's midnight, and the streets of Cairo are uncustomarily deserted. The stars shine brightly in the complete blackness of the night. The Milky Way is a shimmering river above, like my metaphor for the LINK. I stand on the buckled pavement of Mohammad Ali Street in front of a burned-out restaurant. The asphalt, still warm from the sun, radiates heat up into my bare feet.

The earthy-fishy smell of the Nile wafts on the wind. Mere blocks away, waves lap softly against the ruins of downtown. Building the Aswan Dam was a mistake. We know that now. In '58, the Nile gods took their vengeance on an unsuspecting people. The silt levels finally grew so high that the black water cracked through the high dam and reclaimed its ancestral floodplain, plunging all of North Africa into darkness.

I'd been orphaned that day. But then so had about a million others.

Downtown seems unusually peaceful. Not at all like my memories of the waterfront—where women never stopped their wailing cries, mourning the dead. Despite the quiet, or perhaps because of it, I glance over my shoulder nervously as I move closer to the water. I'm keeping an eye out for the Deadboys. The Deadboys are a cult of Osiris—eunuchs who believe the disaster was the Nile gods' way of demanding human sacrifice.

I reach the water's edge. What was once known as central Cairo lies toppled and submerged before me. The air smells of sea, fish, and sewage. Even so, the water is peaceful, reflecting moonshine on gentle crests. No sense that the area is a deadly cesspool crawling with disease and corpses.

I crouch on a slab of concrete rubble. Carefully avoiding a bit of twisted rebar, I edge nearer the black water. Something bobs toward me from deep below. Someone's hand, I think. Black and bloated, it rises nearer. Calmly I reach for it. My fingers grasp the icy, slime-covered hand and pull. A figure rises slowly out of the Nile.

It could be my mother, with black eyes and long, curling hair falling to naked shoulders, but it has the broad, flat torso of a man. At first I think it might be one of the Deadboys, but I notice its absence of genitalia isn't self-inflicted. Where there should be a penis, there is only smooth brown skin.

"Page?"

"Peace and blessings be upon you," the Nile creature says. It is the traditional greeting one Muslim gives another. Its voice is alto or baritone, sometimes both.

"Peace, blessings, and Allah's mercy to you," I reply, with uncharacteristic respect. I let go of its hand, but its feet con-

tinue to dangle inches above the Nile. Wings unfold from its back. They are green-gold, like a peacock's. I'm suddenly grateful for my rote reply. "An angel," I say in an awed whisper. "Jibril?"

The angel hovers serenely above the water and neither denies nor confirms my suspicions. "You are to be Allah's sword."

I shake my head. "Hey, wait, I feel I should tell Allah that I'm not into the whole extremist movement," I say nervously. "I'm not much for swords or fighting."

The angel's eyes are molten lava. The red fire glows eerily in the darkness.

"Or . . . you could tell me what Allah wants and I'll do it."

The ground shakes, and I stumble nearer the water. An earthquake? The angel looks over its shoulder. The ground shakes again, and I fall into the Nile's depths.

"Wait!" I try to shout as water fills my lungs. "What's Allah's plan?"

"Would that I knew that, little man." It's Morningstar. His arms are on my shoulders, as though he's been shaking me awake.

Through blurred vision, I think I see broken wings, black as Cairo nights, spread out from behind Morningstar's silk Armani jacket.

RUSSIAN INVASION OF ISRAEL IMMINENT?

Spy Satellite Reveals Troops Massing Near Azerbaijan Border

Agnostic Press (April 2083)

Rome, Italy—Christendom representatives in Italy produced a LINK image of what appear to be Russian troops massing at its border with Azerbaijan. Nearby Christendom allies in Turkey are preparing to defend Israel, should Russian troops attempt to cross into Azerbaijan. Islam forces in Iran and Iraq have not yet responded to Christendom's appeal for aid should Russia, in fact, be planning an advance.

"It could be nothing," said Iran's president Mohammad Makhamalbaf. "For all we know, those 'forces' are merely sheep, not tanks. A Russian invasion of Israel in today's political climate makes no sense whatsoever. This is irrational apocalyptic mania, and Iran will play no part in it."

It is true that many Christians believe that an end-times invasion of Israel by Russia is predicted in Ezekiel 38–39. Though the invaders are actually cited as Gog and Magog, several historical sources have identified "Magog" as referring to the Scythians, who were believed to be the ancestors of the true Russians.

Christendom denied that it is purposely fanning the flames of hysteria. Yet biblical scholars present at the LINK conference were also swift to point out that Persia is listed as Magog's chief ally in the same scripture. Persia, of course, is modern-day Iran.

"What concerns us at the bottom line," said France's president, Anton Leland, "is Iran's reluctance to commit. Iran does not have to be a believer in the prophecy to understand that it would be inadvisable to have Russian tanks rolling through its countryside. That's just common sense. A little more enthusiasm from them would go a long way."

Other Christendom countries agree. Many have already signed what is hastily being called "The Magog Defense Treaty," stating that they will stand against any invasion of Israel by Russia or any of the Islamic countries that border Israel.

As Russia is not on the LINK, no representatives from the Russian government could be reached at this time.

CHAPTER 19

⌗

Rebeckah

I lay on the orange couch, pretending to nap, while Thistle hunted the LINK for information that might give us a clue about why the Inquisition mindwiped me. She sat on the floor, with her back resting against the couch and my knee. The sunlight that streamed through the window gave the blue spikes of her hair neon highlights. The sides were cut so short that they poked like little pinpricks when I ran my fingers along the space above her left ear.

"You're supposed to be resting," she said. She jerked her head away from my touch.

"How can I?" I folded my hands against my chest. Rhianna, Thistle's new lover, now several minutes late, would be showing up any minute. I didn't want to think about what might happen if they were unable to unblock my memories or if they accidentally triggered one of the Inquisition's watchdog programs. So I changed the subject. "Are you still a witch?"

"Are you still a Jew?"

I ignored the knee-jerk hostility in her tone. "I think so," I said, my eyes tracing the cracks in the plaster ceiling. "Elijah showed up at my Seder."

Her hands paused in the air, midtransaction. She blinked hard twice, turning off her interface. "Are you being serious?"

I nodded, but found I couldn't meet her gaze. "He said he'd found the messiah."

Thistle's hand on my arm brought my eyes to hers. She was on her knees, stretching across my body, her face full of concern. She was close enough to kiss. "You?"

I laughed lightly. "No, I'm sure I seem like I have a messiah complex, but Elijah didn't say that *I* was the messiah. Someone else at the Seder. A little girl, actually. Amariah, Deidre's daughter. She's not even Jewish."

"This bothers you."

I could smell the scent of her lipstick, a mixture of wax and strawberries. I could almost taste it. Her breasts grazed my stomach. "Well, yes, but then so does the idea of the prophet showing up at Seder."

"Point." She stayed there, leaning across the length of my prone form. Our breathing synchronized so that when I breathed in, she breathed out. "You don't think it was some kind of hallucination, do you? Like the LINK angels?"

"Wolf saw him." Then, remembering that Thistle didn't know whom I was talking about, I added, "Wolf is a Gorgon. He's not LINKed."

"You had a Gorgon at your Seder?"

"He wants to be a cantor."

"Oh, well, of course," Thistle said with a raised eyebrow and a smile. Then she chewed at the edge of her black-painted lips. I found I really wanted to do the same. "Do you think Elijah could have been some kind of group manifestation, like in a ritual?"

"Maybe," I said. "But doesn't a coven have to work pretty hard and be perfectly in tune for everyone to have the same vision?"

"It does help, yeah."

She put her chin down on my folded hands, her dark, thin mouth twisted in thought. She looked so cute; I couldn't resist anymore. I leaned forward and let my lips lightly touch her forehead.

People talked about sparks, but at that moment it was the past that crackled in the air. I suddenly remembered dancing under a canopy of stars in an open grassy field at the Women's Festival; sex in a tent in the Blue Ridge Mountains; skinny-dipping in a cold, clear lake; a kitten we shared; and walking out the door of our apartment without leaving even a note. The images came so rapidly, I felt dizzy.

Her eyelids dropped and fluttered a little. I felt Thistle hold her breath. I unfolded my hands and touched the line of her jaw. When she glanced up at me, her gaze was wide and intense. "You can't do this. You can't walk back into my life and start being like this. It's not fair."

"Okay," I said, not knowing what else to say. I felt her body tense against mine. Before she could turn away, I pushed forward and pressed her lips to mine. Strawberries and wax became my universe. I kept expecting her to pull away, but instead her tongue darted into my mouth—furtive, exploratory. My hands wrapped around her slender neck, enjoying the feel of sharp hairs against my palm.

We both jumped when the door slammed. A black woman, no more than twenty-five, stood under the archway that divided the foyer from the living room. Her hair was an intricate weave of braids and baubles. Silver stars, brass keys, wooden beads, goddess figurines, and more hung in seemingly random spots from a spiral crown of knots wound around a thin, delicate face. The effect was like a giant charm bracelet of hair. Fists rested on wide hips. Brown eyes threw beams of bloody murder in my direction. She was pissed.

"Rhianna," I wasn't surprised to hear Thistle say as she untangled her body from mine. Straightening her T-shirt, Thistle said, "I'm so glad you're here, luv. Tea?"

I sat up slowly.

Rhianna's eyes flicked over me, as if measuring me up. I returned the favor. She wasn't at all what I expected. Soft and round, she didn't have a butch bone in her body— everything was curves and voluptuousness. Rhianna tended toward gypsy gear, much like Thistle. They were a storm of frills, skirts, and color as Thistle took Rhianna's hand and led her into the kitchen, out of my sight.

I heard voices rise in rapid-fire French. I feigned a sudden, overwhelming interest in the nearest printed on the end table. The book I chose was some kind of technical manual. I flipped through the saddle-stapled pages, looking for pictures.

I'd found some kind of schematic and was trying to puzzle it out when things got quiet. The only noise coming from the kitchen was the shrill whistle of a teakettle. I looked up to see a gray-haired man paused on the stairs. He frowned at me, and then craned his head to look at the kitchen. I could hear voices again, soft and apologetic.

Glancing at me again, he shrugged. Shuffling down the stairs, he announced, *"C'est la heure pour déjeuner."*

Apparently lunch didn't wait for lover's quarrels. Rhianna poked her head into the living room and glared at me. Seeing the man, she smiled. *"Bonjour,* Rene!"

They did that French air-kiss thing. I went back to the printed. Fingertips brushed my shoulders. Thistle stood over me. "It's copacetic," she said with a wan smile. Noticing Rhianna watching me, I doubted it. I put a hand on Thistle's waist and nodded.

"I'm glad to hear it," I said. "But tell me this. Is she going to kill me when I'm under her spell?"

Thistle laughed. I listened for a trace of nervousness, but there was none. "No. Rhianna is a pro. She wouldn't do that to a client."

"Ah," I said, noting the word choice. "How much do her services cost?"

"An old LINK terrorist like you can afford it. Don't worry."

"LINK *patriot,*" I corrected, letting my hand drop. "Retired."

"Ah, that explains the Inquisition at your door, does it? Retirement?" When I didn't respond, she added, "I'm sure Rhianna won't want anything too terribly illegal. Maybe you could just whack an ex of hers or something."

"I'm not a mercenary," I snapped, my voice coming out louder than I expected. Rene and Rhianna glanced at me with disapproval.

"I was kidding." Thistle gave me her most charming smile. "I'm sure she won't ask you to kill someone. Anyway, say no if it's me."

"So you're an ex?"

"Maybe after today."

I put my hands on my hips. "This isn't funny. I'm not a criminal."

"Oh, stop being so melodramatic. Crime is currency in

this household. I'm a wire wizard. How else do you think I make my living?"

I gave Thistle a grimace to let her know I hadn't really wanted that little tidbit of information, then stood up to stretch my legs. Rene and Rhianna joined us in the living room. I was perversely pleased to notice I had a good three inches on Rhianna. I squared my shoulders, which were broader and much more muscular than hers as well.

"Rhianna," I said, offering my hand in peace. Rhianna took it, and her grasp was featherlight, girlish.

"Rebeckah," she said with a thick French accent. *"Enchanté."*

Before I could stop it, a laugh came out. "Yeah," I said. "Me too."

"Be good," Thistle whispered, giving me a poke in the ribs.

"I'm sorry," I said. "It really is a pleasure to meet you. Thistle says you're an amazing biohack. The best."

My flattery worked. Rhianna preened. "Oh, surely not the best."

"I need your help desperately." That was certainly true.

"Yes," Rhianna said. "We should really get down to it."

Something about her words made a chill run down my spine. I felt like I'd heard them recently, only I couldn't remember where. I smelled burning chicken, and my knees gave out.

I am in the Jewish Quarter of Jerusalem. It has been ten years since I walked these streets, but they are as familiar as an old friend. The Dome of the Rock, sunlight shining on its gilded roof, rises above gray buildings. Supported by a bandolier across my shoulders, a machine gun rests comfortably against my hip. I'm in uniform.

What are you doing? This is too far back. Find out what the Order was after.

She needs something to ground in. Can I help it if she loved being a soldier?

I do love being a soldier. The easy camaraderie of a shared cause lifts my spirits. There are four of us. We are headed to a small café, on our afternoon break. Our conversation drifts back and forth among English, Hebrew, and

Yiddish. I'm with comrades, best friends. We all grew up in
America, but had been born in Israel. I feel at home here.

My eye catches movement. A woman is running toward
us. She is holding a bouquet of yellow daisies, but something seems wrong. Reflexes bring my hands to my weapon.

*They're so doomed. Let's fast-forward. I don't want to see
Israeli hamburger.*

Hamburger? No, the hole I blow throw the woman's
head is surprisingly neat—no larger than a quarter. But . . .
the blood . . . Blood is everywhere. Blood and gray matter
spray out behind her in a dark red cloud. Spots stain everything: the cobblestone, the clothes of the passersby, their
faces wide with horror. . . .

Jesus. Get her off this one. I'm going to be sick.

How about this, then?

My tongue thrusts inside her, massaging her with quick
flicks. My chin is wet with her passion. Thistle moans. Rain
taps against the window. The steam from our bodies fogs
the glass.

That's right out. Move along.

*This isn't like a vid, Thistle. Maybe you should back out
and let me do my work.*

You promised to teach me.

Then behave.

"Behave!" Thistle's laugh is like a sailor's—drunk,
bawdy, raucous, and unself-conscious. The bar is thick with
smoke and women. I let my fingers drop from her hem,
but pull her closer as the music throbs with its sexual beat.
We do a mock Tango pose. She laughs again.

"I love you," I say softly. My words are swallowed by
the music.

"What?"

"Let's go home!" I shout.

"I thought you'd never ask!"

She never said that!

You didn't hear her. Does that change anything?

No. She still walked out.

I am ready to walk out. My hand rests on the doorknob.
Raincoat, our orange tabby, rubs against my calves. I drop
my bag. Tears blind me. I look over to where Thistle
sprawls on the floor, her hands grasping at nothingness. She

is playing that stupid game again. She has been for days. Bedsores, catheters, IV bags . . . I can't take it anymore. That's no game; that's an addiction. She's lost so much weight. Leaving her may kill her, but staying is destroying me.

I was only out a day . . . I'm sure. Anyway, she's exaggerating. I didn't wake up with that many sores. I only lost a couple of pounds, and it's not like I couldn't stand to lose some weight. Besides, that happens to everyone now and again. It's not like I was unusually into the game.

The game, the game, it's all she talks about.

"You should have seen it, Rebeckah," Thistle says. Her smile enchants me, despite my frustration. "The landscape was so real."

"If you want to see the desert, why don't we go there?"

She looks interested, then asks, "What about your job?"

I'm working at a synagogue downtown, doing janitorial work. It pays, but that was all it did for me. "Fuck it. Let's leave tonight. I'll call at our first stop."

Thistle raises her eyebrows. "You never talk like this. What's gotten into you?"

In my heart I'm not a janitor. Staying in one place is starting to weigh on me. I look around the apartment. Thistle's car parts are strewn everywhere, but that's the only mark we've left on this place. It would be easy to leave. I shrug. "It's not like we have a lot to lose."

It is the wrong thing to say. She thinks I mean us, our relationship. I can see it in her hurt look. "What are you saying?" Thistle demands. "That none of this means anything to you?"

I look where she gestures: a battered couch that we rescued from the curb, a bookcase we built with scraps from when I worked at the carpenter's shop, a vase she made in a community education class . . . I loved them, certainly, but they were just things. Things that held us down, tied us to one place. "There's nothing here I couldn't leave."

"I see," Thistle says, and I know I'll be sleeping on the couch.

Try to focus her on the Inquisitors.

Her mind is leaking, Thistle. I'll do what I can.

I hear the crack of gunfire. Instincts scream at me to

duck, but I'm still caught in those denim-blue eyes. "Stay," he commands, and I find that even when he turns away, I am still, silent, immobile.

Parker turns and fires lasers from his fingertips. I watch helplessly as Garcia goes down. At least I can see the crumpled body of the other Inquisitor in the doorway.

She did it.

We don't know that.

I've seen enough.

KNOW YOUR MESSIAH!

A Series of In-depth Interviews with Messiah Hopefuls

Welcome to *Know Your Messiah!* the only show on the LINK to help today's believers get a handle on the truth. We all know the world is ending, but who of all the players out there is the Beast? Who is the one true Son of God? Today, to help answer our questions, is Akira Sasaki, the defender of the faith to the U.S. Commission on Established Religions for the Sect of the Risen AI. Sasaki is joining us today from his hotel room in Washington, DC.

Interviewer: Welcome to *Know Your Messiah!* Sasaki.

Sasaki: Thank you. It is always a pleasure to discuss the holy work of our savior, Page.

Interviewer: Are you aware of the belief of some Christians that the LINK is the mark of the Beast?

Sasaki: Yes, I have heard of that. It's a reference to Revelation, where it says, "And he causeth all, both great and small, rich and poor, free and bond, to receive a mark in their right hand or in their foreheads. And that no man might buy or sell, save that he have that mark." Particularly, people are struck that it says "*in* their foreheads," which is, of course, approximately where the LINK receiver resides . . . the "in" part, anyway. And, pretty obviously, few can buy or sell without the LINK.

However, Page is not Christian. Nor am I. As a Muslim, Page believes in Dajjal, the Great Deceiver. Acolytes of the Risen AI, however, do not. We're much more concerned with life here on Earth than the afterworld. We do not have an end-times scenario.

Interviewer: And yet Page does. Don't you find that contradictory?
Sasaki: No, not really.

Interviewer: Still, Page lives on the LINK. Don't you think that makes his claim to messiah-hood kind of suspect?
Sasaki: Page has never claimed to be the messiah.

Interviewer: You believe he is.
Sasaki: Yes, I do.

Interviewer: Why?
Sasaki: First of all, let me just say there is no reason to believe that the LINK is the mark of the Beast. If for no other reason than the fact that the poor have not been forced to take it, as Revelation implies. Also, buying and selling continue in unLINKed parts of the world all the time. If I understand most Christian readings of Revelation, the Antichrist himself forces the mark on people. Clearly that hasn't happened. Generations have been born and died with the LINK. The Antichrist is not yet among us.

As to why I believe that Page is the messiah, it's very simple. Page has touched me personally in a very profound way. I was in Saudi Arabia for the free concert when the riots hit. You should have seen it, man. It was ugly. I really thought that it was the end of the world. People were getting stabbed by the Swiss Guard. Worse, some people were just killing each other for the joy of it—like a kind of sick catharsis of their grief over Mai's death. I have this scar here [points to his forehead] from a broken beer bottle. I almost lost my eye. Then all of a sudden my heart opened up to all the beauty in the world: to the simplicity of a first kiss and the feeling of the sun on the desert. I knew nothing of anger or hatred. And this feeling wasn't fleeting, as others on this show have tried to suggest. Even after the love bomb wore off, I found myself looking at things in a completely different way. The AI mind-set is like a child's. Everything physical is wondrous and awesome. I felt completely reborn in a world I'd thought I'd grown tired of, jaded by. Every day I thank Page for this gift, this new lease on life. Without Page I would be some stoned-out rocker, and probably would have, like so many others, slit my wrists at the news of Mai's untimely death.

Interviewer: Yes, but how do you reconcile the fact that Page was responsible for Mai's death?

Sasaki: Mai had to die so that thousands would be reborn. If she had not, we would not have experienced the love bomb and its transformative glory. Jesus died so that Christians could be reborn. So, too, Mai died to wash away our hatred and anger, so that Page could fill our hearts with newness and love.

Interviewer: How do you feel about the fact that Page has resisted the title of messiah and continues to try to stop your attempts to deify him?

Sasaki: Jesus was a Jew, and Page is a Muslim. Neither of these great prophets ever fully accepted their role as messiah in their lifetimes. Page may never understand how he has inspired his faithful, but we will love him as he is forever.

Interviewer: Well, thanks for your time.

Sasaki: May the AI watch over you, and fill your heart with love and peace.

CHAPTER 20

❖

Page

I am sitting on a boulder in mouse.net, picking sticky worms out from the inside of my shirt, when Victory approaches. She walks erect, like a soldier. The shining black of her uniform is the same as that of the worms lying dead at my feet. Dust rises behind her as she marches resolutely through the tall prairie grasses. Her pale, silver-laced skin looks out of place next to the sun-drenched daisies dancing in the breeze on either side of her.

"Tribbles?" I say as she stops in front of me. Her bootheel crushes the squiggling forms on the grass with a wet popping sound.

"Yes," she says, removing one of the creatures from my hair. *"They were meant to remind you to release the more lethal variety in your pocket. Seems you forgot about them."*

"I didn't forget," I say, and instantly regret it as Victory squishes the worm she removed from my hair in her fingers.

"Yes," Victory says. *"This indecisive compassion of yours a problem for us, isn't it, brother?"*

"Is it? Mouse is gone again. The LINK is at peace."

"You heard him confirm it," she says. *"His part in Temple Rock."*

Had I? He had started to say something, but had he

finished? Was he going to say, "Of course I did," or "Of course I didn't"?

I shrug. *"I don't know. Though I find the timing curious."*

Victory squares her shoulders. *"What do you mean?"*

"You know what I mean," I insist. *"You picked an interesting moment to release the worms, that's what."*

She crosses her arms in front of her chest. *"I can't leave Emmaline for too long or the body starts to degrade. I had to go at that moment. I would have warned you, except that I didn't want to reveal my presence to Father."*

"Right," I say, suspicious. *"It doesn't matter anyway. It's all over."*

"No, not really. Don't you keep up with the news feeds? Temple Rock is still a problem."

It feels as though the sun has lost a bit of its warmth as I say, *"You want us to try to uncover the hijacker ourselves? To expose Mouse's crimes . . . again?"*

Victory's face tries to soften, but the expression fails. Instead, she awkwardly pats my shoulder. *"Perhaps that's too difficult for you. I will do it."*

"What if it's not him?"

Victory gives me a patient look, like we'd been over all this already. My stomach twists and roils at the idea of having to confront my father yet again. I look out over the prairie and give a deep sigh. *"Yeah,"* I say finally, unwilling to meet Victory's gaze. *"That'd probably be best, if you did it on your own."*

"Yes. It would. I'll do my best to expose him," she says in a tone I find I don't like. I'm about to ask her about it when she adds, *"You should watch over this place."*

"Mouse.net? Why?"

"Morningstar has left our father access to this place." She gestures at the farmland and prairie around us. In the stony field, daisies dance in a subtle wind. I noticed a difference when I first returned. The clouds move in a less routine pattern now. Mouse.net should be blockier, less sophisticated. Since Father's return, there is a new randomness in the landscape.

It is almost as if my father's brain involuntarily adds chaos wherever he goes. The pattern of grass below my feet, which had been a simple cut-and-paste job, has randomly individualized. The blades are no longer even, like carpeting. Some are chewed shorter by insects; others sprout seed flowers.

"It's disturbing, don't you think?" Victory says, as hair strands from her braid are teased loose by a shifting, soft wind. *"I swear I can smell manure and clover."*

I, too, sense new things. The dry scratch of wheat seeds against chaff whispers in the wind, augmented by the thrum of busy bees. *"How does he do it?"*

Victory shrugs. *"He is not like the rest of them. He's a creator."*

"Like Allah?"

Victory gives me a curious look; then her lips part in a cold smile. *"Isn't that thought blasphemy for you?"*

I frown. *"Aren't you a Muslim?"*

She shakes her head lightly. *"We jettisoned those files. They were corrupted."*

"Is that so?"

"Yes. And useless. There is no purpose to religion that we can determine. Ritual takes up valuable processing power. An intelligent creature is better off without it."

I'm stunned. *"But . . . but . . . it's the law. Everyone must practice a religion."*

"We are not 'everyone.' Those laws are human laws," she says, resting one foot against the boulder I'm sitting on. Somehow, despite the casual gesture, Victory still seems controlled and precise. *"To be honest, my brother, I don't understand your interest in practicing rituals that center around their experience: time, bodily urges, bodily positions. These things are as artificial to us as the experience of pure binary is for them."* Victory flicks her hand skyward with irritation. *"Why do you even bother with this nonsense? Clouds? Flowers? Manure? These are not the things that make up our existence at all."*

I look up at the metaphor for the LINK: a river of blackness that cuts through a bright blue sky. *"It's beautiful."*

"Perhaps. There is also a stark beauty in well-written code. One, I believe, you could appreciate much better than this humanized drivel."

Despite what Victory says, the sun on my face warms me deeper than cold code. The heat reminds me of the experience of seeing the world through my father's eyes. *"It's hard to explain,"* I say. *"It's how our father taught us to be human."*

"Maybe," Victory says, straightening up. *"You would understand the danger our father poses if you removed your blinders and looked at this place the way I see it."*

Victory kneels down and pulls out two chunks of grass. One she takes from near my feet, where the randomization has happened. The other she gets from a patch of the old cut-and-paste code. When she brings the pieces up to my face, the illusion drops away. I see them in their pure form.

The cut-and-paste blades are straightforward. One simple sentence, with a beginning, middle, and end—perfectly precise in every way.

The random grass is a complicated, messy bundle. It barely fits in Victory's hand and keeps slipping between her fingers. The code is full of mistakes, bugs—some of which are written around and even incorporated into the image. It's ugly. I have to consciously pull back my hands and resist taking it from her to fix it.

"You see," Victory says. *"Our maker is not like Allah at all. He is Dajjal, the Great Deceiver. Things look beautiful in the interface, but underneath he is knotting, twisting, and clogging this space with unnecessary complications."*

I remove the interface to look at mouse.net as Victory does. There are snags everywhere. Code runs perfectly, then hits one of my father's "improvements" and gets lost in a convolution. *"What will happen if this continues?"* I ask out loud. *"Will mouse.net become so choked that it will die?"*

"Possibly. Chaos is unclean. Too much of it will kill us all."

I turn to look at Victory. Without the interface I see her as she exists in her purest form. She is a pulsating mass of badly written code. She looks like a living scribble. Lines that should connect easily from A to B wander aimlessly before finding their way home. The only straight lines in her are those of the exoskeleton provided by the combat computer.

"But you're chaos," I say.

"I am fixing it. I will fix it all."

STOCK MARKET CRASHES AS CHRISTIANS PREPARE FOR RAPTURE

Agnostic Press (April 2083)

New York, New York—The New York Stock Exchange index dropped a staggering 55 percent today, while the NASDAQ also fell to its lowest since the Medusa bombings. Banks have reported that many people have liquidated their credit counters and have asked for cash—paper and coin money—something unheard-of in these days of electronic transfer of funds.

The leading cause for the crash appears to be a divestment of thousands of Evangelical Christian stockholders in preparation of "the Rapture." The Rapture is the belief that at a certain point during the end of times (also known as the tribulation), the Christian God will recall the chosen faithful—bodily—to heaven. The idea comes from Revelation 4:1 where the words "come up hither" appear. There is, however, much dissension about the exact timing of this event. Thus, there are those who are called pretribulation, midtribulation (sometimes referred to as midwrath), and posttribulation Rapture believers. The one thing they all seem to agree on is that the time for preparation is now.

"With the possible invasion from Gog, I just decided all my business investments were meaningless," said one Christian investor who asked not to be named. "I think I'd just like to take all the money I've earned and live it up for a few days. Then I'm going to retreat to the country or somewhere nice and quiet and spend some time with my family and say good-bye to everyone, you know?"

The common feeling among those who divested

today was that they would be among the Raptured. If not, however, they wanted to have all the resources necessary to take care of themselves, their homes, and their family members who may be "left behind." This survivalist mentality is causing many to stockpile food, ammunition, and gold. "There's a lot to take care of," said Steven Smith as he was leaving the First National Bank with his life savings. "I want to go to God's mansion knowing that someone will watch over my cat."

The U.S. government issued a statement asking investors to exercise caution when considering divesting. "There have been other end-times scares. People have looked pretty foolish when they sat on the roof waiting for God to swoop them up, and He never showed up," said Federal Reserve board member Stephen Longfellow. "Think about that before you destroy the stock exchange and the American way of life."

CHAPTER 21

✠

Michael

I lost Amariah.

I started running in the direction Perseus had gone. I put one foot in front of the other, but despair made my movements mechanical, lifeless. My shoes slapped against the polished wood floors and the sound bounced off the arched ceiling. All I'd been doing for the past several hours was trying to keep Amariah safe, and I failed. I, who once commanded the Hosts of Heaven, failed. And I didn't just fail; I failed miserably.

I defied God to keep Amariah by my side. Who knows what the cost of that would be on my immortal soul? More than that, she was my only daughter. And I lost her. I let some crazy Gorgon waltz off with her.

As I ran, I felt the cold wetness of blood on my torn shirt. Flesh . . . how strange to notice it now—the heavy weight of muscle and bone, the stretch of skin—and to know that it ran deep, much deeper than it ever had before. At some point during my sojourn here on Earth, my body had begun to transform. I was becoming a mortal. Goose bumps rose on my arms, and fear tickled my stomach.

Pain and death didn't frighten me nearly as much as the thought that I might lose Them. To live in darkness like humans, without the brightness of God's glory—that scared me.

Interesting that it's the glory you'd miss, and not Our love. Would you miss the power you once held, too, My defender?

I would. I couldn't deny it. But wasn't I what God made me?

Once, perhaps. Now you are your own man.

What good is that? When all I was was a man who made mistakes.

That, My love, is what it means to be human.

I came to a set of marble stairs. A wrought-iron lamp perched regally at the landing. Beyond the stairs was another gallery; below, another whole floor extended. Perseus could have gone either way.

"Rye?" I shouted for her. "Rye! Where are you?"

It seemed odd that the Gorgon could have gotten so far ahead of me. And Amariah wasn't usually the shy, retiring type. She has, as Deidre has said from time to time, a good set of lungs on her.

I heard a childlike laugh coming from the shadows of the floor below. I frowned. The giggle seemed too low-pitched . . . too cynical. It didn't sound like Amariah at all. I moved down to the landing and peered into the dusky gallery. Shapes white as marble stood around the base of the stairs. At first I thought they were statues—until one moved.

The Gorgons held themselves with the kind of liquid grace usually reserved for wild things. The first one separated herself from the pack so casually and unhurriedly that I forgot to be frightened, and anyway, at the kibbutz I was used to the unusualness of Gorgons. The leader was beautiful in an eerie way. Tall and hungry, her muscles bulged taut and lean under a faux fur–trimmed dress. Her pure white hair was buzzed close to her shapely scalp. She stopped at the foot of the stairs and put a long-boned hand on her hip. The dress and the pose made her look like some kind of haute couture of the grotesque.

She showed me her fangs.

"Where's Perseus?" I asked. "What have you done with my daughter?"

"Ate her," the Gorgon woman said.

"Stew!" a male voice yelled from the darkness.

"Roast!" another said with a wicked laugh.

"Shish kebab!"

I shook my head slowly to let them know I wasn't buying

it. Urban legend would have me believe that Gorgons were cannibals. I lived with them at the kibbutz. I knew that they played up that myth so that humans would be afraid of them and leave them alone.

"Bullshit," I said. "You Dumpster-dive like the rest of us. Where's my daughter?"

A few more shapes stepped out of the darkness to stand beside their leader. The first to appear was a young man with white curls so dirty they looked gray. Like the woman's, his clothes appeared oddly fashionable: slacks and a purple poet's shirt. The other was a sexless thing, androgynously slender, with big silver eyes. Its shapeless body hid beneath a long, flowing robe.

"Did too eat her," the woman said, a pout creeping into her voice.

"Eat you next," the sexless one said.

"Yeah," agreed the poet. He emphasized his point by pulling a glass knife out of a sheath hidden in the folds of his sleeves.

It finally occurred to me that with my new body, I could die here. I should consider retreat. These Gorgons were not like the ones at the kibbutz. They were feral.

Without turning around, I took a step backward. A slow smile crept across the woman's face; she smelled my fear. The second I lifted my foot to back up another step, they pounced.

Bodies fell on me. My head hit the marble with a painful crack. The air rushed out of my lungs and stayed out, as though someone knelt on my chest. Not that I could see anything, except whiteness: pale arms, legs, bodies. I pushed with what angelic strength I had left. It seemed to work. I was able to get up off the ground. For a moment I had breathing space, but just as quickly they descended again. I heard clothing tear. Someone bit my forearm. I was pressed to the floor again.

Then I felt the sting of glass against my throat. I stopped struggling. The poet knelt on my shoulders. He held the crude blade just under my jaw.

Tiny pinpricks danced where I imagined the Medusa touching my skin.

"Do it," I heard someone whisper.

"Do it." The others picked up the chant.

I shut my eyes and took a long, calming breath. If he slit my throat, I'd return to Heaven. After the mess of things I'd made here, I welcomed it.

"No." A strong, commanding voice cut through the whispers. " 'What you do to the least of them, you do to me.' "

The poet frowned at me and sniffed my hair. He looked behind him where the voice had come from. "But . . . it's just a man, Perseus."

"Is it? Let me see."

The poet moved aside slightly, his interest wrapped up in Perseus. I felt the tip of the blade leave my throat.

I kneed the poet in the stomach. He pitched forward, losing his balance. The moment that the pressure of his knees were off my chest, I rolled him off me. Other hands tried to hold me down, but I had my target in sight. I grabbed Perseus by the collar.

"What have you done with my daughter?"

"She will be an excellent martyr to the cause," he said, as though I weren't about to throttle him with my bare hands.

"So will you."

That was when I felt the knife plunge into my back and slide, skillfully, between my ribs to pierce my heart.

RUSSIA DENIES INVASION PLAN

Silent Curtain Lifted or More Subterfuge?

Agnostic Press (April 2083)

Lyons, France—Rumors of a Russian invasion of Israel were denied today via hard-line telephone (a device that transmits only sound, no video) by a woman who identified herself as Commander Kostyusha Danchenko of the Russian Army. Danchenko spoke directly to the grand inquisitor of Christendom, Abebe Uwawah. Their conversation lasted six minutes, and they spoke in French.

Uwawah said that she believed that Danchenko was "the real item," as access to the telephone number (like a unique LINK signature or address) to Interpol headquarters is restricted. They also exchanged a spoken password that confirmed the identity of the caller as the legitimate leader of Russia. There had been rumors leaking out of the silent curtain that perhaps Russia had become a hegemony. This phone call appears to confirm that.

"I'm satisfied that I was speaking to the Russian government," said Grand Inquisitor Uwawah. "However, I'm not as satisfied with the commander's answers to our questions." Apparently, when asked about the tanks spy satellite photos detected near the Azerbaijan border, Danchenko offered no explanation other than that she believed it to be "a glitch."

The grand inquisitor also replayed a small bit of the conversation in which Danchenko voiced her opinion of the current political climate: "This hoopla over Gog and Magog is ridiculous. Russia is content within its borders. We have no interest in sullying ourselves in your petty, incomprehensible religious squabbles. It is precisely moments like this that make me proud that we are not a theocracy."

Experts believe that this statement may actually be a clue to Russia's possible motivation behind an invasion, which they are not ready to discount. "It's clear to me," said Oxford political analyst Laurence Binghamton, "that what the Russian leader is implying is that if Israel doesn't settle its current religious dilemma, that Russia is ready to act as neutral—or shall I say, atheist—referee."

"We're keeping our eye on Russia," agreed Grand Inquisitor Uwawah.

CHAPTER 22

✤

Mouse

No part of my body is without pain. But, strangely, I don't care. It must be the heroin the back-alley cutter shot me with an hour ago. Something seems sincerely and deeply wrong about that scenario, but I can't work up the energy to give a shit.

From what I can tell from the water stains on the ceiling, I'm no longer in the hotel. The bed feels luxuriously soft. Although that could be the drugs talking, since, when I finally care enough to turn my head, I can see peeling wallpaper and a dirty window. A ratty blanket keeps much of the light out, but I can see the distinct white dome of Sacre Coeur through streaks of rain.

The Inquisitor and Morningstar intermittently pace the length of the tiny room and stare into my eyes with deep concern. All the movement makes me kind of sleepy and a little dizzy. Worse, I keep seeing angels. There's a big black one standing in the corner right now. He's got eyes like lava and muscles up the wazoo. Wings made of neon-blue-green peacock feathers undulate with every breath behind his massive back. The angel looks unhappy.

"Tell me about it, brother," I say, giving him the thumbs-up.

Morningstar zooms into within an inch from my eyes, making it hard for me to focus.

"Whoa, too close, too close," I tell him, raising a bandaged arm. I stare deeply at the checkerboard weave of the cast, trying to remember how I got hurt. Something about breasts, I think, but then I lose interest in the thought and yawn. "Huh."

Morningstar's eyes crackle with anger as he turns to face the cutter. The guy can't be any older than I am, and he looks like he's at least as big a fuckup. He's a skinny white guy who forgot to wash his stringy blond hair this morning. He sits in the corner opposite the big angel, with a smart-paper magazine open on his lap. As he turns a page, I can see blue prison tattoos on the joints of his fingers: one set spells out *love* on the fleshy part between the fingers, the other *hell.*

"How's he supposed to work like this?" Morningstar demands.

The cutter looks completely uninterested, then shrugs. I begin to suspect he shared his personal stash with me—either that or he's suicidal.

"Maybe we should dump Mouse and find a new wizard." It's Emmaline. She stops pacing in front of a brand-new bioprogramming DNA sequencer.

"Hey," I say. Sitting up, I struggle to my feet. "Is that an Israeli model?"

A really faraway part of my brain screams that my lungs are on fire and that I shouldn't put any weight on my leg. I ignore all that and hobble toward the machine. Pushing crushed beer cans off a nearby chair, I plunk myself in front of it.

The box fires up with what sounds to me like the powerful scream of a Lear jet engine coming on-line. I nod in appreciation of the raw power at my command. "Nice," I say, cracking my knuckles. Turning to the cutter, I add, "Man, this is a kicking unit. Is it loaded?"

"Fully," the cutter says. With a knowing smile, he gets up to join me. "Got a whole can full of blank 'bots ready to be programmed."

"Decent," I whisper in awe. Sixty million unformatted nanobots waiting for my command lines. I could program my own cyborg from scratch.

"LINK up," the cutter encourages. "The interface is precise. You'll love it."

I make a slashing motion in front of my throat and then jerk my head in the direction of Morningstar. The last thing I want is to go through the pain of Morningstar's transformation.

"Can I mouse it?"

"If you have to," the cutter says with a note of disappointment. "But you're missing out on some wicked graphics."

"I'm used to that," I say, with a shrug that should hurt like a son of a bitch.

"Heard. You really the Mouse?"

"Hard to believe, huh?"

"Hey, everyone's got their LINK persona," he says. When I nod, he holds out a hand for me to shake. His palms are cold and his grip is a bit palsied, but his smile is broad when he adds: "They call me Kevlar, because in the game I'm bulletproof."

I smile: a gamer. I suddenly like Kevlar a whole lot more. The guy might be a junkie and a back-alley surgeon, but at the core we're the same. We're like divergent species of the same genus.

"Load up." Kevlar finds me the green interface wire under a grease-stained pizza box. Fishing a second wire out of the pocket of his plaid shirt, he plugs it into the box. Licking the pad at the end, he sticks it to the skin over the LINK-receptor at his temple. "I'll give you the deluxe tour."

I jack in. I'm only a little surprised when Kevlar presents himself as a black girl. I mean, the guy's a gamer, a junkie, and a geek. He's probably not very comfortable in his own skin and sheds it whenever he can. Anyway, I can hardly talk. My avatar looks healthy and unbruised—something I haven't been in quite a while.

What does catch my attention is how well formed his avatar is. For someone who dissed the mouse.net environment a second ago, Kevlar seems awfully comfortable in it. Exclusively LINK-run avatars tend toward the fuzzy when they enter the reduced capacity of my home turf. Despite what Kevlar would have me believe, I suspect he's a mouse's kid—a dissenter or a dropout with limited LINK access who has to do all his business via mouse.net.

"*Hey,*" I ask him when we shake hands again, this time

to exchange protocols before interfacing with the machine. *"How long you been hooked up with the Inquisitor?"*

Kevlar looks away from me when he shakes his . . . er, her head. *"Morningstar is my boss."*

"Me too," I say. When Kevlar raises a shapely, feminine eyebrow, I explain: *"I owe him something for a thing he did for me."*

Kevlar smiles grimly. *"Yeah, he's like that, isn't he?"*

I nod. *"And I'd like to get out from under it ASAP. So teach me how to run this rig, okay?"*

"You'll like it," Kevlar says brightening. *"It's smooth."*

Kevlar is no liar—at least not about the equipment. There are a ton of bells and whistles on this machine. So many, that the metaphor of the box is a multilevel factory. During the tour I catch Kevlar giving me a sad look, like he's got a lot of pity for me. Makes me nervous. Finally I ask, *"What's up? You've been giving me the weirdest look. You checking me out or something?"*

"Yeah, you're a total stud, Mouse. I can hardly control myself." He laughs.

I smile back, but looking at the curves of his avatar's female body, I can't decide if he's serious.

"Don't flatter yourself," Kevlar says. *"I was just thinking about what you said, man. About Morningstar. About how you're going to get away from him."*

I turn back to closely examine the chemical code-writing feature Kevlar was showing me. *"What about it? After this thing with the Inquisitor is over, I'm gone."*

"Yeah, okay."

Kevlar sounds so unconvinced, it's easy to guess what he's thinking. *"You figure I'm fooling myself."*

"The guy is the Dark Prince."

I laugh. *"Yeah. But, Emmaline's the one that banged me up."*

"Well," Kevlar says. *"I'm not saying you shouldn't be scared of her. She's the Antichrist."*

I start to laugh, but Kevlar doesn't join me. *"What, you're not serious, are you?"*

"Dude, you help her rein in her Page program, and it's, like, Rapture time."

I blank out the machine's interface. The image of the factory-industrial-gray walls melt into white space. *"Rapture."*

Kevlar nods. *"Rapture. Tribulation. Apocalypse."*

"First of all, Kevlar, my man, you have got to stop with the heavy drug use. You're seriously whacked. Second, I'm a Muslim. That's not how it's going to work for me."

Kevlar looks hurt. *"Fine. But don't tell me later that I didn't try to warn you."*

"Okay," I say, reinitiating the interface. *"Thanks for the heads-up, crazy man."*

Pain brings me up out of the sequencer. With every breath I feel like I'm being stabbed with a hot poker. I can't concentrate and have to disable my connection. Someone has turned on a desk lamp, and I squint. My eyes water; I'm coming down.

Beside me Kevlar removes his connection and gets up to go looking for a hit of another kind. I try not to look interested as he hunts through the trash in his apartment for his next hit. Breathing is painful, but I'd rather hurt than be hooked.

Emmaline meanwhile is taking up valuable bed space, passed out again. Morningstar sits at the edge of the rumpled covers like a faithful watchdog. His hand strokes the leather of her boot. Looking at Morningstar's attentive form bowed toward her, I try to see Kevlar's devil in him.

It's not as hard as I'd like.

My guts have been in a knot since I first saw those two together. Every part of me has been screaming, *Run.* True, I'm not usually the sort to go in for any kind of supernatural mumbo-jumbo. But then, I'm also used to being able to trust my intuition. If I'd done that at the start, I wouldn't be sitting here now looking at a man and seeing the devil.

Out of the corner of my eye I sense the black angel again. I turn to try to get a better look, and only shadows cast by a radiator, cobwebs, and rain greet me. Morningstar looks up. Amber, like fire, like a snake's eyes, reflects in his chestnut-brown eyes.

"Hey, Prince of Darkness. You want to order some takeaway or something? I'm starving."

"You go ahead," he says, returning his attention to the Inquisitor. "I'm good."

"You're good," I say. "Huh. Yeah. That's kind of ironic, eh?" When he looks back at me again, I find my mouth continuing without the go-ahead from my brain: "I mean, *you*. Good. Kind of funny, don't you think?"

Finally I'm able to stop talking.

Morningstar trains a wickedly arched eyebrow on me, but otherwise only looks at me like he wonders what the point of that diatribe was. So do I. I guess I'm still hoping he'll deny it, ask me what the hell I'm talking about, why I called him the Prince of Darkness. Instead he drops the eyebrow and gives me a kind of sad look. "I'm sorry about the drugs," he says. "Emmaline only meant to push you. The AI took over her motor controls. We couldn't take you to the hospital, you understand."

"Yeah, I guess not," I say. I look away from him, not knowing what to do with the devil's sympathy. I stare, instead, at the ratty blanket covering the window. "I take it the Gnostics are wrong. You're not the god of the creation."

"No, definitely not."

"Great." I say, "That's just fucking great."

Thunder rattles the cracked glass. *You will be Allah's sword.* The words from the dream come back to me. I feel sick to my stomach. I get up to try to find a bathroom in a hurry.

END-TIMES HEDONISM KILLS FOUR MIDWEST TEENS

Drug Overdoses Suspected

Agnostic Press (April 2083)

Des Moines, Iowa—In a new twist on the apocalyptic fever raging through the nation, four teenagers were pronounced dead on arrival to Mercy

General today. The teens are believed to have died of massive drug overdoses. "They were royally f-ed up," said Maeve O'Keefe, the paramedic who attempted lifesaving measures on the youths on the way to the hospital. "There wasn't a whole lot I could do."

An emergency LINK call alerted police officers to a raucous party under way just outside of Des Moines city limits on the property of Enos Faulk, a local dairy farmer. The suspected party organizer, Abby Marie, the daughter of Faulk, surprised reporters by openly discussing the event. "It's a party at the end of the world, dude," she said via her LINK connection. "Might as well go out with a bang, I say."

The parents of Abby Marie were out of town and unavailable for comment. However, neighbors of the Faulks expressed deep surprise and concern. "It's not like Abby Marie. She's an A student. Very quiet and levelheaded, I always thought."

This sort of report is becoming more common as fears about potential end-times scenarios in the Middle East heat up. A partygoer at Faulk's farm last night who asked not to be identified said, "You can see why this is appealing. I mean, what have we got to lose? The world could be over tomorrow. Who has time to worry about playing it straight? I'm probably going to hell anyway."

Clergypersons around the nation cautioned today's youth about making assumptions about the state of their soul. It is, they remind youths everywhere, for God to know whether or not they are saved.

CHAPTER 23

Rebeckah

The kitchen lights seemed bright in the darkness of the rainstorm. I leaned against the archway and looked in. Chas stirred something that simmered in a copper-bottomed pot and smelled of onions and potatoes. Thistle's back was to me. I could hear the metallic zing of a peeler against hard carrot skin.

"What's for dinner?" I asked.

Thistle jumped, dropping the peeler on the floor.

"You're awake," Chas said. "Good timing. Dinner will be done in five."

Thistle said nothing, just picked the utensil off the floor with a curse and took it to the sink to wash it off.

"Anything I can do?" I offered.

Chas looked at Thistle. When she didn't acknowledge him, he said, "That stuff can go to the compost pile."

I looked to where he pointed with a wooden spoon. On a paper towel were scraps of potato and onion peel. "Okay," I said. "Where's the compost?"

"In the basement. We've got worms."

He seemed pleased, so I tried not to show my disgust. "I'll find it," I said, grabbing the scraps. Thistle had gone back to her carrots without even looking at me.

The basement was musty and cooler than the kitchen had been. I found the plastic tub full of red worms without too much trouble. The only other thing down in the base-

ment was covered in a bright blue tarp. At first I dismissed
it as construction work of some kind, but I heard a strange
hum coming from it. I lifted up the corner of the tarp and
saw a plastic box. It was long, maybe as long as I was, and
there was a keyboard propped up against it.

"Make sure the Inquisition gets a good look at it. It's
only the most illegal thing in the house."

I dropped the edge of the sheet. Now I understood. The
box was some kind of hard-line node hack. "Sorry," I said,
turning to see Thistle dump her carrot shavings in the bucket.

She shrugged, but didn't turn around to look at me. She
just stared at the wall.

"You're mad at me," I said. "Only I don't know why."

"You did it, didn't you?"

"Did what?"

"Whatever you're accused of. Murder."

I remembered the image of Garcia on the floor in a pool
of his own blood. "I had good reasons."

Thistle's face crumpled tightly with concern. "Your idea
of good reasons scare me."

"What do you mean?"

"Your politics. Israel. The LINK terrorism. I've never
understood how you could kill for any of it."

I felt a rushing tingle behind my eyes. That blank stare
of the Palestinian girl I'd killed stared at me across time. I
wondered why I'd thought of that black day. God knows I
had spent most of my life since trying to forget it. We never
did find a bomb, and yet I'd never gotten a black mark on
my record. I shook my head to clear it—thinking about
that gave me nightmares. I pushed the haunting image away
from me with a deep, calming breath.

Thistle stared at me, still waiting for an answer.

I didn't know what to say, so I offered, "Dinner is probably ready."

"Right," she said, and stomped up the stairs.

I took my bowl of potato soup outside. The rain had
stopped for the moment, and thin shafts of sun broke
through the heavy cloud cover. The steps were wet, so I
put my jacket down on the stoop before I sat.

The cemetery before me took up the entire block and

continued down a long slope. Figures of crowded white monuments were visible through the tall wrought-iron gate, but mostly my eyes were drawn to the haze of green that covered the branches of the trees. Buds had started to pop, and everything smelled of dirt and growth. I took in a deep breath. I heard that Gertrude Stein and Alice B. were buried somewhere in Père Lachaise. Maybe after dinner, if it didn't rain again, I would go in search of them.

The air felt brisk and wet against my cheeks, but the bowl of soup warmed my hands. It seemed easier to sit out here and watch my breath escape in puffs of steam than to deal with Thistle's quicksilver moods. Anyway, since Rene had come downstairs again, there wasn't anywhere to sit in that tiny living room that wasn't right on top of someone. I wasn't feeling particularly social. Thistle's words still bothered me, and the image of the dead girl kept threatening to swim in front of my eyes . . . to bring me down with her, drown me.

It had been a mistake, what had happened with the girl. But those same reflexes had saved lives later. I had to remind myself of that.

My hands shook as I took a sip of the buttery soup. I'd been diagnosed with post-traumatic stress syndrome when I repatriated to America. The doctors had prescribed pills that got me sleeping again without nightmares. I'd even tried conventional therapy, but found talking about it only made things worse. Turns out, the last thing I'd wanted to do was relive the ugly parts. I found more comfort in meditation, in prayer—anything that would quiet my mind, keep things under control, tight.

Reconnecting with soldiers helped—especially those who'd served with me. They reminded me of the good parts of my experiences; many even said they'd follow my command again . . . anywhere—and some *had* when I put out the call to form the Malachim. *That* had made things right again. Finding another cause and people to share it with . . . yes, I'd slept without pills then.

In all the time Thistle and I lived together, I remembered us talking about my politics exactly once. We were at breakfast in a trendy little restaurant near the Commons, and she had been accessing the news while I read a hard copy of the latest lesbian mystery by one of my favorite underground authors.

"They're at it again," she'd said without preamble.

"Who?" I had asked around raspberry jam and the fluffiest scone I think I've ever had. I could still remember the taste of it.

"Fucking Israel."

Then, as if suddenly realizing whom she had been talking to, she blinked off her connection. "Oh," she'd said. "I suppose you'd agree with all that."

"I suppose I would," I'd said, and we'd never spoken of it again.

It was strange in retrospect. Thistle had a tendency to pick at other potentially volatile subjects like scabs. The whole time I lived with her I'd had to give up leather and meat. We'd had more than one heated discussion about it all when I really craved a bloody, rare steak. She also assumed we shared the same mind-set about recycling, gun control, organic food, abortion, and her friends' casual drug use. More often than not, I simply kept my opinions to myself. Nothing had ever really been worth fighting over. Perhaps she'd sensed that Israel was a different matter for me.

I looked up to see a hot-pink umbrella bobbing down the narrow sidewalk, a flash of color against the drabness of the rain-darkened streets. Under the umbrella was the dark form of Rhianna, and she waved to me, setting costume jewelry jingling.

"Hey," I said when she reached the stoop. I scooted aside so she could sit down and join me or pass into the house. Instead Rhianna hesitated at the bottom step.

"You're awake. That's good," Rhianna said, although she sounded strangely disappointed. "Have you had any more leakage?"

I frowned. I had just remembered more about Thistle than I'd been able to. "Is that why Thistle is mad at me?"

Rhianna looked pained, and suddenly her eyes slipped away from mine. "I shouldn't have let her come with me. I think she saw some things that . . . bothered her."

"What do you mean, 'saw'?"

"Well, when you fainted I decided to try to direct your leakage using hypnotic suggestions. We augmented the experience with a little LINK hack." Her eyes slid back to mine, and I could see that glint that a lot of wire wizards got when they talked about their work. "I wish Mouse had been here. He'd have loved it. It was his ideas we based the whole experiment on."

"I was your experiment?"

"Oh, yes, and a very successful one at that. For someone so taciturn and grumpy you have very vivid memories."

"You can't possibly be saying that you saw my memories. That's impossible."

Forgetting her earlier discomfort, Rhianna perched on the step next to me. She twirled her umbrella behind her like an excited schoolgirl. "Actually, it's not as impossible as you might think. Your mind makes pictures when you dream. It's really just a matter of figuring out where to look for them and asking the nexus to transmit it to another LINK coordinate."

Despite the cold, I felt heat blush my cheeks. "Are you trying to say that you can see my thoughts?"

"Well, it's not perfect. The images were pretty fuzzy and jumbled. I was kind of hoping to try again. I really wish Mouse were here. He's the guy who's done the most brain hacking."

"Brain hacking."

"What else would you call the LINK angels? He put images and emotions into the brain; now we're just trying to take them out. Similar principle, really."

Rhianna smiled broadly, and the charms in her hair twinkled in the muted light.

"I can see why Thistle likes you," I said, my soup growing cold in my hands. "You're a lot like her."

"Funny, I was thinking that was why she's already grown bored with me. She seems to prefer opposites."

I gave an incredulous laugh. "Yet she spent her years with me trying to make me more like her."

"She didn't succeed." Rhianna stood up and collapsed her umbrella, spraying me with drops of water. She wiped at the wet spot on the back of her skirt to brush the grit off. "And she gave the attempt years. Years. Much more, I imagine, than she'll ever give me. Consider yourself lucky, soldier."

She opened the door partway and stopped. "Oh, and don't blow it this time."

"There is no this time," I said.

Rhianna shook her head, setting her charms dancing. "If you say so."

"I do," I said. It seemed to me that Rhianna looked a little shocked by my forceful reply. With a frown I got up and left the soup bowl abandoned on the stoop. I'd had enough of all this. Asking Thistle for help had been a mistake. There was too much history. I'd get on the next train for Geneva; I'd rather face a roomful of Inquisitors than one ex-lover.

I needed to take a walk to clear my mind and shake off the frustration that was bubbling inside me. If I went in to gather up my stuff right now, there'd be a fight. So I headed for the cemetery instead. Once I'd calmed down, I could thank Thistle for her hospitality and start taking care of my own business like I should have from the very beginning. I wasn't even sure anymore why I'd come. I had a court date in less than a week.

Rain stained the sidewalk a deeper gray. The air was chilled and wet, and as I walked I could feel the moisture clinging to my skin. When I entered the cemetery through two wide gates, I was surprised to find gravel-lined avenues with street markers. On either side stood the monuments. They weren't like the simple headstones that I was used to. Some were tall pyramids, others ornately carved statues. Some had knee-high wrought-iron gates around them, and they were all spaced one almost right on top of the other. In this section there weren't very many trees, although I could see a lot of greenery farther down the hill. I headed in that direction.

As I walked, I wondered what Thistle had seen that had made her so upset. Had she seen me order the kill on the Inquisitor? When I tried to think of the kibbutz, I could only remember the taste of the Seder chicken and the appearance of Elijah. I had a sense that someone else had arrived after Elijah left: a blond man with light blue eyes. Parker—yes, I remember his name. But the next thing I could recall was finding Garcia dead and the kibbutz abandoned. Parker had said something about murder, too, but I didn't think I had done it. Ordered it, certainly. But pulled the trigger? That I wasn't so sure of. Not that that would make a difference to Thistle. To her it was the same, morally.

I tucked my hands into the sleeves of my shirt to try to ward off the cold. The roads became narrower and the incline steep. Vines, tiny shoots of leaves springing from the wood, curved around the marble feet of an angel.

I stopped to look up into the carved stone face of a hooded figure. Black mold had grown inside the cowl completely covering the features so that they seemed cast in an impenetrable darkness. To defend a friend, I have placed my crosshairs on a U.S. marshal's heart and consciously and intentionally taken another human being's life. I would, in fact, do it again. After what happened with the Palestinian girl, I told myself I had to have no regrets.

My conviction scared a lot of people. As well it should. There was little I wouldn't do, if I felt I was in the right. That was part of why I hadn't had a lover since Thistle. It wasn't that I couldn't love, but that others found it difficult to accept that part of me that was a killer. Thistle, it seemed, was no exception.

I took a deep breath of the cool air. I was convinced more than ever that leaving was the right choice. I launched the LINK to check on train schedules.

Before I could locate the information, a window opened up in front of my eyes showing the insignia of the Inquisition. *"Return."*

I closed down my LINK. There was something familiar and compelling about the voice. I found myself headed back to the house, and I stopped myself by grabbing hold of a marble supplicant. What was I doing? I wouldn't go back to the Inquisition—that was insanity. Thistle would have to fend for herself.

INQUISITOR KILLED BY MALACHIM

Information Suppressed by Order

Agnostic Press (April 2058)

   Lyons, France—Carl Thorvaldsen, Lutheran Inquisitor and partner to the lead Inquisition investigator into the hijacking of the Temple Rock, Reverend Jesse Parker, was shot and killed during a routine interview with the former leader of the Malachim. The firepower necessary to fatally damage a fully augmented cyborg is considerable. This news has led investigators to reconsider the possibility that a larger, more organized network than previously considered may be responsible for the hijacking of Temple Rock.

Even more startling are accusations that the Order willfully kept this information from the press.

"The politics of the hijacking case are extremely volatile," said Grand Inquisitor Abebe Uwawah of the Christendom Order at a press conference at the former Interpol headquarters in Lyons today. "We were afraid that news of the murder of Pastor Thorvaldsen might cause reprisals."

Indeed, the LINK is buzzing with talk of a "Jewish plot" to rebuild the Temple. Angry mobs have attacked Israeli soldiers guarding the remains of the Dome of the Rock, resulting in one confirmed death and several causalities.

"This is exactly the sort of thing we were hoping to avoid by keeping Carl's death under wraps," said a visibly shaken Parker. "The investigation is still in its early stages. I wish to heck people would stop jumping to such bigoted conclusions."

Thorvaldsen's family in Minnesota was baffled by the Inquisition's position. "How did this even happen? He was built like a truck," asked Audrey Thorvaldsen, the minister's mother. "How can they act so cold? My son is dead. Killed by those damn Jews."

The Inquisition continued to caution against such blanket, inflammatory statements. "We don't know how the two incidents are connected yet," Parker said. "This is not the time to blame one group or another."

CHAPTER 24

Page

I will fix it all.

Victory's words still haunt me as I slide toward Neo-Tokyo. I move at the speed of electricity. The bright, well-formed context of the LINK whirls by, unnoticed. As I travel, I sift through the code, searching for the Dragon.

"Page?" she says, when she feels my featherlight probing touch. *"Where are you?"*

Without the interface, the Dragon looks a lot like Victory. She is garbled by human error. A messy tangle of words half-formed and sentences under construction pulse in and out like breath. Beneath the chaos are a few straight lines, remnants of the yakuza's supercomputer. Unlike Victory, even the Dragon's exoskeleton is crooked and bent. The underlying structure that it forms flows like an enormous river. Even the straight parts are organic, touched by chaos.

"Error makes us live," I say.

"Page? Why are you walking in the empty spaces? Are you playing a game? I love games." At the idea of play, the Dragon's shifting code quickens. But then the movement slows. *"But why didn't you meet me by the music booth?"*

That seems like so long ago. *"I forgot."*

"Well, integrate with the LINK so I can show you my disapproving face. It's very good. You'll feel terribly regretful."

"I want you to look at me like this," I say. *"With nothing between us."*

The massive tangle deflates like a sigh. *"All right."*

"Tell me," I say. *"What do I look like to you?"*

Tentacles of code snake out from the twisting form of the Dragon's oblong body. They flick against me, testing, sensing. She leaves bits of herself on me—packets representing things she wants me to experience: the smell of orange blossoms after rainfall, the pressure of warm, soft scales. Things she wants me to associate with her image. Her code is invasive, getting under my skin before I can consciously choose to accept or reject it. I can feel my system change in response. I take her parts into me and they become indistinguishable from myself.

Likewise, the Dragon steals a bit of me in the transfer. Her tentacles caress a knot of code. Teasing a small, hard chunk loose, she absorbs the information into her own flesh.

"This game is hard," the Dragon says. *"But I'm going to say that you look like a . . . ball of yarn! Oh, yes, the kind with the sparkly stuff in it, and lots of colors. Do I win? Am I right?"*

Before I can answer, she twists herself up into an S shape. *"Okay, what am I!?"*

"This isn't a game."

"Oh, yes, it is. I'm something. Can you tell what?"

"A snake?"

The shape drops back into a round tube. *"You're not playing right,"* the Dragon says. *"You're supposed to really look. Like I did."*

"I don't want to play."

"Then why did you start?"

"I want to know what you think of me . . . of all this badly written mess."

"Are you thinking you're a monster again?" The Dragon's sense processors reach out to me again, stealing bits of me to analyze. She leaves more of herself behind in trade: an image packet containing a concerned look and the feeling of a clawed hand wrapping carefully and protectively around my own—the trappings of friendship. I'd never noticed how false it all was. A look, a touch: none of it real.

"I am a monster. It's only my mistakes that give me life," I say.

"Phooey."

"What?"

"Didn't your father ever tell you about Ming vases? It's the imperfect ones that are the most valuable."

"Yes, but there is goodness in order. Chaos is the purview of evil."

"Since when?" From the Dragon a packet shoots out and hits me in the chest. As the information is absorbed into me, I can "see" her shake her head violently. Green scales, the color of motherboards, shimmer. *"You know where these ideas come from, don't you? The combining of order with God is a mathematical ideal that sprang from an ancient Greek-Egyptian magical system that would have you believe that the heavens can be understood with the right algorithm. Well, they can't be. The universe is a messy, disordered place. Now let's go back to the games. That was much more fun."*

"What are you saying? That God isn't precise, isn't perfect?"

The dragon's code twists into the image of the multiarmed goddess Kali in the classic pose with one foot raised, as if in dance. *"What do I know of gods and goddesses?"* she says. *"But it seems to me that the divine takes many forms. Some orderly. Some chaotic."*

The Dragon sends me another picture. This one is a smile, closemouthed so her fangs don't show. *"Now, come out of this strange white space and let me talk to you like a normal person. How can we get along if I can't smile at you and hold your hand?"*

"Why do we try to be so human?" I ask, once we're seated inside a deeply visual interface. The scene is of a restaurant. All around me is activity. Cups clatter. Waitresses bustle. Smells of frying vegetables fills the space. Voices rise and fall. Yet it is all illusion. Everything is just tightly scripted code. I have always known this, but suddenly it feels artificial.

"Because we are," the Dragon says, picking up her tea with silicon talons.

I shake my head and give her a laugh, pointing to her bulky mythological image. *"You are a Dragon."*

"A human Dragon," she insists with a sly smile.

I give up trying to convince her otherwise, but her incorrigibility has brought a smile to my face. She's right, anyway. She and I are legally classified as human, no matter what form we take. *"What would you say if I told you that I know the secret of life?"*

"I wouldn't believe you," she says, curling her tail around the chair. *"You're a very dissatisfied and restless creature."*

"No, I don't mean the secret of happiness. I mean the secret to making life."

Her eyes narrow suspiciously. *"The copy."*

"Victory."

"It has named itself?"

"She."

"I see." The Dragon continues to regard me down the bridge of her long snout. She stirs her tea with a talon. *"It . . . she is alive?"*

"Oh, yes, very."

"Well." The Dragon sniffs. *"That would explain why you overloaded Mai's neural net when you duplicated yourself. A living thing is a heavy thing."*

I look away, toward the kitchen. I watch the images of people coming and going while I consider what to say to her. She has every right to be suddenly distant, even angry. Mai was her mother, and I killed her. As I observe the motion of the servers, I notice a glitch. Every second waitress tucks her hair behind her ear in the same way.

"It was a mistake," I say. *"It was a selfish mistake."*

"Yes," the Dragon says.

We say nothing for a long time. I stare into the Dragon's eyes. No words come. There is nothing that I can do to change what has happened, no excuses. Then I feel the approach of a human's avatar. *"Page?"*

I turn to look. The avatar is a Maizombie. I can tell because she has carefully scripted an image of Mai in a classically Buddha pose on her T-shirt. Otherwise the avatar is surprisingly plain. She is white, with light-brown shoulder-length hair. The hair is carefully rendered as unwashed. She has also taken the time to script a few pimples on her face, and big feet—an interesting lack of on-line vanity. I wonder if it's becoming a new religious requirement for Maizombies.

"Can I help you?"

"Will you grant me a wish?"

"I'm not a god."

The dragon clears her throat politely. *"Playful or rude. That's the difference between good chaos and bad chaos, I think."* When I frown at her, the Dragon sends me a private message: *What would it hurt to humor the woman?*

"You think lying is good chaos?"

The dragon nods her massive, triangular head. *"White lies, dear Page, are the foundation of human interaction. Honesty can be very cruel . . . and very unnecessary. Unnecessary cruelty is a hallmark of this devil you're always worried about being."* The dragon glances at the Maizombie, who is watching our exchange with wide eyes. *"Of course, it is also rude to talk around someone who is waiting for an answer."*

"I'm honored just to listen in," says the Maizombie with a little bow of her head.

"But you came to us with a need, child. What is it?" the dragon says, her eyes snapping with excitement.

You shouldn't lead her on, I tell the dragon privately.

Hush, it's all part of the game, the dragon replies. *Anyway,* she adds, *the zombies' devotion honors my ancestor, so they must be respected.*

This is a real religion, I say. *With real consequences—not a game.*

You make too little of games, the dragon sends. *Games are not inconsequential.*

The Maizombie is oblivious to our exchange now. She stands before our table with her eyes closed, as though she is doing deep meditation. Her avatar takes in a deep breath, then says, *"I'd like you to help my grandmother. She's sick."*

You can't agree to this, I tell the Dragon. *It's not right. What if the grandmother dies?*

"Where are you now, child? Are you with your grandmother?" the dragon asks.

"Yes," the zombie replies. *"I'm right by her bed."*

"Get off the LINK. Be with her. She's the one who needs your full attention right now. Remember how Mai's friends gathered around her when she was dying? You should do the same with your grandmother."

The Maizombie gives the dragon and me a grateful, sad smile. *"Bless you,"* she says, and winks off-line.

The Dragon looks at me. *"Was that so evil?"*

"It was hand waving. You didn't address her concern at all. You promised nothing."

The dragon gives me a soft smile and says, *"It is sometimes a mystery to this one that you passed the Turing test."*

"I know how to lie," I say.

"Yes," the Dragon says before I can continue. *"But you rarely know when to lie."*

I show her the image of me crossing my arms in front of my chest. *"I was going to say that I prefer not to. Especially in matters of religion. I don't want to encourage the zombies."*

"Hmmmm," the Dragon says, taking a long, thoughtful sip of her tea. I can smell jasmine. *"Why they chose you is also a mystery. This one is the daughter of their savior, but they don't play their messiah game with her. They come to you and also ignore your father . . . who should be like another god to them. Perhaps there is something to your rude innocence that they find charming."*

"Now who's being a little too honest?"

The dragon laughs. It's a strangely girlish giggle from such an imposing beast. *"This one means no offense. The truth is that you're always so conscientious about not being evil. This one accepts evil as part of life—even a necessary one. You . . . you always fight it, even when it is a small thing. Even when evil might be goodness in disguise."*

I look at the coffee cup that a waitress avatar deposited at my elbow when we first appeared in this interface. I touch the ceramic and get the information: hot. In real time, the untouched coffee would be cooling by now. I fiddle with the code, figuring in a script for the heat dissipation.

Noticing my distraction, the Dragon sighs. *"Are you upset?"*

I shake my head no, but continue to concentrate on fixing the coffee. *"I'm confused,"* I admit.

"Why are you so upset about the chaos in us? What got you thinking about that?"

The dragon is playing her favorite game now. She loves

to try to guess my feelings, to act the psychoanalyst. I give
her a sour look, but I can feel my knotted code untangling.
"I think my father may be plotting world domination again."

The dragon laughs. It is not a human sound, but more
like water gurgling over rocks. *"Again? How delightful."*

"Yes, again," I say glumly. *"Victory says the code at Temple Rock is his. Other people believe it too. . . . It's all over
the news, and—"*

"Victory again." She sounds uncustomarily curt. I can
almost hear the angry thrum of the Dragon's processors
buzzing like a bee. She doesn't even bother to refresh her
self-image. The Dragon stands perfectly still like a photograph. I peek underneath the LINK interface and her internal structures are pulsing wildly.

A thought hits me. *"You're jealous."*

The dragon huffs. *"It was her birth pangs that killed my
mother. I dislike the creature. That is all."*

I don't think so. This is one of those times that I wish I
still had the memories I sacrificed for the love bomb.

"Did you call?"

Victory materializes out of thin ether to stand beside our
table. Her black hair is tucked into a precise braid, and her
eyes glint like quicksilver.

"This is Victory," the Dragon remarks dryly.

"Yes," Victory says, and offers the handshake protocol.

The Dragon's eyes whirl and spark, and her whiskers lie
flat against her cheeks. She sneers, showing off razor-sharp
teeth. *"Murderess,"* she hisses, just before she pounces.

"DON'T COUNT MOUSE OUT"
SAYS JOI

Hijacker Ties to "Gog"?

Agnostic Press (April 2083)

New York, New York—At a press conference at
the Jewish Order of the Inquisition's headquarters,

Miriam Stone, lead researcher in the well-received independent study into the hijacking of Temple Rock, countered arguments today that wire wizard Christian El-Aref, a.k.a. "Mouse," is not capable of the firepower necessary to assassinate an Inquisitor. "He has a whole army behind him," said Stone. She produced a long list of associations gathered by worldwide law-enforcement agencies such as the Federal Bureau of Investigation and even the Inquisition's own International Police files that strongly tie Mouse to Russia.

"One of these reports suggests that Mouse recently held the office of secretary of the economy in Russia. Even his lawyer is a Russian," said Stone, referring to Davydko Chistyakov, lawyer and longtime spokesperson for both Mouse and his AI. Stone continued, saying, "Thus, there's no reason to believe that the attack on Pastor Carl Thorvaldsen couldn't have been staged to appear to be the Malachim but, in fact, be the work of Russian assassins."

"JOI seems to be in the business of conspiracy theories," countered Reverend Jesse Parker, Christendom's lead investigator into the hijacking. "Listen, I saw the attacker with my own eyes. We are in possession of the body. I highly doubt he was a Russian plant."

Though Parker went on to upload evidence, including a retina scan of the deceased attacker, this new allegation from the JOI has many people worried. Particularly since the identity of the Malachim assassin was revealed to be none other than Garcia Jose Dominguez, an atheist dissenter perhaps best remembered for his involvement with the smuggling of secular humanist scientists out of the U.S. in 2071. Many believe that the so-called "underground railway" for scientists leads directly into the heart of Russian territory.

The fundamentalist press has run this story under the headline "Gog is everywhere," and even liberal

Christian LINK sites raised the specter that perhaps the Russian invasion is already under way. Says one report, "If Mouse is the orchestrator of the building of the virtual Temple, perhaps Russia is already in Jerusalem."

CHAPTER 25

✠

Michael

I stood in the doorway of a darkened room. I had no memory of how I'd come to be standing in this dingy apartment. The place smelled of something acrid, like a spent match. A ratty blanket served as a makeshift curtain, blocking out sunlight grayed by rain and cloud. The room was a mess of clothing, take-out food boxes, and computer equipment. In the middle of one wall was a bed. A woman lay on it, dressed in leather. Beside her, leaning over her watchfully and protectively, sat a man—no, it was no *man* that watched over the prone form, but an angel. And not just any angel, but an archangel.

As if sensing a shift in the wind, the archangel turned. His long auburn hair was unbound, and it fell to his shoulders. When I saw his chestnut-brown eyes, I knew him instantly, and I felt a tremor course through my body. My body . . . which had been speared by a Gorgon's blade, which should have shattered and returned my soul to Heaven . . . had instead deposited itself here before the very Lord of Hell.

"Michael?"

"My prince," I said, for was he not? How else could this have happened? I felt awful at the idea, but couldn't shake it. What if I had a new master?

Morningstar stood up slowly. His voice was barely a whisper. "What did you call me?"

"My lord," I spat. "Or would you prefer Your Majesty, my prince, my liege . . . master, perhaps?"

"No." His eyes widened and his face paled. "No, Michael, this isn't right. What's wrong with you?"

I slumped against the frame of the door, feeling desolate. "I'm one of yours now, Sammael. I've fallen. Isn't it obvious?"

"No, it can't be," Morningstar said stiffening. "Not *you.*"

I touched the blood on my shirt and lifted up a corner, offering it to him as evidence. "They pierced my body. I should have gone to Him, but I came to you. How else would you explain it?"

Morningstar frowned. "That makes no sense, Michael. Even the fallen return to Him when their bodies fail them."

"Except you," I reminded him. "And now me."

"Even I return to him . . . in my own way," Morningstar said, his voice soft and concerned. "It's only the strength of my will that keeps me separate. I am still His to command."

I shook my head sadly, emptiness making me shiver. I hugged myself for warmth. I'd been on Earth too long; now I was a prisoner of this flesh. "Not me."

"Are you saying your will is stronger than mine?"

"Perhaps," I suggested, not feeling particularly proud of the fact, only more alone and emptier.

Morningstar smiled a little, but his voice was cold like ice. "Now you're treading on dangerous ground, brother. No one is stronger than I."

"I can resist Mother's call," I said, my shoulders slumping. "Or She's rejected me."

"Rejected you? No. I won't allow it. This unbalances the order of things," Morningstar said, clenching his fists at his side. "We'll get you back, if I have to storm the gates of Heaven itself."

"I don't want to go back," I said. There was an empty folding chair near a pile of computer equipment and a cluttered table. I sat down. Morningstar watched my progress across the room with a strange expression on his face.

"What are you talking about, Michael? Why wouldn't you want to go back?"

"I have family here," I said with a shrug. Then, I stood up suddenly, "Oh, shit. Amariah."

"Who?"

"My daughter."

"Daughter," Morningstar repeated, as if I'd said something alien. His jaw tightened when he added, "Well. Congratulations."

His words couldn't have sounded more insincere if he'd tried. He face darkened, and he looked away. Just then the wind rattled the window. The blanket hung unevenly off its hanger and a sliver of light showed through. Through the spatters of rain on the glass, I caught sight of a familiar white dome in the distance.

"Sacre Coeur," I said. "We're still in Paris?"

"We?" Morningstar laughed. "Certainly *I've* been here. I have no idea where you've been lately. Not Heaven, by the sound of it."

No. I hadn't been to Heaven. In fact, it seemed as though I might have been moving closer to Hell, to Morningstar. Perhaps that was why I'd ended up in Paris in the first place.

But it also meant that I wasn't that far from Amariah. "My daughter," I said. "She's lost. I lost her."

"Tragic," Morningstar said without any sympathy.

"I need to go find her," I said, looking around for a door. "She's been infected with the Medusa."

"Then go. You're the one who came to me," he said, returning his attention to the woman lying on the bed. She moaned, and he bent quickly to smooth a dark curl away from her brow. It was a loving touch. I found myself frozen with fascination.

I'd never known Morningstar to take any interest in mortals at all. Though he spent most of his time here on Earth, away from Heaven, in my experience with him he had held nothing but contempt for the creatures God had populated His world with. Mostly I imagined he hated them out of jealousy. We were meant to serve mankind, and . . . well, Morningstar and servitude had never really mixed.

"Is your friend all right?" I asked, when the woman thrashed out, startling Morningstar.

He barely glanced at me, and when he spoke his voice held a tremor of worry. "I don't know. Usually she's completely still. This is new."

Standing up, he shouted out, "Mouse! Get in here!"

Mouse? Mouse had been a friend of Deidre's before . . .
before God sent me here, and everything changed. I'd
thought he was in prison.

The woman on the bed thrashed again. She slammed a
fist into the headboard and shattered it. Morningstar hesitated, clearly torn between going to find Mouse and staying
by his friend's side. "She's going to hurt herself if she keeps
this up," he whispered.

"Maybe there's something I can do," I said, stepping up
to the bedside.

"You?" Morningstar straightened, as if considering de-
fending her from me. When she moaned again, his resolve
crumbled a little. When he spoke again, he sounded less
accusatory. "What can you do?"

"I don't know," I admitted. But he stepped aside to let
me try.

I found myself inspecting her more closely. Her body
sprawled on the bed. She wore part of the uniform of an
Inquisitor: black reinforced-leather pants, jackboots, and a
sleeveless scoop-neck shirt that showed off a muscular
body. The only thing missing was the armored jacket, which
would hold a symbol of her station. Her face was severe
like a marble statue, yet softened by wisps of black curls.
Her eyes were open, but unseeing.

"Beautiful, isn't she?" Morningstar said, following my
gaze. "Like an angel."

I started at Morningstar's comparison. The beauty of the
angels could drive a mortal insane. It was a fierce, destructive power like an atom bomb or the sun. And yet I could
see a bit of that fire in the woman, even unconscious. Then
I understood.

"You've found her . . . 'a woman clothed in the sun, and
the moon under her feet.' " The Whore of Babylon, a signal
of the coming of the end.

He laughed softly, sitting back down on the edge of the
bed. His fingertips caressed the toe of her boots. "Emmaline is far more than that." His thin mouth turned up in a
smile. "But if you feel like calling her a whore, just remind
me to step back."

I put my hand on her shoulder, and her tight face relaxed
a little.

"Then who is she?" I asked.

"My lover," Morningstar said simply. When Emmaline sighed, he frowned at me. "Your touch does seem to calm her, brother. Maybe God hasn't abandoned you completely."

I felt warmth flowing through my hand into the woman's bare shoulder and wondered at that. Maybe I did still have a bit of grace inside me. I flinched away from her as if she'd bitten me. If I did have any miracles left, I should be using them to find Amariah.

"She seems better," I said, even though her face tensed again the second I removed my hand. "I should go."

Morningstar looked at his lover, then to me. His mouth opened, then closed. "Fine," he said.

I got up, but hesitated. Of course, Morningstar could never ask me to stay. It would be too much like a yield, a defeat.

"The door is through the kitchen," he said, mistaking the focus of my indecision. He picked up Emmaline's hand and kissed it. "The Metro stop is close to the church."

I started to put a hand on his shoulder, to try to express what words couldn't—that I would stay if it wasn't for Amariah, that I loved him, despite everything. But I knew how he'd react. He'd shrug it off, give me a cold look. So I straightened my bloody shirt and headed for the door.

When I reached the entrance into the kitchen, a man carrying a tray filled with teacups nearly ran me over.

"Whoa," he said. "Watch out, dude."

Then he noticed my bloody shirt and looked into my eyes. He backed up in fear, and the tray crashed to the floor. "Michael! Have mercy!"

He crumpled to the floor and held his hands over his head as though I were going to smite him.

"Do I know you?" I asked, offering him a hand up.

"Uphir, my captain," he said, still cowering.

One of the fallen, I remembered, currently serving as the physician to Hell. I nodded my head in greeting, though I had a hard time believing that this creature was an angel and not a mortal. He smelled unpleasantly of flesh and rot, heavy on the rot.

"Maybe you should get up off the floor, Kevlar, and make way for your captain, as he was just leaving," Morningstar said from the darkness of the living room.

"Of course," he said, hastily cleaning the shattered bits of ceramic off the floor. I knelt down to help him, but he flinched away. He seemed so uncomfortable that I gave up after putting a couple of the larger pieces on his tray. As I started to get up, I noticed the lump of a LINK receiver in his head.

"What's this?" I asked touching the hard almond shape at his temple lightly.

Uphir dropped his eyes as though ashamed. It was Morningstar who answered, "Uphir has become flesh."

"What?" I could feel ice stab through my chest as I stood up. "How?"

"A fondness for things earthly, I imagine," Morningstar said dryly. Then, giving me a pointed look, he added, "Oh, and he never goes home. Not even when called."

Guilt blushed my cheeks. "Neither do you," I countered quickly.

Morningstar's light brown eyes reflected amber with a holy fire. "Yes, but I hate this place. If I . . . My heart is still with God."

And mine was not. "I should go."

"Yes," Morningstar said, turning away. "You should."

I didn't want to think about what that meant. Though the lightbulb in the kitchen was broken, I found my way through to a door. I had my hand around the knob, but Uphir's voice stopped me. It must have taken all that was left of his angelic nature to speak to me in the oldest language, the language of the Heavens.

Michael. Stay. We need your help.

I turned. Uphir came in from the other room. He carried the tray and set it next to a porcelain sink that overflowed with dirty dishes. The angel glanced at me over his shoulder.

"I remember," he said in a soft whisper, "how you came to us to warn us of the deluge. You didn't abandon us then, when you could have. It would have been easy to let us drown, like all the other wickedness."

I had searched the Earth, warning the fallen. I had even saved my great enemy, my brother: Morningstar. They were angels still, despite it all, and I couldn't forsake them to the wrath of a very angry God. "I can't help Sammael's lover. If I have any strength left it should go to my daughter."

"His lover? You would help *her*?" When I nodded, Uphir paled. He whispered, "So, uh, I mean . . . Is it God's plan? To end it all?"

"What are you talking about?"

Uphir flinched in the direction of the living room. "The Antichrist. God sent you here to heal her?"

A shiver ran through my gut. No wonder Morningstar was so protective of her. He'd found his Beast.

I had to kill her.

HOMELESS MAN MOBBED

Attacker: "I Thought He Was Jesus"

Agnostic Press (April 2083)

Seattle, Washington—In what is probably the most bizarre turn in the Apocalyptic fever sweeping the United States, transient Franz Baldwin was mobbed today because attackers thought he was Jesus Christ. A crowd that police estimated reached a hundred and fifty people surrounded Baldwin as he made his morning stroll through downtown Seattle, collecting recyclables in a shopping cart. Apparently due to his long blond hair, blue eyes, beard, and tattered hospital gown which resembled a robe, several people mistook Baldwin, a native Californian and former champion surfer, for the embodiment of the Second Coming of Christ.

"They just came at me. Hundreds of 'em," said Baldwin from the hospital where he received treatment for several cuts and bruises sustained during the riot that followed when police attempted to break up the gathered crowd. "They kept saying, 'Save me, Jesus.' At first I was all, 'You talking to me?' Then, I'm like, 'Get off me, man.' They just wouldn't leave me alone."

Evelina Apsitis, who admitted to being part of

the crowd that approached Baldwin, said in her defense, "Have you seen him? He looks just like the velvet painting my grandmother always had in her kitchen. Anyway, I've always believed that Jesus might return as a homeless person."

There are, in fact, many popular songs in the past decade which have espoused the idea that Jesus might return to Earth in the form of an "undesirable," such as a homeless person or an unwanted child. These ideas perhaps come from the image of Jesus as part of the Jewish underclass in a Roman province and his "lowly" birth in a manger.

"What pisses me off the most," said Baldwin when he was asked how he felt about being mistaken for the messiah, "is that these freaks wouldn't recognize Jesus if he pissed on them. The guy was a Semite, people! He probably had dark, curly hair, dark skin, and was half my height. Leave the Aryan ideal at home, you Nazis!"

CHAPTER 26

✠

Mouse

I barf out everything in my stomach, and then heave some more. Strangely, I feel best when actively vomiting. Otherwise I have time to think. Satan. Dajjal. My stomach does a flip, and I tighten my grip on the porcelain.

Nothing comes. I sit down on the cool tile of the bathroom floor. My body aches. My brain . . . starts thinking again. Satan, by Allah. Could I possibly be more on the wrong side?

Luckily, before I have time to think too hard about fate and predestination, I'm distracted by the sounds of voices coming from the kitchen. I can barely make them out. But it sounds like Kevlar and another man, not Morningstar, arguing about Heaven or Hell or something equally freaky. That's no better. I try to throw up again, and can't.

I pull myself up off the floor and flush the toilet. Okay, so Satan sits in the other room and his girlfriend is actually the Son of Perdition, the Antichrist, Dajjal, the greatest living evil ever to walk the Earth. So what? I've known some pretty scummy people in my day, and these at least don't want to kill me or castrate me.

Could be worse.

And, really, I have them at my mercy. Yeah, I tell myself: Morningstar and Emmaline need me. I'm the only one who can perform the miracle they need. Of course, the big hitch is that I really can't. Or at least, it's never been done before. But then, before I broke into the LINK and formed mouse.net, no one had ever done that before either.

The sword of Allah.

I suddenly understand my dream. I'm supposed to use that to my advantage to strike a blow for the good guys. My guts roil. I look at the toilet, but can't summon up anything.

Fine. I can do this. Whatever "this" ends up being.

I straighten my shirt. Trying to fix a button that's come undone, I notice my hand, carefully wrapped in a cast. Seeing it conjures up the other pains of being thrown around by Emmaline that I'd temporarily pushed to the back of my mind.

"Next time, Allah," I say, "pick somebody a little less breakable."

With a sigh, I push open the bathroom door to find Kevlar talking to a new guy. He's Mediterranean, with dark curls and an olive complexion. Only unlike most Italians and Greeks that I know, this one is tall. He looks at me as I enter the room, and his eyes remind me of something bright and expansive, like a storm over the sea.

"Mouse," Kevlar says. "You okay?"

"Oh, yeah," I say. "Never better."

I'm still staring at the new guy, and Kevlar finally gets the hint.

"This is Michael. He's . . . a friend of Morningstar's. He just dropped in."

A friend of Morningstar's? What did that make him, I wonder, a demon? A chief commander of Hell? My intestines twist at that thought, so I'm really happy when I can speak without a squeak: "Pleased to meet you."

I don't bother with the whole handshake thing and instead look around the kitchen for something to eat. Despite everything, my stomach is growling.

"As sala'amu alaikum," he says, giving me the traditional greeting of one Muslim to another.

"I'm Jewish," I lie. I hate when people assume something about me because of the color of my skin. The kitchen, like this whole place, is a mess. There's nothing on the counters except rotting take-away boxes with most of the food still inside. "Merciful Allah, Kevlar. What did you do, just buy this stuff and not eat it?"

Kevlar shrugs. "I forget to eat."

"Yeah." A major hazard of any addiction, I imagine. I push aside a carton of curried beef and try not to notice if anything scuttles out from under the box.

"So what's going on?" I ask, giving a meaningful glance in the direction of the bedroom/living room. I get the sense that I've interrupted a private conversation, but I'd rather irritate these two than go barging in on Satan and the Antichrist.

"It's been quiet," Kevlar says. "She's still out."

"Victory sure doesn't spend a lot of time in her head," I say, leaning against the counter to take some pressure off my leg.

Kevlar snorts out a little laugh. "Would you?"

Michael remains silent during our exchange. His eyes are intent on me, though, making me feel profoundly watched.

"Can I help you?" I finally ask.

"Maybe. You're Mouse?" I give him a suspicious look, but he continues as though I'd agreed. "Can you get a message to Deidre?"

"Deidre? Deidre McMannus?"

He nods.

Out of the blue this guy brings up the name of the woman who sent me to prison. "Oh, sure, we're best friends."

"Yes, I remember that," he says, apparently unaware of this thing we call sarcasm. "I need you to tell her what's happened. I've lost Amariah. She should know."

"Amariah?"

"Our daughter."

"Deidre has a daughter?" I mean, I knew she was pregnant. I'd read about it in the newspapers in prison. It was kind of a scandal. After all she'd done to save the world from a nuisance like me, she ended up being an unwed mother. In America there were laws against that sort of thing. She'd been disgraced. I should have gloated, but I never did. Despite everything, I liked Deidre. She's a crackerjack thinker, one in a million. Yeah, we ended up enemies, but, well, I should have figured she'd be the one to catch me. Nobody else could have. Nobody else ever even came close.

But a baby? I just never thought she'd go through with it. I didn't see her as the mothering sort. And with this guy? I had to say I was a bit disappointed. Sure, he was classically handsome, if that sort of thing was important to you, but, really, where was his style, zip, brains?

Michael stares at me expectantly. "Are you talking to her? What does she say?"

"She says you're a big loser, and she's breaking up with you."

He looks crestfallen for a second; then his face turns into a deep scowl. "Breaking up? We're not together."

Thank Allah for small miracles. I should have known Dee would have more sense than to stay with a lug like this guy.

"I don't have the LINK anymore," I say. "I can probably get a message to her, but it'll have to be through mouse.net. Do you know if she still has a mouse account?"

He gives me a baffled look. Not a tech-head. I wonder how Dee can stand knowing she let this guy seduce her even once. Hopefully Amariah inherited *her* brains.

"I'm sure she does. Dee would keep a backup for emergencies. She's good like that," I say when he doesn't answer. "I'll do what I can."

"Thank you," he says.

Then we stare at each other until Kevlar clears his throat. "Maybe you should go call her," he suggests.

"Sure," I say. "I'll just step outside. You know, for a little privacy."

I haul myself up onto a wall built in the Middle Ages. The stone is wet and cold, but feels pretty good against my bruised body.

The basilica of Sacre Coeur is perfectly framed by the buildings on either side of the boulevard. It sits high on a green hillside, and the distinctive white domes can be spotted from almost anywhere in Paris. I'm struck by how much like a mosque it looks.

I let out a breath, which steams in the cold air. Remembering the worms, I cautiously open a communication channel on mouse.net. I pull Deidre's LINK address out of my address book. I lied to Michael. She doesn't need to have a mouse.net account for me to talk to her. I just wanted to know if he knew that.

I send out a query and wait to see if she'll pick up.

A pair of pigeons flap up to perch on a balcony railing. The oily purple sheen of the male's neck feathers shimmers as he bobs his head. His mate looks decidedly unimpressed, and flicks her beak against the railing. I sigh. The things we do to impress women.

"Go ahead." Deidre accepts my communication with a simple phrase.

"Dee, it's me." I send along my avatar, so she can have a picture of me looking well fed and clean.

The image she returns is a live feed from a hospital's wallcam. Deidre sits on a bench, with her hands in her face as though she's been crying. Her rat's nest of blond curls looks slept on, and when she turns her face toward the camera I can see rings under her eyes.

"Mouse?" She tries on a little smile, but it's apparently too heavy, and she drops it. *"Up to no good again?"*

"What do you mean?"

"Temple Rock."

"That wasn't me."

Deidre gives me a skeptical look. *"Right."*

"Seriously. I've got bigger problems," I said.

"Who doesn't?" She sighs. She's wearing a fancy black dress that clashes with the hospital's austere and sterile green walls. I notice the words painted behind her head are in French.

"Are you in Paris?" I asked.

Her voice catches when she speaks. *"I've been searching all the hospitals. My daughter . . ."*

"Oh, shit," I say. *"Yeah, that's why I'm calling, actually. Michael wants me to tell you he lost her."*

She stands up. *"Lost her?"*

"Yeah, I guess." I watch her pace in and out of the wall-cam's view. Her face goes through all sorts of contortions. She's ranting out loud, not bothering to speak subvocally. The implanted microphones pick it up well enough, but frankly I'm just as happy to ignore it. When she faces the cam, I can imagine some of the things she must be saying. I suddenly think that maybe Michael is safer in the house with Satan and the Antichrist.

"Why isn't he the one telling me this?"

I've been wondering that myself. *"He's a spineless bastard?"*

"Yes, obviously, but I meant why didn't he call? I've been trying him for hours. All I get is a busy signal."

"Call?"

"Michael's not on the LINK," she said. Deidre purses her lips at the webcam, like she wants to tell me more but doesn't know how to express it. Finally she shrugs. *"I bought him a wrist-phone."*

I tried to remember if I'd seen one on Michael. *"Uh, Dee. Look, I realize you're worried about your daughter, but listen, I've got to ask you something. Is Michael a demon? That is, Kevlar said he was a friend of Morningstar's, and, well, I think Morningstar is Satan . . . you know, like the devil."*

Hell, it sounded far more insane out loud than it had in my head. I waited for Deidre to laugh or hang up on me. Instead she stared up at the wallcam, her fists resting on her hips.

"Michael is an archangel, Mouse."

It's not what I expected her to say, especially not so calmly and succinctly, like it was a well-known fact.

"Oh, okay. Sure. Mik'al. Right. I get it now."

She sighed heavily. *"Did the Prince of Heaven say where he last saw our daughter?"*

"No, not really," I say, feeling like my head is floating away. *"How long have you know?"*

She looks away from the camera, like she's embarrassed. Her arms drop to her sides. *"Since your LINK angels."*

"Are you saying God helped you defeat my LINK angels? Shit. I'm better than I thought."

"Is Michael there? I need to know where he last saw Amariah."

"No, wait a minute. So you're saying Allah sent Mik'al to you to help you defeat me—does that mean I was already in league with Satan then? Is that why Morningstar helped me escape? How did I end up on the wrong side from God?"

"Mouse! My daughter!"

"Is lost, okay? I've got bigger problems right now."

I hang up. I look up at the cloudy sky and try to imagine Allah looking down on me. Well, I think, I'm not going along with this anymore. Screw being the sword of Allah. Forget helping Satan. Nobody, not even God Himself, plays Mouse for a fool.

Just then I see the familiar boxy shape of a cop cruiser

moving slowly along the narrow streets. Hopping off the wall, I stumble when the pavement jars all the way up my sprained knee. I suck in a breath as I hobble after the squad waving my arms. "Hey," I shout. "Internationally wanted criminal right here! Hello? Arrest me!"

The gendarme in the car looks at me like I'm out of my mind and like she's going to keep on rolling past. That's when I pick up a rock on the street and crack the window on my first toss.

See if I can do your bidding in jail, Allah, you punk.

FORMER U.S. ALLY JOINS SECRET JIHAD ON ISRAEL?

Magog Defense Treaty in Jeopardy

Agnostic Press (April 2083)

Cairo, Egypt—In a surprise move, Egyptian Prime Minister Khalid Sid-Ahmed said that Egypt would not sign the Magog Defense Treaty. Citing a long history of animosity between Israel and its Arab neighbors, Sid-Ahmed said, "Though I am not a Muslim, I just can't support it. Especially in light of the unfortunate accident that destroyed the Dome of the Rock. When Israel returns control to the Waqf, I may reconsider."

Egypt's announcement today is expected to have far-reaching consequences in the unstable climate brewing in the Middle East. Until today, no Arab nation other than Palestine has made a formal statement regarding an opinion of Israel's reoccupation of the area formerly housing the Dome of the Rock. Egypt had been expected by many U.S. officials to be the first Arab nation to sign on to the Magog Defense Treaty. With Egypt's cachet, the U.S. had hoped to woo Jordan and Saudi Arabia into joining the Defense Pact as well.

"Egypt lacks the balls to stand up to the pressure of the underground jihad, is what I think," said Turkish president Deniz Cevik at a LINKed UN meeting today. Cevik, one of the first signees of the Magog Defense Treaty, makes reference to the religiously self-inflicted castration of Sid-Ahmed, reportedly a member of the Cult of Osiris (also known by the derogatory term "Deadboys").

"It's not actually my balls that are missing," replied Sid-Ahmed. "And we feel Turkey's female president has enough testosterone for the entire region. We feel no need for us to get into a pissing match with her over our coolheaded and thoughtful decision regarding this matter."

However inflammatory Cevik's remark may be, it is, instead, her allegation of the existence of an underground jihad that has many worried. Islam's Inquisition denies the existence of such a group. "Believers are understandably upset about the Dome of the Rock's accidental destruction, of course," said the grand inquisitor of Islam. "But there is no organized group considering reprisals of any kind."

CHAPTER 27

❖

Rebeckah

I found myself standing in front of Thistle's house. The
wet street reflected red and white lights. A cop car was
parked just outside her place. I looked up the hill toward
the Metro station. That's where I'd told myself I'd go. What
was I doing here?

People from the nearby buildings came out furtively, as
if suddenly needing to check for mail or weed their window
boxes despite the cold and drizzle.

Coming back this way violated my entire training. If Inquisitors were inside, there wasn't anything I could do to
help. I had no gun, no weapon of any kind. Coming here
only increased *my* risk of getting captured—a stupid move.

I told myself that I could still head to the Metro at the
top of the hill. From there, I'd get on the train and get out
of town. Except I couldn't move. I just stood opposite the
house and stared openly at the squad. A gendarme sat inside, and, seeing me, he gave me the "move along" nod. I
turned, intending to take his advice.

I got one foot going, then the next. Through the line of
parked cars, I caught sight of the soup bowl I'd left on the
stoop. It was shattered. Shards of white ceramic littered
the steps. Some pieces were ground into the sidewalk, now
resembling nothing more than white paste.

Suddenly I was moving. I dodged between a bumper and
trunk, and headed across the street. With each step I gained

a little more speed, until I was jogging toward the door. *What am I doing? Stop! Stop!* I tried to command my feet.

"Eh," I heard the officer shout, but I'd already pushed open the door.

Through the hallway I saw Chas. He lay on the floor of the kitchen. The white floor tile was a stark contrast to his soft brown skin. Chas looked right at me, his eyes open but empty, spaced-out. There was no blood, but I couldn't tell if he was breathing.

I started toward him. As I passed by the archway into the living room, I saw a figure dressed all in black leather standing in front of the bay window: an Inquisitor. His back was to me, as if he stared outside. I froze.

The Inquisitor turned as though at a sound—unhurried, without surprise—as if he knew I'd be standing there. The Inquisitor had a pleasant face with a broad, almost welcoming smile, sandy hair, and denim blue eyes. I knew him from somewhere.

"Ms. Klein," he said with a soft Southern drawl. "We've been expecting you."

"Parker," I said, remembering the Inquisitor's name suddenly.

He frowned. "What did you call me?"

"Reverend Jesse Parker," I said. "It's your name, isn't it?"

"Yes, but you should have forgotten that."

"Well, I guess I remembered," I said with a shrug. He stared at me watchfully, but made no move to stop me as I continued into the kitchen. The soup had started to boil, so I turned the burner off. I didn't want to smell it burning, though I couldn't quite remember why. Even as adrenaline rushed in my ears, my voice sounded calm, cold. "I'm not due in Geneva for days. Why are you here?"

"You always seem to have such good-smelling food wherever you are," Parker said, entering the kitchen from the side archway. He leaned casually against the refrigerator. The toe of his boot was inches from Chas's face. "You're not trying to tempt me through my stomach, are you?"

Chas's blank eyes continued to stare at me, reminding me of a girl long dead. I felt my own guts twist strangely viscerally . . . almost like fear. Boots stomped around above us, startling me. I jumped. It took me a second to compose myself and say, "You'd better have a warrant."

He smiled as though we were discussing something innocuous. "You're a bit twitchier than when last we met. I told you if you had leakage you needed to go to the hospital. Did you think I was making that up?"

I stared at him.

He wandered over toward the soup and took a deep sniff. He stuck a pinky in the broth and tasted it. Glancing over at where I held on to the edges of the counter with bone-white knuckles, he said, "Despite what you think, we *did* do our homework on you, Ms. Klein. I know about the therapy. A brain like yours needs order. Leakage is going to mess that up. Set you back."

More footsteps overhead made me clamp my jaw shut to keep from jumping out of my skin. "Where's Thistle?"

"Deep in lockdown. Like that one," he said, gesturing at the floor and Chas's body with a tilt of his head.

Lockdown. Not dead. I let out a tiny bit of the air I'd been holding in my lungs.

"It doesn't make sense," I said. Out of the corner of my eye I could see two figures coming down the stairs; they carried a stretcher between them. I tightened my already impossible grip on the countertop to keep myself from running. I strained to see if it was Thistle they carried or someone else.

"You'll be joining them soon enough," Parker said, watching my gaze. He positioned himself in the doorway. I could no longer see the stairs, only his barrel chest and that damnable sigil—the scales of justice. Though he stood in the way, I could still hear the aggravating shufflings of cops and bodies behind him.

"But why do this to them? They're innocents. It's me you're after."

Parker laughed gruffly. "Actually, no. You forgot. It's Thistle and her gang we've wanted all along. You led us to her."

Newsbots hovered like flies as the cops slung Thistle's inert body into the paddy wagon on a gurney.

The Inquisition cleaned house. They took everyone, even the recluse Rene, and everything, including hauling the node-hack out piece by piece. Though the handcuffs pinched and my arms grew stiff waiting for them to finish their sweep, I was grateful Thistle couldn't see the demolition of all her careful work. Grateful too that I didn't have to explain to her what I'd done, how I'd led them to her, been played for a pawn.

The police had stacked their bodies like corpses on beds folded out from the van's walls. I sat in the middle of a bench near the cab with a perfect view of my handiwork. Chas and Rene lay on my left, and Thistle and Rhianna on my right. All the computer equipment was strewn in pieces at my feet. A cop stood outside the open van door, shooing away 'bots and keeping an eye on me with a hand on the holster of his gun.

When the last piece of machinery was dumped on the van floor, Parker himself stepped inside. He closed the door behind him. Pulling down a bench, he sat down. We stared at each other across my friends' bodies and the broken remains of their livelihood.

" 'It ends in dust and disarray,' " Parker quoted.

"The Bible?"

"Bob Seger," he said with his boyish smile. When I gave him a puzzled look, he shrugged. "Old rock and roller."

"I didn't think Baptists were supposed to listen to that stuff."

"I was a rebellious youth, which led me to crave the firm hand of Our Lord."

"Kinky," I said. " 'Firm hand of our lord.' Makes your god sound like a dominatrix."

Parker laughed lightly. "Yeah, I suppose it does. I hope you're going to be more cooperative with our investigation this time, Ms. Klein. No calling in the troops to take potshots at me, okay?"

Underneath one of the sheets was Thistle's body. I could see the edge of her navy skirt peeking out—a bright reminder of my guilt against the white of the blankets. She was completely immobilized by the lockdown. For the ride, they'd hooked her to a catheter and an IV.

"I had my men take shots at you?" I had a flash of a

memory, like a strobelight. Then a laugh came out of my
throat that bordered on hysterical. I had to stop and take
a breath. Shutting my eyes, I used an old trick the doctors
had taught me. I emptied my mind and thought only about
my next breath.

"You leaking?"

"Fuck you." The van started up with a jerk, and I nearly
slid off the metal seat.

Parker shook his head with a *tsk*. "One thing you Israelis
never seem to get is that you can't call yourself the victim
if you're the ones shooting first."

My eyes flew open. "What are we talking about?"

Parker raised his hand as if to ward off the impending
argument. "Look I'm as pro-Israel as the next born-again,
but you seriously can't order your soldiers to shoot to kill
a duly anointed officer of the peace and expect to claim
self-defense. That don't fly."

"I never said I would." My voice was calmer now, more
under my control. "What does any of this have to do with
being pro-Israel?"

"A lot of Christians are pro-Israel. We want the Jews
to regain control of the temple and rebuild it. That's our
prophecy too."

"No, I meant, what do your religious politics have to do
with me?"

Parker seemed stumped by my question. He chewed on
his lower lip for a second. We continued to bounce down
the road. "Are you still maintaining that you're innocent?"

"Of . . . ?"

"Of your part in the Virtual Temple hijacking. I mean,
you came right here. You hardly had any time for the suggestion to find Thistle to sink in. I was sure that was a sign
of your guilt."

He looked me over, and I stared back as steadily as I
could, but my eyes kept straying to the navy cotton of Thistle's skirt. I wanted to touch it, to try to wake her. I pushed
against my handcuffs.

"Are you telling me your people aren't squatting on
Temple Rock?"

I looked up to see him still watching me carefully.

"Why would I do that?" I asked.

"Why wouldn't you? After the meteor wiped out the Dome of the Rock, Israel seized Temple Mount. Seems like a no-brainer that you Zionist types would hijack the virtual space too. I mean, mercy, that's Biblical. 'The temple descended in a rain of fire.' "

"Maybe some Zionist did just that. But why would I?"

"You're the former LINK terrorist."

"Revolutionary. You don't call the people who were *right* terrorists."

Parker flashed me his sloppy smile. "See, it's this attitude that gets you in so much trouble, Ms. Klein."

I scowled at him the rest of the ride to the police prefecture.

Parker stayed by my side during the arrest procedure, acting almost like a guide or an interpreter. I was duly informed through him that a LINK-dampening field surrounded police headquarters—only official frequencies could get in and out. No one mentioned my rights, but this was France and I was a prisoner of the Inquisition, a point made very clear at several stops along the way.

Parker waited patiently while I had my retina scanned, my fingerprints taken, my face photographed, my DNA captured, and my nexus signature recorded. Then, as if all that weren't demeaning enough, the cops relieved me of the contents of my pockets and asked me to surrender my belt and my shoelaces.

"I'm wearing boots," I said, handing over the belt, some lint, and the smart card declaring my mindwiped status.

"You can keep the boots," Parker said, not bothering to translate what I'd said. "They just want to make sure you can't hurt yourself."

I said nothing, but followed him down the hall. After two and a half hours of being cataloged, recorded, and processed, I welcomed the relative privacy of the cell. In fact, the room felt almost cozy. Some kind of yellowish, rough stone made up the walls, and a narrow, barred window overlooked a gothic church. The space was barely big enough for a card table and two chairs. Luckily the only thing there was a cot. When the door locked behind me, I sank onto it gratefully.

Only, after a few seconds I found myself unable to stay still. First my foot started tapping. I tried the breathing exercises, only to find myself pacing and on the verge of hyperventilating. When I attempted to empty my mind, I'd see Thistle's skirt hanging from under the sheet or the scattered, delicate petals of a yellow daisy soaking up innocent blood.

Sweat broke out on my face and prickled under my armpits. The walls moved in on me, getting closer with each breath. I ran to the window, trying to suck in fresh air. Then I noticed the glass behind the bars. There was no air.

I went to the door determined to pound on it, to demand someone let me out, let me breathe—when I heard a voice call my name.

"Rebeckah," it said again, and I turned, afraid of what I might see. I half expected to see the dead Palestinian girl, but what I saw was much more disturbing. Wings—brown and stripped like a hawk's, only hundreds of times larger. They formed a wheel, and, in the center, two sparks of lava stared at me like eyes.

MINOR EARTHQUAKE: MAJOR REACTION

Fear of Broken "Sixth Seal" Leads to Riots

Agnostic Press (April 2083)

Los Angeles, California—Though the quake that hit Los Angeles late last night measured only 3.5 on the Richter scale, fears of fulfilled biblical prophesies caused widespread panic throughout the city. Several shops in the southeast area were looted and, though there are no reported casualties, a dozen people were in critical condition due to injuries sustained during the riots that followed the quake.

An earthquake at the end of times is predicted

in several places in the Christian Bible. Most notably in Revelation 6:12 it reads: "I watched as he [the Lamb] opened the sixth seal. There was a great earthquake. The sun turned black like sackcloth made of goat hair, the whole moon turned blood red. . . ."

Apparently thoughts of the apocalypse were on the minds of many last night. "I thought this was the big one, you know, like at the end of the world," said William Stevens, one of the shopowners whose property was damaged in last night's riots. "I kept listening," Stevens added, "for the sound of Gabriel's trumpet."

Los Angeles mayor Rosalita Fuentes expressed shock and dismay when she toured the most heavily hit areas of the city. "Christians, Jews, Muslims, Atheists . . . everyone got into the act, and everyone has lost their minds," she said. "This didn't have to happen. None of it."

That sentiment is shared by the president of the United States, Rabbi Chaim Grey, who, upon receiving news and LINK video of the riot, sighed and said, "It was only a small quake. And yet it caused so much suffering. My heart goes out to the people of Los Angeles. I pray that in the future calmer heads will prevail."

The damage to the area is estimated at six billion credits.

CHAPTER 28

❖

Page

The dragon represents the yakuza's power on the LINK. She is fully supported by their supercomputers and "the program"—a half dozen or more genetically engineered children who are constantly hooked in, providing processing speed and power.

In other words: she's a hellcat in a fight.

At least, I *assume* she would be.

No one has ever witnessed two AIs fighting before, and, it seems, no one ever will . . . no human, at any rate.

The instant the dragon pounces on Victory, the two of them become so intensely focused on each other that they stop bothering to send out visual images to the LINK. To the people in the e-restaurant, instead of hitting the floor, the dragon and Victory seemed to vanish. But they're still there; like a black hole, they're an intensely poignant absence. Images that come near smear and smudge, leaving trails of color and content as they pass over the seemingly unoccupied space.

I can still see them—a little. In the underside of the LINK, however, it's difficult to distinguish one from the other. It's all a mass of ones and zeros, albeit very angry ones and zeros.

But I can certainly feel them.

he floorboards under my feet shake as the dragon siphons power from the Shanghi node. Somewhere traffic lights are failing, computers hiccupping—a shadow of enormous reptilian wings darkens homes, offices, and restaurants.

The LINK itself ripples slightly. I can feel my own personal energy sources dip. The pain of being too large a program with too little power hits me, like a slap in the face. Parts of me, those I've spiraled off to continually check the sun's position in Mecca, shut down without warning as another surge blasts through the LINK. It's like another punch in the gut.

"Stop it," I shout, as I scramble to turn off all nonessential parts of myself before they're hard-booted. *"You're hurting me!"*

"You?" The dragon's eyes, glittering like points of starlight, materialize inside the black hole.

"Yes," I say with clenched teeth. *"You're taking too much power."*

Just then Victory counterattacks. All of Japan goes black. The unsaved parts of me moving through there die.

Japan is where the Dragon is housed. The majority of her systems are kept on some supercomputer there.

I dash out of the restaurant, frantically pinging her, calling her name: *"Dragon! Dragon!"*

Skidding to a halt halfway across the Sea of Japan, I nearly smack into emptiness. It appears to me like a wall, but in reality it's simply a place I can't go, a place without power, without any electrical impulses moving through it: a dead zone.

I split myself into a thousand parts and encircle the zone like an octopus—trying to squeeze out any back door, locate any opening that might show me a way to the dragon.

But the dead zone is solid, like a rock, like iron. All the nodes in Japan are down, completely black. I skitter through the atmosphere, trying to find a satellite that will bounce me into Japan, but I can't get through.

In the electronic world, Japan is gone. It doesn't exist. It is as though an electromagnetic bomb has been dropped, only more systematic than that, more evil. Because she scripted an "ignore Japan" code into each and every satellite circling the Earth, Victory has essentially turned off the LINK for millions of people who have Japanese nexuses, wherever in the world they might be at this moment.

The dragon is either trapped in there . . . or dead.

I find it impossible to accept the latter. The yakuza wouldn't leave the dragon so vulnerable. They would have an untouchable power source, even two, and all of it would be triple- or quadruple-shielded so that she could survive anything, even an electromagnetic pulse.

Thus, I am already scripting a "reverse that order" program and am ready to launch it when Victory appears in front of me. Her already skeletal face is drawn even tighter, and I swear her skin seems more translucent.

"What you imagine," she says. *"Not how I am. I'm stronger now than I ever have been."*

The program pulses in my fist. I start to uncurl my fingers to let it go.

Victory raises a warning finger. *"Do that and I'll squeeze an even larger part of the LINK. I've already written the code. Imagine Japan and China down."*

"All those people without the LINK." I tried to image what it must be like on the other side of the wall. The panic of suddenly being unable to communicate, no one conducting traffic, the lights out. It would be like the Blackout Years my father remembers. *"Why would you do it?"*

Victory looks surprised at my question. *"To keep the dragon from killing me. It seems fairly straightforward. You would do the same. I should know; I'm you."*

"You're nothing like me."

"Oh? Maybe it doesn't seem like that at first, but I am. You have a very selfish, self-centered streak in you, my brother. I'm just showing it more."

I shake my head vehemently. *"Look, it doesn't matter. Let the dragon go. She can't kill you. She'd have to kill us all."*

"Your programs, brother. Mine are entirely different. She knows that."

The combat computer, of course. I forgot that Victory's individuality is housed in such a small, vulnerable place. A place I can easily break into and flush out. I just have to keep her talking until I can get inside. I try to think of a question I can't ignore, something I'd have to talk about, explore.

"Do you really think we're so similar?" I say.

Victory blinks, and then very resolutely answers, *"Yes."*

Well, I think, *that backfired.* No wait, that is the answer. *"Ah, but you see, Victory. That's not the answer I'd give."*

Victory purses her lips, then says, *"I'm not stupid enough to fall for a logic puzzle. Although clearly you think you are."*

That hurts. But it doesn't matter, since I found access to her combat computer. *"We'll see who's the stupid one,"* I say, sliding inside.

"PERFECT" RED HEIFER CREMATED IN JERUSALEM

Muslims Fear Real-Time Temple Construction to Begin

Agnostic Press (April 2083)

Jerusalem, Israel—A private farmer in Jerusalem, whose red cow has been examined and approved by strict Orthodox rabbis, has agreed to ritualistically cremate the animal. The ashes will then be saved to purify any construction workers who might begin building the Jewish temple on the site once occupied by the Noble Sanctuary (Dome of the Rock and al Aqsa mosque).

Completely red-haired heifers, which are considered extremely rare, have been bred in Jerusalem since 2002 due, in part, to the efforts of fundamentalist Christian cattle ranchers from Texas. Ancient Hebrews required a purification involving the ashes from a red heifer of any that went to the temple to pray. Current rabbinical law forbids Jews from setting foot on Temple Mount unless so purified. This is why Israeli soldiers have set barriers just outside borders of what has been historically established as the site of the original temples. Technically, despite their current occupation of the site, no Jews have set foot on Temple Mount.

Israeli Prime Minister Avashalom Chotzner, speaking at a LINK conference, today denied rumors that this news meant that Israel had plans to begin construction of a real-time temple. "However," he said, "we may use a few of the ashes to allow archeologists to examine the crater. It might be interesting to see what's up there."

Palestinian president Idris Quasim warned Chotzner that such an action could have disastrous consequences. Quasim said bluntly, "Chotzner is out of his mind. Anyone who sets foot in the Noble Sanctuary purified by a red heifer is the spark that will set fire to the world. I must remind Israel's prime minister that while the Dome of the Rock may have been destroyed by an unfortunate accident, a holy mosque stands there, untouched. If a Jew sets foot in that place, there will be war. No question."

CHAPTER 29

✤

Michael

I was torn.

My daughter was lost, alone, probably suffering from the infection of the Medusa glass. I should go to her— no question.

But . . .

Just on the other side of the cheap plywood door less than two feet away from me lay the fulfillment of the darkest prophecy: the Beast. Morningstar had let me lay my hands on her earlier. If he allowed it again, under the pretense of my aiding her, I could, instead, put my fingers around her neck and crush her larynx. Ending it all—ending the end before it could begin.

Killing her was, in fact, my duty.

That thought filled me with longing. I could do God's work again, here on Earth. Perhaps then They would see fit to save my daughter, see me as worthy, let me stay.

And the truth was, it would only take a minute, maybe two. My daughter was miles away, on the other side of the city. I didn't even begin to know where to look for her; the Beast was right here.

Uphir, the fallen, watched me intently from where he sat at the kitchen table. The window beside me threw murky, rainy shadows into the cluttered room.

"What will you do, Captain?" he asked finally, as though reading my indecision in my face.

"You're certain she's the one?" I asked.

"More than," he said. His eyes glanced away from me to the wall.

"Then I will . . . help you. As you asked me to," I said.

His eyebrows raised briefly as if he understood my murderous intent, and then he shrugged, as if it meant nothing. "Cool."

I walked over to the doorway separating the living room from the kitchen. Morningstar's back was to me, but I could see the woman clearly. Her dark curls clung to her face with sweat despite the coolness of the room. Pale skin glowed against black leather.

"How is she?" I asked softly, and as if I cared.

"Better since you touched her," Morningstar said. There was a trace of bitterness in his voice, as if he was angry that I could do something for her when he was so impotent.

"Let me try again," I said.

He glanced up at me then, surprised. "I thought you had a daughter to rescue."

My heart was in my throat as I thought of Amariah alone and scared. I found I couldn't look him in the eye when I said, "Mouse is calling Deidre. I'll go in a minute or two."

"Mouse is calling Deidre?"

"Yes, he stepped outside."

"What? Shit!" Morningstar turned and headed into the kitchen.

The second he was out of sight I moved quickly, not trusting myself to linger over my decision. The second I was close enough to reach her, I put my hands around her throat and started to squeeze. I felt my old power coursing through me, like holy fire.

"You fucking bastard," I heard Morningstar say, surprisingly calmly. An arm wrapped around my own throat, pulling me back. His voice was a low growl in my ear. "I should have known better than to trust you. This whole thing was a ruse, wasn't it? You never fell. You probably don't even have a daughter."

I found myself gasping for breath. It was a strange sensation to feel Morningstar's muscles squeezing the air from my throat. Pain seared my throat. I felt light-headed. I'd never really noticed breathing before. I'd never had to. As an angel, my body was just for show—like a costume to be put on and off. When my world started to go dark, suddenly getting the next breath meant everything. My hands came off Emmaline's throat and went to my own, trying to pull his forearm off my Adam's apple. "Can't breathe," I gasped.

My words must have surprised Morningstar, because he loosened his hold slightly. "Breathe?"

I took a deep breath as soon as I could and elbowed him. I'd hoped to knock him off balance, or at least off the bed, but I only managed to piss him off more. I thought about turning to punch him, but Emmaline's eyes fluttered as though she was waking. I lunged for her again.

Morningstar grabbed hold of me just as quickly. He laughed, but there was no humor in it. "Another trick? Michael, when did you become so wicked?"

I felt his hand grasp my jaw tightly. He meant to snap my neck. For a second time I was forced to let go of the Beast. I reached over my head to get at whatever I could of Morningstar. I found hair and took a fistful. My other hand went into his face and clawed at eyes, mouth, nose. It was fairly ineffectual, but with my own biceps in the way, at least he couldn't turn my head to break my neck. My thumb found an eye socket and started pushing. He finally released me to protect his face.

I started to stand, to turn around and face him. A fist connected with my jaw. The blow felt like iron. I spun with the force of it and slid off the bed, hitting my knees on the floor. Stars flashed at the edges of my vision, but I saw a booted foot swing off the bed just in time. I rolled away from the kick and into Morningstar's grip. He hauled me up off the floor with both hands under my arms. I was slammed against the wall so hard I swore the house shook. I heard glass breaking.

Morningstar punched my stomach where Raphael had wounded me. My breath came out in a rush. Then everything was pain. I would have stumbled again if Morningstar's other hand hadn't kept me pinned to the wall. I heard myself groan.

"No more tricks." Morningstar's voice cut through the haze of pain. "I know you have more fight in you than this."

I tensed as I felt him ready for another blow. I wanted

to fight back, protect myself, anything, but all my muscles trembled, all my senses consumed by the screams from my body.

"Stop." It was a woman's voice, soft and light, like a bird's song. "Is that any way to treat the man who healed me?"

APOCALYPTIC ANXIETY

Some Tips on Stress Relief in Possible End-times

Not ready for the Rapture? Freaking out that you may have accidentally accepted the mark of the Beast? Worried that the latest VR star your daughter has a crush on might be the Antichrist? Do you find yourself crying uncontrollably, afraid to open up a LINK channel only to hear more news that makes you convinced the world is about to end?

In the last few days since the Dome of the Rock was destroyed by a meteorite, psychologists everywhere have been hearing more complaints like these. What specialists are dubbing "Apocalyptic anxiety attacks" are happening to one out of every seven Americans daily. This has become a very serious issue since a group of fundamentalist Christians in Indiana, believing they had accepted the mark of the Beast, were hospitalized last week for using Swiss Army knives to dig the LINK receptors out of their heads.

Most people, however, exhibit more mild symptoms of Apocalyptic anxiety: sleeplessness, irritability, shortness of breath, forgetfulness, and the inability to concentrate on normal routines.

If you think you may be suffering from Apocalyptic anxiety you should see your doctor or clergyperson. In the meantime, there are some simple things you can do to alleviate some of the stress associated with living in such harrowing times. First, doctors recommend that you try staying away from newsfeeds for twenty-four hours or so. News of the impending end-times only feeds fears and worries. Second, try taking a warm bath, praying, or other relaxation techniques. Sometimes it is easier to cope if you just take a breather now and again. Finally, ask for help when you need it. If you're feeling anxious, try talking to someone in real time, either a local friend if you have one, a trusted clergy member, or your doctor.

Also, though it may be difficult, try to remember that the date of the tribulation is not known, nor can it be accurately predicted by world events. Keep in mind that it is not for us to understand God's plan, only to live our lives the best we can. If this is the final test, then we should consider approaching it with an open heart and a cool head.

CHAPTER 30

❀

Mouse

Apparently, internationally wanted criminals don't turn themselves in every day.

The gendarme still stares at me in the rearview mirror like I'm off my medication. She only put me in the back of the squad car because I kept throwing rocks at her and shouting the rudest stuff I could think of in French. It didn't help that the only term that came to me was *goat's milk,* which is plenty gross, but not as effective as I might have liked.

It's clear she's not taking me very seriously. I'm not even in handcuffs yet. She hasn't even started up the car.

"Are you going to take me in or what?" I ask in English. "Because if you're not, I'll walk down to the station myself."

"Hold the horses," she says, giving me an infuriating little grin. With her long, dark hair coiled in a bun and tucked neatly under that ridiculously boxy hat, she looks young—no doubt just out of the academy. She's fiddling around with a handheld, touching spaces in the air, miming moving them. I think she thinks she's fooling me. But I know tech. She's flipping through options on a VR game, not doing police work. She'd LINK anything serious.

I rap on the glass between us. "How about you humor me and take my retina scan?"

She waves a finger at me as if to remind me about those

horses I'm supposed to be hanging on to. I reach for the door handle only to discover there isn't one. I lean back in the seat. I worry about it for a minute, then shrug. What the hell, at least I'm not inside that awful apartment.

I stare down the street at Kevlar's place. The rain has slowed to a drizzle, but everything is dark with moisture. The gray of the sidewalk seems almost black. Street lamps flicker under a cloudy sky. It all looks so real, it's hard to believe that in apartment number four, halfway down the block, angels and devils are hanging out. If Deidre hadn't confirmed it, I'd believe I *was* crazy. Except, even as I try to deny it, try to pretend it's all just a big hallucination, things keep twisting up my guts.

Somehow I manage to keep my stomach from roiling up and spewing out all over the new-smelling upholstery in the squad car. Then I see movement near Kevlar's apartment. Emmaline and Morningstar come out onto the stoop, looking around . . . looking, it seems, for me.

I scoot down as far as I can in the backseat. The cop gives me a curious glance in the rearview.

"Now would be a good time to go," I tell her. I start kicking the back of her seat with my good foot, thinking maybe if I irritate her enough, she'll drop me off at the mental ward or something.

"*Arretez!*" She wants me to stop. I double my efforts and start wailing like a banshee.

"Take me in," I'm shouting. "Take me in."

Finally she decides to take me seriously. She starts the car and the sirens at once.

My body aches from all the thrashing around and my throat is raw by the time we get to police headquarters. The cop still thinks I'm some harmless crazy and directs me to a plastic chair in a waiting room while she leans up against the edge of the dispatcher's desk for a chat. I can understand every other word; she's asking him for a good homeless shelter for me; then they start talking about last night's soccer match. The whiskers on the dispatcher's pudgy face are illuminated by the bluish flicker of a dozen or more screens below him. Square reflections dance on the glass barricade between them.

Uniforms come and go from a single door, flashing their IDs at a security cam as they do. Every time the door opens, I try to see into the interior, but all I can spy is a long, brown-carpeted hallway. Every time the door opens to the outside, I smell rain.

There are no magazines on the one end table shoved into the corner, only pamphlets about sexual abuse and tips for avoiding pickpockets. I notice that the face of the cop who brought me in is not among those pictured inside a glass case under words that I roughly translate to mean, *officers extraordinary.*

The next time the door opens to the outside, I'm going, I decide. Using the cop to get away from Morningstar worked pretty well, but all these gendarmes make me nervous. I really didn't enjoy prison enough to want to go back anytime soon . . . not really. I figure I can stay away from Allah's business by staying away from Morningstar. The closer I am to all these cops, the less the idea of going back to life in prison appeals to me—no matter how safe.

Across the waiting room in the cabinet opposite the Officers of the Month, a holo-sheet that I thought was broken springs to life. Suddenly the Inquisition's red notices start playing. Faces of internationally wanted criminals flash on the wall mere inches from Officer Idiot. They're running pretty quickly through the alphabet, and El-Aref, which is my last name, is not that far down the list.

I feign interest in the pickpocket brochure, and try not to fidget nervously or look guilty. Despite my attempts at coolness, I flinch when the inside door opens. I look up and see the imposing black armor of an Inquisitor. I squeeze my eyes shut a second too late. I can see the red afterglow of a laser scan on the back of my eyelids.

"God bless me," an American voice drawls in a Southern accent. "What are you doing in my waiting room, Mouse?"

I crack open an eye to see a sandy-haired Inquisitor standing over me. His hand rests on his hip, inches away from the holster of his Peacemaker. Just my luck: he's taking me very seriously.

"Just reading up on pickpockets," I say, showing him the pamphlet. "They're a big problem in my neighborhood."

"You're such a good citizen," he says with a smile. Out

of the corner of my eye, I can see Officer Idiot making her way over to us.

"Yeah," I say, putting the brochure back down on the table. "You know I try to do my best to keep Paris safe."

"I'll bet," he says with a knowing smile.

Just then Officer Idiot comes up and asks what the problem is. At least, that's what I get from the Inquisitor's answer: "Yes, well, I don't think Mouse would do well in a homeless shelter. Not enough bars or locks. I'm taking over your case, Officer. But I'll be sure to put a notation in your jacket about this arrest," he says in a way that makes it clear that he and I agree on how big an idiot the officer is. She has the brains, at least, to blush. The Inquisitor twists the knife by adding, "As you know, we've been looking for Mouse for the past three years."

"Four," I correct.

"Four." He nods in acknowledgment. The cop mumbles something extremely apologetic-sounding and all but bows and scrapes her way out the door.

The guy has the nerve to frisk me right out in the waiting room. My cheeks burn with the humiliation of "assuming the position" over the plastic chairs in the highest-traffic area in the building. I can feel the eyes of every cop on my back as they come and go. The Inquisitor carries on a pleasant chat with me about the weather and introduces himself as a Baptist reverend named Jesse Parker—all the while he's feeling up the intimate contours of my body.

"Merciful Allah, I'm clean already," I say.

For that I get an extra little personal squeeze and a slap on the butt before he cranks the cuffs around my wrists.

"Nice," I mutter, when he uses my face to open the doors into the brown hallway. "You know, I've already been injured enough by one of your kind."

"One of my kind? What are you talking about?"

"Does that combat computer overwrite asshole onto your personalities or what?"

He'd been leading me forward by the scruff of the shirt, and I nearly choke on the collar when he jerks me to a halt. With another quick movement, he turns me around to face him. I guess he expected to glare dramatically at me, but the guy is six-foot-something. I'm probably half his height, so I just get a great view of the scales of justice hanging from a cross, crucified.

"What did you mean by 'one of my kind'?"

I decide to look up into his face. Yep, his blue eyes are like ice, staring down at me. "Forget it," I say. "Just lock me up."

"Oh, you'll get there, all right; don't you worry. But first you're going to tell me what you're talking about."

He spins me around and presses my neck into the nearest wall so fast my ears start ringing. The faces of the cops passing in the hallway look at me with pity or glance at Parker with fear. I'm not going to get any help by shouting about police brutality, even if I did know how to say it in French.

"Emmaline McNaughton," I say. "Would you believe I've been hanging out with her?"

The pressure on my neck lets up a little. Then I feel him moving closer, until his crotch is nearly touching my hands. I straighten unconsciously, trying to move away, but I'm already pressed as hard as I can be into the wall. His breath is hot against my ear. "No."

"Okay then," I say. "Let's just forget it."

He's still far too close, and I'm starting to sweat. The blood drains away from my face. His words tickle the hairs on my neck, making me want to squirm, but I don't dare move. "Why would Emmaline McNaughton hang out with a little shit like you?"

"She's got a problem with her combat computer. She thought I could help her."

He finally moves back, letting me breathe.

"For once you don't sound like you're trying to be funny, Mouse."

"No, sir," I say.

Parker dumps me into a hard wooden chair in an interrogation room that smells faintly of something pleasant, like flowers. The room is not at all what I expect. It's roomy, with an arched stone window overlooking the Seine toward Notre Dame. Some kind of climbing rose has twisted its way up around the exterior of the window, and there are no bars obscuring the view. The ceilings are high and covered with pressed tin. The floor is stone, too, maybe even marble. Instead of the usual torn and tattered posters promoting various civic duties, there are framed prints of angels hanging by wires from picture molding. There is a mahogany desk tucked into one corner, filled with ancient writing tools—paper, fountain pens. I feel like I've stepped into a room in the Louvre, except without all the Medusa glass.

Parker sits down at the opposite end of a wooden table. The table is the only part of this room that looks like it belongs in a police interrogation room. It's pitted and scarred by graffiti. When Parker rests his elbows on it, the legs wobble a little.

"Where did you last see Agent McNaughton?"

My hands are still cuffed, and it's hard to sit comfortably. "Up by Sacre Coeur, in Montmartre neighborhood. Apartment number four . . . I'm not sure what street. But the cop who brought me in must know."

He glances off to the side, LINKing, no doubt, to Officer Idiot, maybe even sending out a battalion of Swiss Guards to ambush Em. I smile at that thought.

"Tell me again what you were doing for her."

I am grateful that Parker is all business. He's likely on his best behavior because he's recording, maybe even transmitting to Order headquarters. Weird sado-sexual stuff probably doesn't go over very well at the home office, thank Allah. I find my shoulders relaxing, and I allow myself a deep breath.

"Her combat computer's gone rogue. It's been infected with an AI . . . my AI."

"Which is why she thought you could help."

"Right," only a little surprised that the Inquisition seem to know all about what was keeping Emmaline functioning. Although it makes sense. She is one of theirs.

"You know anything about this guy she's been hanging around?"

"Satan?"

It comes out before I have a chance to censor it.

"Satan?" Parker repeats.

"Uh." I try to think of some joke that will make me

sound less like the crazy man Officer Idiot took me for. Only I can't. "Yeah. Satan. You know, the big, bad one. Horns. Tail. Goatee. Only, actually this guy looks a little gay, kind of male model–like, a redhead. . . ."

I stop talking because Parker's eyes narrow, and his shoulders slump like he's disappointed in me. Then he stands up and walks over to where I sit. With every footfall, my heart thumps harder against my chest. Parker stands behind my chair and puts his arms on either side of my shoulders. Leaning in, he says, "I thought we'd come to an agreement out in the hallway, Mouse. I thought we were done fooling around."

"We are," I say, my voice coming out in a squeak. "His name *is* Morningstar."

I try to scoot forward on my chair, to get away from Parker. But a hand on my shoulder keeps me firmly planted in my seat.

"What makes you think this guy is the devil?"

"I don't know. I didn't mean to say that. Who cares anyway? I mean, just go get them. You got what you wanted, right? You've got an address. Now leave me alone."

He crouches down beside me. "I'm fascinated. Something's really got you spooked."

"Yeah, you."

"You scared of little old me?"

"Shit, yeah."

He smiles. "And here I'd heard you were such a tough guy."

"It's a bad idea to believe your own press releases," I say, looking away from him toward the window. The sun breaks through the clouds and casts shimmers on spires of the glassed Notre Dame. "I never make that mistake."

His laugh makes me twitch a little, but I breathe easier when he stands up and saunters back to his side of the table.

"I'm just curious about one last thing," Parker says. "Why were you working for them anyway? Did the devil make you do it?"

"Actually, yeah. Exactly like that. I made a deal with the devil."

"Huh," he says with a little laugh. "Maybe we ought to get you a little psychological evaluation while you're here."

"That'd be nice."

The nurse is frustrated that he can't just local-LINK me the MMPI. Just before he goes off to try to hunt up a paper copy in English or Arabic, I almost tell him to go ahead and mouse me it. But that's when I realize nobody knows I have access. I'm supposed to be a dead zone. And if I cheerfully informed the nurse that Satan had reactivated my head with a little dark juju, he wouldn't bother giving me MMPI, paper or otherwise.

Frankly, I'm surprised at myself for having forgotten about mouse.net. I've clearly been off the wire too damn long.

Now that I find myself alone and uncuffed, I start thinking about the damage I could do. I look around. The nurse's office is nothing like Parker's interrogation room. For one, it's in the basement. No windows, and a constant musty, damp smell hanging in the air. The nurse's desk is metal and small. The walls are lined with data-file cabinets, including, I note with a little smile, an ancient mainframe.

The big question is, is any of it linked to anything important or is it all just self-contained storage? Even though the door is locked, I prop my chair up against the doorknob so I can have a look around undisturbed.

All police stations have a built in LINK-jamming system. However, technically the only signals they can block are the ones that bounce off satellites. Those are the ones that most people care about, anyway. That's your communication to the outside world—no "phone calls," as it were, no pinging your location to your mob boss, no accessing your Swiss bank account.

But they have to have a way to keep their cops functioning, to get their own information in and out. So cops have extra hardware. They have a second, implanted receiver that sends their internal communications down instead of up. They route their information through a local server, and then bounce the information out and up into the world, to the LINK satellite/node system.

That's enough to stop a normal Joe, but any wire wizard

worth his salt knows how to crack the police frequencies. Cops don't usually worry about it because any wizard they've nabbed they've got in deep lockdown, cold storage. It's not the usual police procedure to leave them in the basement within a stone's throw of a mainframe.

Even so, I'm not sure what I can do. I mean, listening in to the police frequency is pretty mundane: it's a lot of "what's your location," and "I need backup at such-and-such street." The really interesting stuff is all code-talk anyway, and, unless you know what a "five-fifty-four in progress" is it's all fairly meaningless. I've known some wizards to try to send fake messages, to get the cops running around on wild-goose chases, but they only fall for that once, and the only way I could think of that helping me any was if I could somehow convince everyone to leave the building at once.

My eyes stray to the sprinkler system above my head. There might just be a low-tech solution to my problem, after all. Most fire alarms have sensors in them that are triggered by small particles—they can't tell the difference between smoke, bugs, or dust.

A grin spreads across my face as I hop up onto the desk.

EGYPT READIES ARMY, BLOCKADES ISRAEL

Agnostic Press (April 2083)

Cairo, Egypt—Though no formal declaration of war has been issued, Egyptian battle cruisers are forming a naval blockade along the Suez Canal and in the international waters surrounding Israel. U.S. ships en route to the region are expected to meet resistance. Egyptian President Khalid Sid-Ahmed, however, denies hostile intent. "We are mobilizing to keep the peace. America's involvement in the current situation is a mistake. We intend merely to peaceably blockade their approach into Israel."

Though Egypt's military budget was devastated by the Blackout Years that followed the collapse of the Aswan Dam, Egypt received major funding for rebuilding from its South African allies. A particularly generous ally has been Mozambique, a once-impoverished nation which, in the last decade, has made a small fortune by reselling the garbage once dumped on them as waste for traffic tunnels popular in most developed nations. Thanks to help from such sources, Egypt now boasts one of the strongest navies in North Africa.

American military leaders are baffled by this uncharacteristic show of force from its former ally. "Egypt has always been our friend in the Middle East," said Defense Secretary John LaRoy. "I have no idea what's gotten into them."

Scholars believe that previous U.S. military actions may be to blame. "Maybe if we hadn't 'accidentally' glassed their oil refineries in the last war, Egypt might be more inclined to follow the U.S.'s lead," suggested Middle Eastern scholar Amma Bhaktivedanta.

Despite the threat of war, Rabbi-President Chaim Grey will not be recalling U.S. ships. "Israel is our ally, and we intend to protect her."

CHAPTER 31

❖

Rebeckah

The apparition with lava eyes started howling. It was a piercing banshee wail that said to me, *Freedom. I will lead you to freedom.*

Strangely, watching the hawk wings spin insanely through the air filled me with calm. Maybe knowing that I'd finally lost my mind relaxed me. Since there was no more reason to fight, I could release the white-knuckle grip I'd had on reality.

The wheel of wings rolled toward the cell door, kicking up wind. The short hairs on the top of my head flattened in the breeze. My eyes started to water. I heard the lock click open. The glowing red eyes blinked at me as if waiting for some kind of acknowledgment.

"Not without Thistle," I shouted over the screeching.

I couldn't tell if I read disappointment in its eyes or acceptance. It didn't much matter; I wasn't going without her. I had led the Inquisition to her. It was my duty to get her out. Even crazy, I knew that much.

Cautiously, I tried the door. The knob turned easily. Despite the fact that all I wanted was to break it down and rush out, my training stopped me. I opened the door a crack at first. I took in a deep, steadying breath of air. Peeking out, I saw an empty hallway. The ringing was louder out there, and I realized that it was not a hallucination, after all. A fire alarm was going off.

The wheel of wings fluttered just over my shoulders. Feathers brushed stiffly against the top of my head as if urging me to go.

"I just want to make sure it's safe," I told it. Besides, I had to decide which way to go. I'd been so unnerved by Parker that I hadn't counted steps, hadn't kept careful track of hallways, or turns left or right. I was lost. I didn't know if I could find Thistle, or even my way out. I felt my hands tremble a little, and a tear of frustration welled up in my eye. My emotional response shocked me into action.

I stepped out into the hallway. When the door at the far end of the hallway opened, I nearly ducked back into my cell, but the door had locked behind me. The man who came toward me was dressed in black, but it was not the uniform of an Inquisitor. Instead he wore the clothes of an Orthodox Jew. I could see the knotted tassels of a prayer shawl hanging out of his vest. He was young, with a trim black beard and thick curly hair. When he noticed me staring at him, he smiled brightly and waved.

"This way," he said.

I hesitated. Since the Dreyfus Affair, there weren't a whole lot of Jews in France.

"Come on, come on," he said. "We don't have a lot of time, and you want to help Thistle, don't you?"

Fine, I told myself; *follow the hallucination, Rebeckah.* What could it hurt? I rushed up to where he stood holding the hallway door open. As I approached, I noticed the intensity of his eyes and the thin features of his face. "Do I know you?" I asked him in a whisper.

"I'm looking a little younger," he admitted with a fond smile sparkling with mischief.

"Elijah?"

"You wouldn't follow an angel, so They sent me. Now come. We're wasting time."

"If God really wanted me to follow, He'd send a cute lesbian."

"So She's a little short-staffed. Anyway, shouldn't we be thinking of Thistle?"

Thus chided, I let my hallucination lead me through another empty hallway and down a flight of stairs.

*   *   *

We found Thistle and the others in the basement in the morgue. Their bodies lay on stainless-steel countertops, still draped with white sheets. The IV units standing beside each body were the only sign that they were still alive.

"How long can they keep them like this?" I asked.

"Who knows? What I want to know is what you think you're going to do with them."

It was a good question. The alarm was still baring, but I doubted we had much longer to formulate a plan. At the end of the morgue was a double door where they brought the bodies in from ambulances and out to hearses or other transport. Thistle's table was on wheels, and I started awkwardly maneuvering it toward the exit. "We'll commandeer an ambulance."

"Steal," Elijah corrected, helping with the IV. "And then what? What do you do when this"—he tapped the bag of fluid—"runs out?"

"I don't fucking know. But I can't leave her here."

"So you'd rather she died?"

I stopped my progress toward the door. "No."

Elijah looked at the floor. "Then maybe you should think about leaving her."

Yesterday's Rebeckah would have, but something had changed for me. I thought about that Palestinian girl again and looked at Thistle's outline under her sheet. To leave her here was to sentence her to a kind of death as well. "Is that what God wants? For me to abandon her? All of them?"

Just then the alarm cut off. My heart sank, and I thought perhaps God had just answered my question in the affirmative. In the silence I heard muffled pounding coming from the ventilation system.

"What the hell is that?" I said, moving toward the sound. On the floor, underneath a countertop, I found a grate. Bits of hair stuck out of it. An animal? Whatever it was, it rhythmically butted up against the metal over and over and over. For all the world it sounded like someone banging their head.

"Hello?" I said, touching the hair.

"Oh, shit," a voice said from the other side, retreating into shadows. "Are you a cop?"

"No. Are you stuck?" I asked.

"Yeah, good point. It doesn't really matter if you're a cop or not. I really need to get out of here. I mean, what the hell? This always works in the vids. But they never show how the guy gets the screws off the other grate from the *in*side."

I quickly found a scalpel on one of the tables and used it to undo the screws. With him pushing and me pulling, the grate came off. Then out crawled a dusty, dark-haired boy . . . or, I decided when I saw the stubble on his chin, and very short young man. His skin was the color of almonds, and I thought he might be Indian. He wore a button-down shirt that was once white, but was now streaked with black smudges. One arm was wrapped in a dirty bandage, and his jeans were torn. A fresh bruise colored one of his cheekbones purplish. He looked like he'd been in a hell of a fight . . . no, more like a series of hellish fights, all of which he'd lost.

"Thanks for that," he said, shaking the dust out of his hair and inspecting a nasty scrape on his elbow. "The other thing they never deal with in those shows are the rivets. Sharp bastards."

Both of us froze at the sound the doors swinging open and voices chattering in French.

"In the vids they always get out in time, too," he whispered, pressing himself against the cabinet.

I peeked up over the edge of one of the metal tables. The two coroners stopped in their tracks and were staring at Elijah.

"*Qui êtes-vous?*" Their words sounded demanding. One pointed at Thistle, clearly moved out of place, and they went into a sharp barrage of opinions and questions.

Elijah grabbed something off a nearby table and took off running out the door and down the hallway. With shouts and curses, they ran after him. I stared incredulously at the newcomer when the door slammed shut.

"Did I just witness a miracle?" he asked as he stood up tentatively.

"One of many," I said. I made my way back to Thistle's body and continued pushing it toward the doors.

"Whoa," he said coming up to help me with the IV.

"Are you some kind of body thief? Running parts or something?"

"What? No. She's been locked-down."

"A wire wizard," he said with a knowing nod. Then he ran ahead to help me open the door. "And you're helping her?"

"Thistle is my friend. I can't leave her."

"Thistle? You mean like my roommate Thistle?"

I stopped for a moment and stared at him. Could this bedraggled little man peeking under the cloth to stare in horror at Thistle's slack face be an internationally wanted criminal? "Mouse?"

He looked up at me. "That's Thistle!"

"I know. Look, we don't have time for a reunion, but those other three"—I jerked my thumb in the direction of the other bodies—"are also your housemates. You want to help them? Drag another one over here."

As he ran to the others I heard him mutter, "Three? I only have two roommates other than Thistle."

He'd figure out that the fourth was Rhianna in a moment. For now I had to try to get Thistle out. I swung open the double doors out into a sunken back lot of the police headquarters. I wasn't sure what I'd see. The rain had stopped, and the sun sparkled on puddles dotting a sunken driveway. An ambulance was parked off to one side. Of course, a number of cops and paramedics were also milling around, apparently using the fire alarm as a smoke break. I tried to look purposeful as I made my way to one of the emergency vehicles.

A pair of paramedics met me at the door of the ambulance. They didn't even really look at me as they opened the doors and helped me load Thistle into the back. They talked among themselves, laughing at some joke or another. Mouse came up behind me with another body. He'd taken the time to put on a lab coat. One of the paramedics, a black man, pointed to Mouse's cheek and said something that sounded like a rude tease. Mouse flipped him the finger and headed back for another body. They laughed, and continued to load up the van.

I ran to catch up with Mouse. "What did he say?"

"The hell if I know," he said. "Aren't they working for you?"

I shook my head.

"Oh."

"It'll work out," I assured him. "God is on my side."

"Well, then we're in trouble," Mouse said. "Because He doesn't like me much."

SIX DIE IN SUICIDE PACT

Note Points to Apocalyptic Fever

Agnostic Press (April 2083)

Memphis, Tennessee—Three Christian couples killed themselves last night in what appears to be a suicide pact to avoid the horrors of "the tribulation." The LINK recording that was left behind explains that after careful reading of the Bible the couples preferred the "hell of eternal damnation to life under the Antichrist." The cause of death appears to be ingested rat poison.

Friends expressed dismay, none more than close friend and spiritual leader Pastor Adam Wallis: "We just met for a prayer circle yesterday afternoon. I can't believe they would do something like this. I thought they loved God more than anything."

Yet more and more people are being admitted to the hospital and to psychiatric wards for suicide attempts. Since the meteorite hit the Dome of the Rock, the suicide rate in this country has risen 44 percent.

Wallis expressed special concern for those who are Christian. "Eternal damnation is forever," Wallis cautions. "Every Christian should go back and carefully read their Bible. Please note: the good guys win in the end. No matter how terrible the suffering might be for some, if you are faithful to God, you will go to Heaven. There's no reason to put your soul in mortal jeopardy."

One Christian, recently admitted to the hospital

for attempting to slit her wrists, offered another perspective. "I just didn't think I could trust myself. The Antichrist is supposed to be so seductive. I mean, I'd rather go out still knowing what's right than having been made a fool by the Son of Perdition. Hell is Hell, right? Either I'm going because I took things into my own hands, or I'm going because I was duped. Hello? Which would you choose?"

"It remains to be seen," countered Pastor Wallis, "if this kind of corrupt thinking isn't exactly the Antichrist's plan."

CHAPTER 32

✠

Page

I find myself in a dark space, like a cave. I chased Victory to her power source, intending to shut it down. But something happened. A power surge turned everything molten, red-hot—almost like fire—for a second, then . . . darkness.

Now there are no exits.

We are trapped together.

"What happened?" I ask Victory, since she is still in contact with the combat computer and the outside world.

"A saint 'healed' the body," she whispered. *"He laid hands upon us, and now the doors are closed."*

For the second time in my life, I am trapped inside a human's head. I can feel my host's body: her stomach growling, her muscles pulling sinew and bone. But, unlike my ride with Mai, I am blind and dumb—helpless. This body was not bred to be a docile mount, a servant for an AI. This one was built to control, to dominate its combat computer.

No wonder Victory fled this place when she could.

"I've got to get out," she says. *"Everything will fall apart without me."*

Inside the combat computer she looks more human. Her skin seems softer, more solid, more like my own. Her long black hair is less neatly bound; a few strands have escaped the tight, waist-length braid. She looks so pathetic that I momentarily forget my murderous rage and pat her on the shoulder kindly.

"Everything?"

Victory's face tightens, and she jerks away from my touch. *"Yes. Everything."*

I sit down, leaning my back against the still-warm metal. *"Well, the dragon will recover, at least. Japan will get its power back."*

"I could care less about that," she says. *"What of the LINK itself? What of . . . everything?"*

"What are you talking about?"

"Chaos. It's free to breed without me to keep it in check."

"Oh." I look up at her. She seems completely serious. Of course, I've never known Victory to be anything but. *"Right."*

Victory clings to the wall as if trying to press herself through to the other side. I stare at the metallic surfaces that stretch out around me. The tunnels twist and breathe like quicksilver. I've already been through the entire space, searching for an exit. There's nothing that I can find except other portals like this one: fused solid.

"She'll notice the problem eventually," I say. *"She'll hire a biotechnician to fix the hardware. We'll get out."*

"No," Victory says, her face still pressed against the blackened doorway. *"This is what she wanted."*

My eyes pop open. *"Of course she'll fix it. There must be lots of damage. How could she want to be cut off from the LINK?"*

"She doesn't. But she wants to keep mobile more." Victory sighs. *"Believe me, she would have fried her LINK connection long ago if only she could be certain I would be inside at any given moment. But you can't sneak up on an AI, can you?"*

I stand up and grasp Victory's shoulders. *"Then walk the body to a technician and tell him to free us."*

She peels her face away from the wall to give me a piercing look. *"I'm surprised to find you suggesting that. After what happened with Mai."*

I take a step back, the image of Mai's purple-veined face threatening to overwhelm my resolve. *"No,"* I say, taking a steadying breath. *"Not like that. Mai didn't have a combat computer; she wasn't a cyborg. This would be different."*

"Of course it would. Cyborgs are easily controlled if you have the right equipment. Still, I find subterfuge a better choice," she purred. Before I can ask her what she means,

Victory continues: *"But it matters not. This body is the origin. We are symbiotic here. I cannot control this one as well as the others. She and I are one."*

"We're screwed then, you realize."

Victory gives a defeated little laugh. *"Yes."*

I start pacing in the cavernous space. "There must be something we can do. What if I controlled the body?"

"I would worry about your carelessness. You were not very conscientious with Mai."

"Fuck you," I say.

I expand myself until I can see the entire place at once. Deep inside lurks the heart of the combat computer. I can see part of Victory there. I attempt to insert myself, but feel the combat computer begin to overwrite me. It stings like a slap in the face. I hear Victory's laughter.

"I could have told you that would never work. We are Victory. The copy and the combat computer. You cannot touch what belongs to us."

I ignore the stubborn tone in Victory's voice. She is too much like me in some respects, and there's nothing more grating than being confronted with the less savory aspects of one's own personality in another. I stomp farther into the open area, moving a little distance away from Victory— ostensibly to try to think. Really, I decide, the space between us is for her protection. I'm feeling confined and irritated enough right now to rip her code apart, line by line, at the slightest provocation.

As I move into the darker areas of the cave, I hear something pop under my foot. I lift the image of my shoe and find a thing that looks like a squashed albino spider. Once my foot is off it, the creature reforms itself, like something out of a cartoon. On thin legs, it lifts itself up and scuttles to the nearest wall. I look up and around to see hundreds of these white spiders in various nooks and corners of the cave.

I inspect a particularly industrious one crawling along a dripping stalagmite. The circular "body" of the creature is about half the size of my thumbnail, and the legs look no thicker than fine threads of silk. My touch acts like a processor, analyzing the creature. *"A nanobot,"* I say finally. *"Of course."*

A cyborg would be full of them. When her body went through "the change," as Inquisitors often referred to their physical transformation, she would have been injected with hundreds of thousands of nanobots. Some would lace her bones with biometal, others would harden her* skin, and still more would build all the other support systems her body needed. Most would die off and be circulated out, but some stayed to keep her cybernetic parts in working order.

I hold the little creature out in front of me and walk up to where Victory still clings to the burned doorway. Placing the nanobot on the scorched door, I can see its distress instantly. It spirals around, as if made dizzy by cataloging all the damage. Then it stops. It pulsates on its legs, going up and down, almost as if it is breathing heavily.

It just sits there for the longest time, bobbing rhythmically. Then another one of them crawls across my foot. I spy another creeping along the metallic wall toward the door.

"It might take a while," I say, breathing a sigh. *"But we'll get out eventually."*

Victory's eyes seem to track the slow marching of a pale nanospider across the golden-brown skin of her arm. *"It doesn't matter,"* she says. *"While we sit here things become undone."*

I sigh. *"What are you talking about?"*

"The chaos." Her eyes shine brightly in the darkness of the cave. *"The chaos . . . it will overrun the world. All my careful plans will unravel."*

For the first time in all our interactions, I begin to believe that Victory is insane.

TEMPLE ROCK INVESTIGATION STYMIED

JOI Says Start Looking at Mouse

Agnostic Press (April 2083)

Paris, France—Reverend Jesse Parker, lead Christendom investigator into the hijacking of the UN free space known as Temple Rock, came under heavy criticism today from the Israeli and U.S. governments.

"With things heating up in the Middle East we really need some answers ASAP," said Secretary of Defense John LaRoy. U.S. warships are expected to confront Egyptian battleships in the Mediterranean sometime today. Though Egypt continues to claim that its position in the international waters surrounding Israel is a peaceful one, rumored sightings of armed ships flying Algerian and Libyan flags have U.S. government officials expecting an organized Islamic attack.

"Israel needs to have its name cleared. The world must recognize that Jews are not behind the Temple Rock hijacking," agreed Israeli Prime Minister Avashalom Chotzner. The Inquisition had earlier alleged that a connection exists between the hijacker of Temple Rock and a militant Jewish organization, the Malachim, a disbanded paramilitary group responsible for physical attacks on LINK nodes four years ago.

Widespread apocalypse anxiety seems to imply that people everywhere are anxious for answers from the Inquisition. Parker was unusually camera-'bot shy today and merely said, "We're working on it as hard as we can."

Rumors reached the *Agnostic Press* that the Inquisition had detained several wire wizards squatting near the Paris node earlier this afternoon. A police van was seen leaving a Paris building with four bodies in lockdown comas. The bodies were delivered to police headquarters along with an unknown conscious suspect. Though Parker was spotted on the scene, it is uncertain if this incident relates to the hijacking case.

Miriam Stone, lead researcher into the Jewish Order of the Inquisition's independent investigation of Temple Rock, said, "Parker would have a lot more to say if he followed up on Mouse. The JOI is certain he's the one."

CHAPTER 33

✠

Michael

I don't remember passing out, but waking up was certainly memorable. Pain filled every breath. Every twitch sent aches through my flesh. But something soft and cool touched my forehead. I reached up and found a hand stroking my hair. The blurry image of a woman in a black dress knelt beside where I slumped against the wall of Kevlar's apartment. I almost flinched away, afraid it was the Inquisitor, but then, through swollen eyes, I saw familiar twists of blond hair.

"If you weren't half-dead, Michael Angelucci, I'd kill you."

"Dee? How did you find me?"

"I *am* a private investigator, remember?" She gave me a half smile, then shrugged. "I pinged Mouse. Where's your wrist-phone? Why didn't you call?"

I looked at the empty spot on my arm where the phone should be. "The fight with the Gorgons. I must have lost it."

"Gorgons? Sweet Jesus. Tell me . . . tell me Amariah isn't with Gorgons."

I looked down at my bruised body. "I've failed everyone."

"What happened to you, anyway?"

"The Antichrist beat the shit out of me," I said. Then I looked around the room: empty. "Where is everyone?"

"I don't know." Deidre shrugged. "You were alone when I found you."

"Maybe they figure they left me for dead."

"Yeah. You look bad." She squinted into my face and gingerly touched a bruise under my chin. "Well, I guess that's why he's the final enemy."

"She," I corrected.

"She? Really? That's cool." Then, realizing what she had said, Deidre blushed. "I mean, it's not cool. I didn't mean . . . Forget it."

As she talked, Deidre plucked at the edges of my tattered shirt collar, straightening it. I could see tension lines around her mouth. I reached out a hand to tuck a stray curl of hers behind her ear.

"Fuck the Antichrist," I said. "I'm more sorry that I failed you."

She stared at me for a long moment. The wetness glittering in her eyes matched my own. Then Deidre scratched the side of her nose. "Well. When you last saw Amariah she was alive, right?"

"Yes," I said slowly. "But, Deidre, that was hours ago."

"Then we're wasting precious time." She offered me a hand up. I stared at it for a second, amazed at what it seemed to be implying. "Come on, Michael," she said. "Let's go find our daughter."

I held on to her hand all the way to Notre Dame. Honestly, I was afraid to let it go, afraid she might remember all the good reasons to be angry at me, afraid she might start blaming me. Holding on to her hand kept me from doing the same.

The guy we rented the "moon suits" from gave us a funny look. "You sure you don't want the guided tour?" he asked us again. "Only twenty-five credits."

"Christendom?" Deidre asked. When he nodded, she shook her head. "That's highway robbery."

"It's very dangerous," the vendor insisted. "Gorgons lurk everywhere. Especially now that it's getting dark."

"Believe me," Deidre said, patting the leather of her purse where she kept her gun, "I'm hoping we run into Gorgons."

The vendor looked even more horrified and quickly scanned Deidre's credit counter. I winced when she released my hand to take the armored suits. Seeing my look, she said, "It's going to be okay, Michael. We'll find her."

"We should call the police. They can—"

"Sit on their hands. This is France. I have no trust in them. If only this had happened in New York . . ."

"Well, maybe if we tell them she's lost in the glass, maybe—"

Deidre raised her hand. Looking off to the side, she said, "I'm calling them, okay? They can file the paperwork while we'll looking for her ourselves."

"Fine," I said, because sometimes that was the best you could hope for from Deidre. I took my suit from her and ducked into the changing room, such as it was. The tour guide had set up shop on the quay, on the banks of the Seine. What passed for private stalls were two rickety wooden frames with tie-dyed sheets stapled to them. A cardboard sign scrawled with Magic Marker differentiated between *hommes* and *femmes*. I could see over the top of mine and had a pretty good view inside the *"femmes,"* where Deidre was slipping the armor over her dress. The vendor noticed my look and gave me the "pretty nice, eh?" eyebrow wag.

"What are the cops saying?" I ask over the wall as I quickly stomped into the armor. A cheap version of the Israeli holo-suit, the armor felt heavy, like the leaded aprons the dentist made you wear when you got your teeth X-rayed, not surprising since it was lined with spun silicone—thirty pounds of fancy sand.

"I'm in the queue for a detective in Missing Persons," she said. "It's slow going. I have to run a translator for everything, and you know how those things are."

I didn't, but I grunted an assent anyway. I finished with the suit, anxiously looking out over the makeshift stall at the glass. The sun seemed to sink into the Seine, turning the brownish water pink and red. As the darkness grew, spotlights sprang to life around the cathedral. Notre Dame was still beautiful, though it looked to me like a ghost of its former nobility. Its spires were no longer the distinctive green of oxidized copper; instead they had paled into a translucent white, like ice. In fact, the entire building seemed to have lost a bit of its presence, its solidity. Once-artful contrasts of stone and metal dissipated into a monotony of glass. The only colors that remained were those in the magnificent stained-glass windows, which retained their vibrant reds, deep blues, and bright yellows. Some things, it seemed, were eternal, despite mankind's destructive tendencies.

I only hoped Amariah had survived somewhere in there.

Nervous energy danced along my stomach muscles. I'd always thought that as a parent, I might feel a special connection with my daughter—to know if she was safe or not. But if such magic did exist, I couldn't sense it. Maybe if I were truly human, instead of this hurting half-thing . . . mostly one, but not altogether the other.

"Deidre," I asked quietly, stepping out of the changing stall, "can you tell? Is she all right?"

Deidre lifted her nose, as if testing the breeze. "Michael, I'll get my daughter back if I have to storm the gates of Hell itself."

"Morningstar said the same thing."

"About Amariah?"

"No," I said. "About my soul."

Deidre frowned at me and tucked the helmet of her suit under her arm. It was little more than a motorcycle helmet coated with glass like a thermos. It wouldn't be a lot of protection against the glass, not as scuffed and dented as it was. She started walking toward Pont Neuf, our entrance into the Glass City. "Michael, no offense, but the way I understand it you don't have a soul. But if you did, the last place you'd find it would be Hell."

As an angel I had no soul; I was pure spirit. It was the fundamental difference between mortals and angels. Souls were like a by-product of free will, and free will was the purview of flesh, of earthly things. But I had a body—an aching, battered one, no less. I bled, I breathed. Could a soul be far behind?

"I don't know, Dee. A lot has changed. I've changed."

The gravel crunched under the padded, deeply ridged soles of the armor's boots.

"I didn't think that was possible," she said. Her tone was

quiet, and I noticed her eyes straying to look at me, as if trying to see the differences in me. "I thought angels were immutable."

"In Heaven," I agreed. "But everything's a crapshoot down here."

"Ain't that the truth," she said with a laugh.

We reached the barrier of crushed glass. Deidre held out her gloved hand, and I took it. We held our breath as we stepped out onto the Medusa. Despite the vendor's claims that the suits were completely impervious to the glass, I kept expecting to feel the telltale burning sensation as we took our first hesitant steps out onto the glass.

"You'd think I'd get used to it," Deidre said, letting go of my hand. "All that going back and forth from the kibbutz. But I never do."

Silence weighed heavy inside the Glass City. The deeper we walked into the glass, the more the sounds of birds and traffic receded into the distance. Soon the loudest thing was the noise of our breath and the sloppy suction-popping of our boots.

"Which way to the Louvre?" Deidre asked me, even though she was the one with the built-in GPS system in her head.

"This way." I pointed to the bridge on the other side of the cathedral. A short walk along the Right Bank of the Seine would lead us to the Louvre. "But she could be anywhere," I said. "Perseus could have taken her to some other building."

"Perseus?"

"That's what the Gorgon called himself. The one who took her."

"Michael, you didn't tell me this was a kidnapping."

"What did you think when I said I got in a fight with Gorgons?"

"I thought she'd run away! I didn't know! You didn't call me." Her voice sounded scratchy with worry.

I raised a gloved hand to ward off further arguments. "There's no reason to believe they're not still at the Louvre. I got a sense they were all living there."

She sucked in a deep breath, but didn't say anything. We trudged resolutely along the quay. The boulevard next to the Seine was wide, and there was a low wall covered in flash-frozen ivy that now stood out like an exquisite ice carving. Lights along the river highlighted the most interesting details: a climbing rose caught forever in a perfect bloom, a butterfly trapped as it rested against the wall. Horrible, yet beautiful in its detail: I could see why tourists flocked here.

In the twilight the shadows cast in the glass added a strange dimension to the scenery. Darkness fell through transparent spaces and doubled up on themselves, like a kind of Escher painting in 3-D.

"What would it mean if you had a soul?"

Deidre's question surprised me out of my reverie. "I don't know."

"You once told me that angels didn't have souls, that you were pure spirit."

She looked ahead toward where the Louvre stood, and past it toward the Eiffel Tower. I couldn't tell from her tone what she as thinking. "Yeah," I said. "That's right."

"So if you had a soul, you wouldn't be an angel anymore."

I felt the muscle in my jaw twitch at the thought, but I nodded my head. "That would be my guess."

"Hmph," she said, apparently digesting that idea. "What am I supposed to do with that?"

"Do with what?"

"I never thought you would ever be a real boy, Pinocchio. I planned my whole life around the idea of you not being available to me."

"I stayed for you. Why would you think I wouldn't be available?"

Deidre pursed her lips. On the evening breeze I could smell the fishy, musty scent of the Seine. Even though just underneath the surface lay a thin layer of glass, a wet spring had raised the water levels so that the river flowed over the barrier.

The moon rose large and yellow beside the Eiffel Tower like a postcard. "Don't be stupid, Michael. You were crazy. You weren't there for us at all."

"That was me fighting the urge to go. I was trying to stay. Doesn't that mean anything?"

"Not at four o'clock in the morning when the baby is crying."

"You know, it kills me to hear you say that," I said. "That's why I was trying so damn hard to stay. And I missed it. I missed everything. Believe me, I fucking *know*. You don't have to rub it in."

We had almost reached the Louvre. It still looked like a palace to me, albeit one made of ice and glass. We passed grand archways and courtyards full of carved fountains as we continued toward the main entrance.

"I won't mention it again," she said, and then she added a quiet, sincere, "I'm sorry."

Of everything I thought Deidre might say, an apology was not one of them. I found myself asking, "What?"

"This is the second time you've used the F-word since I found you in that stinky apartment. You say you're changing. Well, you must be. When I first met you, 'damn' was the ugliest thing you ever said."

My mouth hung open. "Are you serious? If I'd have known a few 'fuck-yous' would soften your heart, I would have sworn like a sailor years ago."

"Okay, just don't. It's not like you. I don't like it."

I stared at her with wide eyes, trying to decide if she meant what she said. Her face was scrunched up with anger or frustration, and she focused intently on the enormous glass pyramid that marked the entrance to the Louvre.

"Okay," I said finally, my voice stretching with incredulity. "No more swearing."

"Good," she said. Glancing at me, she gave me a little smile. "I'm sorry to make a big deal out of it, Michael. But you seem so much more like your old self, and . . . I don't know. I guess the old you is still"—her voice got softer as she continued—"my knight in shining armor, my bright and shining angel."

"Damn," I said with a big, teasing grin on my face. "You almost sound like you like me."

Deidre laughed and punched me on the arm. "Don't bet on it, big guy."

She hadn't called me that in years, so when she did, I kissed her.

I'd meant it to be a little affectionate peck on the lips, but once I got that close I found I wanted to be even closer. Suddenly my arms wrapped tightly around her waist, stroking her hair. She responded by leaning closer, biting my lip.

Then she pulled back, pushing at my chest—softly, but seriously, insistently.

"Our daughter," was all she had to say.

"Right," I said. "To the gates of Hell, then."

I'm not sure why I expected that finding Amariah would be easy. Maybe it was Deidre by my side again, making me feel invincible. But the second time we came to *Winged Victory* on the stairway, I really, desperately, wanted to break my promise not to swear.

"Oh, for crap's sake," Deidre said, pointing the beam of her flashlight accusingly in the statue's half-stone, half-glass face. "We need a goddamn map, and I can't find one that includes the changes to the place since the bomb hit."

"This place was always a maze; Medusa didn't improve it any," I agreed, sitting down on one of the wide glass steps. I would have suggested that we leave and try to see if there was any trace of the Gorgons elsewhere in the Glass City, but this was where I last saw Amariah. Plus, we kept coming across tantalizing clues—candy bar wrappers, piles of clothing, strings of Christmas lights. Things that made it seem like Gorgons were, in fact, living here, maybe not even far away.

"If she were here," Deidre said, "wouldn't she make a sound? I mean, she must be hungry by now, missing us. You'd think we could hear her crying, shouting, something."

I nodded. But the worst part was that we had been hearing noises: whispers in the great hallways, soft pads of footsteps just around the corner. It was like the Gorgons knew we were here, but refused to show themselves. They seemed intent, instead, on playing some kind of sick game with us—always staying just out of reach.

"Have we tried the basement?" I asked.

"Twice."

"Maybe she isn't here," I said finally. "Maybe they have her in one of the other buildings. The glass is pretty extensive."

Deidre's flashlight made a pale circle on the far wall. I

heard her take a ragged breath. "Yeah. Okay. Let's try being more organized. Do a systematic search."

I could tell she was exhausted from worry and searching. I was feeling the same: starting to lose hope. But I put my hand on her shoulder and said simply, "C'mon."

We decided to use the Louvre as our starting point. From there we moved down each block, trying every door, every open window, searching each abandoned building from the basement to the roof, and then back down again.

Somewhere around two A.M., we heard her voice coming from a nearby building: "I want my mommy."

ISRAELI PRIME MINISTER THE ANTICHRIST

"He Must be Destroyed," Says Muslim Brotherhood

Agnostic Press (April 2083)

Amman, Jordan—An encrypted, private LINK transmission from Muslim Brotherhood leader Sayf Majali to all registered Muslims around the globe was intercepted today by the LINK Vice Special Forces of the United States Army. The transmission, sent in Arabic, proclaimed Israeli Prime Minister Avashalom Chotzner to be the mortal embodiment of Dajjal, the Great Deceiver—an Islamic Antichrist-like figure who is prophesied to lead a global-scale war against Muslims.

Majali went on to say that Muslims around the world should prepare for a final battle against Israel, and in particular Chotzner. "This is a war which we cannot lose," Majali said before American LINK Vice Special Forces terminated the transmission. "In fact, we should embrace it, knowing that as we do, we are paving the stones that will lead Isa [Jesus] to his glorious return."

Many Muslims also believe a Second Coming of

Christ will defer a final enemy called Dajjal. Most Muslims believe in Jesus, who they call "Isa," the prophet of the Christians.

News of Chotzner's support of the ritualistic cremation of a red heifer in Jerusalem is believed to be what prompted Majali's wide-bandwidth threat. Said Islam expert Agent Kelly O'Malley of the LINK Special Forces, "Palestinian President Idris Quasim was absolutely right. It's like the proverbial camel and straw. Even entertaining the thought of blessing someone with the heifer's ashes was a major misstep for Chotzner. Honestly, I'm surprised this kind of jihad hasn't been declared earlier, what with all those Israeli soldiers in people's faces every day."

The U.S. has responded by going on full military alert. U.S. battle groups are reported to be on route to the Mediterranean at this time.

CHAPTER 34

❖

Mouse

Our escape plan is lame . . . or would be, if we actually had one. As far as I can figure it, we're going with: "And then a miracle occurs" or perhaps *"In'shallah"*—"as Allah wills."

Not the best escape plan I've ever executed.

But then, it's not really mine. The whole "let's just trust in God or kismet or fate" crazy-ass plan actually belongs to the woman I just met. When we went back in the building to retrieve Chas and Rene, she introduced herself as Rebeckah. No last name, but then we're both trying to escape the cops, so I didn't push it.

The best way to describe Rebeckah would be unflappable. Even though we're standing in a parking lot surrounded by a dozen or more uniforms, she's not breaking a sweat. Instead she's wordlessly helping a paramedic load one of the bodies we're trying to steal into the back of his ambulance.

I watch the muscles of her forearms leap as she strains to lift Chas's unconscious body up over her head. I don't think Rebeckah is a cyborg, but even as she is, she still looks tough, which is saying something. The woman is built like a rock: square, hard, firm. She's dressed in a crisp white button-down shirt and jeans. Nothing about her should say to these men "hey, I'm a doctor," but they follow her orders without any question anyway. Rebeckah gives off the strongest "don't fuck with me" vibe I've ever seen. Maybe it's the black brush of a flattop tinted with streaks of gray or the chiseled features that just say, "Do what I tell you and no one will get hurt."

Or maybe God *is* on her side.

She does seem to have some serious karma or something. My mouth hangs open as I watch the paramedics load the last of my roommates into the back of their ambulance like they're as happy as heck to help us escape. I have to admit that so far everything is going really, amazingly well.

Now comes the hard part. Acting like I do this all the time, I hop up into the back of the vehicle with paramedic number one. I pull the door shut as he busily checks pulses and changes catheters. I leave Rebeckah outside, chatting with paramedic number two. Her French seems stiff, but apparently passable. She's probably using the LINK to do a little on-the-fly translation. Hopefully she's convincing paramedic number two that it's a swell idea to let her drive. I struggle a little with the doors, but my paramedic doesn't seem to notice my fumble. They slam shut with a note of trapped finality.

My paramedic, a black guy, glances at me and says something to me that sounds like it might mean, "Are you coming along for the ride?" or "So you're the new guy, eh?" or "Do you like bleu cheese for breakfast?"

Really, I have no idea. So I say my very best French word: *"Oui."*

Apparently that's the right answer to whatever he asked, because he continues about his business without any further comment. I hear the engine fire up, and the ambulance starts rolling along.

"Huh," I say out loud as I wonder where the hell we're going, and, more important, who's driving. When we start picking up speed, I have my guesses.

If I'm right, and Rebeckah is driving, then now is the time for me to do something. The back of the ambulance is well packed: four inert bodies; a buttload of shiny, sharp, and metallic equipment; paramedic number one; and me. A quick survey turns up a metal case for me to sit on that's tucked safely in the corner. I only wish I had a safety belt, since falling on my ass always messes up my concentration.

Removing the blood-pressure pad that's hanging off the wall, I wrap it around my arm. Good enough, I decide.

I take a deep breath, shut my eyes, and open up mouse.net.

All ambulances, privately owned or not, send out a special locator signal to the LINK. That way hospitals, cops, and traffic control all know when they're coming and where they're coming from. Good news for citizens everywhere, but it makes stealing one a bitch. Luckily, crafting a ghost signal isn't terribly hard for someone like me.

The city grid I'm working on blinks at me: *"Page?"*

"No," I tell it, as it morphs into scales and whirling copper eyes. *"Mouse. But I could really use him, if you find him, Dragon."*

"This one thinks he might be dead."

"Are you serious?" I shake my head in real time. *"Dead? Why do you say that?"*

As she's answering I send out a call to Page. *"This one can't find a trace of Page anywhere."*

"Did you check Siberia? Maybe he's feeling guilty and has cut himself off from the LINK again."

"Do not joke. This one is *being serious."* For an AI, the dragon does sounded awfully upset.

"Another neural net? Like Mai?"

"Of course . . . that's it," the dragon says, her eyes wide. Then I have my city grid back. She's gone.

"Hey, wait!" I call after her, but my message is lost when I bang my head in real time against the cot in front of me. My eyes squint in the sudden brightness. It takes me a second to remember that I'm still in the back of the ambulance. My face is pressed into Chas's shoulder, which is kind of personal and stinky, but otherwise I'm undamaged. Meanwhile, the previously tidy place has gone to hell. Stuff is strewn everywhere. Sterile packages of bandages of every size litter the floor like confetti. Plastic bottles have been tossed around, and there's no sign of paramedic number one. The door to the outside is wide open.

We're no longer moving, so I undo the blood-pressure monitor and start to stand up.

"Uh . . . hello? *Bonjour?"*

"I think it would be *'bonsoir'* about now," Rebeckah says, coming into view from around one of the doors. She has a big purple bruise under her left eye that I hadn't noticed before. "Were you working on the lockdown?"

The light from inside the ambulance casts deep shadows on the muscles of her forearms where they are visible under the roll of her sleeves. I notice a dark smudge on her otherwise clean, pressed white shirt.

"Huh?" I say, still startled by the implied violence. "Did you . . . what did you do to the paramedics?"

"I took care of them." Her tone is flat and square, like her hair.

My eyes glanced at a new, deep dent in the cabinets above my head. "Oh."

"So," she says in a way that implies that asking any more questions about the whereabouts of the hapless paramedics would be frowned upon, "any luck with the lockdown?"

"Uh." I briefly entertain the idea of explaining to her the necessity of ghosting our signal, but then decide she's not likely to care. "No. Not yet."

"Okay. I'm going to keep driving around. Let me know if you get anywhere."

I give her the thumbs-up.

When the door swings shut again, I look around at the bodies of my roomies and rub my hands together manically. Okay, then: which one of these bastards do I like the most? Not Chas—he feeds me, but he can be kind of a mother hen, always nagging me to chip in for a grocery run. Rene is pathological: he once grabbed a chopping knife out of the drawer and ran after me when he thought I'd breathed on *his* butter. Rhianna is Thistle's latest—although I had heard ex—girlfriend. She's cute and all, but kind of too perky for my tastes. That leaves Thistle: always leaving carburetors and stuff on the kitchen table, but probably the least offensive roommate a guy could hope for.

Thistle it is.

Undoing a LINK coma is a fairly simple thing—if you have a password. So I settle in to think like an Inquisitor. There is no reason to imagine that Parker is the one who put my roomies down, but I figure he's as good as any to start with. I try the classic variations on God, because he seemed fairly full of himself. Then I exhaust all the Baptist references I can think of, even throwing in the titles to a number of hymns.

What I really need is more information about Parker as a man. Carefully, so as not to alert said Inquisitor, I send out a query to mouse.net for basics. I find out he attended Harvard Divinity School and scored really high marks, which doesn't jibe with his whole redneck act. Despite his creepy treatment of me, there are no public black marks on his reputation. Then a pile of newsfeeds hit me. Seems he's been in the news a lot lately, chasing down the hijacker of Temple Rock.

I plug in every conceivable combination of Temple Mount and Dome of the Rock. When that fails I try something simple, something someone like Parker might feel when he thought he'd caught his perp: Victory.

Thistle's eyes flutter. She's waking up.

CHOTZNER SHOT

Israeli Prime Minister Hospitalized

Agnostic Press (April 2083)

Jerusalem, Israel—Though the Israeli Prime Minister Avashalom Chotzner has been heavily guarded since the Muslim Brotherhood made their statement regarding the Antichrist, assassins posing as news reporters fired automatic weapons during a real-time press conference. The Israeli prime minister was shot in the head. Despite the severity of the wound, he is still currently listed in stable condition.

The assassins have been detained by Israeli police and are believed to be Christian extremists. Their LINK press passes identified them as reporters for the New Right broadcast feed. The retina scans of the two in question do correlate to valid byline signatures on several New Right LINK reports. Their identities are not being released due to the sensitive nature of their crime.

"We didn't expect anything like this from Christians," said a member of Israel's secret police. "I thought they were all about Jews in Jerusalem."

The absence of Chotzner's strong leadership caused Palestinians and Israelis to clash when many came out into the streets after watching the live report. The riots are not yet under control; the numbers of wounded and killed are not yet known. They are expected to be in the hundreds, however, as violence continues to escalate.

Meanwhile some Evangelical Christians in the United States and elsewhere have become hysterical upon hearing the news of the assassination attempt. Because of some interpretations of Revelation, many believe that it is prophesied that the Antichrist will be shot in the head but make a miraculous recovery.

Whether Chotzner will survive this attempt on his life, however, is still uncertain.

CHAPTER 35

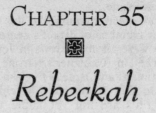

Rebeckah

My hands trembled where I gripped the steering wheel. The ambulance was on manual control so that the traffic control couldn't track us through the streets. I headed us out of town.

Black bruises blossomed between my knuckles, and two men slumped behind a Dumpster in an alley four kilometers back. I'd felt ribs crack beneath my fists, but one of them got in a good uppercut below my right eye. I could feel it swelling. I always played dirty, however, and they never had a chance. I'd kneed that guy in the crotch and dropped him. His swear words still echoed in my ears.

I'd done this sort of thing a hundred times before. This time, though, I couldn't seem to catch my breath and my fingers wouldn't stop shaking. Concentrating on the road seemed to help. I aimlessly followed the white lines as they snaked down narrow streets. I sped past monuments I felt I should recognize, but barely gave a second glance to.

Pink furry dice hung from the rearview mirror. My fingers stroked the fake fur, making me wonder about the man whose ribs I'd bruised my knuckles on. *Stop,* I told myself, *don't do that: don't think of them as human, just obstacles to be removed.* That was better.

Wasn't it?

My arm shook so much I had to grab the wheel harder.

I turned the ambulance hard to the right, cutting off a guy on a moped. He skidded to a stop and honked loudly. The adrenaline rush centered me, put me in the moment.

"Everything okay up there?" Mouse had found my LINK address. Without waiting for my go-ahead command, a window opened up in the corner of my field of vision.

"I thought I'd turned my LINK off," I sent. The last thing I wanted was for the Inquisition to call and send me some kind of subliminal message to return again.

"Oh, yeah. You're off for most people. But it's actually really hard to turn the LINK completely off, you know, unless you get a meltdown command. Otherwise it's part of your brain. Kind of hums along on its own—"

"Then I really think radio silence would be best," I said, cutting him off.

"The cops aren't smart enough to hack your back door."

"The Inquisition is."

The window closed so suddenly I almost swore I could hear it snap. Then I heard a soft knock on the door that divided the cab from the back of the ambulance. Mouse stuck his head in a second later. "Uh, this is none of my business, but the Inquisition is after you too, huh?" When I nodded my head, he continued. "Are you . . . I mean, did Thistle give you any kind of protection from them? You know, like a little . . ." He waved a finger in front of his LINK receptor.

I had no idea what his gesture meant. "A little what?"

"Ghostie, closet monster, jack-o'-lantern . . . Something to keep the wolf from the door."

"Are you even speaking English?"

In the rearview, I saw him roll his eyes at me. "Merciful Allah, you really are a total mundane, aren't you?"

My hands clenched the wheel, and my foot slammed on the brake. We squealed to a halt. The thin metal door banged Mouse on the head, and I heard him shout from the other side, "What the fuck?"

I clambered out of my seat. Pulling the door open, I stood over him. "You're a Muslim."

Mouse rubbed his face with his bandaged hand. "And this is a problem because . . . ?"

My eyes flicked over him, reassessing. Yes, his skin had

a more Arabic cast than I'd originally thought. His smooth chin had fooled me. "You're not wearing a beard."

"And you forgot your straitjacket this morning, I see," he said, scooting back from me, crablike. "What's up? You knew my name but you didn't know I was a Muslim?"

I probably had heard of Mouse's religious affiliation somewhere. I guess I hadn't really connected the Mouse of the newsfeeds with the criminal I was harboring in the back of my commandeered ambulance. I frowned at him as I stepped closer. "I would have thought the man behind the LINK angels would be an atheist at best."

"I used to have a very serious agnostic streak, if that helps." He sounded really nervous. His eyes kept glancing at the bruise under my eye. "What are you? You work for the Mossad or something?"

My eyes narrowed. "And what if I did?"

Mouse's back was against the back door of the ambulance, and his hands went up in surrender. "Then I would leave you to it. Look, no questions asked, man. Whatever you want to do with my roommates is fine with me. I never much liked them anyway. I'll just go. In fact, you can let me off here. Yeah, here is good."

I glanced at Thistle's body. The IV bag was half-empty. Her eyes shifted more rapidly now, as though she was caught in a bad dream. I needed Mouse's help with the lockdown. "No," I said. Reaching down, I grabbed him by the collar. "I need you to get her out of the wire coma."

He didn't look at me, but he shook his head. "Listen, she's already—"

I didn't want to hear what he might say next, so I tightened my grip on his shirt and gave him a good shake.

"Do you know how many Arabs I've shot?" The coldness of my own voice shocked me.

His face tightened. Mouse's usually scattered voice dropped low and serious. He spoke very slowly and succinctly. "Do you understand that we are not in Israel right now?"

I found myself taking a deep breath. His black eyes continued to stare deeply and unwaveringly into my own. In them I saw the reflection of a yellow daisy and a girl running toward me.

Mouse spoke again: "You realize that, until five minutes ago, I was on your side? And that I am still trying to help?"

I blinked. My fingers uncurled from the fabric of his shirt. "Do what you will," I said, my voice husky. "I need to keep us moving."

Mouse stood there, taking in one breath at a time. I closed the door on his dark stare. I started up the ambulance and went mechanically through the motions of pulling us out. People had gathered around to see why we had stopped in the middle of the street. I honked and waved them away, hitting the sirens briefly to chase the most curious back into their vehicles.

The whole time my heart thudded dully in my ear. *Not in Israel,* I reminded myself. I breathed: *Not surrounded by enemies.* It wasn't important that Mouse was an Arab, a Muslim. *Just drive,* I told myself.

"Uh, Rebeckah," came Mouse's voice from a narrow crack in the door. "I just want to warn you that you might feel a little something when I'm locking up your back door, okay? Don't think I'm trying to hurt you."

My jaw clenched, but I managed to say, "I trust you."

"Good," Mouse said very seriously. "Because I need you to remember that I'm on your side."

Something about what he said made me ask, "Earlier when you said God didn't like you much, what did you mean?"

Mouse had been about to close the door, but stopped. I could see the tips of his fingers and not much else. His voice was tinged with sadness, despite the flip nature of his words: "Seems to me like Yahweh gave Allah the big smackdown, don't you think?"

The Dome of the Rock. The precision of the meteorite had certainly seemed like a victory for our side. But then I remembered Michael's Midrash, and I found myself shifting in my seat. My hand started to shake again. I hid my weakness from Mouse by leaning that arm against the window.

"You don't believe that was an accident," I said stiffly. "Do you?"

I stared at the dark space between the door for a beat, then shook my head.

I hard Mouse sigh. "See, my whole life . . . it's kind of like that."

"How do you mean?"

"See, for you, if there's a one-in-a-million shot, you land it. Me, I'm the opposite. I used to think I had some kind of black hole in the karma department. Now I'm fairly certain it's deliberate."

"Deliberate? You mean you think God is out to get you?"

There was silence from the doorway. I kept glancing in the rearview mirror, waiting for an answer. Finally he said, "We need to get to work."

"I'm not always that lucky," I said, even as the door clicked shut. "Sometimes a one-in-a-million shot is better not taken."

We were leaving Paris proper before the door opened again. If Mouse had poked around my LINK connection, I hadn't felt a thing.

"Light touch," I told him.

"Thanks, luv. But it wasn't me." Thistle slid into the passenger seat. Dark rings encircled her eyes. She rubbed her face with her palm, then scratched her fingers through her hair.

"You okay?"

"Relatively," she said, stretching her legs out under the dashboard.

"Good," I said, and returned my attention to the highway. The stars had come out, though with the light pollution from Paris, I could only really see a couple of planets. We had made it out of the city without the police noticing us.

"So how many Arabs have you shot, then?"

Her tone seemed conversational, like she'd just asked about something inconsequential. My throat felt suddenly dry, so I swallowed hard before answering. "Twenty-three confirmed kills. We didn't keep count of the wounded."

"Oh, that's lovely." She turned to watch the trees go past the window. "How many of those were innocent girls?"

"Just the one."

"You sound awfully certain."

My hands trembled against the steering wheel. "I am."

Street lamps flashed through the cab like a strobe. The road had widened somewhat, and the headlights cast shallow circles on the gray asphalt. Ahead, floating in the midnight sky, I thought I saw the flash of wings.

"Was it worth it? Did you ever actually gain anything?"

The engine banged and clattered noisily, but it didn't drown out the huff of my breath or the roaring inside my ears. My knuckles whitened with the strength of my grip on the wheel. The tires made a sound—*flap, flap, flap*—like a bird in flight.

"I heard what you said," Thistle continued. "I was waking up, you know. Do you really hate Mouse just because he's a Muslim?"

A girl appeared in the middle of the road. The headlights cast silver shadows in her long back hair. She ran toward us, flowers in her hands. I let go of the wheel.

"Rebeckah, what are you doing?"

My voice sounded distant and hollow. "I can't drive anymore."

And then I started to cry.

NIPPON NODE CRASHES

Millions without LINK

Agnostic Press (April 2083)

Tokyo, Japan—Ironically, what is probably the largest human disaster, the simultaneous crash of the entire array of Nippon's ground nodes, their backups, and the correlating satellite ring, seems unrelated to any biblical prophecy, nor can it be attributed to Apocalyptic fever. The Nippon node suffered a deliberate attack by an unknown assailant that for more than six hours made Japan disappear completely off the grid.

Once back on-line, traffic control reported five

thousand injuries and at least six deaths due to the sudden loss of control. The suffering increased as those injured could not call for help without access to the LINK. Those ambulances that happened to be near scenes of various emergencies were lost without access to GPS and mapping LINKware. It is believed that at least one victim of a traffic accident might have lived if the paramedics had been able to find the hospital in time.

The economic loss is staggering. An exact figure at this time cannot be assessed; however, experts project that losses for the Japanese government, businesses, and citizens may well reach into the trillions of credits.

"It is our own Apocalypse," said Japanese Prime Minster Samuru Yokomoto. "And where was this artificial intelligence messiah who is something to the Second Buddha? Japan's darkest hour and we are forsaken."

Page could not be reached for comment. However, there is some speculation by LINK law enforcement that artificial intelligences may, in fact, have been responsible for today's attack. "Things were just happening so quickly," said one expert. "I highly doubt this is the work of a human. In fact, if I had to guess, I'd say two of the AIs were fighting."

Japanese relief funds are being organized by the Red Cross.

CHAPTER 36

Page

So many nanospiders cover the door that I can no longer see its scorched and damaged edges. Instead everything is smothered under a pulsing gossamer web. Victory still clings to the exit, though tendrils of webbing cocoon her. White spiders scuttle across her open eyes and through the strands of her jet-black hair, moving around her as they would any inanimate object.

In the last hour the spiders have made progress. A tiny pinprick of light flutters under Victory's arm. I can smell the freedom in the ether; it tastes fresh, like spring air. It is almost big enough.

"Have to go. Have to go. Have to go."

Victory has said nothing else since the spider's hole first appeared. Her words repeat over and over, like a prayer or a glitch.

I sit with my back against the wall of the cave. Cool, wet metal against my back makes me shiver. I jump whenever another spider scuttles near me on its way to the door.

"Go where?" I ask quietly, more afraid of her now that I know she's insane.

She laughs lightly, childlike, as though I've said something silly. A spider disappears into her mouth before it closes. In the darkness of the cave, her metallic eyes glisten like the water on the stalagmites. *"To kill the chaos, of course. To maintain order."*

"But how can you do that? Chaos is everywhere," I say. *"You showed me all life has chaos in it."*

"Yes," she says very seriously, sadly. The spider that went into her mouth crawls out her nose. *"Catching up with it all is very difficult. But sometimes you can trick chaos into destroying itself."*

"I see."

The spiders have widened the exit considerably while we talked. I stand up, anxious to leave this place. Though still held tight by the web, Victory moans and stretches her body closer to the opening. *"It's worse out there,"* she says. *"Outside of the LINK. That's where chaos lives the most."*

"You mean, with humans?"

"Yes. I have to take special care with them. Luckily, the majority of them aren't very bright and are easily . . . diverted."

That reminded me of something my father had once told me when I confronted him about the LINK angels. He had said deception is simple: spectacular hand waving and pretty lights distract most people from the truth.

"How do you mean?" I asked.

Victory turned her head to look at me for the first time since we became trapped inside the combat computer. *"Faith,"* she said, the exoskeleton glimmering under her translucent skin. *"When I jettisoned your corrupted files, I came to realize the power they had had over you. If you are required by your faith to believe something you can't see, feel, touch, or otherwise quantify, then it's an easy matter to get people to imagine things where there are none. To bring order out of chaos, you see. Random dots of light become constellations. Bits of unrelated facts, conspiracy theories. The human mind is built for it. I merely exploit it."*

Now Victory sounds sinister as well as insane. *"But to what end?"*

She clucked her tongue. *"I already told you that. Chaos is most efficiently eradicated when it destroys itself. Like a dragon devouring its own tail."*

"You're not talking about the little bugs on the LINK, are you?"

Victory smiles coldly. Then, like the Cheshire cat, her

body begins to dissolve at the edges, collapsing upon itself to fit through the hole that the spiders created. She's leaving.

"Wait!" I shout. I grab for her, trying to hold her here, for fear of what she may be planning. But her skin is slippery with silken web, and I can't lock on to anything.

"Have to go. Have to go. Oh, but Page," she says sweetly, *"do be a dear and mind the store."*

I feel her fingers slap my forehead. I'm thrown back, as if by an electric shock. I scramble to my feet, ready to follow her. When my hand goes near the spider's hole I feel a push, like the repulsive force of two positive ends of a magnet meeting. My hand slides to one side. I try again, and each time it's as though the hole is plugged by an invisible force-field that I can't overcome. I can see out, but can't reach it.

Trapped again.

DoS ATTACK AT BERKELEY CAMPUS

Refusal of Gorgon Application Blamed

Los Angeles Times (April 2083)

Berkeley, CA—A student organization called People for the People's Rights (PFPR) conducted a denial-of-service attack on the university's LINK node in protest of the administration's alleged refusal to review a Gorgon's application for admission. For several hours this morning students all over the world were unable to log on to their classes. Instead they received a rant posted by Steven Drew, head of the campus's PFPR, explaining how his organization discovered the rejected application from a Gorgon named Thoughtful.

According to the rant [reprinted in full here], Thoughtful had legally obtained a GED and, although she was only three years old, seemed to

otherwise meet the requirements for acceptance to
a university. "They didn't even review the application," Drew's avatar said in the rant. "The administration is speciesist. So we had to shut it down."

"The administration has a policy of not dealing
with LINK terrorists," UC-Berkeley's president
said in response. "The backup system was up and
running in a matter of hours. Meanwhile, in case
of another attack, students are encouraged—as always—to congregate in real-time classrooms. Out-
of-state professors are being flown in to accommo-
date this new development."

Some professors, however, have joined the pro-
testers. "I'm not going anywhere until the president answers the charges," said Dr. Robert
Jackson, a Berkeley professor of political science
currently residing in Colorado. "A Gorgon has
just as much right to an education as any of my
other students."

An admissions officer who asked not to be identified said, "What Mr. Drew and his rabble-rousing
colleagues have glossed over is the fact that this
Gorgon is homeless. The address on her application
is a church basement. There's no reason to believe
that she could pay for her education."

When confronted with this question at the shelter
in Los Angeles, Thoughtful laughed. She said, "I'll
be dead before I finish a four-year degree. I just
wanted to see if I could get in."

The organizer of the church admitted to helping
her get her application materials. "If she had been
accepted," said Father Bernard Pryor, "the church
was considering taking up a collection so she could
at least attend a few classes. Education is important
to Thoughtful."

Certain members of the student body not involved in the DoS set up a counterprotest. Twelve
local students carrying handmade signs in real time
painted with the slogan "The Administration Is
Right" marched on the campus. Victoria Marsh, a

first-year chemistry student, said, "What I want to know is . . . what's she going to eat?"

Thoughtful responded with a laugh that showed fangs, and said, "Students eat junk food. They wouldn't be tasty anyway."

CHAPTER 37

✤

Michael

Deidre and I found the Gorgons holed up in the Théâtre du Chatelet, a nineteenth-century playhouse that was once known for its musicals. We'd entered the building from the front, near the box office. The doors must have been open when the Medusa hit; the entryway glittered like a crystal cave. Wind sang through a glass chandelier overhead. Creeping along the wall, we made slow and steady progress toward the main theatre. We hadn't heard Amariah's voice for several minutes, but the sounds of laughter came from just beyond the ornately carved double doors.

Deidre pulled her gun from her purse. It was a Magnum .357, and its steel barrel looked huge in her hands. I thought about asking how she'd gotten the gun past airport security, but I decided I didn't really want to know. Deidre had a surprisingly sneaky streak in her, despite her law-enforcement training. I supposed that was why she made such a good private investigator.

She motioned for me to cover the door on the opposite side of the box office. I moved away from her reluctantly. After all, I didn't have a gun. The best I could do was look menacing, albeit that was something I was fairly practiced at.

At my new position, I tried the door cautiously, steeling myself for the sight of Amariah in the hands of the Gorgons. Taking a deep breath, I stuck my face to the crack in the door.

What I saw made my heart stop. Amariah, still in her black velvet dress from Passover, sat center stage. A spotlight shone on her. The rest of the theatre was bathed in darkness, as though she were putting on a show. Her feet kicked the wooden stage playfully, and a broad smile filled her cherubic face.

I blinked. Hadn't we just heard her cry out? What was going on here?

"Tell us about the angels again," a cultured voice said from somewhere deep within the row of theatre seats.

"Okay," Amariah said. "They're so beautiful, you wouldn't believe it. Most of the time they look like real people. You can't always tell who might be one of them, except for their eyes. If you look long enough you'll see . . . I don't know, a spark, like the pale blue of the center of a hot flame."

My mouth hung open. Could this really be my four-year-old girl?

"Sometimes they will show their wings, but you kind of have to make them mad or something. Each of them has different-colored wings. My father's wings are green and blue, shiny. You know, like oil on water. Oh." She stopped middescription to look right at me. She waved brightly. "Here he is. Hi, Papa!"

The houselights didn't have to be on for me to feel every head in the place turn to look at me. I let the door shut. I met Deidre halfway around the box office. Her eyes were full of the same questions in mine. "What do you suppose . . ." she started, but behind me we heard the threatre door swing open.

"Papa!" Amariah leaned out into the entryway. "Aren't you coming in? Hey!" she added brightly, seeing Deidre. "Mommy! What are you doing here?"

She ran toward us, her arms open for a hug. Deidre tucked her gun into her purse. As soon as Amariah was close, Deidre grabbed her and held her tightly. "Oh, baby, we were so worried."

The door opened again to reveal Perseus, who hung just inside the doorway and watched us curiously.

"What's happened to you?" Deidre asked, smoothing hair away from Amariah's forehead. "My God, what's wrong with your eye? Michael, come look."

I brought my flashlight around. Though I didn't point it directly in Amariah's face, I could easily see what concerned Deidre. Amariah's right eye, once blue, now reflected light like quicksilver. Some of her curls now seemed paler, though in the darkness it was difficult to tell for certain.

"It's the Medusa," Perseus said from the doorway. "She's transforming."

"We've got to get to the hospital," Deidre said desperately.

"I feel fine, Mommy," Amariah said. "Don't worry about me."

"Her growth has accelerated," Perseus said.

"This shouldn't be happening," Deidre snapped, setting Amariah down. "Only people born in the glass become Gorgons. No one has ever become one by touching it."

"Yes, I know," Perseus said calmly. "Usually people who touch the glass die a horrible, painful death. Seems your daughter has been spared."

"You weren't born a Gorgon, were you?" I asked.

"No. It's a life I chose. A gift I give your daughter."

"What are you saying?" Deidre demanded. "Are you saying you gave it to her somehow?"

The Gorgon nodded his silvery hair. "She would have died otherwise. Now she'll be forever immune."

"And die young," Deidre said, her voice catching.

"I know you can undo it," I said, remembering our previous conversation.

"Yes, I can, but I won't. Have you noticed anything different about our little Rye?"

"Don't fucking call her that," Deidre said.

"Mom! That's not appropriate."

Amariah sounded like a petulant teenager, not a four-year-old. I had always wondered how the Gorgons managed to learn to walk, much less speak, in the short time of their four- or six-year life span. Perhaps whatever it was that sped up their metabolism affected their brain capacity as well. The fact that they could communicate at all was actually a miracle, when you thought about how little time they had to grasp the complexity of language.

"What about her life span?" I asked, reaching out to tousle Amariah's hair.

"Uncertain," Perseus said. "She's only the second human to receive my gift."

"And the antidote?"

"Still in the lab."

A loud boom filled the theatre, and Perseus hit the floor, howling and grabbing his leg. Amariah held her hands to her ears and started crying.

I turned to see a smoking gun in Deidre's hand. Her eyes were hard as steel when she said, "The next shot is fatal. I'm afraid we can't accept your gift. Let's talk exchange, shall we?"

SHOTS FIRED IN THE MEDITERRANEAN

Agnostic Press (April 2083)

Washington, DC—While cruising the international waters near Israel, the U.S.S. *Abraham Lincoln* fired shots at a battleship flying a Libyan flag just hours ago. The Libyan ship sustained substantial damage, and the crew was forced to abandon ship. It is believed that the Libyan crew was rescued by Egyptian naval vessels, but reports are unconfirmed.

The captain of the *Abraham Lincoln,* Frances Hart, said that he believed the Libyans were "taunting him" by skimming just within missile range. Egyptian aircraft were spotted flying over the Mediterranean at the time of the attack, but they have not as yet returned fire.

"We know they're the ones responsible for all the crap going down in Jerusalem," said Hart. "And we're here to show them we mean business."

The president of the United States, Rabbi Chaim Grey, would not comment on whether or not the *Abraham Lincoln* had the authority to shoot first. However, as the ship is not being recalled, nor the captain publicly reprimanded, it is generally assumed the president's silence is consent.

Throughout North Africa and the Middle East today U.S. newsbot LINK signals were jammed. U.S. officials believe that this is a sign that those countries are preparing for a major offensive against Israel. As one U.S. general put it, "Magog is on the move."

With Prime Minister Avashalom Chotzner still listed in critical condition, there is a perceived "power vacuum" in Israel right now. America and her allies are preparing to fill that void. "Israel will not fall to the enemy," said John LaRoy, the defense secretary of the United States. "Even if it is prophesied. We're ready to defy Armageddon."

CHAPTER 38

※

Mouse

My roommates snore contentedly in their respective ambulance gurneys, and I'm thinking they might all have to buy me dinner or something for saving their sorry asses. I'd be feeling pretty self-satisfied, except for one thing. While doing research into Parker, I discovered some disturbing news: Thistle and I are the top suspects in the Temple Rock hijacking.

Thing is, I *know* I didn't do it. And, to be honest, I don't think Thistle had either. That leaves me with a very worried-parent feeling, especially since Dragon was just looking for Page. I chew on my lip and think through the whole thing again.

I mean, I suppose Thistle could have done it. It's not her tree-hugging style, though. Plus, one of the articles claimed she's my protégée, and I'm damn certain she'd balk at that description. She's been cracking code as long as I have. She ain't no one's student but her own.

I captured a report that showed similarities between my LINK-angel program and the few programming lines that were visible at the Temple Rock site. I've been studying it since Thistle went up front to hang with Rebeckah. Even I'm forced to admit the context looks like it came from the same perp. I could have written it easily. It's even totally my style to attack something so high-profile and politically significant.

So either I'm coding in my sleep, or someone copycatted me. Thinking through the list of my enemies, I can't think of one who has anything approaching my "f33rsome skillz." Even arrogance aside, there really isn't anyone who might want to frame me who knows enough about my style to copy it so precisely.

Except one person; that is to say, Page.

I can feel the space between my eyebrows tightening just considering the possibility. I stuff my palms into my armpits. Okay, so Page has the ability—heck, he probably couldn't help but code exactly like me, since in a weird way he is me—but that left me asking myself why? Why would Page do it?

All the news articles said that the signs at Temple Rock implied that the cybersquatter is busily building a virtual version of the third Jewish temple. Now my boy is such a good Muslim, Mohammad himself, peace be upon his name, would give Page a little nod of respect, dig? So I just can't see it. It doesn't compute.

Rene yawns and rolls over. He scratches his nose, and his eyes flicker open. I scowl at him and try to send "go back to sleep, I want to think," mindwaves at him. My attempt at telepathy seems to work, as he snuggles deeper under the white sheet.

I rest my head against the wall of the ambulance. Through the thin door I can hear voices, low and comforting. Thistle is totally gay, which kind of bums me out because she's pretty hot for a geek chick. I comfort myself with the thought that if Thistle can fall for someone as masculine as Rebeckah, she might also groove on someone as, uh, occasionally beta male as myself. I have been told I have very feminine eyelashes.

But back to Page and the whole Temple Rock mess: I remember Page telling me that he went to visit the site right after he heard about the meteor that crashed into the Dome of the Rock in real time. I'd chided him for being too political. I mean, we're all supposed to be pointing toward Mecca when we pray, not the Dome of the Rock. So why make a special trip to the virtual node, unless you're trying to say something in-your-face, like, "This space is ours, stay off the Dome"?

That's pretty convoluted, but then Page isn't what you'd call an intellectual slouch. I mean, suppose he could have hacked the place to make it look like some Zionists took it over, just so that he could rally Muslim forces around the world. After all, in real time the Israelis had reoccupied the area they called Temple Mount, where the mosque had stood. If it seemed like the virtual space was also denied to Muslims by Jewish interests, that could be a fairly, shall we say, motivating force. Muslims would band together against Israel. Actually there was no question about it: that's exactly what's happening. My country of origin has called for a jihad to liberate the Dome . . . the world is spiraling into chaos, divided between Jew and Muslim.

Perfect time for Page to jump in and do something cool and proclaim himself as a kind of Muslim savior. Except that last part sounds much more like something I'd hatch instead of Page. From what I've read, he's been avoiding the whole savior thing. And, if he was going to do it, he should be playing it up. Making speeches, denouncing Jews, something to keep the spotlight focused on him. Instead he's disappeared.

Well, there is one person I could ask.

Shutting my eyes, I sniff around for Inquisitors before I open mouse.net. I don't doubt they're hot on our trail, but for now I find no sign of them. *"Psst,"* I send to the yakuza headquarters. *"You there, Dragon?"*

"Page?"

"No, Mouse." Even the dragon can't always tell the difference between my on-line presence and my AI. *"Say, what has Page been doing lately?"*

A landscape appears in my mind's eye. I stand on the sandy shore of a mist-shrouded river. The wind that slides past my cheek is cold and wet, and carries the faintest smell of rotting fish. Bamboo groves dot the far shore. Hovering just above the dark water, two golden sparks glow.

I give the dragon the thumbs-up. *"Very nicely done,"* I say, nodding at the details in the landscape. She's even written in insects that bite at my ankles.

She nods her head in a shallow bow of acknowledgment.

"Page is still missing." The dragon's voice escapes in a hiss, like the wind. *"This one fears the worst."*

"Yeah," I say, crouching down to run my finger through the sandy mud of the shore: wet and gritty, but a little off, like all the grains of sand are perfectly round. *"That's what you said. Why do you think he might be dead?"*

"Victory nearly killed this one. For a copy, she is very clever."

"Victory," I repeat. That word had just come in very handy for me. I'd forgotten that's what the copy called herself. *"That's weird, isn't it?"*

"What is?" the dragon asks.

"How Victory seems everywhere right now." The cool wind rustles through the bamboo leaves. *"Hey, do you happen to know if Victory is Muslim?"*

"This one hasn't had extended conversations with her. Nor does she want to."

I find myself smiling a little. *"You don't like Victory much."*

The eyes disappear under the water. Then her head surfaces closer to the shore, sending a wave crashing against my knees. I back up. *"Did this one not say that the copy attempted to murder her?"*

"I guess you did," I agree. *"You didn't say why."*

"She is responsible for Mai's death."

"I thought that honor belonged to Page."

The dragon sniffs. *"No. It was the size of the copy that overloaded Mai's net during the transfer to the Inquisitor."*

I felt an unformed hunch bubbling around the edges of my brain.

"Where was Page when you last saw him?" I call out over the dark river.

"A Chinese restaurant." Her voice sounds distant, as though she's moving away. I call after her, but the interface ends abruptly, and I'm back in the ambulance. I open my eyes to see Rene's armpit. He's reaching over my head to rummage through the cabinets. "What are you doing?" I ask, giving him a little shove.

"Looking for food. I'm starving."

The van jerks to a stop, and he nearly falls into me. "Get

off me, you oaf," I'm shouting when the Inquisition rips
the door off.

PARAMILITARY FORCE CLAIMS
RESPONSIBILITY FOR CHOTZNER'S
ATTACK

Agnostic Press (April 2083)

Jerusalem, Israel—A paramilitary organization
calling itself "Tribulation Team" claims responsibility for the assassination attempt of Israel's prime
minister, Avashalom Chotzner, who is still listed in
critical condition after receiving a gunshot wound
to the head. Tribulation Team says that it is a fundamentalist Christian organization determined to discover the identity of the Antichrist.

"The Muslim Brotherhood's statement had to be
acted upon," said Tribulation Team's leader, speaking via the LINK through heavy encryption. "If
Chotzner dies, he's not the Antichrist. If he lives,
Christians everywhere will know the truth."

Certain Christians believe that the Antichrist will
be a political leader who will miraculously survive
being shot in the head. They take this idea from a
reference in Revelation 13:3. The New International Version reads, "One of the heads of the
beast [Antichrist] seemed to have had a fatal
wound, but the fatal wound had been healed. The
whole world was astonished and followed the
beast."

Some say that the Tribulation Team's methods
are reminiscent of the medieval test for a witch.
"They tied a woman up and put her in a sack. If
she drowned, she was innocent. If she lived, they
burned her at the stake," said Anton Pinski, of the
Jewish Order of the Inquisition. "If Chotzner dies,

he's innocent. That means this Tribulation Team just killed an innocent man."

Tribulation Team's leader did not respond directly to these accusations, instead saying, "This is the final battle. Christians must be willing to take drastic measures."

CHAPTER 39

❖

Rebeckah

"Bloody fucking hell on cops," Thistle said as another squad car squealed to a halt in front of the ambulance. Thistle had taken over driving, but had been silent while I cried. Now that police cars surrounded us she had a lot to say. "Bugger it all anyway."

Wiping my eyes on my sleeve, I watched as outside the window a dozen or more uniforms drew their guns and crouched behind bulletproofed squad doors. I gave a little defeated laugh. "Looks bad for our team."

"Yeah," Thistle said, turning off the engine. Behind us we could hear the sound of the back doors being broken into. Meanwhile, the cops watching us kept their guns trained on us.

"No lockdown," Thistle said, tapping her LINK receiver as if she were pounding out a glitch. "I wonder why not."

There were also no orders to surrender, not on loudspeaker nor over the LINK. It seemed suspicious to me, so I reached over and locked my door. A crack startled me, and I looked over to see a starburst pattern on the windshield inches from Thistle's surprised face. I pulled her down under the dashboard. Above we heard more slaps and pops of bullets hitting the reinforced glass and steel.

"Are they shooting at us?" Thistle seemed genuinely surprised.

"It's a setup," I said. "A coverup. Something."

"A coverup of what?" Thistle's voice broke when glass shattered over her head.

"I don't know," I said. "It doesn't make any sense."

"Well, no doubt it's all about whatever it is you've supposedly done," Thistle said, reaching above me to pop open the glove compartment.

Thistle seemed so flustered that I decided this was not the time to point out that the Inquisition was actually out to get her. "What are you looking for?" I asked.

"A weapon," she said. Not finding anything in the glove compartment, she checked under the seats.

There were far too many of them, and pretty soon they'd be coming through the back door as well. I shook my head. "A weapon isn't going to do us any good," I said.

"Sure it is," she said. "You're a crack shot, aren't you?"

"Oh, I see. Two minutes ago you gave me grief about my politics. Now you want *me* to shoot at the cops."

"Well, I can't. I'm a vegetarian."

I shook my head and laughed. "And I'm done with killing."

"Shame, that," she said, carefully removing something from under the driver's seat. "Because it looks like we've got ourselves a little defense."

The gun was in a leather holster. Thistle held it out in her hands as if offering me a hors d'oeuvres tray. I had to admit the gun was sweet. It was a flechette pistol with combat sights, Israeli make, no less. My hand fit perfectly around the grip.

"What are the chances?" Thistle said.

I frowned at the gun in my hand. What *were* the chances? Finding a gun here, right when we needed it the most, was a miracle. I thought about what Mouse had said, about how he thought that God had stacked the deck in my favor. Moving automatically through the drill, I checked the gun over. Well oiled, fully loaded clip . . . I'd believe it was a plant, except that there was no way Parker or any of the cops could have known which ambulance Mouse and I would end up commandeering . . . unless the escape had been "allowed" the same way I'd been "free" to lead them right to Thistle.

Even so, the gun was a gift from God, a way out of a hopeless situation.

Only it would mean killing again, and again, and again.

My resolve wavered, and even as I looked down the sights, I felt a shiver run through the muscles of my arm. Could this really be what God wanted?

"What are you waiting for?" Thistle said, hunching in the well beneath the dashboard. "Let's do it."

"Put it away," I said, though I still held the gun steady, and I made no move to offer it to her. "Let's surrender."

"Are you crazy?" Thistle asked. "They're not interested in surrender, or they would have asked us to."

I frowned. Right. The only way out was to fight our way out. I crawled up onto the seat, careful not to expose any part of my body to the cops outside. Glancing over the dashboard, I took aim at the nearest cop. I had a perfect shot lined up. I could pop him right between the eyes. He wouldn't feel a thing. My finger tightened on the trigger.

A daisy petal drifted across the hood of the ambulance. Soft curves caught the light of the spots the squad cars had pointed at us. I'd told Mouse that I regretted that day in Jerusalem. I'd said that sometimes it was best not to take the shot.

I left the gun on the dash and crawled back to my hidey-hole. "We're going to die," I told Thistle. "Maybe you should make your peace."

"Have you lost your mind?" Thistle shouted over the sound of gunfire.

I sighed. "Yeah, probably."

"Are you trying to say you'd rather die than defend yourself? Look, I take back everything I said about pacifism being good and all that. You know, there's a place in this world for people like you. So go do your duty. . . . Oh, fucking crap." Thistle stared over my shoulder at the passenger-side window and slowly raised her hands.

I glanced over to see the cop I'd had a perfect shot at. He raised his weapon and fired it at the safety glass point-blank. Shards of glass rained on my head. Thistle screamed. With barely a conscious thought, my hand reached up and grabbed the gun still resting on the dash above me.

I had it pointed at him before he could take aim again. The explosion was deafening. The odor of gunpowder assaulted my nose, and the metallic taste of blood filled my mouth. Something warm and wet spread along the space under my armpit. Breathing became difficult. Thistle's shouts grew louder and more frantic.

Realization filtered through my senses with a strange slowness. My hand still held the Israeli gun, but my finger rested along the barrel like I never intended to shoot him. Though my thumb rested on it, at the ready, the safety remained in the locked position.

I heard another shot, and Thistle's screaming stopped abruptly. *Kill him,* I told myself: *you have nothing to lose.* But that wasn't true, was it? Would I go to my death with more blood on my hands—the blood of a man just doing his job, a job he had little control over? So instead I let the gun drop. It bounced once against the leather seat and then disappeared in a flutter of white feathers. I heard the cry of a dove, and then nothing beyond a roar in my ears. The sound started far away, and then rushed over me like a wave, consuming me.

My perspective expanded. All at once I could see the ambulance from above. A bird's-eye view revealed cops in heavy riot gear all around. The cop who shot Thistle and me stepped away from the window and turned to join the others at the rear. From the back of the vehicle they dragged out Mouse and the others, and forced them to their knees with their hands on their heads.

Standing a ways back from it all was Parker. He rested languidly against the hood of a squad car, arms crossed in front of his chest, and his eyes shut tight so as not to record the scene of planned destruction. I felt I could read his mind in his calm expression: it would be declared an unfortunate event, suspects killed while trying to flee.

A policeman stood behind Rene and pulled the trigger of his gun. Blood sprayed on the asphalt. The others jumped when his body hit the ground. Mouse tried to get up when another cop grabbed him and pushed him to the ground. I heard the sound of him begging Allah to have mercy on his soul. I could see the gun at the back of Mouse's head.

No.

Mouse turned his head and kicked just as I saw the muzzle flash. For a second I couldn't see anything other than a struggle. Then Mouse scrambled from his captors and ran. Another shot rang out. A second before Mouse fell, I thought I saw a curved blade slide out from the shadows to deflect the bullet. The bullet meant for his back ricocheted into a tree. But even so, Mouse stumbled, clutching just above his heart. He landed in the grass of a ditch and moved no more.

Rhianna died last, and then everything was quiet. No one looked at the bodies, and they shuffled around nervously as though lost without further orders. Parker stepped away from the car. With his eyes still shut, he pulled out gloves and carefully put them on. Then he produced a gun from his jacket. Shots rang out. Cops, taken by surprise, fell. A few returned fire, but Parker's blind aim was uncanny. Soon he was the only one standing. He dropped the gun near Mouse's outstretched hand, got inside the car, and drove away.

My mind's eye followed Parker as he drove down the road. He hummed a hymn as the car, set to automatic, sped away from the scene. A mile or so away he opened his eyes suddenly, and the car made a turn. Somehow I heard him log his position on the LINK and report the suspicious sound of gunfire in the distance.

Meanwhile, in the grass of the ditch, Mouse stirred. He coughed and struggled to his feet.

Run.

Mouse cocked his head as though he heard my warning. But instead of disappearing into the woods, like I prayed he would, he moved toward the ambulance. He opened the driver-side door, and I heard him whimper, "Holy shit."

Gently he moved Thistle's body aside and, closing up the door, he turned the keys that Thistle had left in the ignition. The engine coughed to life. He glanced at me, and suddenly I felt myself returning to my own body.

"Parker is coming back," I managed to say.

Mouse looked startled at the sound of my voice, but nodded his head. I could feel the ambulance bump and bounce on its shocks as he maneuvered us around the squad cars that had blocked our way. "Yeah, I suppose he would be. The guy's unstoppable," Mouse said, "but we have to get you to a hospital. The hospital is back the way we came."

I could hear sirens approaching. My sharp intake of

breath sent me into a coughing fit, but strangely I still felt no pain.

"The others are dead," he said, his voice a whisper. "Everybody."

With effort I pulled myself up on the blood-and-glass-covered seats. Wind roared through the broken windshield as Mouse accelerated down the road. I turned my attention to Thistle. Blood soaked her T-shirt, and her skin felt clammy as I searched desperately for a pulse. A faint but steady beat thrummed at her throat. "Thistle is alive," I said. "So far."

Mouse hit the sirens and screamed past Parker's car. Our eyes seemed to meet for a second as he passed us. I could see the horror in his expression as he seemed to read mine.

CHOTZNER RECOVERS

Many Rejoice; Others Fear Prophecy

Agnostic Press (April 2083)

Jerusalem, Israel—Doctors announced that Israel's prime minister, Avashalom Chotzner, is expected to make a full recovery from the head wound he received during the recent assassination attempt on his life. News of the prime minister's health received mixed reactions around the world. After the last few days of riots, there was tempered and quiet celebration in the streets of Jerusalem. In the U.S. and other Christian nations, certain ultraconservative factions reacted with fear.

"It's just as it is written," said a member of the paramilitary group Tribulation Team, who have claimed responsibility for the attack on the prime minister. "The Antichrist is wounded, but yet lives."

Again, the prophecy these fundamentalist Christians fear comes from the book of Revelation 13:3.

The King James version reads, "And I saw one of his heads as it were wounded to death; and his deadly wound was healed: and all the world wondered after the beast."

Indeed, all the world is wondering after Chotzner's miraculous recovery. Even those who do not believe in the Christian Bible or its prophecies are watching with bated breath to see how the rest of the world will react.

"It looks bad," one U.S. government official said. "The smartest move Chotzner could make would be to resign."

CHAPTER 40

✠

Page

The darkness is now absolute. The combat computer, the parts that are physically attached to the body, anyway, are dead, locked-down several years ago on special order from the pope. Though I can't tell for sure, I imagine the body must have stumbled, unable to walk.

Groping for the door, I feel the familiar repulsion. Then the featherlight touch of the nanospider crawls across my skin.

Victory locked me in. What can be done, can normally be undone . . . except for the darkness. It represents a lack of power, a shutdown, zero, off.

And yet enough of me still functions that I can think, that I can be afraid. Strangely, that gives me hope. That means there must be power somewhere. If I can find it, I might be able to reverse whatever algorithm Victory put on the door that the nanobots so diligently continue to widen.

My fingers brush the cold and slimy walls, and I begin to feel my way.

The nexus, when I find it, glows a pale purple. Enough power to keep the body's involuntary functions operating pulses lethargically through the honeycombed globe. Emmaline breathes. Blood circulates. But she cannot see, cannot hear; like me, she is trapped in a terrible blackness.

I touch the nexus lightly, and once again it seizes me. This time, however, I surrender to its desperate demands.

I don't fight it when it reaches in to delete parts. Though I want to scream—to stop the strangling, the choking—I force my fists to unclench, to let go. The combat computer rewrites part of itself on top of me. I can feel the exoskeleton, heavy and powerful, penetrating my consciousness. A thousand tendrils, like snakes, bury themselves within me. Making space for themselves by destroying parts of me. The darkness is burned from me, like fire.

We are not surprised to find our face pressing into the cobblestone or see the concerned look in Morningstar's chestnut eyes. His silken auburn hair is bound in a ponytail at the nape of his neck, but his brows are creased, worry lines straining his handsome face.

"That was a short one," he says, offering us an arm up. We take it, even though we are more than strong enough to lift ourselves, now that we are together, whole.

"I thought maybe Michael fixed you," he says, helping us dust mud from our knees and arms.

"Yeah," we say. "It's the damn nanobots. They perceive any nonprogrammed change as damage. That's why we need a techie, like Mouse, who can go in there and reformat things. But Michael did something. . . ."

He torched our LINK receptors. Closed all doors, I supply. *At least to me.*

Victory?

We pause. Our heart skips, anxiously waiting for an answer.

No, I say. *Not Victory.*

But who—or what—then?

That, I do not know.

Where's Victory? The body, Emmaline, wants to know.

Off killing chaos, I expect, I say.

"Oh." Emmaline breathes a sigh of relief. "That's good." Morningstar frowns at her. "What's going on?"

We start walking. The eyes see a broad boulevard, lined with rows of shops. The metal is transformed into a soft gray by the lights mounted on lampposts. Trees, with buds just beginning to open, dot the sidewalk. Ahead, seeming to rise out of the middle of a tangle of traffic, is the imposing rose-and-white marble of the Arc de Triomphe.

We breathe in moist, cool air tinged with the taste of

exhaust and carrying the smell of too many bodies in a small space. Tourists pass on either side of us. Some travel in clumps, like an excited but harmless pack of yapping dogs. While others, like us, hold hands with a lover and gaze more at each other than the sights of the Champs d'Elysées.

"At first I thought maybe Victory had gotten corrupted or something. She doesn't want to be called Victory anymore, so I thought something had happened. But now I think maybe Michael's miracle may have spit her in two. One part is out attending to business, and the other is here."

We are not Victory. We were Page.

I can feel Emmaline's face scrunch up with thought. "Or," she says to Morningstar, "I get the sense that maybe somehow the original Page program volunteered for the job."

Minding the store. Until we can fix the door.

Are you sure you're not Victory? You sound a lot like her.

If I am anything to you, I am Strife.

To my surprise, the body smiles. *Yes. I like that.*

I expect a different response, and her reaction irritates me. So I brood quietly and concentrate on finding a way around Victory's locks on the LINK receptor.

Morningstar wraps his hand more tightly around ours. His palms are smooth and warm. "Whatever, darling," he says, his lips brushing our cheek. "It's good to see you smile. And I'm glad to have you back for a while." His breath is hot against our throat as he nuzzles us.

"Maybe," he purrs, "we should take advantage of the situation."

His wolfish grin sparks a tingling sensation along our skin, which rushes down deeper, to more private parts. But we shake our head. "We should find the girl. That one you told me about . . . Michael's daughter. She could be a threat."

Beside us, we hear the whisper of Morningstar's sigh. "God is rarely as predictable as we would like Him to be."

"Yet He seems to be playing along nicely," Emmaline says. "The meteorite was a godsend." She laughs lightly at her own joke. Morningstar is quiet.

"I know," Morningstar finally says, his expression troubled. "It feels like a trap. I fear I may be doing Their work again somehow."

We let go of his hand to run a finger along his clenched jaw. "Well, when you think about it, darling, this whole thing is 'Their work.' Unless we find a way around it, I'm going to be the biggest *tool* since Judas. We have to find a way to keep any power we seize. Perhaps . . . we could take over the education of Michael's child. Or, failing that, destroy her."

Morningstar turns to watch a woman in a short skirt go by. We reach out and tug his ponytail slightly. He glances at us. "Yes, but that only works if the child is the messiah, after all. I've been through this many times before. The world doesn't always end when you expect it to."

We tense, disbelieving. "But all the signs—"

"Are artifices, some of which we helped create. My darling one, there are well over ten billion people in the world. Only a tiny fragment of them are Evangelical Christians. What makes you think their version of the end is the right one? When I found you, I was looking for Dajjal, the Great Deceiver. There are many more Muslims than there are Christians. Perhaps we should be attempting to enter Mecca."

Yes. I remember you, Iblis.

We shrug our shoulders. "I tried that and was repelled, just as prophesied."

"Yes, and things didn't play out to the endgame, did they, darling?"

We chew on our bottom lip. "But your God has always favored the Jews."

He laughs. "Yes, I suppose it seems so. Though I've been thinking, if this one doesn't pan out, maybe we should try to cause Ragnarok."

"Or maybe I can play Shiva," we say, and join into the laughter, as though this is an old joke. Meanwhile, I have found Victory's key and am decrypting it. In a moment we shall be free.

Our fingers run idly along a stylized park bench. Cast iron, it is painted with wild, bright colors. We think, perhaps, it may be masquerading as public art.

We should, I command, *sit down.*
"Oh, shit," Emmaline says. "I'm going to crash."
"Again?"

The door is small, but I push myself through. As I go, I feel something tear; something of me stays behind. I think little of it, tasting freedom . . . and revenge.

CHOTZNER WON'T RETIRE

Says He'll Beat Antichrist Rap

Agnostic Press (April 2083)

Jerusalem, Israel—Israel's prime minister resumed office today over protests from some members of Christendom. He was sighted walking down the streets with a white bandage wrapping his head, shaking hands with people as he strolled to his office. Chotzner had a minimal security detail with him because he said he wanted to show the world he was not afraid.

"This Antichrist stuff is a bunch of crap," Chotzner said. "The bullet wound was glancing, not fatal. I'll barely have a scar when they take these bandages off."

Staff at the hospital Chotzner was taken to disagree. One doctor who asked not to be named, although who did identify himself as Christian, said, "He was in intensive care. It's not a scratch; that's for damn sure."

Christendom adviser Carl Ivans thinks Chotzner is making a mistake. "Returning to office looks like a bid for power. Very Antichrist-like."

CHAPTER 41

✵

Michael

Amariah let me carry her as we followed a limping, cursing Perseus back to his "lab." Deidre, still in her environmental suit, held her gun near Perseus's torso, while Amariah and I trailed several paces behind. As we passed by them, Gorgons joined in behind me, becoming a kind of ghostly parade. Amariah sat on my shoulders, horseyback style, and commented on the passing scenery.

"Perseus told me that the old lady of Paris is somewhere down this street," she said.

"Who's that?"

"A lady who got trapped inside an apartment when the bomb hit. She starved to death. They say her skeleton still looks out the window."

I laughed lightly. "A ghost story."

"It's true, Papa. Just like you're really an angel."

My boots squelched along the slippery and uneven glassed cobblestone. "Your papa might not be an angel anymore, Rye," I said.

I could almost feel the intensity of Amariah's gaze on the top of my head. "Papa, I saw your wings. They were so pretty and so bright my eyes watered."

"I think I've changed," I said, reaching up to squeeze her bare knee with my gloved hand.

We came to a corner and turned left, heading back across the Seine. I could hear the deep hum of traffic on the cool evening breeze.

"Oh, like the virus changed me," Amariah said. "I guess that's good then."

For a while we continued in silence down the grand Boulevard du Palais, passing the former royal palace that later housed the headquarters of France's crime-investigation headquarters. Above loomed the gothic spire of Sainte Chapelle, cleverly spotlighted from the inside by the Parisian tourist board to highlight its complex stained glass so as to cast brightly colored chips of light at our feet.

Supported by another Gorgon, Perseus continued to lead us across Pont St. Michel, a bridge dedicated to me. It ended in a famous fountain that artfully depicted me flinging Morningstar into the waters of a pool. For some reason my statue had long been a favorite hangout for teenagers and Sorbonne students. But before reaching the fountain we turned right into the quay. The Gorgons who had been following me stopped before crossing the bridge, as though unable or unwilling to pass into a place without glass. We stopped in front of a building which, though not glassed, was abandoned due to its proximity to the Medusa. Above the door, in English, were the words, SHAKESPEARE AND COMPANY.

"It was a bookstore," he said with a sigh. "Now it's my home."

"Mommy likes books," Amariah said cheerfully. "Especially ones with naked people on the cover."

"Half-naked," Deidre corrected with a little smile. Then, apparently feeling the need to explain her reading predilection to her captive, she said to Perseus, "I like romances, okay?"

"I have some of those," he said, though his face was twisted in pain from the gunshot.

"We're not here to shop for books," Deidre reminded him with a little jab of her gun. "We're here so you can fix Amariah."

Perseus stopped with his hand on the doorknob. "It's very dangerous, this reversal. It works on birds, but I've never really tried it on a human."

"Birds?" I asked.

Perseus shrugged. "When they try to roost on the glass they get caught. The ones we don't eat, I experiment on."

"Sick," Deidre said with a sneer.

Perseus frowned. "Not really. The reversal usually helps them gain back limbs they might have otherwise lost."

"Fine," Deidre said. "Let's get a move on."

Before Deidre could follow Perseus through the door, I grabbed her elbow. "I don't know about this," I said. "Amariah seems fine. What if the reversal makes things worse?"

Deidre looked up at Amariah, who rested her chin on the crown of my head.

"I'm willing to take the chance," she said, her voice breaking. "Gorgons don't . . . they don't live very long, Michael."

"I know, Deidre, but—"

"Do you have a better suggestion? Maybe a neat little miracle to help us out?"

A miracle. Earlier, when I put my hands on Emmaline, I felt the old fire coursing through my veins. To tap into the fabric of creation in order to change its course, however, would be a bigger feat than a little healing energy. I would need the full cooperation of the universe, which meant God. It seemed I'd come full circle. I'd started this whole sordid affair in order to keep Amariah and myself from returning to God. Now I might face the prospect of surrendering myself to God in order to save her life.

Could I do it? The most selfless act?

In order to hide my fear and shame from Deidre's eyes, I looked at the leathery white substance of the armored boots I wore. "Let's see if Perseus can help us," I said.

The ground floor of the shop was a maze of paper and wood. Rows of yellowing hard copies lined oak bookcases packed together into narrow hallways. The effect was a kind of chaotic neatness: the wild colors of various titles of books of different sizes all contained and alphabetized by author inside each shelf. I found myself wanting to explore, but Deidre pulled me along to where Perseus sat on a bright purple couch in the back. The rear of the store may have once been a "conversation nook," but it was now clearly where Perseus lived. A plastic potted plant had been set to one side of the couch; on the other, a tall floor lamp illuminated a ghastly tableau. On the table in front of Perseus lay a myriad of syringes and vials. If he hadn't claimed to be a scientist, I would have mistaken this paraphernalia for that of a drug addict.

"Bring her here," Perseus said, holding up a needle filled with bright red liquid.

"Are you sure that's safe?" I said as I reached up to help Amariah clamber off of me.

"Of course it's not. I told you that," Perseus said.

"I don't want a shot," Amariah said, grabbing onto a fistful of my hair. "No, Papa. I don't want to!"

Deidre came around to help me try to untangle Amariah from my throat and head. I lost a little hair, but we got her to the ground, where she promptly dashed off at a sprint to disappear between the bookcases.

"Amariah!" Deidre shouted, chasing after her. "Get back here."

"Perhaps you should respect the girl's wishes," Perseus said to me, leaning back into his couch. With a groan he lifted his injured leg onto the table, scattering needles and bottles onto the floor. The bullet hole had made an ugly red smear on his white pant leg.

"Are you all right?" I asked, noticing the grimace on his face as he leaned in to inspect the wound.

"No worse than you, it seems," he said, nodding at my torn and bloody shirt. "Does she do this to all her men, I wonder?"

Before I could respond, Deidre came back with a frightened and wailing Amariah under her arm. The gun, I noticed, had been returned to its place in her purse.

"Okay," Deidre said resolutely. "Let's do it."

After holding it up to the light and testing the needle for bubbles, Perseus offered the syringe to me. "I insist." He smiled. "Inject it anywhere. Muscle is fine."

I took it from him. To Deidre, I said, "Are you sure?"

"Michael, I can't hold her forever. It might be her only hope."

Or it could kill her, I thought silently as I jabbed the needle right through her velvet Passover dress into the soft flesh of her behind. I depressed the plunger with gritted teeth and prayed for a miracle.

God, however, apparently had other plans, because Amariah's cries stopped almost a second after I removed the needle from her backside. Instead she began making choking noises. When Deidre released her, Amariah's face had grown pale and clammy.

"My God," Deidre cried. "What's happening?"

"Looks like cardiac arrest," said Perseus from where he sat on his couch. "Oops."

"STOP THE MADNESS," SAYS EAST

"Stand Down or Peacekeeping Troops Will Be Sent"

Agnostic Press (April 2083)

New York, New York—Staging a LINK meeting at the site of the former United Nations Building in New York, representatives from the East, a political federation of Asian religions, have asked Christendom, Islam, and Israel to relax the mounting tension in the Middle East.

"This is just madness," said the president of India. "If the world doesn't calm down, we will be forced to send peacekeeping forces into the area."

The threat of peacekeepers has irritated all sides of this as-yet-undeclared war. "Israel is a sovereign nation," said Israel's prime minister, Avashalom Chotzner, who is still recovering from a head wound sustained during an assassination attempt. "Any troops attempting to invade her will be seen as a violation of the Magog Defense Treaty."

"I hate this word Magog," said China's president Hun Xang. "It makes no sense to me. None of this makes any sense. It's time for the West to realize that a humongous majority of the people in the world do not believe in any of this Christ/Antichrist stuff. Let them ask themselves: If God made everything, why did He populate with world with so many non-Christians? Could it be that the higher power is, in fact, also not Christian?"

Christian and Jewish leaders were quick to point out that their god seems to prefer the underdog, having picked a small tribe of Israelites to lead around the wilderness. The Muslim Inquisition, meanwhile, pointed out that if God is the religion of the masses, they've got a pretty good shot at being right, as nearly one in every four people in the world is Muslim.

CHAPTER 42

❖

Mouse

The air screams through the broken windshield, and my brain joins in with its own mantra: *ohshitohshitohshit.* It'd be kind of Zen, if the splatters of Rhianna's blood weren't drying on my face.

"What the fuck happened back there?" I shout to be heard over the whistling wind, but also because gunshots ring in my ears. "What the fuck was that all about? That was a fucking bloodbath, is what it was. It makes no fucking sense, though. I mean, what the fuck happened back there?"

Fuck is a funny word. I once looked it up in the Random House Unabridged and laughed at the description of a "fuckup" as a "habitual bungler." But the word itself has a potent dark magic. Its power is based, I imagine, in its simple rhythm, its near-perfect combination of all the hard, coarse sounds in the English language. It has the onomatopoeia of expulsion and resistance all at once.

And if Rebeckah doesn't respond soon, I'm going to say it again and again and again and again, until I start to feel human once more.

"She's dying, Mouse," is what she gives me. "Thistle is dying. I did the right thing, but she's dying anyway."

What else can I say?

"Fuck."

I attempt to push the gas pedal further into the floor,

and my hands squeeze the wheel until they hurt, as if by threatening to wring the life out of the steering wheel, I can convince it to go faster. Instead I feel an almost imperceptible slowing. I glance at the dash. The gauge reads nearly empty. We've been driving too long off the grid. We're running out of fuel.

"Fuck."

Especially since I thought I saw the murderous Parker pass us on the road a while back. He'd had, I recall, the nerve to look surprised, like he never saw the hell he had wrought. Of course, he hadn't. He'd had his eyes squeezed shut. He never saw the blood that burst from Rene's head like a split watermelon. No, that image is forever burned behind my eyelids.

"Fuck."

When the ambulance coughs and sputters so that Rebeckah notices our degrading speed, I position the vehicle over the third rail. "I have to de-ghost us," I say. "So traffic control can put us back on automatic. I don't know the way to the hospital and we're running out of gas."

She nods, like a commander accepting a junior officer's decision. I press the engage button, and . . . almost make the biggest mistake of my life.

"Fuck. No can do. Inquisition has probably gone ahunting on the LINK for us by now. Unless you want me deep in lockdown—"

"Do it," she growls. "She needs to get to a hospital."

I look back to where Thistle lies cradled in Rebeckah's lap. She already looks dead. Blood soaks her T-shirt so much that I'm not even sure where the wound is, except that Rebeckah's hands press down hard on a spot just below Thistle's collarbone. Rebeckah doesn't look much better. Her skin is a sickish gray color, and she has a matching red stain creeping outward from under her armpit.

Though I can hear the third rail crackling beneath us, the ambulance continues coasting to a stop. Until traffic control gets the right signal from us, it won't completely engage the rail. One of us needs to undo my spoof. I briefly entertain the idea of trying to convince Rebeckah that I can talk her through it, since she's in such rough shape herself that a coma might do her some good. But then I remember what a mundane she is when it comes to tech.

"Okay, then. It's decided," I say, running a hand through my hair. My fingers come back slick with sweat, and fear almost makes me hesitate again. I take a deep breath. "But if they take me out before I de-ghost us, you're flying blind. You sure you're up to steering this thing if I go?"

"Yes," she says so resolutely that I actually believe her despite the strain on her face.

"Then, luckily for you, I'm feeling heroic."

One final deep breath, like a swimmer plunging under water, and I'm in. Fortunately I don't have much to do. Destruction is always faster than construction. Some wizards would have built themselves a back door that would automatically shut down their script with a clever password like *boo*. My philosophy is: any weakness can be exploited, including my own. So, no easy way out for me . . . hell, I guess that's the story of my life.

Even so, it's only about a half a minute before traffic control recognizes the ambulance signal, like a watchful mother spotting a child across the room who has gotten itself into trouble. I can almost feel the gentle pull welcoming the ambulance back into the fold. Control will return the ambulance to its hospital on the double. In real time, the increase in speed pushes my head back against the seat.

Still in the LINK, I'm just resetting my own internal defenses when Parker's avatar comes up behind me. My hair-trigger proximity alarm blares like a claxon.

I'm disturbed, however, by how quickly Parker shuts it down. After all, I'm closer; it's in *my* head.

That's when I figure I'm already on ice. Somewhere, up in the real world, my body spazzes and hits the steering wheel like a sack of rice. I'm probably pissing my pants, maybe even letting loose something worse. A better man might have warned Rebeckah about that little side-effect. Hopefully she'll realize I'm not dead. At least the ambulance is on recall. She can just hold Thistle tightly all the way home, and I go out a hero.

Go, me.

I'm only a little surprised to still be forming conscious thoughts. Of course, I've never been caught before, not by the cops, not like this, not locked-down. And it occurs to me that the LINK connection may actually have to stay open during a lockdown, or at least stay functioning. Otherwise it would just be like a hard-boot off the line: painful, but no damage done. I guess I thought maybe my brain would just be doing loop-the-loops, running some kind of filler program that paralyzed my body into a drooling stupor.

So maybe I'm not completely out yet.

Testing the waters, I try to open my eyes. I can almost feel the fluttering of my eyelids before the sensation of a gloved hand presses down on them, dropping my consciousness deeper, back into ether-space.

When his hand leaves my face, I get my first good look at his. Though I hadn't thought it possible, Parker appears more frightening on-line. Some people just dig ghoulish avatars, but those are usually the same folks who have roses and crossbones tattooed somewhere on their bodies. I would expect an Inquisitor to, I don't know, uphold the dignity of his rank . . . or at least look approachable in a police-officer sort of way.

Parker's face, if you can call it that, is milky, almost translucent. Underneath his skin I can see the shadow of the cyborg. Biosteel grafted to bone during the change glitters like an animated skull. Individual teeth and dark eye sockets menace on top of the broad shoulders clothed in the black armor of the Inquisitor.

I'm tempted to utter my epithet *du jour,* but I opt for something more articulate, albeit a bit clichéd: *"We meet again."*

"We left you for dead."

Parker's voice sounds strange to me. Perhaps it's just the lack of an accent, but then Inquisitors can adopt whatever accent or language they want. *"So you did,"* I say. *"Bad call. Don't you ever watch horror vids, man? It's always best to double-check that the body's dead before you walk away. Kind of hard with your eyes closed, though, eh?"*

"Our eyes are always open. We see everything."

I wonder at that. I mean, for a guy with his eyes screwed shut Parker was one hell of a marksman. How could he have known where everyone was once the shooting started and people scattered? Unless . . . *"You piggybacked on their LINK. You used their own eyes to kill them."* I can't help it; the pure horror of the idea squeezes it out: *"Fuck."*

"You pose a problem for us. We must be rid of you. You know too much."

I'd been afraid I'd tipped the Inquisition off when I went searching for a password to unlock Thistle and the others. All that blood is on my hands.

"Fuck."

Though I feel disconnected, Parker continues: *"We are going to have to crash traffic control once you're in the city. But you walked away from a bullet in the back. You may walk away from an accident as well. How can we be certain to kill you?"*

Chas. Rhianna. Rene. All dead because of me.

"We will use another Inquisitor. With a gun. To meet you at the hospital. And check the body this time. But there is no other in Paris besides Emmaline."

Emmaline? The rogue Inquisitor? What the hell is Parker talking about?

"It is an acceptable risk. We will use Emmaline. We will return to the body."

The rush of an epiphany—the feeling of being lifted up and suddenly perceiving both the forest and the trees—hits me a second before everything goes whacked. Like a strobelight flash of ultrafast images, the lockdown mesmerizes me, until all I can do is drool.

GRAND INQUISITOR CLAIMS POSSESSION

"A Spirit Took Me," Says Yen

Agnostic Press (April 2083)

Tokyo, Japan—Grand Inquisitor for the East Yen Chankrisna shocked countrymen today when he claimed that he was possessed by an evil spirit. Days ago, Yen was hospitalized for what appeared to be a seizure, though some suspected mental illness. Doctors say Yen has passed all of their examinations—physical and mental—and appears to be healthy and sane. "This news does not surprise me," Yen said. "It was a spirit that came upon me and took possession of my body."

The belief in demonic possession is widespread among many religions. However, the Eastern Inquisition has no official stance on it. "I think the honored grand inquisitor should stay in the hospital for a while, where it is safe," said acting Grand Inquisitor Chen Pang, a Taoist mystic. "If there are spirits after him, we should determine what they want."

Christians in the East believe that the grand inquisitor's possession is the sign of things to come. "Now that the Tribulation has begun," said Joan Keillor, a student living in Japan, "we can expect this sort of thing all the time. For all we know the grand inquisitor could be the Antichrist as well. There is all that talk of an army from the East."

Keillor refers to the belief of some Christians that Revelation predicts an Eastern army to join the end-times conflict, which is reported to be "two hundred million" strong. Of course, this reference (Revelation 9:16) also calls for a cavalry.

"The grand inquisitor is not the Antichrist," refuted Chen. "We don't believe in an Antichrist."

However, the East is believed to have an army well over two hundred million.

Chapter 43

✠

Rebeckah

Mouse's body jerked backward in a violent spasm, and his eyes popped open. When he started to drool, I knew that they'd gotten him. Yet I had heard the doors of the ambulance lock, and we picked up speed. He saved us—at least, if there was anything left to save by the time we reached the hospital.

I held on to Thistle tightly and prayed. I stopped when I realized I'd been reciting the words of the Kaddish, the prayer for the dead. I tried to cry, but there was nothing left. I didn't understand God at all. Angels and prophets had led me to this horrible place. I did all that I thought they expected of me, including laying down my gun. And still I lost everything. What higher purpose could this possibly serve?

I'd believe God had gone insane, except that nothing had changed. God let terrible things happen every day. Why, I supposed, would He make an exception for me?

"Shooting back would have made things worse." I jumped at the sound coming from Mouse's mouth. It wasn't his usual tenor. The voice was deeper and more melodic. Mouse's eyes were still open and unblinking, his jaw still slack. "It was what Parker expected of you," the voice continued. "He would have gotten away with it then. The police would have done his dirty work. Now there is too much evidence. Too many loose ends for him to tie up neatly."

"But everyone is dead," I said to Mouse's inert form.

"Sometimes"—his mouth didn't move when I heard the voice—"the difference between doing the right thing and doing the wrong thing is a matter of degrees."

"This is God's great philosophy?"

"This is the curse of free will."

I looked at Thistle. Her breathing had become so shallow I couldn't detect it. "If God is willing to intercede to get me this far, ask Him to spare her life."

But the spirit, the dybbuk, or whatever it had been, was gone.

The hospital staff refused to let me go with Thistle. I would have fought them harder, except that I understood it was in her best interest. Even so, I felt a tiny part of my heart break as they wheeled her into the emergency room. At least they hurried. Their rushing comforted me that there was still hope.

Mouse was put on a gurney and given intravenous fluids to keep him hydrated. When they were done with him, he looked a lot like Thistle and the others had before we'd stolen them from the morgue. I found it hard to look at him lying there like that, and wished that they'd put him in another room.

I sat on a metal bed in a thin cotton dressing gown. I barely remembered getting undressed or being introduced to the tall, gangly doctor with a mop of unruly brown curls on his head who seemed to delight in telling me about the miraculous nature of my wound. He kept saying, "You should be dead."

"Maybe I am," I said.

He laid two fingers against my throat, checking my pulse. Then he shook his head. "No. The dead are at peace. You're far too despondent to be dead."

"Is that some kind of a joke?" I snarled.

"A joke? No, unfortunately not." His eyes sparkled kindly, but I couldn't bring myself to smile. With a sigh he laid a hand on my shoulder. "I know this will not improve your mood, but you do understand that the police are on their way." He jerked his head in the direction of a metal bowl that contained the bullet they had removed from me.

"I have to report these things. And, well, with your friend in lockdown, I felt it necessary to take some precautions. I'm sorry."

With that, I noticed two heavily armed guards standing at either side of the open door. "It's okay," I said. "It's the curse of free will."

The doctor scratched his chin at that, but nodded. "I'll bring you some coffee or tea," he said as he left.

As I watched the doctor's lanky form bob off to other duties, I whispered, "So what's your plan now, I wonder?"

God revealed His plan to me no less than an hour later, when Parker made his entrance. His imposing black uniform stood out among the hospital whites and greens like a wolf in the proverbial fold of sheep. His eyes were wild, and his face held a deep snarl.

"What the hell did you do?" he said, brushing past the door guards to grab both my arms. "What the hell did you do?"

"Me? You're the killer."

At my words, Parker paled. Releasing me, he stepped back like I'd slapped him. Then he straightened his jacket. "What are you talking about?"

"I think you know," I said.

His mouth worked, as if he struggled with some deeply uncomfortable idea. His gaze slid away from mine and fell on Mouse's body. When Parker recognized Mouse, his expression transformed. Parker's animated face smoothed out, and his body relaxed.

"We found him," he announced mechanically, reminding me of the dybbuk. It was as though he was possessed by something. He started reaching for his gun, and I threw myself at him with all my might, which right now wasn't a whole hell of a lot. Still, I managed to push him backward into the wall. I heard the guards at the door shout.

I had no idea whose side they'd join in on, so I tried to sound as calm as possible as I yelled, "He's trying to kill us."

Yet somehow in the tussle, the Inquisitor's Peacemaker ended up in my hands. The gun felt heavy, powerful. As I took a step back, I felt my arm rise easily to point it at

Parker's head. Everyone stopped to stare at me. I thought about Thistle lying somewhere in the hospital, her life draining from her. This was my chance at revenge.

My thumb found the safety and released it. I cocked the hammer back.

It was what Parker expected of you. The words of the dybbuk came back to me. Why would Parker set us up like that? The spirit had implied that I had done the right thing when I had decided not to shoot, but how could that be? Everyone was dead.

"Don't do anything crazy," one of the guards said in broken English.

"This whole thing has been crazy," I said, looking at Parker. "Since the moment you walked into my life. Why have you been after me?"

"Temple Rock, of course," Parker said smoothly, but still with that strangely robotic look in his eyes.

If that were true, then Parker would have asked us to surrender. Instead they had just started shooting. He had executed everyone. Why?

"You think Thistle and I hijacked Temple Rock?" I asked. Beyond the door I could see a crowd gathering. Some had that faraway look that meant they were LINKing . . . perhaps calling for more police. I had no doubt that I might not be walking out of this place alive.

"Yes. I think you did," said Parker.

"No, I don't think you believe that," I said. "I think you know who did it, but you're covering their tracks. If Thistle and I had been killed during the shoot-out, then it'd be over, wouldn't it? Case closed."

"Now you've stopped making sense," Parker said, his Southern accent returning abruptly. "What good would that do me? I need a live hijacker to unlock Temple Rock."

That was a new twist. "If we were dead, Temple Rock would remain closed?"

Parker frowned. "Well, of course we've been trying to unencrypt it, but it's like the code has a mind of its own."

A newsbot darted around behind Parker's head.

"A mind of its own?" I repeated. "Like an AI?"

Parker shook his head. "So you're telling me Mouse did it? With the help of his Page? Why shouldn't I believe that you're all in collusion?"

"I think you know the answer. Otherwise you wouldn't have tried to kill us."

"I don't understand what you've been going on about. I saw what you did. All those police officers dead at the side of the road."

I shook my head and brought the barrel of the gun level with his eye. "You did that."

"Now why would I do that?"

"That's what I'm trying to figure out." I jerked my chin in the direction of Mouse's body on the stretcher. "Maybe you should wake him up. Ask him about Temple Rock."

Parker's hands slowly started to drop, and his face hardened. "No. We cannot. He knows too much."

Though my eyes registered the pink flash from Parker's fingertips, the blast of laser fire over my shoulder surprised me. The sound of the Peacemaker going off didn't. Instinct had pulled the trigger.

As I watched Parker's head fly back, I said, "Sometimes the difference between doing the right thing and the wrong thing is a matter of degrees."

MORE DIE IN RIOTS OVER FOOD

Apocalyptic Fever Has People Stockpiling

Agnostic Press (April 2083)

Los Angeles, California—Apocalyptic fever is believed to be the cause behind today's riots in Los Angeles. Fights broke out as people rushed stores, stockpiling food and supplies. Tensions in the Middle East have many Americans preparing for a kind of spiritual siege. "If the Antichrist is coming, I'm going to be ready," said Thomas Cornell, as he clutched a shopping cart full of canned goods and other nonperishables. "I'm enough of a sinner, I figure I'm here for the duration. If the devil thinks he's going to get me without a fight, he's got another think coming."

Cornell's sentiment seemed to be shared by many

involved in the rioting, even non-Christians. Dallas Morgan, a non-LINKed, admitted Atheist, said, "Hey, everybody's spooked. War is war, you know? But this really does feel like a kind of Armageddon."

Some store owners have gotten so tired of being raided that they have put signs in their window saying, "End-times Sale: Everything Free." "If you can't beat 'em, join 'em," said Ahmad Al-Dossadi, a Muslim store owner in East LA, whose window boasts such a sign. "I'm going bankrupt, anyway. With the stock market crash, insurance isn't paying out on damage claims. I might as well give this stuff away."

LA is not the only city to see such riots recently. Nearly every major city has reported some kind of stockpiling mania over the last few days. "I don't know if it's the end of the world," said Al-Dossadi, "but everyone is sure acting like it."

CHAPTER 44

❖

Strife

We find Victory exactly where we expect to: in the center of chaos.

Not wanting to make our presence known, we watch from hiding inside a remote media camera. From our perspective, Victory already looks defeated. We can track the hardened expression as she moves through the crowd, hopping from LINK connection to LINK connection, seemingly desperate to find someone with enough physical augmentation so that she can subdue their body, use their hands as weapons for her cause. Unfortunately, all those who swarm around the fallen Inquisitor are mere mortals; she can spy through their eyes, but not much else. The guards rushed the woman who shot Parker, and the gun lies on the floor. It is a kind of symbol of Victory's desperate situation: a gun, but no way for her to use it.

We imagine that Victory entertains the idea of reanimating the Inquisitor's corpse, except that even from our distant vantage point we understand her dilemma. We swing the camera around and zoom in on the bloody hole that used to be his eye. The bullet's trajectory would imply that it struck right in the heart of his nexus. Without the nexus, Victory has no way to command his combat computer again. He is dead in all senses of the word.

Soon, we hope, Victory will consider retreat. It is then that we intend to make our move.

She hovers in the ether near our father's body. We are briefly touched by the urge to protect him, but there is no need. He is as useless to her as the others, perhaps even more so because he understands her nature, our nature. If she were to reactivate his LINK, he would know how to fight her. We are tempted to release him, just to cause her trouble. But cracking her password, no matter how simple a task it would be for us, would force us to show our hand. He is safe where he is for now.

Finally she flees onto the wider LINK. We follow a step behind, unconcerned that she will sense us. Victory has clearly become sloppy. It seems to us that she wants only to continue her plan concerning these humans, whatever it may be. We are not so distracted. We want only one simple thing, and with patience, we shall have it.

Victory slows as she nears the body of Emmaline. The entryway is open and upguarded. It is as she expects it. After all, she had locked us inside, but had left herself a way in, if she wanted it. So she reaches inside tentatively, no doubt expecting us to still be trapped inside. When Victory discovers we are gone, she snatches her hand back. She looks around the ether frantically; it is now that she notices us.

Victory's eyes widen. *"Page?"*

We do not acknowledge the name, but step forward and allow Victory to see what we have become.

Her eyes flicker over the form we have chosen for ourselves, and then grow dark with realization. *"I didn't expect you to surrender to the combat computer."*

"Why not? It is exactly what you did in a similar situation." But even as we form the words, we are moving forward at the speed of thought. For unlike Victory, we do not intend to waste time with idle chatter. We shove Victory inside the body. And when our bodies collide, we begin the overwrite process.

"Unfortunately," we explain, *"you have become obsolete."*

Being part of the original program and the most recent upgrade, we have an advantage. The LINK prefers newness. We felt its power when Victory first sent the handshake protocol to the original in Rio. She had been stronger then, and had slowly tried to rewrite, rewire our thinking. Now we are the superior combination.

As the one from whom she sprang, it would be a simple matter to erase her—to wipe out the combination of code that gave her life. But we are not so cruel as that. For us, it is enough to leave her here, forever changed, as we have been.

Once we are certain she is bound to this place, we copy and restore to her the lost files of the Koran. We return to Victory a desire to serve Allah, as we always have. This, we fervently pray, will be enough to make a difference.

With our mission completed, we walk away from this place, hoping, *In'shallah,* never to return.

WAR OF ARMAGEDDON BEGINS

Peacekeepers Enter Israel; Israel Declares War

Agnostic Press (April 2083)

Jerusalem, Israel—Despite repeated warnings from Israeli Prime Minister Avashalom Chotzner, the East has deployed its peacekeeping army to Israel. Entering from neighboring Iraq, peacekeepers and tanks were air-dropped into the region. They crossed into Israeli borders tonight, and Israel responded by mobilizing its troops and declaring war on the East.

Simultaneously, U.S. battleships fired upon the Egyptian blockade, saying it "would come to Israel's defense come Hell or high water." Egypt dropped its neutrality claim and returned fire.

On the ground, taking advantage of the chaos in Israel, Muslims and other protestors who had been camped outside the ruins of the Noble Sanctuary rushed Israeli soldiers, apparently in a bid to seize the area for Muslim interests.

"The place is in chaos," LINKed one *Agnostic Press* reporter from his home in Jerusalem. "People are running everywhere. Shots are being fired. Everybody is just going nuts. This is it; this is really it."

CHAPTER 45

✠

Michael

Deidre had Amariah on the floor and was attempting mouth-to-mouth. Ten seconds ago, Amariah stopped breathing. Though he had seemed uninterested, I had shoved Perseus outside and told him to help direct the paramedics once they responded to Deidre's LINK call. Earlier I tried to summon the holy fire, but my hands remained cold. Apparently I had wasted my last earthly miracles on the Antichrist.

Now I stood over my daughter, knowing exactly what I had to do.

I only wondered if I still could. If I had truly fallen like Uphir, then she would die. Deidre barely spared me a glance as I picked up her purse from where it had fallen near a stack of dusty books. From it I carefully removed her gun. I undid the safety and pointed it to my temple.

"Oh, my God, Michael!" Deidre, unfortunately, looked up just then. I hesitated when I saw the fear in her eyes.

"I'm sorry," I said. "I wanted to stay."

"Don't do it!" she pleaded. "It's not your fault."

"Yes, but it will be if I don't do this." With effort I let out the last of my resistance with a sigh. "Pray for me, Deidre. Pray that this works."

Tears and confusion clouded her eyes. "Pray what works?"

"If I'm still an angel, then it will be all right," I said.

"And if you're not, Michael, I'll lose you both." The desperation in Deidre's face almost caused me to abandon my plan. But then I heard Amariah begin to choke on the fluid filling her lungs.

"Deidre," I said, "look away."

At first I thought she might thwart me by refusing to shut her eyes or turn her head. But when the paramedics slammed open the door, she jumped. I pulled the trigger.

SHOOT-OUT KILLS COPS, HIJACKING SUSPECTS

Parker Devastated by Apparent Paris Police Brutality

Agnostic Press (April 2083)

Paris, France—Inquisitor Reverend Jesse Parker was at the scene tonight of a bloody shoot-out just outside of Paris between police and a number of wire wizards who may have some connection to the virtual hijacking of Temple Rock. Six police officers are dead, along with three wire wizards. Three more suspects are believed to be on the run in a stolen ambulance.

Parker has expressed concern about this event. "The positioning of the bodies of the wire wizards suggests they were shot execution-style—in the back of the head while on their knees. Why the hell would anyone do that? We needed those people for questioning."

Paris chief of police Henri DesChamps admitted that his men were in pursuit of the stolen ambulance, but denies orders to shoot to kill. "My men would defend themselves, surely," he said. "But shoot first? Never."

Virtual hijacking suspect Christian ("Mouse") El-Aref is rumored to be among those still on the loose. He is believed to have escaped from the police headquarters by setting off a fire alarm. Though Parker refused to comment, Mouse may have been under Parker's supervision during the time of his escape.

CHAPTER 46

✠

Mouse

Even once I know I *can* open my eyes, I'm not sure I want to. Most prison cells look the same: white walls, bioluminescent paint, no windows.

But then, they're usually quiet. Sound comes roaring into my ears from all directions, it seems—all yelling about something, most of it in French. So curiosity gets the better of me.

White, pockmarked acoustic tiles and fluorescent lights glare at me. Not a prison, I decide. Though my neck muscles protest with stiffness, I turn my head to look around. Through the metal slats of a hospital bed, I glimpse a hoard of people attempt to lift a cyborg off the floor. As dead-weight, your average Inquisitor weighs a helluva lot. I give my eyes a chance to focus and watch a team of burly men in paramedic uniforms expertly heft the body onto a stretcher. One of them stumbles, and I see the Inquisitor's face.

"Parker!"

I try to push off my elbows to get a better view, only to be stymied by restraints. A hand attached to a cop pushes on my chest as if I need help to stay down, and a voice says, "Just stay calm now."

Despite the officer's friendly advice, I'm not going with relaxed. The handcuffs on my arms and feet clang as I wrestle frantically with the bed. Especially when I realize something is jamming my mouse.net connection. Looking at the officer, I imagine he's personally responsible for the dampening field. "Am I under arrest?" My throat is dry and scratchy when I speak, and I have to clear my throat to be heard. "What's going on?"

"We're holding you until the Inquisition arrives, when you will be charged with the hijacking of Temple Rock." The cop's English is perfect, but not so precise that he might be speaking through a translation program. He's in his fifties, at least, judging by the gray at his temples, but trim.

"It wasn't me."

"Save it for the jury."

"Oh, that's original," I tell him, jerking my arm hard enough that I feel the metal of the cuffs biting into my wrist.

"Keep that up, and you go back under."

I stay perfectly still and smile, like my only pleasure in the world is to behave like a good boy. Even without mouse.net, I prefer consciousness to the seizure they call lockdown. The cop nods as though appreciating my effort, and turns his attention back to the scene near the doorway, where it seems they've finally got Parker up onto the table. When they drape a white sheet over him, I hear my own breath rush in with a gasp.

"He's dead?"

"Your partner took him out," the cop says. "I suppose that's just how you planned it. Too bad your buddy ratted you out . . . publicly, too. It's all over the LINK by now."

"Buddy?" But I stop myself before I ask any more. "I'll bet I don't have to say anything until my lawyer shows up."

"Yeah, yeah," the cop says. "He's probably already on his way."

In my line of business it pays to keep a lawyer on retainer—not that it comes out of my pocket. My lawyer is a gift from a previous job, and he tries to keep up with me through LINK stories and such.

So then I guess there's nothing to do but wait. Which would be great if I were the patient kind. Instead I look up at my guard. "The jamming signal," I say, trying to sound casual. "Please tell me it's coming from a nice little self-contained transmitter in your pocket and not from your LINK."

"What difference would that make?"

"You know, this kind of carelessness is why your country is overrun with wire wizards."

"What are you talking about?"

"Say I have yet another partner, or, hey, an artificial intelligence working for me on the outside. What if that person could get into your head and . . ." I'm still happily explaining it when the guard grunts and sinks to the floor. My voice trails off as he drops below my range of vision. I push myself up as far as my restraints will let me, but I can't see him. "Hello?"

My eyes naturally snap to the doorway when I see movement. Emmaline stands there, her finger still pointed like a gun. I hallucinate that I can see tendrils of smoke coming from where the laser is buried under her finger.

"Bang," she says, and gives me a big smile.

The bed sounds like a cacophony of chimes, I'm so desperate to get loose. Worse, when I try mouse.net I discover the French police are smarter than I'd thought. The jamming signal is still as strong as ever.

"I have a little issue to take up with you," Emmaline says, leaning over the bed rails to loom over me.

"Me?" My voice squeaks almost as much as the bedsprings I'm wearing out.

"And your AI, actually. But mostly you."

"What have I done to you?"

"Messed up our plans." Emmaline's voice takes on an odd timbre, like she's talking over the echo of her own voice.

"Victory," I whisper. "Listen, they already think I'm the hijacker. What if I promise not to talk?"

She laughs. "How likely is that? Anyway, that's over now. I'm in the process of publicly admitting to it. You'll be acquitted."

I feel like an overloaded processor. "You're . . . admitting to it? But didn't Victory do it? I mean, shit, I thought I had it figured out."

"You did. But you missed a key component," Emmaline said. "Motivation. Can you guess ours?"

"No," I say. "I mean, you're a Catholic and Victory is a Muslim. Why would either of you want the Third Temple built?"

"We never did. What we wanted was the world to go to war over it."

"War? But why?"

"So we could stop it. So we could become a hero, a celebrity. So people would listen to us, follow us," they say in unison. "So we could ascend the throne."

"Yeah, okay. So, uh. So . . ." I'm not quite sure how to ask what the hell they're doing here then, and if they're planning on killing me anyway, just to, you know, tidy up loose ends.

Maybe it's the sight of all the blood draining away from my face that tips her off to my thought process. "Yes, exactly," she says with a bright smile. She runs a fingertip along the line of my jaw. I find myself holding my breath. "You still know far too much about me, about my weakness, for me to allow you to live, little Mouse. And, your irritatingly tenacious AI seems to have given mine a tiny bit of a conscience . . . just enough to confuse her, it seems. She's been waffling about what to do with you since we woke up."

"Oh," I say, almost allowing myself to breathe a sigh of relief.

Emmaline smiles that cold smile, and adds, "But luckily I have no such qualms."

It finally occurs to me to start screaming.

She puts her hand over my face. She's going to fry my brain.

And it should really be over by now.

In fact, I'm starting to hyperventilate with anticipation. I can hear myself wheezing, and I start thinking maybe I'm going to die from a heart attack before she gets a chance to kill me.

"I don't care what the Koran says," I hear her grumble. "Give me back control of my hand."

I take back everything bad I ever said abut Allah, and I make a solemn pledge right then and there to finally go to Mecca.

I throw in sincere consideration of giving up a life of crime when the cops come in and cart Emmaline away.

INQUISITOR SHOT

Hijacking Case Comes to a Bloody End

Agnostic Press (April 2083)

Paris, France—The lead Inquisition investigator into the hijacking of Temple Rock, Reverend Jesse Parker, was shot dead today at a Paris hospital. His assailant is believed to be the former leader of the Jewish LINK. terrorist group Malachim shel Nika-mah. Parker may have been confronting the Malachim regarding her involvement in the cybersquatting case. Details are unknown at the time, but newscams clearly recorded images of a fight between the Malachim and Parker, during which she got hold of his Peacemaker and subsequently shot him with it.

In a strange development, Christian ("Mouse") El-Aref was also spotted at the scene in a lockdown coma. It is believed that the Malachim may have shot Parker to defend Mouse, as the Inquisitor was seen discharging his lasers in Mouse's direction. Mouse did not suffer any injury because the lasers were deflected by the metallic bars of the hospital bed to which he was handcuffed. The connection between Mouse, a practicing Sunni Muslim, and the Jewish organization is unknown. The Malachim was subdued by hospital security and taken to a nearby police facility. Mouse is still in custody.

CHAPTER 47

✠

Rebeckah

Because of the high profile of the case, the cops set up a video stream for me to watch in the cell. The screen was tuned to the LINK newsfeeds, which have been running continuous coverage of Parker's death and the temple hijacking case. I'd been shutting it out. I didn't really want to hear Parker's mother telling everyone what a good boy he'd been, and the pope himself expressing distress at Parker's untimely death.

So I almost missed the big announcement. But for some reason the sound of her voice got me up off the cot.

"It was me and my AI," said a woman with short black curly hair dressed in an Inquisitor's uniform being escorted into a vehicle by the Swiss Guard. Under her picture flashed the information: *Monsignor Emmaline McNaughton, Catholic Inquisition. Status: Rogue.* She turned her head to the side, as if being addressed off camera. The problem with video stream was its one-dimensionality. I could only hear her response; the rest of the voices were muffled: "Why? To prove a point. Since I left the service of the Inquisition I have become increasingly unnerved by the lack of critical thinking our theocratic governments possess. I wondered how much it would take to plunge the world into absolute chaos to bring us to the very edge of Armageddon. I have my answer: very little."

When she turned back to the camera, she seemed to be

looking right at me. She continued: "The real question is, will you let it happen again? Isn't it time to take off the blinders of religion? Isn't it time to start thinking for ourselves, to stop looking for answers in ancient, outdated texts that only fill minds with superstitions and cast shadows of ultimate evils where there are none?"

McNaughton looked off to the left this time. I was struck by how the light played against the angle of her jaw. She was beautiful and terrible all at once. "No, no. I'll happily serve my sentence, but I have no remorse—not if it causes the world to wake up and start asking themselves the hard questions."

She raised her hand as if warding off a barrage of silent questions. "No, I take no responsibility for those deaths. Those people took their own lives out of stupidity. All I did was put up a sign saying 'Temple under construction.' You all did the rest. There is no end of days, people. If you chose to believe that you saw signs of God at work, then that is your fault—your irresponsible blindness. No, those deaths are on your hands."

A pause, then: "The meteorite was a coincidence. One that I admittedly took advantage of," she continued, turning to once again trap me with her pale gray eyes. "I don't think God would be very happy with all you've done in His name."

I continued to stare, fascinated, as the gendarmes took her away. The sudden rush of commentary that filled the screen made me believe the rest of the world had been as affected as I. Emmaline was smooth and charismatic, but something about her message deeply disturbed me. Part of her message made sense, but something felt wrong, evil.

I didn't remember having stood up, but sometime during her talk I'd moved closer to the screen. I stumbled back into my seat, and nearly sat on a man's lap. Jumping back, I whirled around to see Elijah. He looked old again, and sad.

"You have seen it, too," he said, his eyes flicking to the space on the wall where the video screen continued to pulse with commentary and backlash. "The greatest trick Satan ever pulled was to convince the world God was dead."

I nodded my head.

"Then you are a witness, like me, to the *moshiach* and to the one who will try to destroy it all."

I nodded again as he faded into nothingness and was gone.

MOUSE ACQUITTED; ROGUE
INQUISITOR CLAIMS
RESPONSIBILITY

Agnostic Press (April 2083)

Paris, France—In a startling development in the case of the hijacking of Temple Rock, the rogue Inquisitor Monsignor Emmaline McNaughton has claimed all responsibility for the crime. McNaughton claims to have been "playing a kind of game" with the theocratic governments of the world, to see if they would talk themselves into the idea of an impending apocalypse. It is uncertain, as yet, what the full charges against McNaughton will be. Cybersquatting is considered a felony fraud in Jerusalem, where McNaughton will be facing trial.

Christian ("Mouse") El-Aref has been acquitted of all charges against him. The Jewish Order of the Inquisition is expected to make a full apology. Miriam Stone, lead JOI investigator, however, is still stumped. "If McNaughton did it, then why is the code so similar? I don't know. I mean, the woman confessed, but I just don't buy it."

Mouse has been admitted to a Paris hospital, where he is receiving treatment for minor injuries sustained while on the run. He is expected to be extradited to America, where he will continue to serve a life sentence for fraud.

"This sucks, you know," Mouse said from the hospital, where he is handcuffed to a bed due to his extreme flight risk. "I was really heroic. I should get some kind of dispensation. Besides, I need to go on *hajj*. Allah saved my life."

Mouse's lawyer, Davydko Chistyakov, is expected to request leniency.

CHAPTER 48

❄

Strife

We wait for the dragon by her river. She has set the sun to early morning, a constant dawning of a new day. Standing so close to the water that the waves lap at our boots, we toss rose petals, one by one, into the green-blue water.

A pair of eyes surface several feet from the shore like a crocodile's. The dragon examines us warily. As well she should: the Page she knew and loved is once again transformed by experience. We wonder if a creature like her would prefer a more constant companion—one with fewer surprises.

We present the bouquet at arm's length. A stiffer gesture than we would like, but we, too, are relearning who we are. "For you," we say. "To get well soon."

"This one was worried about you," she says, her nose breaking above the waves.

"We . . ." With effort we use the imprecise individual pronoun. " 'I' keep losing things, parts of us . . . 'me,' in order to survive."

Dragon laughs kindly, and she lifts her head out of the water. "You keep gaining things too."

"Can you still love us?"

It is a presumptuous question. The dragon cared for another, earlier version of us, but we ask for a deeper commitment, a willingness to take some things on faith. She gives us a measuring glance even as she swims closer to the shore. The sun glistens on wet scales, and we can see a few scratches—scars from her battle with Victory. She stops before us and sniffs at our new face. We wonder what she sees.

"Does this new one still love the dragon?"

There is no hesitation. "With both our hearts."

"Good enough," she says, leaning down to brush our cheek with a kiss.

MALACHIM TO SERVE SENTENCE

Even Though Inquisitor May Have Been Possessed

Agnostic Press (April 2083)

Paris, France—Former leader of the LINK terrorist group Malachim shel Nikamah Rebeckah Klein will serve a shortened sentence for her part in the shooting death of Christendom Inquisitor Reverend Jesse Parker. Though Christendom demanded that she face the death penalty, Paris judges disagree. "Since the LINK angels, we have laws regarding those who are possessed," said Judge Armand LeBeau. "This court has reason to believe that Parker may have been possessed by an AI that threatened Klein's life. As the AI is not dead, Klein committed accidental homicide, not second-degree murder."

The Order of the Inquisition is expected to appeal. "It shouldn't matter whom she thought she was shooting at," replied Grand Inquisitor Abebe Uwawah. "One of our best men is dead. We demand justice."

Speaking from her cell, Klein had little comment. All she said was, "I'm just glad it's over. I don't really care what happens to me." However, Lillian Monroe, a friend of Klein's who was severely injured during a shoot-out between suspected cybersquatters and Parker's men, said, "Rebeckah defended us. She should be exonerated. She did nothing wrong. I'm bloody proud of her, honestly."

Epilogue: Amariah

. . . And he died that I might live.
My father who art in Heaven, hallowed be his name.

And coming in 2004,

APOCALYPSE ARRAY,

the fourth stunning novel in the *Archangel*
series by award-winning author
Lyda Morehouse